A
KNIGHT
And WHITE
SATIN

Also by Jackie Ivie

ONCE UPON A KNIGHT

A KNIGHT WELL SPENT

HEAT OF THE KNIGHT

A KNIGHT BEFORE CHRISTMAS

TENDER IS THE KNIGHT

LADY OF THE KNIGHT

A KNIGHT
And WHITE
SATIN

Jackie Ivie

ZEBRA BOOKS
KENSINGTON PUBLISHING CORP.
http://www.kensingtonbooks.com

ZEBRA BOOKS are published by

Kensington Publishing Corp.
119 West 40th Street
New York, NY 10018

All Kensington titles, imprints and distributed lines are available at special quantity discounts for bulk purchases for sales promotion, premiums, fund-raising, educational or institutional use.

Special book excerpts or customized printings can also be created to fit specific needs. For details, write or phone the office of the Kensington Special Sales Manager: Kensington Publishing Corp., 119 West 40th Street, New York, NY 10018. Attn. Special Sales Department. Phone: 1-800-221-2647.

Zebra and the Z logo Reg. U.S. Pat. & TM Off.

ISBN-13: 978-1-4201-0884-2
ISBN-10: 1-4201-0884-0

First Printing: October 2010
10 9 8 7 6 5 4 3 2 1

Printed in the United States of America

To my son,
Joshua David

With love and pride—
for the boy you were and
the man you are

Chapter 1

AD 1540

The spoils went to the victor. Always. It was one truth of life that the Caruths embraced and flexed at will. That was before spoils included her.

For members of the warrior clan of Caruth, claiming victory, taking riches, and wreaking vengeance was right and just and exercised without warning, empathy, or delay. To have it turned so completely was causing bitterness to flood her breast until it was rooted in disgust as she watched them.

It was Dunn-Fadden clan. Beggars. Wanderers. Fools. The entire clan was a mass of disjointed factions with none claiming leadership until this surprise. A dark shadow filled the space in front of her, taking her unseeing vision from the few gleeful Dunn-Fadden men ripping apart her home. She focused on their leader and frowned deeper.

"Come." He had his hand out, the one still encased in the falconer glove. The bitterness moved, filling her throat with the acrid taste. "*Nae,*" she told him.

A half-smile played about his lips for a moment and in the next Dallis was atop his shoulder, blinking on the blood-coated, split tiles of the great hall floor, and hating the fact that she hadn't even seen him move.

"You can struggle. I'd like that."

The portion of her anatomy that he was fondling had never felt what it was now. Dallis choked back any reaction as his free hand caressed her buttocks that he'd put on display for the act. And then he was moving, taking sure steps that had her bouncing with each one.

"Dinna' do this!"

He'd reached the steps leading to her tower, as if he knew where her bedchambers were. If she could have stopped the sobbed words, she would have. Dallis sucked her lower lip into her mouth and bit down, holding it in place to keep any further emotion from sounding. She'd been taught better. You never showed weakness and suffering. And pain? There was nothing more painful than the sting of clan censure and hatred. Dallis held her lessons close, started going through them in a prayerlike chant, and still she couldn't stop the shivers. All she could hope was he didn't note them.

He chuckled. He had broad shoulders she'd noted earlier and they shuddered with what was probably his amusement.

"Do what? You're my wife. Taken this night. In wedlock."

"A pagan ceremony, given without clergy!"

He had to have heard her even if he was taking each step like they were level and not steeply assembled. The angle had to be steep. The spiral stairs were a tight and rapid ascent. That's what came of having such a tall, square keep; one that was impenetrable and had never been taken . . . could never be taken.

Until now.

He didn't say anything to her outburst. He didn't have to. She knew the toll she was paying. She just wished all the teachings meant something when butted up against reality. Not fear the solid mass of man that was carrying her? How was she to do that? Mayhap her clan shouldn't have saved the altar of her maidenhead until she was plum-ripe and almost too old. Maybe they shouldn't have dangled the castle, glens, and lochs that came with her hand. Mayhap they should have wed her off to her betrothed, one of the king's most powerful earls, the moment she'd come of an age for it. Any of that they should have done.

In her mind's eye, she could still see the shine of spilt blood below, and how it was being washed by the drip of rain through the roof that had been ripped open when the Dunn-Faddens had first used their battering ram. Dallis had never known the like, never even experienced it. The moment the tree they'd felled hit the doors, the most horrendous roll of the earth had happened, making the floors sway and crack, her mother's prized leaded glass windows warp and then fall inward—creating shards that were difficult to fight amongst and even harder to dodge when wearing slippers—and their blow had even caused the roof above the great hall to split.

They'd reached her chamber, and he didn't have to use a handle to open the door since it was gaping wide from the jamb. The force he'd somehow summoned had affected even here, three stories up the square tower that had been the sign of Caruth power for over a century. He swung wide giving Dallis a sweeping vision of what had been a lady's chamber, decorated with material in a white hue she demanded, but was now little more than hanging strips marking where her canopy had been, an open window where the leaded glass hung in chunks, and chests that contained absolutely nothing.

Then there was her serf, Bronwyn. The girl appeared from the antechamber to stand, wringing her hands and sobbing tears that Dallis didn't have the luxury of crying.

"Get out."

The man holding her ordered Bronwyn out, but the maid did little more than burst into louder sobs.

"Take the wench and get her from the chamber. Take her

below. Use her for sport. Keep an eye out for Caruth clan. They'll have sent a cry."

Bronwyn shrieked louder and there wasn't even anyone near her. Dallis knew the girl wasn't adverse to a romp, and made certain she had a bed to share for her nights. That should have helped contain Dallis's own fear.

"There'll be none to witness the consummation, my laird."

"It won't be an issue. Take her. Now."

The man holding her spoke to three men at his heels that Dallis hadn't known were following them. She gulped, sent the streak of emotion deep, and turned her head sideways, away from them. It was better to arouse anger. That was her lesson. It helped temper everything else. She heard Bronwyn's screams all the way down the hall, and couldn't summon anything except fright.

The door wasn't shutting properly. Dallis hung to his waist as he fussed with it, pushing and shoving and then cursing while she swayed with each movement. The fit had been perfect before God betrayed them and sent the earth heaving. Or maybe it was this Dunn-Fadden and his heathen gods that had the power to make the very earth move with but one hit of a battering ram.

"Now." He had the door bowed, but he'd managed to bolt it, and then he had her on her feet. He backed several steps off and then he just stood there, waiting. He didn't even look to be breathing hard. "What was that said about clergy?"

"Without benefit."

"Unions are held with less." He was unfastening the falcon glove as he spoke, undoing the leather tyrrits that his peregrine had been attached to. She knew he'd own a peregrine without asking. Such a falcon befitted his station.

"And without my troth!" She hadn't agreed to being his wife. She couldn't have. They'd put a bond across her lips, keeping her from saying anything.

He looked across at her, spearing her with an ice-blue gaze

that had caught her attention when he'd first pulled off his helm and shown her the color of them. They still did. Dallis had to force her heart to calm, cease the fluttering that was making her ribs feel tight, and then she had to gulp around an obstruction in her throat.

"Your clan had the choice put to them. They should na' have declined."

He had the glove off, and then he was starting to work at the linkage of his thigh-length hauberk. He was wearing Norse battle attire. It was strange, but difficult to fault. It was also difficult to pierce. She had to wait. The dirk hidden in the back of her girdle would be enough. She just had to be patient until he was vulnerable, and that meant until he had the chain-crafted tunic off.

"And it was na' agreed! Never! I'm trothed already!"

"Get undressed," he said.

Dallis's eyes widened. "I'm na' helping you," she managed a reply, and it was evenly said and without inflection. She was very proud of that.

"I dinna' request it," he replied.

He pulled the hauberk from his body, showing he wore a tunic of gray that was plastered to muscles with sweat. And little else. It was going to be easy to pierce flesh. She just had to keep him occupied—and not with bedding her.

"Why do you wear . . . mail?" she asked, with the slightest touch of snideness. "'Tis na' verra manly."

"Protection. In battle. My father has but one son. Me. There are some that think me a large target. Easiest to see and easiest to hit."

"You are a large target," she replied.

He looked across at her again, stopping her breath for the barest moment with eyes that looked so striking against swarthy skin and midnight-black hair. Then he was frowning at her. She assumed it was from lack of motion, as she wasn't

obeying anything he'd said. His hands stopped fussing with
the kilt knot at his hip.

"True," he replied finally. "I dinna' like to wear it. I'm
forced to."

Dallis eyed his arms, bare now and thick with strength.
There was an obvious sign of muscle on the stomach his tunic
was barely shielding, as well. To think him forced to do anything was a lie. It had to be.

"How?" she asked.

"We've nae time for talk. You ken it. I ken it. Now, take
your wedding dress off or I'll be forced to tear it from your
body."

Her eyes widened. Nothing else on her entire frame betrayed anything. "This is na' my wedding dress."

He smiled, not enough to show teeth, but enough to show
his amusement. "It is now," he replied finally. "And I'd na'
like ripping it."

That reply created shock akin to an ice bath, and her heart
was hammering so loudly, she could barely hear over it.
"What difference . . . will that make?" She stumbled once
through the question, and was amazed her voice didn't
warble.

He'd given off untying his kilt and it helped gain her
breath. And then he made it immeasurably worse by pulling
the gray wool shirt over his head, moving an array of muscle
and baring an expanse of flesh that made her gape. She'd also
slighted him. He wasn't just the largest target. He was the
largest, most fit male she'd ever seen. Anywhere. Even on the
castle list.

One thing was certain. He was in much better condition,
much younger in age, and much more handsome than her
intended husband, who was well-known for two of those
things. Admitting that much to herself was a huge mistake.
She realized it as her mouth filled with spittle and her eyes
widened. She couldn't do a thing about the increase in her

pulse. Someone should have put that in her lessons. He was affecting her too much to think.

"We haven't this much time. I'll na' speak it again. Take off your kirtle, or face having it torn off and going without."

"The king shall hear of this!"

He gave her another smile, wider this time, revealing teeth that probably owed their whiteness to his tanned appearance, and not any care. "The king canna' put asunder a union that's been consummated. I've given off the warnings, lass. I've na' this much patience."

Then he was striding toward her, making her tower room seem small and insignificant and more stark than usual. Dallis backed up, stumbling on long skirts she didn't lift. She couldn't. Her hands were behind her back, fumbling for the dirk with fingers numbed by something she wouldn't label as fear. They were cold. Her fingers were that. The handle of her knife was slender, jewel encrusted, and fit for a lady's hand. It looked the size of a needle when she had it out and held in front of her.

"Stay away from me!" Dallis hissed, waving the small blade in front of her.

He didn't break stride. Not even when he reached her and she had it buried in his left side. There wasn't the sign of anything on his face as she pierced flesh, although Dallis was gagging with the feel of it. The spurt of blood doused her, staining the white with crimson. He had her pushed against the wall with his left hand, and with his right he grabbed the neckline of her serviceable bliant and tore it completely down the middle. Nothing on his features betrayed the slightest bit of pain, or anger, or anything, although the light blue color of his eyes seemed darker. Or maybe it was the shadow cast by heavy lashes in the same shade as his hair.

There was a loud pounding in her ears, and then she realized it was the door. She couldn't think. His weight was stifling her as he used it, shoving his body at her, and making her knees tremble and her back clench. She felt him move, smearing his palm with his own blood before jamming it between her legs. Dallis's jaw dropped, her features flooded with heat and everything on her entire body felt locked into place as he fondled, putting fingers where no man had ever been and forcing a reaction she didn't know anything about.

"Deny that," he growled.

"*Nae!* I—" Her voice stopped.

She saw the door opening from behind him, the hall behind filled with Caruth clan colors. Dunn-Fadden was at the window, the little jewel hilt sticking from his side since her hand had lost grip with it some time earlier, and she was too caught up in stifling all the tremors overtaking her to care. She hoped it killed him.

"Payton Dunn-Fadden! You crazed whelp of a she-wolf!"

Someone called his name and the slur with it. He ignored it. He was piercing her with those eyes . . . fathomless blue eyes, making everything else disappear. She knew it was going to be imprinted on her mind forever; the sight of him silhouetted in a window that was crafted large to let light in, but protected from enemy attack by the sheer height of it. That same light molded him for her, turning solid flesh into a statue of memory and making her absorb it. And then he turned and launched right out her window.

The room was filling with Caruth clan, all yelling and shoving, drowning out any sound of the splash his body would make as it hit the loch. Some even commented on it at her window. After a glance, anyone else was studiously avoiding looking at her; at the ripped gown, the nakedness, and the blood pointing toward . . . what he'd done. Dallis didn't move her eyes from where he'd been standing. She didn't think she could.

Bronwyn fought her way through them then, her arms loaded with what had once been Dallis's canopy of pristine white material. It looked heaven-sent. It was exactly that. She realized it as the maid wound it about her, covering over her nakedness, his blood, and the proof that she was no longer a member of the Caruth clan.

She was the bride of Dunn-Fadden. And that's how she came to be the outcast known as White Satin.

Death wasn't what he'd expected. Neither was heaven. Or maybe it was hell. Either way, there was too much yelling and cursing and shouting for it to be heaven, and way too much softness, filling drinks and cool, soothing linens for it to be the other.

A fire ate away at his side until it took over his entire frame. That had put him in hell. Then the cool cloth upon him had tempered it. There had also been the soothing sounds of lovely singing and words of crooning . . . sounds like his mother had once made when he was a small lad. It wasn't his mother, though. That would have made it heaven, since he was certain that's where she'd gone. So, if it wasn't heaven—he wasn't dead. And it wasn't his mother.

Payton opened his eyes. It was his bed, his room, and his walls. It was the clan healer, Josephine, doing the singing. Nobody had told him she had the voice of an angel. He rather thought she'd be treated differently if anyone knew she could sing as beautifully as she did. He opened his mouth to speak it, but she shoved another spoonful of broth in, stopping him.

"You gave us quite a fright, lad," she said as he swallowed. And then she smiled. "What with trying to swim Caruth loch with a wound such as you had."

"Wound?" Payton asked, and frowned.

"The hole in your side, draining your life's blood away. I did the best I could. It's still an ugly scar. You should ha' taken the wench's sewing needles away a-fore you took her."

"Where?" Payton tried to sit, but coughing racked his chest, weakness took over his limbs, and all he really managed to do was make her cackle. She should have stuck to her singing. It was more melodious, he decided, once the cough had settled to a whiff of sound and he could breathe and think again.

"You were in luck the lass didn't have a bigger weapon. You'd have probably lost your manhood." She gave another cackle after her words. Payton sucked for a bit of breath to answer. It felt like it was burning a hole right through his chest. He let it go.

"I've kept it secret, lad, but you should ha' put a rein on the other lads' tongues. They've been regaling all who'd listen with your exploits. Not without encouragement, either. All and sundry wish to hear. "

"What . . . are you speaking of?" Payton gasped through the entire sentence, and even had to stop for breath midway. She waited. That was another good thing about her. She had so little company most of the time that she always showed courtesy and listened carefully when she had it. Then again, she probably wanted to know all of it so she could add words meant to belittle him.

"Your little foray onto Caruth land. Your wedding of the heiress. Your taking of the keep. All wonderful exploits. All making your da strut about like he's sired the most manly fellow to set foot on the earth." She bent closer, gifting him with a foul odor from her gap-toothed mouth. Payton winced. "You should na' have turned tail and run. You might have been able to keep the tower once you gained it . . . if you'd have told anyone what you were planning, that is."

They hadn't told anyone they were planning on attacking the White Tower. It was a lark while the lairds were at court, undertaken without much thought, no cunning, and after an eve of drinking whiskey. They'd expected to take a chunk of the white rock used to construct the structure as proof that they'd braved it. Maybe steal a kiss or two—if the wenches weren't too ungodly ugly or unwilling. Never did they expect the earth to heave up and assist them the moment they rammed the gate. It was as if God had decided to open the door for them and had even given them the key.

The Caruths within the walls had fought hard, deathly hard, as was their creed. They'd been battle-prepared and hadn't waited to engage in one. There'd been so much blood. His vision was stained with it. That was regrettable. As was Ian's death. Payton closed his eyes. Nobody was supposed to die.

"The king's given you a goodly portion of Caruth kirk, as well."

"He . . . has? Why?"

"Well, only if you can seize it and hold it. 'Tis what your da petitioned for."

"Da . . . petitioned The Stewart?"

She grinned. More of her foul breath touched him. Payton was grateful he couldn't take great, lung-expanding gulps of air at the moment. "Aye. The moment he heard. He's had a blood-lust for the earl of Kilchurning that nothing can stanch. They've been feuding ever since the earl's great-aunt left your great-grandfather standing at the wedding altar whilst she eloped with that Irishman some generations back. You know the story."

Payton groaned.

"Why . . . to ken that his own son filched Kilchurning's betrothed right from beneath the man's nose was beyond great! The laird was crowing. Strutting. Saw his chance and took it. He turned his mount about the moment he learned and went right back to Edinburgh. I dinna' ken if he even stopped for a change of horseflesh. That's how pleased he was at your exploits."

"Da . . . did that?"

"Aye. And all exclaimed over the tale. Why . . . the king's entire court's been a-buzz at what you did. It's highly chivalrous.

They're bandying it about as a sonnet. You might hear it once you've healed enough."

"*Nae,*" Payton whispered.

"Oh, aye. With minstrels. They sing of your attack of the Caruth tower with but a band of ten clansmen. Your taking of the castle . . . splitting the roof wide open and fighting your way in. 'Twas most heroic. And then filching the heiress right from beneath their noses? Na' only that . . . but wedding and bedding with her, too? And all a-fore clan alarm could be given? 'Tis said you've the strength of a demon and the speed of a griffin. Why, they're even saying you're immortal, since *nae* mortal could have done it."

Payton breathed out slowly and a curse went with it.

"Little do they ken the wench stuck a sewing needle in your side, putting you on your back worse than any whore." She was cackling and chortling, and he couldn't decide which was worse, her words or her laughter.

"You need to learn that about women, Payton Dunn-Fadden."

"Learn . . . what?"

"Na' all folk tremor at your passage, young one, although you've done so much to gain yourself that reputation, it will probably be truth now. Na' all men run in fear from you, nor do all the women swoon in ecstasy even a-fore you touch them."

"I'm really tired," he said, more to shut her up than because it was true. He didn't want to hear another word.

"Women. Mark my words, Payton Dunn-Fadden. The women will be falling over themselves to get your attention. Even worse than a-fore. You've a reputation now. You're a dangerous man. A conqueror. Taking no quarter and expecting none."

Payton groaned again. There wasn't any way to stop her words. She wouldn't cease them until she said everything and made it worse. The Caruth wench hadn't betrayed him. She hadn't said a word about it. He wondered why. He couldn't even remember her name. Or her face. She hadn't been remarkable except for the size of her bosom once he'd had it displayed, and even that vision was tempered by a haze of pink-washed pain he'd been looking through. She had brown hair. He thought it was brown. It had been tightly braided about her head, but a few strands had come loose in her struggle to keep from being wed. It looked to be a brown color, interspersed with red; an autumn red, tinged with a bit of orange. Her eyes had been a hazel color, more brown than green. Unremarkable. That's what she was. No great beauty. And she might even be older than his twenty-two years. Maybe. He didn't really know. She hadn't been young. That, he knew.

"We'll start your new lessons with the basics."

"Lessons?" Payton asked. He didn't bother opening his eyes. He didn't care. The entire episode was dreamlike and approaching nightmarish. It was better not to see it.

"About women. And wenches. And what a man's to do with them."

"I dinna' need any help with that, crone."

She laughed again. He ignored her. His mind wandered back to the Caruth lass in that pristine, bare room . . . the white dress she'd worn; the pale, almost translucent beauty of her skin against the large, red ripeness of her lips.

He couldn't fathom why she hadn't spoken the farce, saving both of them from his foolishness. Unless she needed the news that he'd taken a maiden wall, because she no longer owned one. Payton pulled in as much breath as he could and wondered at the insanity he'd made of his life. He'd wed the Caruth heiress, gained himself a reputation and land, and he couldn't even recollect what she looked like? He couldn't truly call it wed, actually. Hand-fasted, maybe. That, they were. But . . . wed?

"Just mark these words, Payton Dunn-Fadden. Mark them

well. Some wenches truly dinna' wish your attentions. You must make certain they've no weapon next time, a-fore you mount them. You might na' survive the next prick." She put back her head and hooted even louder.

That was when the lie began.

Chapter 2

The lie ruled his life. Usually as an ache he barely felt. Sometimes it came as a raging belly of disgust. Sometimes it was muted, whispering through him and making him shudder with what those about him might be thinking. But always it was there, hovering in wait. That was when it was most powerful. When it was dormant . . . and he didn't know for how long. That's what he feared.

Payton took another blow and then another, until he was on his knees facing a sea of mud flecked with his own blood. Then, and only then would the lie subside and go deep into his soul where it would stir the hatred. He had to wait for the self-hate to get big enough and harsh enough. Then it turned everything into a red wash of color that would pump strength back to his limbs.

Then Payton would start to win.

It was ever this way. The battle would be lengthy, allowing the Stewart king time to flirt with his latest mistress, and his lords to wrangle and bet on the eventual winner. By then the King's Champion would be faltering. His legs wouldn't have much feel, his arms would be dead weight attached to his shoulders, and it became a fight simply to lift his shield to ward off yet another blow. This was when the king covered most of the wages. Because somehow the diminutive Stewart knew.

He knew it would happen. He didn't know that the lie Payton harbored was solidifying and glowing, warming until it became hot, and then it got dangerous. It became fire—sending rage to every part of him with every pump of his heart. He gave a warning. He always gave a warning, with a yell so deep and guttural, he could hear the applause already starting before it was drowned out by drums. The king always had drummers at his side, keeping a light prancing cadence of taps throughout the evening until Payton's yell changed it. Then, the drums became one blended thump that kept growing until it was the only thing he heard.

This time went exactly the same. They'd found him a Welshman capable of making a decent fight, sponsored by a nameless prince with a full purse. The Welshman was also covered in animal hide trews and tunic, and smelled worse than a latrine at high summer.

Payton didn't wait until his yell died out. He couldn't. He wasn't in control, anymore. The lie was. It turned him into a hate-filled menace that was feeding off the drumbeat until his movements matched them. His shield felt as light as feathers, his club had the same weight of bread, and he used both to pummel; striking again and again at the man he was facing until they'd call a halt, and even then he seldom heard it at first.

King James usually stopped it with a blast from his pipes, immediately followed by the cessation of the drums. Sometimes, he had to send men onto the field to pull Payton from his opponent. On those rare occasions, it felt like the self-hate was consuming him, frightening him with the intensity of it as he waited for the woman behind it all to open her mouth, branding him a fool, a coward, and a fraud.

The Welshman looked like a mud-covered heap of dead animal. He groaned occasionally, showing his defeat. He was still breathing. He lived. Payton turned away and stalked from them. It was time to hide in his chambers, where his bath and a feast would be waiting for him, as well as a lovely wench to make sure it was all to his satisfaction. He didn't look twice at the Welshman. He didn't care.

They didn't say he fought like a demon without cause.

"Dear Lord!" Dallis gave it as much emotion as she dared. There were too many serfs still about, raising a slight dusting of snow with each footstep as they swept what had once been a stately and beautiful great hall. She looked up and blinked as more snowflakes filtered down from three stories up, showing how frail the latest roof patch was.

"Leroy!" She hollered it loudly, since he was probably outside by now. Most of the Dunn-Fadden clansmen were. They had animals to secure, since the storm hadn't waited as she'd prayed and hoped and worried for.

"I hope you dinna' pay too much for that."

"Of course I paid too much. When would I have grown sense?" Dallis snapped, glaring for a moment at her companion's head before looking away.

"I dinna' say that," the older woman answered.

"I ken as much. I said it so you would na' have to. I already ken that everything I pay for, and everything I do to save this keep is wasted. I'll still do it. 'Twas my inheritance and entrusted to me. I'll na' shirk it."

"Your father dinna' entrust it to you. The king forced him to. That's why it's in this condition while he covers the kirks, fanning the feud with Kilchurning. It was entrusted to that man . . . the King's Champion. Your husband."

Dallis swept harder, but that was the only hint she gave of listening.

Beside her, Lady Evelyn snickered. "'Tis your fault, you know."

"I dinna' control the weather."

"*Nae,* but you do control the fates."

"Nonsense."

"'Tis what happens every time you use what funds he sends to try and exact your revenge. Time and again I tell you, and yet you go against my advice."

"Advise me something I want to hear, then."

The older woman shook her head. "'Twas most stupid this time. The Welsh canna' fight well enough to take him down."

"Leroy!" Dallis turned her head and yelled the name again. If he didn't answer, she was going to have to climb up and out onto the balcony of what used to be her servant's chambers and try and put the woven thatch piece back in position. That was a daunting task. It was going to be precarious and it was going to be cold. Her shoulders sagged slightly as she started hitching her skirts into her belt, revealing a worn underdress.

"Actually . . . now that I think on it, I dinna' ken if there's anyone that fights well enough to win him."

"Somebody will win him. I just have to find one."

"You'd be better served using his funds on his keep, filling his larder, his woodpile, and his treasury. Like his missives instruct."

Lady Evelyn went back to sweeping, before the snow melted and made a mess of the dried rushes. The woman was nearing sixty, and as her niece's chaperone and companion, she should have been sitting beside a fireplace, sewing tiny little stitches into a tapestry to adorn the castle walls. Since every bit of gold that the great champion, Laird Dunn-Fadden, sent toward the upkeep of the castle was gathered up and saved until there was enough to find another warrior to pay for Dallis's revenge, Lady Evelyn was forced to do what they all did: work in order to survive.

Dallis didn't let it bother her. Not today. Maybe after she'd reached the thatch across the roof, seen the damage caused by the storm, and secured it again. Then, maybe she'd feel guilty. But not now. She had too much to do.

It was colder the closer she got to the roof. Dallis ran the steps past her rooms, and when she reached the battlements, she could see why. It wasn't just a storm, it was a horrific wind-driven storm. The thatch was still intact. That was a blessing. It was waving about in the wind since one of the mooring ropes had come loose. Dallis scrambled onto the merlon, settling her buttocks into a cupped area that seemed molded for them, and pulled until her arms ached. The last repair had been the cheapest, and they'd chiseled out a slight line in each crenel for the ropes to hug into. One had itched its way loose. She breathed out the relief as she caught the line and pulled it back into position, and even managed to keep her seat at the same time.

She didn't hear the commotion until she was finished and rounding the stair near the second story. If it was what it sounded like, she wasn't prepared. She might never be.

"The . . . meaning?"

The stammering voice was Lady Evelyn Caruth. Her voice was old and feeble sounding and it hadn't been earlier. It wasn't hard to find the cause. A large retinue of men was filling the great hall, too numerous to count. They wore Dunn-Fadden colors, and they weren't the faded, worn plaid all the clansmen about her wore. Theirs were newly woven, bright with dye, and embellished with pure silver thread if she wasn't mistaken. If Dallis was in control of her own heartbeat, it probably would've stopped. Instead it thudded harder, making it difficult to breathe. She knew instantly who it was. Anyone would have.

It was their laird, the King's Champion . . . and her husband.

"I want an accounting and I want it now. Where is the mistress?"

"I—if you'll allow a-a moment?" Lady Evelyn began, but he interrupted her.

"A moment? The pipes have been blasting my arrival from the other side of the bailey. You've had more than enough time."

He wasn't shouting. He didn't have to. Lady Evelyn reached his midchest and she hadn't much stiffness in her backbone anyway. She was probably close to breaking into sobs. Dallis hadn't much time. She pulled the skirt from her belt as she took the stairs, ignoring the shaking of her hands as she did so. If she cowed the moment she saw him, he'd win. Again. That was not going to happen.

"Here."

He'd taken off his fur cloak and tossed it to one of his men. It didn't mute the sensation of his size. She remembered that. Three years and she still remembered how large, how well-defined, and just how handsome he was. And then he turned his head and saw her.

He might as well have flung a bucket of snow melt on her for the blast of cold that happened. She must have forgotten the impact of his ice-blue eyes, but couldn't imagine how it could've happened. They'd been in her dreams, shadowed her steps, and haunted her every waking moment. It should have prepared her for when she got his gaze again.

"You there!" He was pointing at her. Dallis knew her heart stopped then. She couldn't prevent it. All she could do was ignore it and hope it worked. She sucked for air, lifted her chin, and tossed the loose braid of hair over her shoulder. She hadn't donned proper attire such as a wimple, a girdle, and a dress befitting her station. She rarely did, and today was laundry day so there hadn't been a need. She didn't let it matter. Cowardice didn't gain a Caruth much.

"Yes?" she answered, and was grateful her voice had no sign of the wavering every portion of her body was suffering.

"I demand an accounting!"

Dallis gulped. *Now?* He wasn't even going to see they had privacy? It was going to be difficult enough showing where funds had gone without him guessing the truth. Her eyes went huge. She couldn't prevent it.

"Why is everyone mute the moment I speak with them? Fetch the mistress. Perhaps she'll not cower in fear from me. Go! Now!"

Dallis's mouth fell open as what had to be shock raced through her, turning everything numb. It started at her throat, and it slithered until it reached her toes. He didn't recognize her? Her eyes narrowed before her mouth closed. She had to look away in order to answer. This time her voice did warble. "I'll see her fetched for you, immediate-like, my lord."

"See that you do. Redmond! Find my steward, Leroy. Have him brought before me as well. And stoke this fire!"

Dallis didn't hear the rest. She was running back up the stairs.

His belly was burning and it transferred to his eyes as Payton looked over his keep. He'd sent a large portion of the gold he'd won and this was the result? His eyes ran over the sparse furnishing, the hangings that didn't look to have been repaired or replaced since that fateful day, and he had to swallow the sourness back down so it could keep the lie he always harbored company. He'd expected anger, maybe hatred, but an impoverished keep and nothing in the way of a welcome? His wife had much to answer for.

"Sir?"

The hesitant voice belonged to the elderly woman he'd first met. Payton made her wait. And he made it a long wait. He was doing a visual inspection of his hall. From the looks of it, his wife hadn't even seen to a repair on his roof, nor the large crack across the floor. There wasn't even leaded glass in the window openings. There were shutters. He narrowed his eyes in consideration. The Dunn-Fadden clan he'd left here had seen to the fitting of those shutters. They fit well. Kept the drafts out . . . but allowed very little light in.

The woman cleared her throat again. Payton lowered his chin and glared at her. She backed two paces from him. It didn't give him any satisfaction.

"What?" he finally asked.

"That—that . . . *was* the mistress." She waved her hand in the direction of the spiral stair.

Payton closed his eyes, knew the sickness in his belly was due to the lie he harbored as it roved about, weakening him and making him feel like a lad again. He had no choice but to hide it. Again. "Well," he replied finally. "My luck with women is accursed bad. As always."

"How so?" His vassal, Redmond, asked.

"My keep is a ruin and my wife dresses in sackcloth. Added to that is her visage, and that she's as plain as the day is long. What would you call it?"

Redmond's lips didn't even twitch. Payton liked that about the man. Vast sense of humor. "I call it a waste of good fund. Perhaps with a good cleaning and the proper cloth?"

"Order it, and oversee it."

The elderly woman gasped. Payton looked back at her. "We speak of the hall, old one. Not the wife. I'll gird her alone. In my chamber." His boots made little sound on the spread of rushes in the hall. That was a good sign. This Dallis knew the value of fresh sweet rushes. Good for insulation and for disguising stench. That was one mark in her favor.

He had his foot on the first step before Redmond spoke again. "Make a scan of the woman's sewing basket first, my laird."

Payton's lips twisted as he turned back. He couldn't help it. "I intend as much. Send a contingency of guards back to Edinburgh. I've decided to take His Majesty up on his offer of stonemasons and carpenters. See to that, as well."

"Such gifts come with strings."

Payton nodded. "I ken as much. Don't come up. No matter how much screaming you hear."

"I've na' heard you scream a-fore," Redmond returned. "'Tis shaping into a vastly more entertaining eve than I'd foreseen."

Payton grinned, and turned to take the steps two at a time. They'd fashioned a tight wheel staircase. He had his left hand against the stone as he climbed. He didn't recollect that and he'd been carrying her at the time. It wasn't surprising. He'd been stewed, and rarely tried to remember any of it.

She had the door locked. He discovered as much when he tried to twist the heavy metal handle. She might even have it barred from within. That was going to be difficult. Payton sucked in on both cheeks as he looked at it. He was called the King's Champion. He wasn't letting a door be the thing that exposed him for the fraud he was.

He leaned forward and pushed and felt the wood give just slightly. That was a good sign. The keep had suffered moisture damage and that would give him just the edge he needed. The hall's width accommodated four steps. Payton lowered his shoulder and heaved at her door.

She didn't have it barred.

His blow shook the jamb, but it held. It groaned with the attack, however. The door wasn't far behind, as a heavy thunderous cracking noise accompanied the split that opened right in the center of it, sending large chunks of wood, a cloud of dust, and a blizzard of little slivers into her room with him at the midst of the destruction. Payton was actually amazed he kept his feet, although he had to spin fully and that left him open the entire time to any attack.

Vulnerable. She made him that. And frightened, and defamed, and weak. Always. Just her. He had his breath held until he finished a full circle and spotted her. Where she was had him raising his brows and lowering his head. She'd leapt onto her mattress and was well above him, holding a large

swath of white material against the front of her, and she was
wet. At least, her hair was wet. It was sticking to her flesh and
showing the length of it as it caressed the curve of her hip.
She had a rather shapely hip, too. He hadn't noted that before.

He tipped his head a fraction and craned his neck in order
to see it more fully. She made a half-turn away, to shield herself. White material moved with it. Payton took three steps to
his left and craned his neck again. She swiveled with the
movement and the satin moved with that motion as well. He
had his lips pursed before he moved his gaze to hers.

She didn't look cowed. Far from it. She looked determined.
She also wasn't as plain as he'd assigned her. That was a
pleasant thought. Payton stood to his full height, crossed his
arms and regarded her. The dust from his entrance was almost
settled, and the remnants wavered in the air with flecks of
glint.

"What do you want?" she asked.

He cleared his throat. It was to cover any nervousness.
"The same thing I wanted three years past," he replied finally.
He had his heartbeat under control as well, for nothing about
his voice gave him away. The satisfaction went deep. He had
control of his fraud even in her presence. He felt the cooling
sensation in the depth of his gut. He didn't give any outward
sign to any of it.

She gasped.

"And mayhap . . . more," he finished.

She was going a nice rose shade, and it suffused her skin,
until the material had the same pink shading where it got to
caress her skin. Payton licked his lower lip as she pulled the
material tighter.

"*Nae,*" she replied.

"Strange, but I'm na' at all surprised to hear you say that,"
he said.

"Dinna' you understand the word nae?"

He nodded slightly. "Verra well actually. I just doona' accept it."

"You're na' welcome in here."

"I was never welcome. What of it?" he shrugged.

"You dinna' even knock!"

"You barred me and yon door was na' crafted well. It dinna' withstand the slight touch of my knock."

She looked skeptical, and not much else. "I'm na' ready," she said finally.

Payton looked her over. She was watching for his gaze when he'd finished. "You look ready," he replied.

"You dinna' even recognize me!" She put the slightest emphasis on the words, and then she colored. If Payton wasn't mistaken, it bothered her greatly.

"There are parts of you that I definitely recognize, my lady. Definitely." He knew she had his meaning as she pulled the material even closer to her body. Which wasn't doing much to mute the fact that she had a spectacular form: large round hips, slender waist. . . . He hadn't known that.

"Doona' come one step closer!"

Payton had moved his right foot. He halted at her command. There was a shrill sound behind her words. He'd heard it before. He actually recognized it. It sounded like actual fear. He shook it off and moved his other foot. She backed to the wall and gave a gasp as her nakedness came into contact with the stone. It also made certain things happen behind the sheet she had held to her so tightly that it defined more than it covered.

That was visual, he decided. She had twin crests at her breasts, and they were a healthy size. He remembered her bosom. Payton had to turn his head to hide the expression. He couldn't do anything about the rest of his body. He was only grateful he was wearing woolen trews beneath his *feile-breacan*. Scratchy and warm. And thick. All of which was a good thing at the moment.

"Three years ago you stopped me with a slip of a skean. You verra nearly did what nae man has. I still bear the scar."

"You were forcing me!"

"What of it? Women get forced. Especially women that have been taken in battle." He took another step. She pushed farther back into the wall. Her movement made him stop. He didn't want her cowed and beaten and he didn't know why.

"But I never accepted you!"

Payton blew the snort through his lips, making a sound like the neigh of his horse. "You did more than agree, lady. By keeping silent, you've more than accepted me as husband. And then you added to it by taking my gold, abusing my keep, and doing naught a good wife should."

"Perhaps you should have been a good husband, then," she retorted.

"My thoughts exactly. We've reached accord. Already. This bodes well." He was teasing as he hooked his thumbs under the fastening of his belt. He had a heavy, real silver buckle that the Stewart had crafted especially for his champion. It had a weight and rigidity to it that any other belt wouldn't have achieved. He watched her eyes flit there and then back to his face.

"What . . . are you going to do?" she asked.

"Whatever I want." The rush of power hit the region about his nose and flared there, making a sting for a moment. Payton shook his head slightly. All these years he'd dreaded being face-to-face with her, and having her reduce him to boyish incompetence—and it was for this? Strangely, he didn't like the sensation. He didn't want her beaten, and he didn't want her submissive. But he did want her.

Chapter 3

If he didn't cease looking at her like prey she was going to scream, which would be stupid, and cowardly besides. Dallis narrowed her eyes, muting some of the brunt of his physical presence. She'd had nightmares of coming into contact with him again and thought herself prepared . . . for his size, his bulk . . . his presence. She knew now she'd been fooling herself. There was no way to prepare for such!

He had an even greater impact than he'd had before, if that was possible, and there was a sureness to him that must have been lacking. He had a litheness to his movements, even the one where he'd twirled through the broken door had been done with a sure-footed grace that made it look melodic and elegant. She swallowed but it was more a gulp. He was very handsome, very manly, truly eye-catching, and he looked immensely powerful. It was a shame he was so base-born. A Caruth would never accept a Dunn-Fadden as their mate. Never had. Never would.

Had he been her betrothed, how different everything would be!

She could see that no matter how much gold she'd sent to pay for a challenger against him it was wasted. She should have spent it on other methods that would have gained her freedom and given her back her power in one fell swoop . . . something like poison.

Her eyes narrowed.

"You readied yet?" he asked.

Dallis's lips opened slightly to let the gasp out and everything on her answered him. She watched his eyes flick to her breasts before returning to her face and tried unsuccessfully to stop the blush. Again. The man was maddening. And dense. And thick-witted. And didn't even know what rejection was. She swallowed.

"For what?" she asked with what she hoped was a tart tone. It didn't help that it warbled slightly.

He sucked in both cheeks and started unlacing his gloves. They were leather crafted and worn to his elbows, tightly fastened to his arms for warmth, and that gave her added moments of time as he pulled at the laces . . . first the left, then the right. He wasn't watching his hands, though. He had his chin lowered a fraction and was favoring her with his unblinking stare.

That was too much impact, and she knew he was fully aware of it.

"Our consummation," he finally said, and yanked first one glove off and then the other, turning them inside out with the motion, before swatting them back into shape against his thigh.

This time he had to hear her gasp.

"I . . . thought you wanted . . . an accounting," she replied in chunks of words.

She watched him pull at the immense silver disk of his waist, making sinew bulge in his lower arm with the motion. The claw prong on his belt gave up the fastening and he dropped it, making a heavy thud of sound on the thick white rug at his feet.

"First I secure the right. Then, I'll see to the accounting." He plucked the tucked end of his plaid from the back of his waist, and just kept watching her as the material began unwinding about his waist.

"You never had the right!" *And God curse the squeak in her voice as she said it!*

His lips lifted, making a smile on one side of his face. And then it was gone. As was his *feile-breacan*. Dallis watched with eyes that didn't seem to belong to her anymore as he tipped to one side and pushed the kilt band from his shoulder, allowing the entire mass of woven wool to fall in a puddle at his feet, covering over the silver glint of belt.

None of him was diminishing. She could tell from the way his shirt fell from humps of muscle in his chest that he'd gained even more size to his frame, and more brawn. And more power. Her breath caught, held, pained her, and then escaped. And then she had to gasp another one in.

"Since when has that put a stay on me?" Payton finally replied.

Then he was crossing his arms, grabbing fists full of the garment and pulling it from where he had it tucked into his trews and over his head with a motion designed to shock her into stillness and lock her tongue since the shirt clung to sweat-damp skin on his upper body and nothing else.

Payton Dunn-Fadden was a mountain of brawn, shadowed by the winter light into hills and dales of shadow; he had ropes of tendons pounding in his lower belly with what had to be his heartbeat; and he had a thin line of hair starting at the center of him and running downward . . . to where every thought on her stalled at the mis-match of plaid due to his size and condition.

His clan sett had been sewn into a type of trousers, molding about his lower legs before coming together in a knotted swath of material about his lower hip. There wasn't enough material to hide him. Dallis didn't move her eyes from his face, but that didn't stop her from seeing . . . and feeling everything on her body respond. It was starting with the thump in the bottom of her belly and then it was spreading. Fire flicks of shivers were followed by an ice-melt of reaction, and then that was tempered by the fire again. The ice. The shivers. Then the heat. It was covering her entire frame and making a trembling nobody had warned her about. She'd never seen an aroused man before, especially one of his size, and it just wasn't fair. Caruths learned from the time they were born of battle and loss and what a female faced should she be taken; rape and ravishment included. But not one soul had told her about what would be happening to her. Nobody. All of which was a huge hole in her education.

Dunn-Fadden was very aware of what he was doing to her and she didn't even know why she had such certainty of it. It was in the flick of his eyes when he ran them to where the pinprick darts of her nipples were trying to shove their way through the satin she'd tightened, and then he moved his gaze back to hers.

He stepped free of the mass of discarded garments and put a hand out toward her. Even from half the span of room away, she felt the menace and backed even farther into the stone at her back, earning the chill that contact caused as well.

"Now, come off that perch like a good lass."

Dallis shook her head.

"Please." He said next.

The oddest humming was running through her ears, making the word have a melodic and muted cast. Dallis shook her head again.

"I'm na' a patient man," he said next.

Dallis shook her head again. He sighed. And then he was coming for her.

The wall had no give to it and that left her only two choices to escape him: left or right. The headboard would impede her on her left, so she chose the footboard, with a slide of her body and then a lunge. She didn't get there. She was screaming as he grabbed at the satin and yanked, pulling with one hand and reeling her in like a salmon caught in the burn. It was made easy for him with the way Dallis clung to the material, digging her nails into the fabric and halting her cries for the fight, just before finding out his chest was just as hard and unyielding as it had looked when she was slammed against it. The only good thing looked to be that the samite had wadded between them, creating a barrier of material to keep the scorch of his skin from hers.

He wasn't breathing hard while she was sucking for air and then shoving it out rapidly, making her dizzy with it. And he was chuckling. Then he was holding her glued to him with one arm, while the other hand was busy lifting a hank of her hair and then, God help her, what had to be his tongue was on the back of her neck and sending a blizzard of tremors all over and then through her. There was nothing to hold to, either. Her hands were still gripping the white satin and they were now trapped together where he had her molded to him. Her legs weakened, trembled, and gave, dropping her weight. Payton shifted as he felt it, going to a knee on her mattress and placing her in the depression made by their combined weight. She collided with the bare flesh of a thigh against her backside and then even that was altered as he reached his conquering arm lower, gathering a handful of her rump in order to pull her up, lifting her so securely against him, it was difficult to breathe and impossible to move.

"Nae . . . please." She huffed the whisper between breaths that were difficult to take from the position he had her in. And then he made it immeasurably worse, by putting his entire mouth against skin and sucking his way along her jaw until he'd reached her chin, the movement forcing her head backward and making her bow slightly over his bent leg.

He grunted his amusement, feathering the breath across her gapped lips, and that was even more tortuous, she decided.

"Nae . . . Wait," she whispered again.

"For what?" He'd disconnected his mouth enough to say

that and with the words against the moisture he'd just put on her chin, came even more shivers, making it immeasurably more vibrant.

"The . . . door," she stammered out.

His left hand, the one that had been holding her head and pinning her in position for him, was moving, sliding over her shoulder and then down an arm, and back. Again. That was tempered by his huff of amusement as he lifted his head to look at her. He smiled, genuine amusement filling incredibly blue eyes, and Dallis couldn't halt the widening of her own as her heart lurched so queerly and completely it frightened her.

"Ignore it," he replied finally.

Then he was shadowing his eyes with his lashes and lowering his head, lifting her again, using the hand at her rear to hold her and the one at her shoulder to make certain of it. Dallis only had time to gasp in a breath before his lips were on hers, fully, completely, and totally.

Time stalled. Her breath was right behind it. And her hands were like twittering baby birds as clenched fingers of material fluttered at her breastbone. There was a moan happening, a deep-throated murmur as his mouth sucked at first gently, and then with more purpose, and then with full-conquering effect. Dallis's lips held for a moment and then gave to the marauding twist of his tongue and then she was experiencing waves of heat ebb and transfer through her and into him, and then back, as he flicked again and again to the caverns of her suddenly willing and voracious mouth.

She wasn't aware of the answering moan that came from her as her limited knowledge of sensation was shattered and then leveled to dust. The whorl of emotion he was stirring she'd never before known, never before tested, hadn't even been aware of. Nothing in her night-time dreams had warned her of the spiral of passion he was putting into place. Nothing had been close. She didn't feel him moving, going to his haunches on the mattress and bringing her with him, settling her into the triangle support of a bent leg, until the heat and rigidity of his arousal came into contact with her material-covered belly, making everything on her go oddly alert and focused and frightened.

"Nae . . ."

Dallis managed to pull her mouth from his long enough to say it before he had her lips again, this time lapping at both upper and lower before taking the upper into his mouth with such a delicate suction action, she was crazed with how it felt. All the while the hand at her rear alternately squeezed and lifted. Squeezed. Lifted . . . and then held her against his arousal time and again, while everything on him alternately shook and then stiffened.

His other hand wasn't unoccupied or lazy. That one was about her shoulders now, supporting and holding her and making certain she couldn't put deed to word until nothing about her was in denial except her mind, and even that her body was betraying.

He was pushing her backward, using his kiss for the tool, his upper body for leverage, and his hands to guarantee her movement until her head and shoulders reached the pillows, placing her in an arch over his bent leg. Dallis's hands moved then, releasing the satin to mold against the hard mounds of his chest, where the feel of his bare flesh against her palms was nearly as vicious a sensation as his tongue had been.

"Nae," she mouthed again the moment he released her lips.

"Why now?" His voice was lower than before and it wasn't whispered. And he was looking at her with a blend of anger and something else she didn't know enough about to name.

"I . . . doona' ken," she stammered, and earned herself another huff of amusement.

"Doona' fash yourself, then. I ken well enough for the both of us."

He released the arm at her back, sliding it away and making

her skin suffer the colder temperature of the bedding at her back without his warmth, and that impression was only slightly offset by where he'd moved it.

"Nae . . . please?" Dallis was begging and hated the pleading tone in her voice as much as she hated the urge that made her say it.

"You'd best be begging for what I can give, lass."

He was whispering it against the sensitive tissues of her lips that felt sucked raw, and then he was moving his mouth along her jawline . . . to her neck. And then he was lacing her chest with trails of fire-laced wetness he'd tongued into place. His hand was helping, and Dallis felt him at the edge of her satin, pushing it down, slapping slightly at the fingers she was putting in his way. She'd given off trying to hold him from her with her hands, and was using them now to keep him from seeing . . . touching . . . tasting.

The material slid lower, pushed by his tongue as well as his fingers, and his chuckle was making everything worse. Dallis pulled each breath in with a tense motion and let it out with a hiss as she struggled, hearing a slight rip of cloth, sensing air, and then the defeat as her nipple popped free. Then, the other. And then she was slamming her eyes shut to all of it.

That was *worse*.

"You're pleasant fair, lass. Ripe. Soft. Womanly. Perfect . . ."

She heard his whisper through rasps of breath, felt the caress of air, and then arched in shock as what could only be his tongue claimed a breast tip, lapping all about her flesh with precision and skill, and making everything on her react. She had her eyes scrunched so tight the most vivid yellow light arced through her lids, joining the riot of pleasure that started in her nether region and then swelled through her entire frame, turning her into a quivering mass of delight as his tongue gave way to his entire mouth and the suckling drove her to the brink of eroticism and then shoved her right over it. The yawning chasm of pleasure she fell into cradled her for whole moments of time as Payton toyed with her flesh, moving his ministrations from one to the other nipple, and at one point placing them in a conjoined position so he could slather both with attention at the same time.

Dallis was kicking against the bed, lurching and shoving herself against him, into him, and holding wads of hair in her fingers as she hung on, shivered, moaned, and then shrieked with the eruption of pleasure.

"Oh . . . dear God. Sweet . . . sweet . . . Oh!"

She was mouthing the words and then she was screaming them. And it was Payton orchestrating it, huffing a bit between his ministrations to make certain of a response. Then he was moving the white satin lower, lifting his weight from her with one arm, while the other slid the material down . . . revealing the flatness of her belly, and swell of her hip . . . the reddish colored hair of her woman-place. And then he swore with a deep guttural tone, while the mattress bowed and then rocked with his exit from it.

Dallis was afraid to open her eyes at first. The position he'd left her in was indefensible, open and wanton and female. There was nothing about her that looked to be fighting him, either.

The sound of movement at the door had her moving her head, pulling the satin from her knees at the same time. It was Payton. He was maneuvering the door back into the portal preparatory to dropping the bolt on it. It probably wouldn't hold, but it was better than the yawning opening of before. He was breathing extremely hard. And then he turned.

Dallis gaped. Her entire frame started shuddering and she had to slam her eyes shut again, and hope he wouldn't see the awe and fear before she could stanch it. He was still clad in the plaid trews, but they were hooked on what he possessed, delineating a weapon Dallis instinctively knew was going to cleave her apart. And worse. She wanted it. Desperately. With a craving she didn't know how to contain. . . . And with the lowly, base-born Dunn-Fadden laird.

"There. That should hold."

His words were gruff and he was nearing. Dallis didn't open her eyes. She didn't move. She was trembling with the effort of stopping her response to everything he did.

"You were right a-fore. The door should be shut. Barred."

"What?" She whispered it through cold lips.

"Nae man sees my wife. Na' now that I ken how glorious she is."

The bed dipped with his entry into it and then he was fitting himself beside her if the movement of the mattress was any indication. Nothing on her was fighting it and yet everything was. Dallis kept her eyes closed, denying the knowledge entry.

"Why did you cover again?" he asked from a position above her head, every breath ruffling strands of her hair.

She shook her head.

"You'll na' say?"

She shook her head again.

"Why na'?"

He was fitting a finger along her collarbone and sliding it along flesh that was so sensitive, the motion raised a riot of goose bumps.

She shook her head again.

"I appear to have marked you. Na' good."

"What?" Dallis whispered again. Nothing he said made sense. The way he was holding himself from her made less of it.

"We've but started, lass. You ken?" he asked.

Dallis shook her head again.

He grunted. "'Tis a good thing, that. And bad."

"What?" She slit her eyes open. He was heaving for breath, toying with a lock of her hair and turning such an uncertain look toward her that she frowned. The King's Champion . . . hesitant and unsure?

"'Tis a verra good thing that you ken naught of tupping. The act of it."

He had such amazing blue eyes! Eyes that looked akin to pools of warmth, holding such depth and soul it was difficult to gaze into them! Dallis blinked.

Since she'd come of an age for a betrothal, Dallis had been warned of the beauty of the Dunn-Fadden clan. Everyone was. She'd thought it a story to make the girls shiver in anticipation of their own wedding bed. More than one of the older matriarchs of the clan had told her to stay from the spell of their beauty, since that's all a Dunn-Fadden would ever claim. That, and poverty.

And here that beauty was. Right before her.

"I would na' have it bandied about that my firstborn be a bastard."

"What?" She wasn't pretending the confusion. It sounded in her voice.

He smiled slightly. "Our offspring. Their legitimacy. Due to your maidenhood. Despite your age, you still possess it?"

"My . . . age?" She was bristling, and that had the exactly right effect on her senses and her emotions.

"Doona' take offense. A man wishes a maiden to wife. 'Tis just . . . you're just . . . Uh . . . well. . . ." He stopped and swallowed and looked sheepish.

"Don't say it," she warned.

"You've some years to you," he finished.

"Payton Dunn-Fadden!"

"What?" he replied.

"I am na' auld! I am definitely na' *too* auld! And you have nae right to infer such! None!"

She'd gone into a sit, pulling her legs under her and he hadn't stopped her. In fact, he wasn't doing anything except grinning. Widely.

"What?" she finally said.

"Good. You've conquered your fear."

"I'm na' a-feared."

"We'll work on the lying tongue later."

"What?" Her voice was raising along with her torso and she had to keep the satin against her skin with one hand since it was locked under her legs.

"You were a-feared. And now you lie about it."

She slapped at him, losing the satin on one side at the same time. It didn't help that he caught her hand midslap, and then used it to pull her off balance, right up against him, shoving her entire backside into view since she had nothing at all to cover it. He held her in place with one arm about her torso, while the other trilled down her back, cupped her buttocks and then slid to a thigh.

Dallis gasped at the shock, and then she was warm with the blush. And then she was just all-over warm as he continued stroking her, to the midst of her back . . . down over her curves and nearly to her knees with his reach.

Payton grunted a guttural sound and then huffed a sigh. "As I said a-fore. Nice. Pleasing. Womanly . . . Perfect."

"Get your hands . . . off me," Dallis replied, but she had to swallow midsentence to get it out.

"How about my lips?" he inquired.

The sound she made wasn't an oath, but it was close.

"I'll take that for an aye," he murmured and then brought the captured hand to his lips and proceeded to touch his tongue to the fingerpad of her index finger. Then, he moved it to her middle finger, then to her ring finger, and Dallis had wide eyes on him the entire time, while needles of sensation ran down her arm to her elbows, moved from there to her back, and made everything heated again. Everything.

"You doona' wear the ring?" he asked finally when he'd given off sucking at her fingernail and pulled back a fraction.

"What . . . ring?" The throaty whisper couldn't be hers, and yet it was.

"The one I crafted. Designed. Paid for. Meant for all time to be put on your hand. For all to see. You belong to one man. Me."

"Oh. That ring," she replied with a flat tone.

He looked heavenward for a moment before lying back, making the bed groan more than she was as he pulled her atop him. Dallis locked the satin to her with an arm as she moved, bringing it with her and creating a barrier even as she split her legs to straddle him. Then he just lay there, holding her with hands like talons and heaving great breaths that moved her up and down with each of them.

"Aye," he finally replied, moving his gaze back to her face from her exposed bosom where the material didn't reach. "That ring."

"Oh." She was failing. In everything. Dallis should have registered that as her legs quivered and then slackened and then squeezed to him without her giving the order.

"Why doona' . . . you wear it?" he asked, lifting a brow with the question.

Dallis shook her head on the reply.

"Why na'?"

"'Twas Dunn-Fadden clan. It bore the Dunn-Fadden seal."

"True," he remarked, putting his mouth in a bow position with the word. Dallis concentrated on that, rather than the hard abdomen she was perched atop that kept thumping with each heartbeat against her inner thighs. And then she had to ignore the hands that were sliding around her torso, using the pressure of his forearms against her thighs to keep her from moving. She felt his movements at her buttocks, fumbling with the material he still wore. She caught a breath. Shoved it out. Caught another one.

"You are Dunn-Fadden clan," he remarked through his teeth. Dallis's eyes flew wide as heat touched her backside, scorching and branding and owning her so that her entire body broke out in a sweat of tremors.

"Always. From this day forward. Ever. Mine."

The blue of his eyes darkened, warning her as much as the pressure of his hands lifting her fractionally, holding her for raw moments filled with harsh breathing and the shake of his arms while he shoved the white satin aside, and then she was yanked swiftly down atop him and impaled.

Dallis sucked in on the scream as pure fire tore through her, branding and owning her, and then she started beating at him, silently and viciously and repeatedly, not even seeing through the blur of red in her vision. And she was sobbing. Dallis Caruth never cried. She'd have died first.

"Hush, love. Hush."

There was more he crooned in a low timbre of voice that was accompanied by his hands; he held her to him with one and the other wiped at her cheeks with the satin. And all the while he was rocking beneath her, slowly and gently and to a rhythm only he heard.

"Cease this," she whispered.

"Oh, nae. Na' now." He was smiling as he said it and then he was crooning nonsensical words again, and rocking hard enough to make the bedstead creak with it.

"Please?"

"Never."

"But . . . you hurt me."

"Could na' be helped, love. You had a maiden wall to breach, and I'm na' a small size."

"You're still hurting me."

One side of his mouth lifted. His hands continued moving her forward and backward. "Give it time, love."

"How . . . much time?"

The pain wasn't as intense, nor did it burn anymore, but it was definitely tender and raw and his movements were making everything jumpy and sensitive.

"A bit," he answered.

"But you hurt me," she repeated.

This time the huff of amusement was hard enough to cool her belly with the force he gave it.

"I ken as much. 'Tis only fair."

"For what?"

"The pain you give to me."

Dallis straightened, earning a groan from the man beneath her, but he didn't stop his rocking.

"Pain?"

There was the slightest smirk on his lips at the way she said it and then he slit his eyes open, caught her gaze and nodded.

"Definite . . . total . . . pain," he replied, and then he went back to his crooning and rocking.

"Where?"

The ripple of laughter went all through him and transferred from where her hands were balanced on his chest and where they were joined, until she trembled with it as well.

"Now what?" Dallis asked.

"Doona' move. That's what."

She wasn't moving anything. He was. Still. Although he wasn't humming anymore. He was still moving her up and down, increasing the speed proportionately each time. He was sucking in small gasps of breath, too, easing them out and then doing it again, making a pout each time. That was visual and stirring and showing every bit of his handsomeness. She didn't feel remotely like weeping anymore, either. What she felt was flickers of sensation coming from where he had her linked to him, to flit about her frame and lift every bit of hair she possessed.

"Payton?" she whispered.

"Aye?"

"I doona' understand."

He chuckled then, caught her to him with a sit-up of motion to halt everything, groaned, and then started shaking.

"Sweet Jesu'. I'm na' sure I can stay this . . . much longer."

"Stay . . . what? Where?"

"This!"

He slammed his mouth against hers, pulling her into an embrace of unbreakable strength with one arm, while the other held her loins exactly where they were, and then he was moving, shifting, pulling, and tearing and making everything hurt again. And if he'd give her a moment from the assault on her mouth she'd tell him of it.

And then she was on her back, her legs wrapped all about him, and holding for dear life as he started pummeling her body with his, leaving off any small movements to make large, heavy lunges that made the entire mattress sway while the creak of the bed was louder than ever. And he was crooning love words again between kisses.

"Ah lass. Lass. Love. That's it. Sweet! Sweet! Ah . . . Jesu'!"

Dallis held to him as he arched upward then, filling her entire vision with a red flush happening all over him, and the deepest, most heart-rending sobbing noise came with it. Dallis had her hands full of him, her arms wrapped about him, finding that holding to him was lifting her from the mattress as well, and then he was shuddering, the massive arms holding him making the bedstead rattle for a differing reason before he collapsed heavily, pushing every available bit of air from her body since he landed directly atop her.

"Pay . . . ton?"

The name came out in two parts due to not having enough breath to say it. He groaned slightly and then snorted. Dallis tried again, and this time, she trilled a finger along his side. The response this time was a roll to the side of her with his upper body. It didn't separate them and he was still shaking and twitching there. Dallis reddened despite herself as she looked down at them.

"Jesu', Mary. *And* Joseph. Where did you learn to tupp,

wife?" He lifted his head to ask it before dropping it back to the pillows again.

"Well!" Dallis pulled in the surprise and anger and tried shoving away from him, but that was as successful as shoving at a loaded cart would be.

He was chuckling then, and moving his head sideways to rub his chin along her cheek. "Dinna' take more offense, Wife. Just get the damned ring on your finger."

"I . . ." She stopped. She didn't know how to tell him she'd sold it.

"If you've lost it, I'll have another crafted. Larger. With a larger stone. I might just make it with a chain, too. Attached to me."

"What? Why?"

"Because you are . . . without one doubt . . . the most amazing woman I've ever had. Ever."

I . . . am?"

"Oh, aye."

Dallis couldn't believe the ripples of joy that cascaded over her at the praise. And then she stopped it. This was the Dunn-Fadden clan laird heir. She shoved again at him.

"And cease that."

"But Payton. I have to wash. I have to . . ."

He opened one eye and stopped every thought with the blue-lit color made easy to spot since he had both eyebrows lifted.

"Oh, nae. You're na' to move. Na' yet. Na' for some time. And if you complain more, I may make it a larger span a-fore I allow you from my marriage bed. Jesu'! You're that good, lass. That good. I hope I survive."

"Payton!"

Chapter 4

The disgust started the moment he disengaged himself from her and rose from her bed. Dallis knew what the sensation was and welcomed it, and then used it to temper and cover over what she'd done. She'd failed clan creed. Not only had she been taken by an enemy, but she'd failed to exact the proper revenge for it. It no longer mattered about the funds she'd used against him, or the sleepless nights she'd undergone plotting her vengeance, nor what emotion she'd vowed to show him if he dared be in her presence again. She'd schooled herself to show nothing but disdain and hatred.

And her own body had betrayed her!

She could hear him fussing with the basin of water at her long dresser, splashing a bit. That raised the gall, as well. He was washing the proof of her maidenhood from himself. Her blood . . . not his.

It was better to stay buried with her face in the mattress than witness any of it. Maybe that way, it would all stay hidden.

"Wife?"

The title was smoothly said and in a low grumble of voice, alerting her to his approach. Her back tightened.

"My name is Dallis," she replied in a stiff voice.

He chuckled and the mattress bowed with his weight.

"I ken as much," was his reply.

"Then use it."

There was silence for a bit and then there was a slap of a wet cloth upon her backside, followed by her gasp. And that was accompanied by a jerk in the bed he couldn't help but feel.

"Here."

His warning was too late, but she should have known a man whelped by a she-wolf had little manners and less sense.

"Wash yourself."

"Nae."

"We'll work on obedience to your husband after we work on your lying tongue," he replied.

Dallis pushed her teeth together to halt the immediate response. She couldn't do anything about the pull of breath that came with it that was loud enough he heard it. And would know what caused it.

"So do as I say. Wash."

She shook her head, rolling her cheek against the satin sheet.

There was a moment respite before what had to be his hand came down on her buttock. Fully and with a loud slap.

Dallis whirled onto her back, making the mattress sway as much as their mating had, and she was glaring at him when it was done. He wasn't witnessing her expression, primarily because he wasn't looking at her face. He was looking at her bosom and liking what he saw.

She pulled at the bedding and almost had it to her breasts before he stopped her with a fist full of material directly between where she held it. Despite her straining against his one hand, all that happened was a slight ripping noise somewhere in the fabric and his amusement feathering every breath across her exposed skin, lifting rivers of shivers she'd die before she admitted.

"I said, wash yourself."

Now, he was talking to her bosom.

"When you've gone."

He pulled on the coverlet she held, raising her into a sitting position with the motion and proving the power in just one arm, as well as her obstinacy in not letting go.

"What makes you think I'll leave?" he asked.

"You got what you wanted. You'll leave."

He swung his gaze to hers and even steeled for the contact, she had to force her jaw not to slacken when she got it. She told herself it was due to his handsomeness and not any other reason, and then worked on believing it.

"Do you na' listen, either?"

Dallis straightened her back, which was pure stupidity, since that just made every bit of her jut right at him, catching his glance before he moved it back to her face again.

"Say something I wish to hear. I'll listen."

"You're a bonny one, Wife. Right bonny. I'm man enough to appreciate it. And hold on to it. You ken?"

"That is na' what I wish to hear."

Both sides of his mouth quirked, and the line beside his lips followed as he smiled. And she didn't need to note any of that!

"I suppose you're wishing it was your intended husband in your bed and at your side . . . and with the right to your body?"

"Nae man has the right to my body. Including you. Especially you."

It would help if he wasn't rubbing the sheet between his thumb and fingers with a mesmerizing tempo, right between her breasts. It would also be beneficial if her body wouldn't note that he was doing so. Nearly touching her. And all that was made worse when she couldn't prevent the tightening of her breast tips at the possibility of such an event.

"And with the proper size and prowess to grant such satisfaction to you that your skin still tells of it?"

If there was a purgatory ripe enough to place him in, she hoped he'd fall into it and then stay there!

"I dinna'—", she began.

"Kilchurning is too small to satisfy you, Wife. Much too small. Near shamefully so."

"How would you ken?" Dallis shot back.

"Wenches talk. And gossip. They're heavy with their praise, while blunt with their stings."

"You listen to women's gossip?" Now it was her turn to put amusement in the words and she did so with such satisfaction, she was probably glowing with that. Which was a better thing than the other reason, the sensual response he was lifting in her. That she was definitely keeping hidden.

"When they're beneath me and I've failed to keep their lips busy with something else . . . aye."

Dallis's face fell. She felt it. "Get out." The tone she used would have made Leroy's eyes puff up with unshed tears. She already knew that. The man holding her sheet didn't seem to be affected in the slightest.

"When I'm good and ready to. And na' one moment a-fore."

"Now, Dunn-Fadden. Out."

"We've been wed years, *Dallis*." He emphasized her name, and she tried to tell herself that at least he'd used it this time. "I'm your husband. Dunn-Fadden clan . . . which makes you Dunn-Fadden clan. Legal and right and justly."

"You are na' my husband!"

"Would you be carin' for a repeat? I'm man enough to bed you again. And willing, as well. Or, perhaps you'd like to test that."

She couldn't control the response her body was giving him, and watched as he saw it. All of it. He scanned from the tight pinch of her nipples to the slight opening of her lips to gasp breath in and then caught and held her gaze from beneath lowered eyelids. It wasn't her fault! She wasn't versed in what to do when a man lowered his voice, moved a fraction closer to her. Or maybe it was the pulling on the sheet she held that took her closer to him, but it had the same effect, and all of it was to demonstrate the status of his arousal. Dallis had never been around a virile male before Payton Dunn-Fadden. The Caruth clan made certain of that. And she'd never had a man place that manliness in her face before. She didn't even know they did such.

She settled with shaking her head.

"You surrender? Already?" He was pulling her closer as he said it, and she either had to go with the sheet or give it over and be naked. Either was bad.

"I doona' wish a . . . repeat," she whispered just before knocking her shoulder into his chest. Both his arms went around her, locking her where she was, and then she knew what was worse.

He snorted, the air from it tormented her shoulder while what had to be his mouth touched at her neck. "Your frame says different."

"We both ken . . . I canna' prevent . . . you from taking me," Dallis stammered it in a throaty whisper. "You're too . . . strong."

"I'm fond of your wording even if it's a lie."

"Payton—." What was meant as a curt tone, came out breathless and warm.

"Aye?" he murmured against her skin.

"Why . . . are you doing this? Now?"

"Why na? I've an estate to secure and a wife to do it with. And I find her womanly and ripe and verra pleasing to the eyes. And the touch."

"Nae, I . . ." She was losing her thought to his tongue against her shoulder as the spot sparked, and then warmed, markedly and rapidly.

"And now I wish an heir."

"A . . . bairn? You wish a bairn?"

"What man does na'?"

He was rolling her in his arms, placing her fully against his chest and putting her in a twist since she refused to split her legs to straddle him.

"But—."

"You've too many words and none of them worth the listen," he replied.

She shoved at him and gained herself stronger bands about her torso. And not much else. "But . . . we already did that," she stammered.

Payton hooted what was probably laughter and it lifted her with it. It also lifted his mouth from her. "Once? You believe I'll gain an heir with but once?"

She nodded.

He grunted, settled back onto the bed, and then pooled her into the cavity of his thighs, causing a contact with his arousal that speared her in the lower back. And that caused him to stammer. "'Tis possible . . . I've heard. True enough. Dallis, lass. With enough luck. I've about spent my share of luck. Aside from which . . . I want to."

"Well, I don't."

"Jesu', Wife. Do you never tell the truth?"

He had every right for the confident way he said it, since she'd taken off shoving at him and had her fingers threaded through his midnight hair and was sliding her own mouth along his jaw preparatory to securing his kiss.

"It is . . . the truth."

She lost the last word against his mouth as her lips melded to his, and the moan that escaped them probably had more of her voice to it than his. She'd worry about that later. After he left. And when her conscience returned from wherever it had hidden.

"The next thing you'll be speaking is that you wish it was Kilchurning gracing your bed and pleasuring your body."

"Kil . . . churning . . ." She split the name with her breaths, but that was his fault.

"Aye—"

"Kilchurning!"

The guttural cry coming through the door interrupted him. Dallis's eyes met his for a fraction. She watched the black of his enlarge to overshadow the intense light blue color and wondered at her sanity in noting that.

"Laird Dunn-Fadden! 'Tis Kilchurning!"

"Where?"

Payton yelled it as he shoved from her, making a buzz in her ear with the volume of voice he gave it. He pushed her into the mattress in order to spring to the floor. From there he went to a squat, shoving aside his discarded clothing for his weapons. Dallis pulled the covers to her chin and shimmied to the far wall, putting her back against it and ignoring the cold from the stone.

"Here!"

He growled it as a dirk was tossed her way, landing in the sheet at her knee. *He's giving me a knife?* For a scant moment she felt like giggling, and then put it aside.

She didn't have time for such an idea. Payton's tupping with her had taken the choice away. She didn't have the luxury of wedding Kilchurning once she proved her virginity. Like before. Now, all she had was the right of captive.

"Well? Where?"

Payton was at the door, pulling the bolt out of its socket, rather than lifting it. He wasn't wearing a stitch of clothing.

It was the man that had been with Payton earlier. In the shadows of the hall he looked even more massive. And he was fully dressed. Dallis caught his glance and went so warm with the blush the wall at her back lost its chill.

"At the woods. Inside the demesne."

"Jesu', Man! You interrupted me for that?"

Payton straightened and pulled himself into a full stretch,

while Dallis tried to ignore the winter light as it caressed sinew and muscle and buttocks. It wasn't possible! She had to turn aside.

"You were warned," his man continued.

"Aye. 'Tis why I posted guards. You ken that."

"I also ken our numbers."

"So? Each one is worth three men. And he'll be spent. 'Tis a fair ride from Castle Kilchurn," Payton said.

"Unless he encamped closer."

"Why would he do that?"

"To gird you in this accursed tower the moment you're spotted outside Edinburgh's high walls . . . what else?"

"Only if he had warning. Who would give him that?"

Both men turned and looked toward her. Dallis could see it from the corner of her eye. She kept her gaze fixed to the footboard. She supposed they thought they were whispering.

"'Tis a blizzom outside. Kilchurning is daft."

"The man is burning with vengeance. Warms a body in the coldest of climes. You ken this. 'Tis your own creed."

She waited for Payton to answer, then had to look at what was taking so long. He'd donned the shirt and was shaking out his plaid, prior to winding it back onto his frame. And then he secured it with the immense silver belt of the King's Champion. "You sent Daws?" he asked, when the belt was affixed.

"And Graham. To Edinburgh. Upon your order."

Payton nodded. "We're ten then."

"Aye."

"And Kilchurning?"

"Forty." The man in the hall shrugged. "Perhaps more. Less. 'Tis difficult to be certain in the storm. Dugan dinna' wait around to count fully."

Dallis was going cold again. And it wasn't from any element outside her body anymore. Forty . . . or more? Against ten? Payton was mad.

"Heat the oil. Prepare the pitch. Gather the men. Check for an armory. If I still possess such. And see if there's a catapult with any service to it."

The man in the hall nodded, and didn't move.

"What are you waiting for?" Payton asked.

"You."

"I'll be down shortly."

"I'll just wait that event. Right here. Watchful."

Payton probably had the same expression she did. Dallis didn't need to verify it. She felt mystified and Dunn-Fadden looked it as he turned his head toward where she was still shoved against the wall. She raised her brows and shrugged when all he did was stare, and then relaxed as he turned back to his man. She hadn't even known she was tense.

"What for?"

"The wife." His man gave a nod in her direction in the event anyone questioned who that was.

"We've more worries than a lone woman, Redmond."

"She has one of your dirks. I want it back. On your person."

Dallis had forgotten it. So had Payton, although the outline was easy to see amidst the mass of white satin all about her. She watched him glance there and then to her face.

"She'll have need of it," he replied finally.

"You planning another romp?" Redmond asked. "Now?"

Payton chuckled. "Nae. I'm planning a battle. With your help. Go. See to my orders. I'll be down shortly."

"She's already proven treachery, My Laird. Dinna' gift her with your life."

Payton turned back to his man and lowered his voice so far Dallis couldn't catch what more he said. It must have reassured him, for the hulk turned and vacated the space he'd been in.

And then she had Payton's full attention again. But at least, he was dressed. That didn't help much as he moved across the floor to stand at her bed, feet apart and hands on his hips. He flicked a glance to the knife and back to her face. Dallis kept everything blank.

"If I allow you yon dirk, will you use it properly this time?"

"This . . . time?" She had to clear her throat of the dryness to get the words out.

"Kill the man who claims you without the right. Doona' just stick him in a non-vital spot."

He moved a hand to the scar at his left side. It wasn't necessary. She already knew what he meant.

"You dinna' have the right."

He lowered his chin and regarded her through his eyelashes. "'Tis why I gift my blade to you now. Use it. But doona' go for his manhood. 'Tis powerful hard to spot."

"Payton Dunn-Fadden!"

The name carried a bit of sob at the end of it. That matched the blur she was looking at him through. God was cursing her worse than ever to make it so! She wasn't crying and she definitely wasn't heart-sore at anything attached to him. She cared little that he was facing a force four times the size of his and was making plans for defeat. She was Dallis Caruth. She cared only what it meant to her. She didn't even care if he had his head cleaved clean off his shoulders. She didn't care—

"Or so I've been told." He stopped her thoughts with words, accompanied by a grin. That expression creased his forehead with one small line across it, while one black lock decided to caress the spot as well.

"What?" Dallis wasn't feigning the bewilderment. She was infused with it. Which was better than thinking herself saddened at what could be his demise, and her freedom from him!

"His manhood. Dinna' go for it. Go for a soft spot in his belly. Right here." He pointed to a spot above his belt. "Na' only will that prevent him from taking what's mine but t'will make his death a surety, as well."

"Payton?" The name was whispered.

"Aye?" he asked.

"I dinna conspire with Kilchurning."

"I dinna' ask if you had," he replied.

"I have na' even seen the man since . . ." Her voice trailed off.

"Since a-fore our wedding?" he supplied.

She nodded.

"Good. A loyal wife is a great asset to a man. One who cares and protects her husband's property in his absence is an even greater one."

Her eyes went wide and she knew he was watching for it. As well as the color in her skin as she blushed severely. Heat spiked through her, followed by a pallor severe enough to make her dizzy with it. And through it all, he didn't even blink. That much of his intense stare was too much. Dallis moved her gaze slightly and focused on the open door behind him, with the bolt that was broken and lying at an odd position on the floor, rather than upright beside the door in preparation of being lowered into place.

"I still dinna' betray you with Kilchurning," she finally answered.

"And I repeat that I doona' ask it. Here. Take the blade. Protect what's mine."

"Yours?" She was showing emotion and bit down on her tongue to still it. She'd been taught better!

"I'm speaking of my heir. Should God be gracious enough to grant that you carry one. Here. Take it."

Dallis looked. He held the blade out toward her, handle first. And then Dallis had it in her hand and was testing the weight. A good silversmith had smelt it for him if the balance was any indication. She tested it briefly and looked up. And watched him leap backward with both arms out.

"Dinna' fash yourself, Dunn-Fadden. I'll na' carve on you. Na' yet, anyway. Mayhap . . . later." Her attempt at humor would have worked better if she could curb the odd sensation that might be sorrow and loss.

His grin was back and it had a devastating impact on her tongue. And her heart. Dallis didn't know what the sensation that made her heart lurch in a huge motion was. She didn't want to find out, either. She was too afraid.

"You'll protect my heir? Should we have created one?"

Dallis blinked the moisture away and nodded.

"Better than you protected and cared for my keep?" he continued.

"Damn you, Payton! Can you na' just leave?" The feeling overtaking her was so close to crying it wasn't to be borne! Dallis pushed her teeth together and shoved her chin up and blinked until the room went back to being just a room.

"You'll keep it safe?"

"I kept my silence for a reason. Dinna' it ever trouble you what it might be?"

He shrugged. "I doona' know the workings of a woman's mind. I dinna' ken any man who does, either."

"You looking to be carved on already?" she asked.

He shook his head. "Only speaking my words a-fore I meet my maker. As short or as long as that could be."

"There is only one thing worse than you. And that is the laird of Kilchurning." She whispered it.

"Truly? Why?"

"Have you na' seen him?" She shuddered.

He grunted; straightened; lifted an eyebrow; speared her with a gaze that had her heart doing such antics she didn't know how to stop it, and then he tossed his head back and laughed. It was such a full and hearty noise that it brought his man, Redmond, from wherever he'd been hiding. And two others as well.

Chapter 5

The protected land surrounding his castle that a lord could ride and return from on horseback was known as a demesne. The area that Payton Dunn-Fadden claimed stretched out in three directions since there was a loch covering the entire back side. The area was just as cold, sodden with newly fallen snow, and filled with misery as it had looked to be from the crenels they'd been patrolling and checking from before finally spotting movement. The Kilchurning was approaching and he wasn't doing it with speed. That meant Payton had to use the same stealth; moving on foot—leaving the horses in the stables, where they were warm, well fed and groomed, and bedded down for the night.

All of which was useless to contemplate when he had more pressing matters to attend to.

Payton whistled softly, and accompanied it with a lift of his white wool and fur-covered arm. He wasn't surprised to see the lump of white at the edge of his vision turn into a clansman, and beyond him was another and then another. Payton pointed and knew they'd look to where silent, dark-clothed masses of men were moving, circling about the edge of the meadow. That proved at least one thing.

Kilchurning may be one of the king's landed earls, but he wasn't a powerfully cunning one.

Only a white covered bulk had a chance of hiding amidst the snow-covered heather of Payton Dunn-Fadden's land on a wintry eve. The mass of Kilchurning clansmen turned into individual spots numbering more than forty. Payton gave off counting when he reached fifty. And then he was communicating the tally to his man Redmond and waiting while it was transferred all about the line of white-clad lumps fronting his castle.

Then he gave the sign to wait.

There was no telling what Kilchurning had devised once he got his men set. It was going to be interesting to find out. Payton's keep within the bailey hadn't been repaired from the damage of three years past, but there wasn't one gap in the stone of the curtain wall that an enemy could use. None. The mass behind them was solid and secure and impregnable.

Which made it even more odd that Kilchurning would try and gird it with such a small force. It was a worse plan than the one hatched the night Payton had gained the castle. The irony made him grin and that just gave him an ache in his front teeth from the cold. It was better to stay grim and silent.

He gave the motion to move behind the Kilchurning clansmen and start taking them down. Every man had enough twine to capture ten men and tie them up, orders to get at least three, and the command to do it in silence. The silent part was the easiest, since the snow muffled the sounds of scuffling well enough.

It also made things slippery, the fog of air breath-enhanced, and the scene fantasy-driven. That was just and fair, and worked to their advantage more than the Kilchurning clansmen, since none of them were expecting the snow to turn into solid bulks of armed men. Payton had five of them down, choked to silence with a forearm to their windpipes and then gagged and trussed up before Kilchurning reached the gatehouse.

It took time, though.

His men appeared to have done as well and it was some satisfaction to note through snowflake-dusted eyelashes that each of his men claimed four to his credit. That meant perhaps a dozen Kilchurning marauders left. It wasn't as satisfying to see they'd reached the castle gate and were some distance off, though.

Payton pulled his bow from behind him, looked to each of his men and then nodded. They had orders to wound. Disable. Not kill.

The man challenging his castle had vengeance in his veins. Payton could understand. If such a treasure had been stolen away from him, he'd feel the same. Kilchurning deserved a set-back; a defeat; a ransom paid from his clan to crippling effect on his treasury. He didn't deserve death.

Payton hand-picked his Honor Guard from the warriors of Clan Dunn-Fadden for such a thing. To kill a man was easy. To take him was a deed worthy of a champion. That's why he'd ordered it so.

Aside from which, if they killed Kilchurning, there'd be an accounting to make to the Stewart king who leveled fines for such things as clan wars. Payton was already indebted to the spiteful diminutive monarch.

He would take Kilchurning by surprise, defeat him soundly, exactly as he'd done on the challenger list at Edinburgh more times than a man could count, and then see him settled in the dungeon. Then, he could go back to the pleasant pastime of enjoying his wife's bounty.

The thought warmed him, and he had to shake his head at such foolishness.

Kilchurning was yelling something, probably Dunn-Fadden's name and a slur on his family, and then a command to yield. All of which couldn't be heard distinctly, but Payton put it into place in his mind, anyway. He had to guess at the events, since nothing made much sound against the muffle of falling snow.

A dull thud filtered through the night as what had to be a battering ram hit the solid wood doors of his gate. Then came another thud. Followed by another. Somewhere in the center of his castle complex he heard the sound of a bell being rung, and that was exactly as he'd planned, in the event Kilchurning got through to them. The clansmen within were already warned and armed and ready.

Kilchurning yelled out another slur on Payton's mother and accompanied it by another hit with his battering ram. Then another. That was a waste of good wood. And needed to be stopped.

Payton jogged along the wall, skimming his fingers along stone which not only helped him with direction, but helped with the slide when his feet couldn't hold the steps he forced on them. The rock surface also made hand-holds for pulling himself back up from the cold wet snow-mash that was blanketing everything.

He lost his bow at one such slippage, scraping his knuckles on the ice-covered rock and losing feeling in his hand long enough to temper the pain. That might be beneficial if he hadn't gained both boots full of snow and started a cold ache through his ankles and into his calves. Payton huffed the breath, gained his feet, searched fractionally for the bow, and shrugged it off. In close enough proximity, an arrow worked well enough.

He could tell he was close. The thudding was transferring energy into the rock at his fingertips, and the noise was louder. It was accompanied by a worse sound, that of splintering wood.

He could also hear the slurs Kilchurning was leveling at him.

"Whoreson! Bastard cur! Whelp! Come out of there and meet me like a man, Dunn-Fadden!"

Another booming thud hit the gate. Payton slid onto his haunches then, earning himself what felt like slices of dirks along the back of a thigh and into the other knee. He knew once it warmed, it would probably prove exactly that, since ice proved knife-sharp and he'd used it as such before. He pulled himself up, glanced at the red-streaked snow, and felt the worry start.

The lie was missing. His gut told him of it.

Nowhere in his body was there a core of emotion or a depth of anger large enough to change everything into rage and hate and a lust for the win. He needed the drums. He needed the crowds. He needed the lie. He hadn't known it until then.

"Come out, coward!"

Payton was within shot of them, and could have easily pegged Kilchurning's throat if he had his bow and wished to. As it was, he stopped for a moment, pulled in a breath and looked about him for the others.

Nothing.

"If you will na' come out, Dunn-Fadden, I'll take your guts and twine them about your roof!"

Such a thing would at least untwist them, Payton decided, feeling a twinge in his belly that had nothing to do with championship fighting, and everything to do with fear. He dared not take this many Kilchurning clansmen by himself.

The felled tree hit the door again with punishing force, although the thudding sound of it was still muted with the damp. Payton saw the men advance into the stone portal itself as the men sensed the give in it, before they were all shoved backward as the bolt once more held.

Well-aimed arrows would have changed everything, stopping them in the confusion of a hit on legs or arms and making them drop their ram. If only he hadn't fallen and lost his bow! Payton pulled his sword from the scabbard with his right hand, shoving aside the fur-lined wool cape to make the move, while he gripped an arrow in his left, twisted both in his hands as he gathered courage, and then time stopped as the sound of chain moving filled the night, pulling from the embrace of the bolt as it unlocked his gate.

Light started as a slice onto the mud-trampled snow, and then broadened until it lit on more than two dozen Kilchurning clansmen, all wearing the same look of astonishment. There was another shadow in the midst of the light, turning from a sliver into a long, form-pleasing woman-size. And then Payton heard his wife speaking.

"Laird Kilchurning. All you had to do was send word."

And Payton went berserk.

It wasn't the lie after all. It was him.

The deep guttural cry filled his chest, boomed out through his throat, and heralded his entrance into the light, and when he slid on the snow-mixed mud, he turned it into a purposeful motion, slicing through the legs of the men he slid beside, and ending up slammed against their battering tree. Where that would have felled him, he turned it instead into an arc of movement and leaped across the wood, slicing another man's chest with his sword, while the arrow went into a different throat.

He didn't need a drum, either.

Red filled his vision, turning the mud and snow mixture into a realm of hell. Payton slammed and chopped and fought his way through them to Kilchurning. He ignored the blows to his back, shoved aside the pain of a blade as it slid across his belly, missing his vitals by inches, and welcomed the agony of an arrow as it embedded in his shoulder. Kilchurning was backing, the fear on his face a goad to Payton's rage, and when he'd finished with the Kilchurning laird, he was going to take his wife's slender white throat and slit it, too.

"No, Payton! Nae!" He heard the screams behind him, ignored them as much as he was ignoring the new pain of another blow, this time in his left buttock, taking him to a knee, before he was up again and advancing, and feeling the Kilchurning's fear as if a drug.

Then he had the man pulled to him, with a fist about the brooch he'd used to clasp his kilt band to his shoulder and Payton was pummeling as much of him as he could reach, ignoring the new pain of a blow to the side of his head, while shaking off the instant dancing of firelike dots. He saw a huge fist coming at his face . . . a fist with a very recognizable ring on the little finger. A ring he'd designed and had crafted and created so it could grace the finger of his lady wife. For all time. Proving she was his. Showing the world that Payton Dunn-Fadden had burst through the bonds of poverty and filth and degradation and gained himself not only a castle, but the heiress to go with it. But only as long as he held it.

And then he knew oblivion.

Don't hurt him! Don't kill him! Don't hurt him. . . .

The litany went through her like an unfinished sonnet, unspoken and filling her with an emotion close to fear. It was worse than the feeling that had already iced over her entire frame, making it difficult to don her presentation attire, and even harder to make the movement to the door, and give the order to open it before they caved it in. It was the same sensation that kept her standing, aloof and pale and trembling, frozen with a chill the winter couldn't dent.

The scene outside the gate was a mix of groans and blood, bodies and clamoring from male throats too numerous to count. And amidst the sea of green and yellow plaid marking a Kilchurning . . . was the lump of Payton.

One of the Kilchurning men kicked at him. Aside from a rocking movement his boot caused, and the return back to a sodden lump of red-colored white wool, nothing happened.

Dallis had her hands clasped to where pain was radiating through her breast and willed herself out of the scene. She didn't know what was wrong with her. She'd wanted him dead, hadn't she? The emotion close to fear moved then, clogging her throat as Kilchurning . . . or perhaps it was one of his closest men, pulled a claymore and advanced on the non-moving lump that was Payton. Dallis was grateful then for the lump her throat harbored. The screams didn't make any sound. She only knew she was making them, and suffering them, and gagging with them.

Pain. That was it.

She remembered it at the same time another man pulled another claymore from his side to follow the first man. Dallis shoved a hand behind her and beneath the jeweled girdle at her hips, pricking the soft tissue of her thumb pad with the dirk Payton had given her. Again. And then she pulled it forward and bit on it. And then she started begging God to make the pain greater than the one in her breast.

Before they reached Payton, the ground started turning into a shaft-filled quagmire, filling with arrows that rained through the falling snow, peppering the ground all about Payton, and then starting to move outward. One landed in a thigh . . . a foot. Dallis heard the cries and started backing, yelling at Leroy as she went to pull the door shut and let Kilchurning escape as best he could.

They were too few and Dallis couldn't prevent the Kilchurning laird and most of his men, bloodied and bedraggled with the storm and their battle, from pressing into the castle ground of the lower bailey before the door shut. And worse. They'd brought their battering ram with them.

She exchanged a glance with Lady Evelyn, accepted the woman's censure and felt her frame sag. But only slightly. She couldn't win if she didn't continue planning and altering to what was needed.

Behind her, they were jamming the door closed with not just the nearly split beam that had been the old bolt, but they'd shoved the felled tree across the portal as well.

This was not what she'd planned, although greeting the man slated as her husband had been her intent when she'd opened the door. She had no other choice. That's what one did when facing defeat and capture. Alter the plan. Welcome the conquerors. And get a chicory-dandelion soup into them.

"Good eve, My Laird. Welcome—"

"Get the men into the hall! Onto the tables!" He shouted it, interrupting her and drowning out her welcome. He pointed at one of his clansmen. "You—Riley! See she's locked up. Back in her tower, of course!"

"But—" Dallis started to exclaim.

"And dinna' eat or drink anything!"

Kilchurning turned one eye to her, pinning her in place and then he smiled. Dallis knew then what fear not only felt like but what it tasted like: metallic, sour, and bitter.

He'd altered since the one time she had seen him, on the day of her betrothal. He'd gotten even older and balder, which was apparent as he tossed the cloak away. He'd also gotten a larger paunch. He was probably uglier as well, although the cut above his eye, the bloodied nose and the face full of beard didn't help with the assessment.

"You!" He was pointing at another of his men. "Get outside and locate the men! He canna' have killed all of them!"

"But . . . the champion—"

"Lies in his own blood. That's where that whelp is! Use the Chieftain entry. It still exists?"

He was asking Lady Evelyn. That woman didn't have enough sense to keep her knowledge to herself. Dallis watched her nod her head rapidly, like a baby bird. The woman had little sense and no backbone.

"See him there. Go! Call the clan! You canna' hold this property with a small force. And why is she still standing there?"

A rough hand gripped her upper arm, propelling her forward. Dallis didn't turn to see who it was. She didn't care and her mind was already moving to the next problem.

Chapter 6

The woman was made of ice and her form felt just as cold. And unforgiving. But her curves were full and ripe, and calling to him. Payton liked that, above all. Curves this slick needed caressing. Loving . . .

And then somebody ruined everything.

"Payton?"

The woman turned into ice water and started surrounding him, her limbs cloying and clinging and pulling him under. Then he was swimming, the act bathing every bit of him with chill and frost. Then he started breathing the ice water in with every pained inhalation. And drowning.

And then he started coughing.

"Get him up. Now!"

The command belonged to Redmond. The ice belonged to the sea of snow melt he was lying in, and the drowning sensation was due to breathing in his own blood with every inhalation.

"Red . . . mond." Payton whispered.

"Dinna' talk!" The hissing came from Redmond. "Just get your arse on the sheeting!"

Sheeting. They were making beds. At least he knew how to

do that. His legs didn't belong to him, though. Nor did his arms. He wasn't certain about the rest either.

"Nothing . . . moves." Payton was panting with the effort of telling them the issue and losing.

"Christ! Send for the laird!"

"Nae . . . na' my da!" Payton forced his lips to say it but nothing worked there anymore, either.

They were shoving him, making the ice water mess slosh into his face, and that just made everything that was paining him turn to agony. Payton concentrated as the frost-woman formed again and started calling for him, kissing him with lips slick with ice and breath tinged with frigid cold. She was cold, but she took the pain away. He'd pay her later. She was worth it.

"I told you this would happen."

Dallis swiveled from contemplation of the gray skies that were all the day was bringing them and looked across at her companion. Lady Evelyn was perched atop a long stool, her back straight, her gray hair beneath a mantle of pale blue silk, and a deep frown between her eyebrows to join the other wrinkles lining her face. It was exactly the picture that a lady of the castle should be presenting as she concentrated on her tapestry.

It was also wrong. Ladies of an occupied castle didn't sit sewing and chatting when a usurper held their property. They plotted revenge.

"I beg to differ with you, Aunt. You most definitely did na' tell me Kilchurning would be warring against me. Nor did you mention he'd be holding my castle and treating me like a prisoner for near five sennights now!"

"Treating *us* like prisoners," Lady Evelyn replied to her handiwork.

"Us? You can come and go at will! You are nae prisoner."

"Should you swear the man fealty, he'd probably grant you the same," Lady Evelyn replied.

"Never." Dallis hissed. "He has nae right to hold me. He has nae right to hold my castle. He has nae right to dismiss my servants and put idiots in their place that canna' even cook a decent meal!"

Dallis shoved at the untouched platter of under-cooked venison they'd sent her way. And then she was pushing the heavy leaded glass doors to her oriel open to heave whatever her belly contained over the balcony. Again.

Behind her she heard her aunt clicking her tongue. "I'll ask for a nice gruel to be delivered a bit later for you. It will soothe your ills."

Dallis passed a hand across her mouth and grimaced. "You'll do naught of the sort. Have a dirk delivered, instead. I'll show him fealty!"

"Kilchurning was to be your lawful wedded spouse, Dallis."

"He can rot in hell! I'll never accept him. Na' now."

"You should na' spend more time out in the elements. Come back inside. Your cheeks redden and you ken the chill you'll catch."

Dallis stepped back into her tower room, pulled the glass back into place, and shivered. Her aunt was right. The day held a cold the flames in her fireplace couldn't defer. She couldn't fight anyone if she got sicker . . . and it was without cause. She'd never been ill a day in her life, and now each morn, she suffered. It was enough to make a high-born noble-woman clench her teeth to prevent any anger from sounding. Dallis hadn't the same control. She realized it as she kicked at the platter of food they'd brought, congealed now in its greased sauce, and losing a joint of meat as it rolled into the rushes.

She should have listened to lessons of deportment better.

"I'll na' catch a chill. I'd na' be so weak a-fore him."

"Which is why he bides his time and ignores any pleas on your behalf."

"Who would dare plead for me?"

"Well, doona' look to me. I'm na' that dense."

"It's na' Leroy Dunn-Fadden, is it? The worm. Why dinna' my great late husband, Payton Dunn-Fadden, gift me with a steward of immense stature and a good sword arm? Why did he leave a spineless meal-sop of a man? I'll tell you why. Because he had nae regard for me. Which is why I returned it."

Lady Evelyn made the sign of the cross about her, leaving off her needle for the motion.

"Now what?" Dallis asked, crossly.

"Leroy Dunn-Fadden lived up to the duties entrusted to him. He dinna' plead, and he was nae meal-sop."

"Then, where is he?"

"Kilchurning has a rule, Dallis. He lives by it . . . and he'll die by it. Anyone who serves a purpose is put to that purpose. He has the more comely of your wenches serving . . . well, they're serving. They then spend all day recovering from their service."

"Recovering?"

"'Tis a decided chore to service that many men. At night."

Dallis knew she was blushing. Thanks to Payton, she knew what such service meant now.

"Kilchurning's put the strongest men to shoring up the castle defense, others are put to squiring for his knights and caring for the horses. Anyone who spoke up and claimed a skill, he put to work. He doesn't na' have the sense to check. You already ken he doesn't have an eye or nose for who can cook and who canna'. Anyone else . . . is put to the sword."

"And . . . Leroy?" Dallis's heart sank on the name.

"He dinna' claim to cook. He claimed to be your guard."

"Oh dear God." Dallis went to her knees on the floor. She still felt the cold stone through the heavy voluminous velvet of her skirt and the three layers of linen she'd used for warmth beneath it. That was why she was shivering. It wasn't reaction to what she'd just been told. It wasn't!

"How many did he put to the sword?" she asked.

Lady Evelyn shrugged. "I dinna' ken for certain. I dinna' think you interested."

"Of course I'm interested! They're my . . . people! My . . . clan. What there is of it. Damn him!" If she got loose, she'd find him and—

"If we were in the gate tower, you'd na' have to ask. You could simply look out from your balcony and count the heads he's skewered and put out on poles as a warning."

Dallis swallowed. Quickly and rapidly. She shook her head before covering her face with her palms. Nothing was working. Her belly was churning the warning.

"He dinna' get enough of them, though. I do know that much."

"How . . . do you ken?" The question was hesitant, unlike her normal assertive way of speaking. She'd worry over that later.

"'Tis what he says," her aunt answered.

"So, now he talks to you?" Dallis raised her head from her hands and looked over at her aunt. The woman was bobbing her head and nearly smiling. She'd worry over that later, as well.

"Everyone talks amongst themselves while I'm about. They think me dense." The woman shrugged. "I let them."

Dallis opened her mouth to reply and shut it. Opened it again. Shut it again. And stared.

"I'm a frail, elderly spinster. What harm can I possibly do?" she asked.

Dallis's lips twitched.

"Aside from which, I am not a Dunn-Fadden. I'm Caruth. Should the Kilchurning still wish an alliance . . . ? Well. I'll be clan."

"An alliance?"

"Who is going to stop him? You? I think na'. 'Tis you he's wishing the alliance with."

"God damn the man!"

"'Tis unlucky to damn others, Dallis. And we're going to need as much luck as the others."

"What others? Who in this farce is lucky?"

"The Dunn-Fadden clan outside in their own crofts when you decided to open the gate and invite their enemy in. They were lucky."

"I had to open the gates! You were there. You saw it. One more shove and he'd have busted through! A surrendered castle is sometimes spared. A castle that is taken gets razed . . . and all within suffer. I did it to spare us!"

"That is your fault as well. I told you. Did you listen? We knew the wood was weak and the bolt rotted clean through. That's what happens when the elements leak from split stone above it. That's what the Dunn-Fadden heir sent funds to fix. I doona' think it was for buying his death. Perhaps you should have listened to my warnings. We would na' be here having these words."

Dallis blew out a sigh and ruffled the loose hair at her forehead. "If Kilchurning had to send me a companion for this past fortnight and ten, why did it have to be you? Is he hoping to wear me down with your words of guilt?"

"I *am* your companion."

"Only through the vagaries of fate," Dallis grumbled.

"Nae. Through the untimely demise of my betrothed. Had he lived—?"

"You'd have seen him to an early grave with your words, instead of the ague that took him. That's what would have happened."

That was contemptible, and she knew it. Dallis watched her aunt's shoulders dip ever so slightly. The woman was a spinster with a sharp tongue. Worse, she was probably right with her words. That's what smarted the most.

"Forgive me, Aunt Evelyn. My tongue betrays me. I over-spoke on that."

"Bide your time, Dallis. 'Tis what everyone else is doing."

"For what?"

The woman shrugged again, turned back to locate her needle and then started sewing again. "You should join me, you know."

"At sewing? My castle is overrun with vermin and you suggest sewing to cure it?"

"Makes the wait seem more tolerable."

"What are we waiting for?"

Dallis's knees were getting cold from staying on the floor and the fire could use another log on it before too long. She was looking at that when her aunt answered.

"You."

"Me? If he's waiting for me to swear fealty, he's going to die of auld age first! I'll never pledge my troth to that man!" She was on her feet and getting warmer with the emotion behind the words. The fire could still use another split log. Dallis busied herself at that, poking the ashen remains of a log until the embers glowed red again, and then adding one from the stack that the servant kept replenished, when he wasn't bringing her noxious smelling meals. Which reminded her as her belly rumbled. She was hungry now.

The past days had all been crazed with the same odd illness. First, to heaving all morn until she shook with the spasms, then to ravenous hunger. There was no explanation for such illness and she wasn't telling anyone of it! She'd been keeping it hidden for over a fortnight now. It was just more bad luck that Aunt Evelyn had witnessed it today.

"Would you be carin' for a bit of gruel now, Dallis lass?"

"Depends on what I have to do for it," she grumbled, settling the log into place with the tongs and then replacing them. The hearth needed sweeping, but it was glowing warm. Dallis swiveled on it, putting her back to the warmth.

"I'll tell them it's for me. I'm the one has sworn fealty. I'll have to answer to your father should we meet again in this lifetime. 'Tis me who bears the brunt of clan censure. Na' you. All you have to worry over is Dunn-Fadden."

"Why? He's . . . dead." Dallis felt her heart twinge and ignored it. Again.

"I dinna' mean the son, Payton. I meant the father."

"Laird Dunn-Fadden? Why?"

"The man only gets to keep the Caruth Dale where he built his castle, if the son holds on to this one. 'Twas the Stewart king's ruling."

"Oh." Dallis had forgotten.

"So all bide their time. All."

"For what?" The words said as sourly as the taste in her mouth.

Lady Evelyn bent to her task, speaking again to the field of heather she was stitching in minute detail onto the fabric.

"The Dunn-Fadden clan has been gathering. Just outside of arrow range. For days now."

"I have naught to fear from my father-by-law."

"I would na' be so certain."

"He'll want Kilchurning's blood. As do I. I've naught to do save welcome him and my release."

"Perhaps."

"Why must you always be so cryptic! Say what it is and let the blame fall! The Dunn-Fadden will revenge the fallen and I'll get my keep back from Kilchurning's grip. Dunn-Fadden will have his own castle back and I'll have what I always wanted. Freedom. I dinna' see what I have to worry over."

"Perhaps," came the answer again.

"You are so maddening!" Dallis burst out.

"Come. Pick out a color and sew. Mind you doona' pucker it as much as last time. I had to take out all your stitches."

"Then why ask it of me? You ken my lack of skill. I was na' trained to needlecrafts. I was trained to run a household, keep a hearth fire burning, fill a larder, balance accounts . . . brandish a dirk. Revenge an ill. I was na' trained in sitting about worrying!"

"You admit to worry? Odd. I've seen you pace with intent, rail with anger, and screech with fury. I've na' seen worry."

Dallis chewed on her fingernail in thought. Her aunt was right. She had been pacing. She was not a shrew, though. Lady Evelyn was.

"I over-spoke again. I meant waiting. I sit about waiting. Not worrying. I leave that bane for the spinsters of the world."

Lady Evelyn sighed this time. "Your barbs doona' affect me today, Dallis lass. You have made me too satisfied. I'll be the first to let them ken the wait is over, and they'll have what they want."

"Are you daft? First you tell me I must bide my time, and now you drift into being fey by telling me the wait is over? And all without sense? This is na' companionship. This is argument."

"You want bread with your gruel? I'll go and order it."

"I want to be let free! Grant me that and I'll find my own meal."

"He allows you the run of the tower. You're free."

"Up. He allows me this floor and the turret. This is na' freedom. 'Tis worse than a caged bird! At least a caged bird is given something to perch upon! And food worth the eat."

"You canna' go to the turret anyway. Na' today. The weather forbids it. In fact, 'tis so cold, the garde-robe is almost too far to venture unless the need is too great."

Dallis didn't need the reminder. Even with the fire at her back, it was still chilly in her rooms. That's why the ladies of the castle kept to their solar in the winter months. That room was directly above the main hall and shared a fireplace with it. If Kilchurning had a bone in his body devoted to chivalry, he'd have known that and made it available to her and Lady Evelyn.

Dallis shuddered. She was being greedy and selfish and heartless. What was a bit of chill when she still had her head? Nor was she being forced into a differing bed each eve. All she was really suffering was enforced boredom, Lady Evelyn's tongue, and badly prepared and cooked meals.

"When is Dunn-Fadden going to attack? Do they ken?"

"Nae. 'Tis why he's had his men on orders to patrol in two shifts per day. On rotation. Constantly watchful. And then he sends them to their rest. He does na' ken how draining that is."

"Draining? How?"

Her companion giggled. "You think your wenches un-skilled in the love art? Please, Dallis. 'Tis a woman's greatest weapon."

"Aunt Evelyn!" Dallis was shocked. It sounded in her voice.

"They also ken the best way to weaken a man is to get a bit of wine into his gullet. A bit of wine with a bit of hops and St. John's Wort in it. Just a bit. Na' enough to flavor it, but enough to make a man drugged and slow in his actions. 'Tis my own concoction."

Dallis kept her mouth from dropping open with an effort. It was difficult to form words for a bit. "I thought you swore the man fealty," she said, finally.

"So does he," the lady replied.

"Aunt Evelyn. You have nae honor."

The old woman looked askant at her and winked before going back to her sewing. "When you've reached my age, you learn something about honor."

"What?"

"You learn survival is what matters. Then shelter, food, good ales. One thing you've done right since wedding the Dunn-Fadden, Dallis lass. You've learned how to get the proper age of your lager. You brew a hearty ale. Kilchurning and his men are most appreciative of it. Most. Should he win the day, I'll be rewarded while he finishes drinking the kegs dry. Should he lose?" She shrugged again but was still talking to her tapestry. "Well . . . I've proved my loyalty as a member of the Dunn-Fadden clan with my potions. Either way, I survive. I call that a win."

"You let the choice of two evils decide itself," Dallis commented.

"What woman can choose between two evils?"

She had. "What of me?" Dallis asked in a small voice she hated.

"Dinna' look to me for the answer. 'Twas na' me opening the gate and welcoming his sworn enemy, Kilchurning, while his lone son perished. You'd best hope for a Kilchurning win."

Dallis felt the twinge again deep in her breast at mention of Payton's demise. It was painful. And mysterious. There was no reason for sorrow. She was close to getting what she wanted. What she'd always wanted. The death of her husband was a foregone conclusion. It shouldn't hurt and make her eyes water up strangely.

Yet, it still did. Again. She had to turn her face aside to hide the moisture in her eyes and blink rapidly as she watched the flames.

"Brighten up, Dallis lass. With what I suspicion, I'd guess your acceptance into Clan Dunn-Fadden will be easy. If he does na' take your head for getting his son killed, that is. I'd talk fast if I were you."

"Of what?"

"The bairn you carry."

That's when Dallis's mouth really did fall open.

Chapter 7

"That looks a bit like the Dunn-Fadden crest. A bit swollen and misshapen, but that's a thistle . . . see there? And surely as I'm standing here, that thistle is wrapped about a falcon claw. See that?"

"Hush." Payton's lips moved. His teeth hurt badly enough he knew the words were being formed, but nothing came out. He couldn't get a deep breath, either. The armor wrapped about his body guaranteed it. He settled with grunting. That didn't do much either, although it sounded like bubbles forming in his nose.

"Jesu'! He's awake! And hush a bit! Your da will have my arse if he knew we were here, visiting you. He gave strict orders. We had to wait till near dawn."

"Mar . . . tin?" Payton choked out, splitting the name in half.

"Aye. And Seth-the-Silent. At his side is Davey . . . and you ken he's never about without his little brother, Alan, so we have the whelp with us as well."

"My cousins?"

"The same. Here. We brought you a dram of whiskey. 'Twill do you more good than the broth they keep on the fire just for you. Here. Drink up." The words were accompanied by the touch of a sporran to his mouth and Payton gulped before they drowned him with it. Then he was choking, making it impossible to breathe.

"Payton?" Martin's whisper held fear. They all knew why. The Dunn-Fadden laird was a bull of a man and could make grown men cow with his temper. Payton kept from making noise while he sucked in blessed air and vowed silently to get even. And then his chest wall ran into the abutment of armor about his chest and belly.

That bit of nurse-maiding he'd take up with Da. When he was well enough. It was bad enough being forced to wear a chain tunic when he was younger. This amount of armor was going to make him look pampered and effeminate. Aside of which, it was going to be difficult to put up a decent fight if he were encased in steel plates like the Sassenach.

"Here now. That's enough of that. We'd best leave the hard spirits for the men. Try this instead. Now, sip on the broth like a good lad."

Payton spit it out at them. The dribble of it on his lower lip showed how poorly he'd done that, as well.

"What's . . . been done to me?" *Aside from my wife trying to get me killed.* He wheezed between the words and somebody mopped at his lip probably using a tender motion. It still hurt.

"You took a cleaving. And a hacking. That was followed by a general amount of beating. And then a bit of a chop. Or mayhap it was two chops. It looks like the fellow landed more than one blow to your face, and bother me if it doesn't look like he used your own family crest to do it with."

"My . . . face?" Payton asked.

"Dinna' fash yourself. You're still just as bonny," Martin replied. "The scar will na' even show. It's that close to your scalp. You can lift your hair to show it off to the lasses when you like, though."

Payton tried growling instead, making it vibrate through his throat where it hurt less.

"What? You doona' think of things like that? We do. Doona we, lads? All lasses love a scarred man. Makes him dangerous."

"Mar . . . tin," Payton tried for the growl again, but it sounded ridiculous, even to him.

"What? You ken that truth as much. The lasses love a big, scarred man. Love him well, they do."

"I'm . . . wed," Payton replied.

"Sweet mother of God. Listen to him. Claiming to be pious. It's the head blow, it is. He's barely lucid. Best give him more broth."

"Damn . . . Martin! I am na' mad."

Payton's words ended with another cough, since they'd shoved a spoonful of broth into his mouth. If he could use his arms, he'd show them. Even weighed down with metal plate, he could still take out Martin, Seth-the-Silent, and both Dunn-Fadden cousins, Davey and Alan.

"Somebody keep an eye out for the laird! And Redmond, too!"

Payton's eyes went wide on Martin's whisper. And what it meant.

"What . . . are you up to?" he asked.

"Alan's never seen a battle wound. I promised him a peek."

"You . . . what?"

"Just a small bet I've made that he canna' stomach gore from a battlefield. The lad says he can, and further claims I sully him without cause."

"I will na' just lay here while you—you. . . ."

Davey was the one chuckling. "Well, since your da has you all trussed up like a prize goose, I doona' see why you won't just lay there. Like a good lad."

"My da . . . did . . . what?" *It isn't armor?* he wondered.

"Flesh takes time to knit and you were fighting anyone that tried to get you quiet. Losing blood and spilling your guts and making a fine sight. And that was a-fore the fever," Martin replied.

"Fever?" The word warbled.

"Aye. Fever. You were burning with it. And raving. And yelling. And fighting. There was na' one of us to hold you down. So it took all of us."

"You . . . held me down?"

"Na' me. 'Twas me doing the rope tying."

"Damn, your rotten—!"

"Here lad. Have some more broth."

Payton's spate of cursing was cut off by more of the soup as Martin warned him a moment before shoving the spoon in. He had to resort to glaring as he swallowed.

"Your da says you was birthed from a she-wolf, and he must be right. Any other man would have bled to death long since. Or perished of the fever. But na' you. Oh, nae. You even curse and fight them when they spent all that twine stitching you back together. And then they wasted a good volume of whiskey to bathe you in, as well. You dinna' take to that well, either. Let me tell you."

"I'm going to be sick."

It was Alan retching out the words. Martin was grinning and raising his eyebrows and looking like it was very hard not to laugh.

"And then everybody got to worry over your head wound. And how mayhap you'd never waken. Then, you started mumbling . . . the oddest things."

"I doona' wish to hear," Payton replied. He knew it was a wasted breath even as he made it.

"You told everyone about the starlike scar on your rump. You remember. The one just above the right thigh—"

"Cease, Martin!" Payton interrupted him, and there wasn't much weak sounding about his voice anymore.

"Everyone had to look. And discuss. I dinna' tell them how it got there."

Payton blew out the breath he hadn't known he was holding.

"He dinna' have to. You did!" That was Davey.

Payton knew he was reddening. And warming. And then sweating.

"Na' one soul knew we'd shaved that bit of the latrine seat up to see how long it would be a-fore any noted it. And how many arses we could spike. 'Twas na' my fault you went and forgot. And then you had to go and confess it!"

Martin's voice held the disgust while snickering happened from the others, including Alan, who no longer sounded like he was ill.

"Now we have to pay a fine. To the laird's coffers. Due to your loose mouth."

"A . . . fine?"

"Seems you're na' the lone Dunn-Fadden with that particular scar. It's a family trait now, we might say. Wouldn't we, lads?"

Payton groaned aloud. It didn't stop them.

"We've na' got all night. As soon as morn comes, they'll be poking at the fire and coming in to check on you. We'd best na' be here when that happens."

Payton roved his eyes about the coarse, thick walls. He was in a siege tent, and now that dawn was starting to stir light through the sides, he could see the heavy lengths of hemp it had been woven from.

"Why . . . am I here?" he asked.

"Why are you here? Have you na' been listening to me explain it?" Martin pulled in a lung full of air. "You took a cleaving. And a hacking. Some chopping. A blow—"

"In a siege tent! I already ken—!" Payton halted the rest of his words when a new ache from just below his breastbone twinged into being. And then it felt sticky again.

"Oh. We have the siege tents because we have the castle under siege."

"We . . . do?"

"'Tis actually your da, but we're assisting," Martin explained.

"Aye. I gather the firewood. Alan assists me," Davey added.

"Why?" Payton queried.

"In the midst of winter, a fire is a good thing. Aside of which, the men like the meat cooked."

Payton sighed. That even hurt. "Why did we . . . put a siege . . . on the castle?"

"Your da is right fond of the Dales. And his own castle. He is na' giving all that up without a fight. And whoever holds the keep gets the lands. Or whoever has the heiress gets the keep. Or whoever keeps the heiress gains the land. I disremember the wording. The Stewart King's edict was too long."

"Kilchurning . . . has my keep?"

"Aye."

"And . . . the wife?" Payton continued.

"Her, too. Has her locked into her tower, I hear."

"You . . . hear? From who?" The pain radiating just about everywhere was turning into darts of fire. Payton kept working his mind and mouth in order to ignore it. It wasn't working.

"That serving wench tells us. Lass by the name of Bronwyn. You recollect her? She's right fond of Seth-the-Silent. Tells him everything, she does."

"But how . . . does Seth tell you?"

"Pictures. The lad is verra good with a stick in the snow. Except last eve. She must have told him momentous news last eve, because he was all red and odd acting when she left. And he's been drawing pictures of your da ever since. Haven't you, Seth?"

Snickers from Martin, Davey, and Alan answered him. Payton narrowed his eyes. Seth was bobbing his head in agreement.

"She . . . is na' being harmed, is she?" Payton asked. If Kilchurning had put one finger on her, Payton was killing

him. Dallis Caruth Dunn-Fadden was not to be harmed . . .
until Payton got his hands on her.

"Nae. From all accounts, your wife is crying and pacing
and in mourning over your sorry arse."

"Liar!" Payton gave the word too much emphasis. The
twinge of agony that arced through his torso was the reward.
He drew in a shallow breath and eased it back out. Then he
did it again.

"Well . . . perhaps it is a tiny lie. But you are on your
sickbed. I doona' wish you fretful. Aside from which, I have
a bet and time's a-wasting."

"I think it's started bleeding again," Davey said.

"Perfect," Martin replied. "Come along, Alan. Time to see
the wound."

Payton groaned again. Concentrated. And tried ignoring
the sensation of pain throughout his torso. Then a leg. His
entire shoulder. Even his forehead where they had him bound
to the bed. "Which . . . wound?" he asked finally.

"Which one? The one from the broadsword. Be-Jesu', but
it's big. And deep! Near cleaved you in twain. And right
across your belly! I dinna' ken a man could withstand a blow
like that."

"Alan . . . get me the light! Bring it closer! Na' that close,
you fool! You'll burn him."

Payton blinked rapidly on the quick singe to his eyelashes
from their candle. And then he was glaring at his man through
an upturned glance. All of which muted the pain somewhat.

"Quickly now, lad! Look. And then hurry! Payton's gone
and torn some stitching open. You should take more care of
this, Payton Dunn-Fadden. They'll have to put that twine back
in. And it was hell the first—"

His words were interrupted by the sound of Alan's retching,
which was covered over by the sound of horses arriving. A
lot of horses. And they were accompanied by something truly
heavy and large if the rumble of sound from its passage could

be believed. There was a collective moment of silence in the tent from all of them. And then Alan broke it.

"Ah-oh," he said.

"You're saying they went into the tent? With my son? Martin? And my sister's lads? And none stopped them? Where is MacCloud?"

"Christ. And his mother, Mary." Martin's whisper answered the booming sound of Payton's father's voice.

"What do I keep you all about as guards for? And what the blazes are they doing in the tent?"

"We heard his speech. We checked. He's awake. And coming to nae harm." That had to be one of the laird's Honor Guard with that announcement, and then the tent flat moved, blasting the interior with cold air.

"Why dinna' you say so sooner? He's awake? Payton? Lad?"

Alexander Duncan Dunn-Fadden was a bear of a man, eclipsed in size only by his son. He had silver-streaked black hair and brilliant blue eyes, proving to the world that the King's Champion was definitely the Dunn-Fadden laird's offspring. There the resemblance ended. Unlike Payton, the laird claimed a full black beard and a fire-scarred face no lass would swoon over anymore. The beard was the only sign it bothered him. He shoved his way through the trio about Payton and dropped to a knee. Payton had never seen worry in his father's face, nor moisture glazing his eyes before. His own widened.

"Thank the lord. Payton? Son?"

"Aye?" Payton whispered.

"You're awake. And lucid."

"Aye," Payton repeated.

The laird cleared his throat. "Well. You're in luck . . . that Kilchurning just winged you." There was an odd warble of voice in the midst of the statement.

"In . . . luck?" Payton replied, feeling the familiar pull of resentment whenever he was about his father.

"Aye. Saved me the trouble of it. And if I ever hear of you leaving your Honor Guard and taking on an entire clan without benefit of a sword to your back again, you'll na' survive the whipping I'll give you. I guarantee it." The hand his father put atop his head trembled.

Payton swallowed to kill the emotion. And then he nodded.

"Good. Remember that. Hell's fury is na' as great as your da's will be. And should you ever put me through another fortnight and ten like this, I'll make certain you canna' walk for a month!"

The laird ruffled a bit of Payton's hair and then lifted back to his feet. Then he was clearing his throat of an emotion it was impossible for a Dunn-Fadden laird to have, in order to start speaking. The man was out of Payton's range of vision, but loud enough anyone hovering near the tent would have no trouble with the listen.

"Follow my orders this time! And get another warning sent over to the Kilchurning! He's bound to have heard the arrival of my onager and kens what that means. Spent nigh a sennight getting the catapult ready, what with twisting the ropes for the right tension and greasing the wheels. Now 'tis time to get serious. Tell him he has three days!"

"My laird?"

Payton wasn't the only one surprised to hear his cousin, Davey Dunn-Fadden, address the laird. Near everyone in the tent had the same reaction of indrawn breath.

"What are you all standing about denting the good earth with your weight while you watch my son get well? You there! MacCloud! Get us some rocks. Take these four sorry arses with you!"

Davey cleared his throat. It was a pathetic sound. "My . . . laird?" he said again.

"Make them about ten stone each. Any heavier and the

onager canna' launch them! Take a wagon." He was moving away, the door was shoved open again, if the drop in temperature was a good indicator, and then he was standing in the portal, with the door flap open while Davey tried again. Payton wasn't the only one shocked by his cousin's actions.

"My laird! You need listen to me!"

"Dinna' I put you in charge of the firewood?" Alexander Dunn-Fadden asked.

"Aye," Alan agreed.

"Then haul your bones out to the woods and get me some! A-fore you go, get some more broth in here! My son is wasting away while we tarry! And get the healer! It appears he opened his belly up again as well. I'd best na' hear it was you lads causing it, you ken?"

The door flap dropped as Payton's father exited. And then it lifted again. Dropped. Each time with a blast of cold air.

"But . . . Seth has words . . . for you!"

Davey had never shown much in courage. Payton knew he wasn't the lone one wondering what had gotten into him.

"Words? The mute?"

Payton's father roared with laughter after his announcement. It was said at a volume no one in camp could avoid hearing it. Payton heard it clearly enough, but had to hold his breath to hear more. Davey's voice came as a mumble of sound, but it was easy to listen to the laird's answer.

"Are all of you gone deaf? Get your carcass moving! Stones! I need a goodly amount of them! Take both wagons! 'Twill take some to get the measure of the walls! And the height. And mind you, I need logs as well!"

More of Davey's mumbling came then. It was impossible to make out what he was saying since he must be moving away and Payton was bound into position and couldn't move closer to the walls. He could always count on his father's booming volume, though.

"Big logs! And get me some carpenters! We've got to build

a siege tower! I'm na' taking that bastard's occupation of Dunn-Fadden property another sennight! You say he talks with sticks? Draws what he means? Are you fashing me, lad? I would na' continue it, if—"

Davey's voice was high-pitched as he interrupted the laird and Payton caught a breath at his cousin's daring. He fully expected to hear a slap after such a thing, but all he got was silence after Davey's outburst.

Cursed silence. There wasn't a damned thing he could do about it, either.

All of which lasted long enough to get the healer crone to her knees at his side, twisting a bit of whiskey-soaked twine between her thumb and fingers, and making Payton long for the oblivion again. Josephine gave him a gap-toothed smile just before she poked the needle through his flesh, and if Payton wasn't as stiff as a board already in preparation, he'd have gone that way with the fresh prick of pain.

"Any harm! Any at all . . . and I'll have him skinned a-fore I plant him!"

His father's voice preceded his entry into the tent again, sending cold dawn air into the enclosure and making the torch light waver. Payton held himself stiff, expecting any moment to feel the whip his father normally didn't spare. Instead he got the laird at his side again, with a grin on his mouth that split his beard with the white of teeth. Then Payton got a beefy hand on his shoulder, rocking him slightly from the stiff position he was maintaining.

"You've done it, lad!"

"I . . . have?" Payton queried.

"Aye. Justly and rightly, too. And with little time, as well. I'm that proud of you, son. That proud."

Payton narrowed his eyes a bit, and would have frowned except the bond at his forehead holding him in place didn't allow him movement enough since it was rubbing against where the Dunn-Fadden thistle-wrapped falcon claw crest wound was still scabbed.

"I doona' ken . . ." Payton started, and then just let the words end. He'd never received such full approval from his sire. And here it was taking place, not in the Chieftain's Rooms as would be orderly and proper, but in a siege tent outside the demesne of his castle, with the clan healer Josephine as a witness, and with a string of twine hanging from somewhere in his belly since she'd stopped her sewing. He shook his head.

"I've done sent those fools off for stones, too."

"They're needed for the catapult," Payton replied.

"Na' now. The laird of Kilchurning canna' ever have the castle, nor can he have the dales. If I continue this assault, I'll cause harm to my property. And that I refuse to do."

"'Tis my property," Payton told him.

His dad grinned wider. Then he chuckled. "Aye. So, 'tis."

"You're calling off the siege?"

"Nae. Never that. I just have to wait. Nae need to blight the walls. Anything done will need rebuilding."

"You'll let him win?" Payton's lower lip dropped slightly.

"The man canna' have a win. Na' now. We do."

"I doona' understand." He didn't either. Only a fool would claim a win when they were outside the demesne, in a tent in the midst of winter, while an interloper held their castle. And he knew his father wasn't a fool.

"The king's edict was clear. The castle and lands are all yours if you hold them and keep control over them. And that means you have to keep the heiress to your side." His father rocked back on his heels and rubbed his hands together as if that explained everything.

"I am na' holding much at the moment," Payton pulled in a breath as Josephine went back to her task, pricking and pulling at his flesh.

"Well, your son will."

Payton went slack-jawed as he lost his breath. Then he lost his stiff post. And then he just lost feeling, as giddiness overtook everything else. Then, he was smiling larger than his father.

"My . . . son?" he choked out.

"'Twas Seth's news. I've done given the group of them the day off. I'll give the entire camp the day off! 'Tis that wondrous!"

"My . . . son?" Payton said again.

"Aye. And my grandson."

"My . . . son?" Payton said it yet again, although in a stronger tone.

"Takes a bit to get used to, I ken."

"My son!" Payton's voice was back. He didn't even feel what Josephine was doing to him. He didn't feel much of anything except joy.

And then the worry started.

Chapter 8

"When do they plan on sending me food today?"

Lady Evelyn looked up from her incessant sewing on the tapestry, but she didn't reply before getting back to her work. She did set her lips tighter, but other than that, she looked engrossed in her needlework, and not like she was listening to her niece's complaints at all. Just as she'd done last week, and the week before, and all of four months plus a fortnight!

"And even when they do send something, all they manage is watered-down broth! There is na' even meat to the broth they cook! I doona' even get a crust of bread. Do I deserve such punishment? And for what? I've been a model prisoner!"

"You tried to escape last Sabbath," Lady Evelyn replied.

"Poorly. Obviously. And is that reason to starve me now?"

"Most clans could have, and would have, done worse. You ken it as well as I do. The bleached skulls mounted at the gate tower are mute testimony of that."

"I have value. They will na' do that to me."

Lady Evelyn clicked her tongue. "True. You are also difficult. You complained until that poor man ran from you this morn."

"That was because they send swill worse than pond water!"

Dallis made a face at the door before looking over at her aunt again.

"'Tisn't something they wish to do, Dallis lass. They're sending the best they have."

Dallis snorted with an unladylike noise, "The best they have?"

"Aye. And Laird Dunn-Fadden wants it that way. 'Tis why every man to Kilchurning's forces is at the gate as we speak."

"How do you ken that?"

"Because I heard the latest taunt. And was there when he tossed a meatless joint over the wall with his catapult."

"A joint?"

"He's got his clansmen filling the grounds outside the gate, just outside of arrow range. They're roasting four venison carcasses over open fire, all browning nicely and filling your fields with the most heavenly smell."

"That's unfair . . . and making my mouth water."

"'Tis exactly what he's done to Kilchurning's forces, as well. The entire castle is watching, with mouths watering and bellies taunting."

"Why would he resort to such a thing?"

"I believe Dunn-Fadden's lost his patience, and I'm a-feared I ken why."

"Why?"

The older woman sighed heavily. "I told the Earl of Kilchurning of the bairn."

Dallis's eyes went wide. "You did . . . what?"

"Aye. I told them! Someone had to."

"How could you?" Dallis was past the four month mark of carrying a babe, and beyond an increased bosom, little of it showed. She was wearing the same clothing, keeping herself covered whenever another was in the rooms, and she was going to keep it her secret and hers alone. Until she could get to safety.

"I had to. 'Tis the lone way I could get meals of substance for you!"

"You call that substance?" Dallis asked.

"'Twas the best they have. They slaughtered the last animal a fortnight ago. There is na' much else worth the eat. Complain to the others if you like. They're at starvation's door."

"This canna' continue!"

"Which is why I told Kilchurning. He's got to make that Dunn-Fadden see sense! He's got to realize that further siege will harm his lone grandson . . . if Dunn-Fadden even knows about the bairn. It was foolish, I ken. But I was hopeful they'd end the siege and do this fairly."

"It dinna' work, did it?" Dallis asked.

"Na' unless you think cooking meat within smell of the gate is an end to it."

"Men! The least they could have done was send us a meated joint. Mayhap through our window. Right there."

"Men are na' smart enough for such. Too much brawn. Nae sense. You just keep pacing and walking. 'Tis best for the child. And they'd best start negotiating with Dunn-Fadden for that venison. That's what they'd best—!"

A strange air-sound followed by a thud interrupted her. Dallis gaped at the huge claw that latched to one of her fur rugs as it slithered along the floor in a jerking fashion and then clanked against the wall, digging deeply into the stone.

"Look! A grappling hook!" She was pointing, but it was unnecessary. Lady Evelyn was watching the dark stone where the hook was latched, looking incongruous with a dangling white rug as an accessory.

"Perfect shot!" The announcement carried too much sound.

Perfect? Payton felt the gut-clenching reaction the moment he'd launched the hook, knowing he'd swung it at too low of an arc, he'd let it fly a moment too soon, and he'd sent it with too much force. Consequently, it wasn't high enough to snag a merlon of the crenellation, but was instead going to fly with precise force, right into her room. And right near her.

He hadn't aimed to send a hooked weapon of battle into a room where his wife was imprisoned! He could have hurt his bairn. Or the vessel. The possibility of either caused him such emotion, he had to blink it rapidly away. He spent the time awaiting any scream from the rooms above by wiping his palms along the kilt grazing his thighs, where the damp melded with the black, white, and green of his plaid.

He didn't know that fear weakened a man, made his palms wet, his belly clench, his eyes moist, and his limbs tremble. He didn't dare let the others in the boat know of fear's effect. It was bad enough that he did.

"Doona' just sit there wasting time! Go get her!" That was Davey.

Seth-the-Silent wasn't saying anything—as was his creed, Dugan was smiling, while Alan was just bobbing his head and looking in awe at Payton.

He motioned for Redmond to precede him. They'd already decided it when Payton had bested the others last eve. At every challenge. He was still the strongest, now that he'd healed. Easily. There wasn't anyone else he'd trust with lowering her from the tower. It was his chore.

But the lass thought Payton dead. Her reaction at finding that false was bound to be entertaining. It had been an amusing thought before they'd concocted this rescue. Now, he couldn't risk the woman's screams of shock or her rage at finding him alive. Although a dead faint might be helpful in getting her out of the tower in the sling they had. Either way, they couldn't risk it.

Redmond was first. He had to get it announced and the reaction handled before Payton got there with the sling. He knew Redmond wasn't desirous of his task. The man nodded once at him and started climbing.

Payton watched him get halfway before moving forward.

* * *

"Oh my. That Dunn-Fadden has more smarts than I credited him with." Lady Evelyn had a note of amazement staining her voice. She'd also given off her seated position and moved to stand beside Dallis. They both watched as the thick rope attached to the hook moved back and forth by a finger-width of space in more jerking motions as something heavy climbed it.

"He couldn't have created a better diversion than those deer carcasses, either. How else could he get you spirited away without alarm? It's brilliant!"

Dallis wasn't arguing. She was watching, breathing shallowly as the rope slid back and forth in a sawing motion and keeping her hands clasped for lack of something better to hold to.

"He'd better have sent a sturdy clansman or two as well. I'll na' have you injured by the rescue, brilliant though 'tis."

A hand came over the edge of her oriel and then the other. Dallis didn't know she was holding her breath until the head of Payton's second-in-command came into view. It was all right, then. He was sturdy. He was known. And he was going to see her rescued, and then protected, and for certain well fed.

He pulled himself over the balcony and then fell into a heap into it, where he sat for precious moments breathing hard. Then he rolled onto his knees, lifted himself up and started walking toward her, speaking as he went.

"Good. You're quiet. Did you secure the door?" His voice was gruff as he asked it, before he reached her and then went past.

"I'm a prisoner. Why would my door na' be secure?" Dallis answered, and was forced to swivel to one side to grant him room.

"From the inside. Jesu'!"

He'd reached her door and pulled her bolt into position, making a creak of noise from the unused metal bolt it was fastened with.

"There." He announced it before walking back toward her.

"You hurt?" he asked when he was an arms-span from her, and being held at that distance by exactly that.

Dallis didn't know why, but something about the man's demeanor was frightening, although she'd never admit it. She'd never been looked at with such distaste and distrust. She stood for several moments, hands holding him off and watching him breathe hard.

"Nae," she finally answered.

"'Tis said you carry a bairn," he said.

Dallis looked over at Lady Evelyn. That woman had her eyes wide, was shaking her head like a clock pendulum, and was holding her tapestry to her like a shield.

"Did you have to tell everyone?" Dallis asked.

Lady Evelyn didn't answer, but the head shaking got worse. Dallis turned back to the man at her palms.

"Well? Do you or doona' you?"

He was running his gaze insolently over her before meeting her eyes again.

"Aye," she answered.

He grunted, whether in approval or not, she couldn't tell. Then he was pulling a length of cloth from his belt.

"Is it Payton Dunn-Fadden's bairn?" he continued.

"Nae other man has touched me," Dallis replied.

He grunted again and draped the piece of material over her hand. As a sling, it was going to be severely inadequate.

"What am I supposed to do with this?" she asked. "Tie my hair back?"

"'Tis a gag. For your mouth."

Dallis's eyes went huge. "I will na'!" she announced.

"You'd force my hand? I would na' wish the bairn harmed."

"But I *want* to be rescued. Why would you gag me?" she asked.

"An arguing woman needs silenced. Especially during a rescue."

"I'll na' argue," she replied.

"You'll na' scream, either?" he asked.

"Do I look to be screaming?"

He pulled in a breath and shoved it out in a long, heavy sigh. "Payton dinna' warn me with sufficient words," he replied.

"To what?" Her tone was acidic. She couldn't help it. She'd heard the Dunn-Faddens possessed beauty. She'd also heard they had a dearth of wits that went along with it. And here she was facing a perfect example of it.

"The argumentative nature of his bride."

"Show me a rescue, and I'll cease the argue."

"I have na' got time for this."

He had her swiveled with her back against him and the gag in her mouth with such speed, Dallis couldn't comprehend it at first. Then she was biting hard on the material and screaming her anger. And then it all turned to iced shock as her husband materialized from her balcony, tossing a lump from his back onto the stone floor as he went. She was in luck the clansman was holding her when her legs refused to do it.

"She took the news well, I see," Payton said as he approached them.

Dallis had sagged against the man at her back, forcing him to hold her weight up. And with Payton's approach, everything weakened even further. She could barely function past the loud pump of each heartbeat and the tremble overtaking everything. He was alive? The reaction was sending pings of emotion through her jaw and into her scalp, and bringing tears to her eyes.

Dallis couldn't decipher what the emotion making her reel

was. She told herself it wasn't joy, or something so closely akin to it, they meshed. And then she worked at believing it.

He's alive! Not only alive . . . but well; recovered, fully and totally. And he was stunning. Even more so than before, as the frame blocking the sunset proved. He loomed larger and more menacing with each silent step nearer. Or it was her own ears silencing his movements. Dallis couldn't hear over the rushing sound in her ears. Payton looked even larger than before, more muscled, more powerful. It wasn't possible, but nothing in front of her eyes disputed it.

"Evening, Wife."

He'd reached them and stopped, close enough she could see a vein pulsing in his throat, which was the level her gaze reached. Then he smiled with such loathing, his upper lip curled with it. Dallis dared not look higher.

"Doona' bother with a greeting. I can see you're . . . occupied."

"Payton." The rumble of voice came from the man holding her, making her back vibrate with the name.

"Aye?" Payton replied.

"We na' got time for such."

"We've got time. I'll make sure we do."

His voice was sending cold shivers up her back and nothing about the man behind her warmed them away. It was at his tone, and the hatred it carried.

"Later. We've got a rescue on our hands at the moment."

"'Tis true?" Payton asked.

Dallis glanced up at him. He wasn't asking her. He was directing his words to the man holding her, as well as his gaze.

"Aye."

He glanced down at her and then away, gifting her with a fraction of time that imprinted even more cold. Everywhere. She started shaking with it.

"Fair enough. We take her. With care. The spinster first."

"We dinna' make arrangements for her."

"When they find her gone, they'll do two things, Redmond. Punishment first. Then, the chase. We take the spinster, too."

"What do I do with the wife while we lower her, then?"

"I'll handle the auld one. You've got your hands full as 'tis."

"Payton." The warning tone was back in Redmond's voice as it rumbled through her again.

Payton didn't answer. He'd dismissed them and spun around to approach where Lady Evelyn was cowering. Dallis watched as her father's sister looked smaller and more insignificant than ever. Especially when she was pulled to Payton's side and taken to the balcony.

The lump he'd tossed there proved to be a mesh sling. Nobody said a word as Payton unfurled it and plucked Lady Evelyn from the floor to bundle her into it. Then he was wrapping a rope about his waist, lifting the bundle of woman and netting and lowering her. Dallis watched his movements with unblinking eyes. He had his back to them in a slanted stance. Red-tinted sunlight was outlining every bit of him, delineating the strength and maleness she'd thought lost to her. She was afraid it would be imprinted on her eyes even when she closed them.

She couldn't halt the sigh and was afraid the Redmond fellow heard it as he chuckled. That gave her the impetus needed to close her eyes to the sight, turn her head, and lift her chin. Nobody knew. Nobody was to ever know. If she'd mourned the masculine beauty of her husband—and been tormented over it, that was her secret!

With closed eyes she didn't have to watch anything more of Payton when he'd finished lowering her aunt. She didn't have to watch his approach, or hear it, since the running water sound in her ears effectively muted all of it.

She still knew exactly when he was standing in front of them. Every bit of flesh on her body was warning her, as the gooseflesh rose, prickling all over her.

"You ready?" Payton replied.

"You asking me or the wife?" The man holding her responded.

"I'll na' speak to her again until I have the time. And privacy."

Dallis jerked. They both knew it. There wasn't any way to hide it.

"In that event, aye. I'm readied."

"Bring her. Doona' over-touch her, but bring her."

"How am I supposed to do that?"

"Carry her," Payton replied.

"Nae."

"What do you mean nae? You canna' say nae. Bring her."

"You bring her. You married her. You seeded her. You carry her."

"I'm na' certain I can touch her, Redmond." Payton's voice sounded unsure. Worried.

"Why na'?"

"She carries my bairn."

"So?"

"I'm a-feared I'll hurt her."

Redmond snorted at that. The rush of breath grazed the top of her head, reminding her of how bare it was. She should have donned a wimple when he'd first appeared, or had the sense to find a cloak. That would have been better than wasting time arguing.

"You canna' hurt the bairn yet, Payton. It does na' even show yet."

"That is na' what I meant. And you know it."

The shivers wrought by just his voice were worse than the words. Dallis ignored where they were lifting every hair on her body and tightening her nipples against the fabric of her shift. It wasn't in pleasure. It was abject fear. She swallowed to still it.

Redmond sighed. "All right. I'll carry her. For now."

A stranger had overtaken her body, for Dallis Caruth would never have been so pliant and weak, while a man she barely knew lifted her to his chest and walked across her chamber. She wouldn't have lain docilely when he placed her into the netting and entwined the top together. She would have done more than untie the gag and hold her hands to her face and suffer the tremors as both he and Payton held to her ropes and lowered her in a spiral of motion down the castle wall.

She would have stopped the tears, too.

Chapter 9

"The wife will be cold, Payton."

"So?"

Dallis figured it was Redmond speaking on her behalf, since night had descended while they'd been doing the same from her tower window, making it difficult to see. They'd brought a small lantern but it was stingy with its light. Redmond's words were accurate, for where they'd placed her in the bottom of his skiff was definitely cold. It was wet and lonely, too.

Dallis huddled into a crouch atop the mesh that had been her sling, and tried to keep out of the very bottom where an inch of sea water from the loch, ice-melt cold and smelling of brine, sloshed about. Their rowing motion created more wet from the spray that came over the sides with each wave, too.

"So, give her your cloak."

"I'm na' concerned," came Payton's answer.

"Well, I am."

"Then give her *your* cloak."

There was lull in their words while those closest to Dallis avoided looking her way, or remarking on the words. They were all more secure on their benches and they were drier. They were all cloaked as well. Even Lady Evelyn sported a large plaid cloak on her frail boney shoulders where she was perched atop a small keg behind the oarlock. She didn't appear to get a bench either, but she looked infinitely warmer and drier.

"'Tis na' my bairn she's carrying," Redmond replied finally.

There was a heavy sigh, followed by a general shifting feeling over the entire structure as their momentum slowed. The boat rocked from side to side as something heavy skimmed along the middle of it. She knew it was Payton and stiffened for whatever he would do. Then, she felt the heavy wool of his cloak dropping into place atop her. It was a heavenly experience, warmed as it was by contact with his body, and filled with the smell of him. She spent several long moments enjoying it, before lifting her hands to fling the cloak off. It was a satisfying emotion to watch as it landed in the brine water at his feet.

"That was a waste. And now 'tis wet." Disgust filled the words as he snatched it up. Nobody answered him. The boat rocked gently with the motion of his passage before he was seated again, his cloak back atop his shoulders, and then the rowing commenced again.

"An unwell wench canna' produce a healthy bairn," Redmond remarked as the boat got underway again.

"She will na' take it. You all saw."

"Payton." The reply was just one word, and then silence dragged.

Dallis concentrated on counting their movements, filled her senses with the sight of Payton's broad form whenever the light slithered that way and wished the warmth of emotion from watching him canceled out the elements. He had his back to her and the cloak was a bit wetter than before, since it defined him as he moved. Redmond had the other oar and was facing her.

"She's going to get ill. And then she's going to slow us

down. And then she'll be in danger of losing your heir. Is that what you want?" Redmond said again.

"A bit of silence is what I want."

"Payton."

"The wife is stubborn. You saw. She did not accept my cloak. I doona' think her as cold as you say."

He was wrong. She was much colder than they suspected. If they weren't moving and if it was daylight, her shivers would be impossible to ignore. That's what came of nothing but non-nourishing broth for a diet and little in exercise.

"Payton, if you lose that bairn, you'll have naught."

"I have the ability to create another. So heave off."

"Kilchurning has a full two days head start on us, and now you think to saddle us with an unwell wench who is breeding?"

"Would you please cease speaking of my condition?" Dallis spoke up, trying to sound haughty and aloof. That wasn't what happened. The chattering of her teeth ruined it. There was no hiding how accurate Redmond had been with his observations. It was her own fault, too.

"I forbid you to give her your cloak, Redmond. I dinna' care how cold she is. She can take mine, or have naught."

There was a huge sigh happening, and then the boat was changing momentum again. The same rock of movement accompanied a body down the middle of it, and if it was Payton again, she was going to spit at him . . . after she took the cloak.

"Here, My Lady."

It was the Redmond fellow. He hadn't brought her his cloak, after all. That bit of wool was now atop Lady Evelyn's shoulders. Dallis had possession of the plaid one. She didn't waste any more time getting the material about her, swathing everywhere except her eyes and nose, and holding it from the inside with hands that shook.

"Redmond . . . you're a wretch," Payton remarked.

"I prefer the word chivalrous. 'Tis much nicer."

"I hope you freeze."

"Perhaps we could get the boat moving at a decent speed, and it will na' be an issue. You rested enough?"

Dallis didn't know how they did it, but the speed did pick up, and that just had more wave water coming over the side, more wind at her eyes and nose, and more muscle getting moved on the back she was still watching. It also seemed to do what Redmond had said it would, since neither rower looked remotely cold.

They should have planned better, since the loch was leagues wide and it was sheer madness to cross it, when there were so many coves and inlets available. They'd also be at least a half day's ride from the Dunn-Fadden camp when they made land. Nothing made sense.

Fog settled about them near the center of the loch, where the water was the deepest and coldest. Redmond and Payton didn't change their rhythm. They'd been matching each other since the cloak episode. They set a punishing pace, more for speed than endurance. And yet, endurance was what they needed to cross this loch. Dallis watched as the other clansmen nodded off and some appeared to be dozing. For certain Aunt Evelyn looked in that state, since she'd pillowed her head on a wad of Redmond's cloak.

Still Payton and his man rowed, grunting occasionally. The fog thickened to the point the men were mere blobs of constantly moving darkness, ceaselessly pushing and then pulling, their energy creating a fog of its own about their forms with released heat. It was a mostly cloudless night. The moon-touched fog about them proved that, making the lamp they'd mounted on their pole useless and superficial. It also made the scene surreal.

Dallis watched them the entire time, marveling in the strength and power they were both exhibiting. She watched even as her eyelids drooped, her belly rumbled with emptiness, and her legs cramped from sitting atop them. Such discomfort was as nothing in comparison. And then they scraped something.

The other clansmen moved as if they'd been wide awake the entire time, leaping into the water to haul the boat in, while Redmond and Payton sat, slumped slightly as they heaved for breath, their oars dangling above the water. Dallis stretched slightly, and then yawned and watched her aunt do the same. She probably should have spent some of the crossing in sleep. That way, she wouldn't be feeling so out-of-sorts and odd.

"Dugan! Seth! Call Martin. Get dried off. And get the horses."

Payton had recovered from the row if his voice was any indication. He was moving as well, with his man right behind him. They didn't leave the boat as much as fall over the side of it. Dallis's lips curved as she watched that.

The ice sting of the water was reviving. As was the feel of land beneath his boots. Payton pulled himself out of the water with sheer willpower and a hand-hold of water-sculpted rock. The pace they'd set was stupid. And wasteful. They still had a half day's ride to where he'd told the others to pitch the tents. It was going to be harder to sit a horse if both arms were shaking over the exertion of the row they'd just done.

It was Redmond's fault, he decided, and narrowed his eyes at his companion.

"Cease willing it had gone different and order the women fetched from the skiff," Redmond said, as if Payton had spoken aloud. "You have the lass. Soon you'll have the property again. All you have to do is reach Edinburgh and His Majesty's ear. The keys will be handed over."

"I have to gain strength enough to turn them," Payton joked.

"Then find it. We've still a ride to make."

"I ken as much."

"And a wife to keep seated while you do so."

Payton groaned. "You take her. I'll take the spinster."

"You give tongues too much to whisper of. Estrangement should na' be one of them. 'Tis your bairn. Your wife. Your property. All of it."

Payton stayed in the crouch, holding to the rock and welcoming the heat the anger was bringing to him. It felt like the scar on his left temple was thumping in tempo with his heart. She'd tried to kill him. Then, she'd betrayed him. She'd nearly had him killed. She'd made him look an unchivalrous wretch in front of his men. She unsettled the elements about him and made him unsure. Now he had to give her a seat with him on his horse? Within his arms?

"None here would speak. With anyone. At any time." He reasoned it aloud from his position holding to the black outcropping of rock.

"Why give cause?" Redmond was pulling himself onto the same rock. He was also breathing heavily from the exertion. "Think, my laird. You're nae fool. Then, order the woman fetched. Doona' fash it. I will do as you say."

Payton watched his man climb past him and disappear in a mess of wet plaid. Then, he was following. Sometimes, he hated Redmond MacCloud.

Payton knew they were to ride double. By necessity. The Dunn-Fadden laird would note twelve horses missing, more than the six they'd filched. If his da had more sense than bravado, he'd have been the one to steal the heiress and be on his way to the king and sure victory, rather than trying to get the Kilchurning laird into a hand-to-hand battle on the field. Payton shook his head. Alexander Dunn-Fadden was a hard man. No sense trying to change him now.

So be it.

Payton had selected the stallion he'd bred and raised, the Clydesdale named Orion. The stallion already had a long saddle on him making it easier to sit two. Payton had prepared a bundle of dry clothing, spare plaid, and hard bread. He knew he had to take another with him, riding pillion. At least for this portion of their journey. He just hadn't thought through that it might be *her*.

He shoved it all aside and climbed to the paddock Martin was guarding.

The volume of horseflesh, milling about as they had, was putting steam into the air, making the mist sparkle with what light the moon would part with. That made it easy to spot where Martin held them. What was harder was getting Payton's legs to climb to the small, flat meadow atop a bluff, open to the elements and brushed with a winter breeze that frosted clothing and chilled limbs. Payton was cursing silently when he reached the snow-flecked heather and stood, searching for Orion through the opacity.

As always, he felt the pride from owning such a magnificent creature, since his Clydesdale stood a half-hand taller than anything else they had. He was also nearing. The misted light was weak and fog grazed as it stirred with the passage of the horse as Seth-the-Silent led him.

The mute clansman handed Payton the reins and waited, as if he already knew. Payton pursed his lips in thought, cursed again to himself, and said it.

"See that the wife is escorted here. To me."

The man's face broke into a grin before he left.

While the man went for his burden, Payton opened his bags to pull out dry boots of a soft leather so they'd fold easily, and then he had another *feile-breacan* unfurled before his fingers grew too iced for the movement. Already the leather of his boots seemed melded to him and the clasp of his belt gave him trouble. As did the brooch at his shoulder. Frozen fabric dropped to his feet, and then he was rubbing briskly all over his body with the dry plaid prior to donning it. Then the spare length of wool. Then he was munching on a hard biscuit. He had time. On the other side of the horses, he could sense Redmond doing the same.

He was in the saddle and feeling surprisingly content, when Seth loomed from the whiteness, holding Dallis by her arm. It didn't look like she'd come easily, if the angry sound of her words and sodden look of Seth were indicators.

"I am na' a sack to be handled so roughly! And unhand me!"

"Seth?" Payton asked.

She stopped her tirade at his voice. It looked like she even slowed her step since Seth had to resort to pulling at her. All of which was satisfying. He couldn't tell what expression she had on her face when she neared his side, since she had the plaid cloak swathing all of her, but he could hear the disdain well enough.

"I am na' riding up there with you," she announced, as if it were so.

"You are," Payton replied.

"You're soaked through and iced. It will hurt your precious bairn."

Payton grunted. "Hand her up, Seth."

"Aside of which, this Seth fellow is na' capable of lifting me. He near dropped me getting from the boat."

"Is this true?" Payton asked. Seth hung his head, but he was pointing at Dallis as he did so.

"Seth tells me you made it difficult for him."

"You should have beached your craft on land a-fore un-loading it. 'Twould have gone easier."

"Too deep. Can you mount yourself, then?"

"You should have picked a cove with a beach then . . . and I am na' riding with you."

"Redmond?" Payton asked it, and lifted his head toward where the man was standing, watching silently.

"'Tis said Caruth clan possess sharp tongues and sharper wits. I can see the truth of both now," Redmond answered.

Payton groaned before answering. "'Tis your plan," he replied.

"Perhaps she canna' ride and tempers the fear with the argue?" Redmond suggested.

"Get me a horse," Dallis spoke up. "I'll ride."

"Perhaps," Payton ignored her outburst. "Perhaps na'. We doona' have that choice. We may have to tie her."

"Na' if you hold to her. Help her keep a seat. 'Tis a long ride."

"This is na' a good idea. You take her."

"She is na' my wife," Redmond replied.

"Will you both cease speaking of me as if I were na' here?" Dallis asked.

"Aside from which, you ride Orion," Redmond announced. "You ken he's the strongest. 'Tis why you chose him."

Payton grunted. "You bring twine?"

"Never without it." He was pulling at a bundle of it the man always kept wrapped about his sporran.

"He is not tying me. I am not riding with you. And I have tired of this man-game," Dallis continued.

"On four?" Redmond asked.

Payton nodded.

"Doona' start counting," Dallis warned. "Either of you."

"One," Redmond announced.

"Just as we did in Aberdeen. Hook to crook," Payton said.

"Two," Redmond replied.

"I'm warning you—!"

They moved before three. As always. It was the best way to get a drunken clansman atop a horse for the ride home. His wife's squeal was cut off as Redmond wrapped both arms about her from the back, locking her arms in place as he lifted her. Then, he moved forward so that Payton could grip her beneath the arms and haul her up, swiveling her sideways so her buttocks fit between his thighs and her head beneath his chin. He had his arms tightly about her, listening to the rapid pace of her heart, while he waited for the sting of her anger. All of it had taken less than the count to four. He was rather proud of their execution, since he'd never had a drunken clansman in front of him before.

And then something happened. Something horrid. Payton pulled in air on the pressure inside his chest that he'd never admit to. That would never do. Ever. In the span of a heartbeat, he worried over it. Hated it. Tried to kill it. Nothing worked. He had to release the inhaled breath and gain another. Not only did she feel wonderfully soft within his arms, but she had a particular smell he'd thought imagined. And then forgotten.

She wasn't moving. She wasn't even breathing. He was starting to worry over how he'd get the wench to take her own breath, when she eased it out. Payton didn't move anything on him. Anywhere.

"Payton?"

Her whisper was going to undo his stiff stance with the soft, breath-filled way she did it. He anchored his legs more firmly about the horse, hardened his arms, and concentrated. The thump of heartbeat hitting his scarred temple got louder.

"Aye?" he asked finally.

"'Tis hard to breathe."

She squirmed slightly and received a further tightening of his arms about her before he could prevent it. He had to consciously force his own limbs to relax. Just slightly. She sighed a response. Payton had to turn his head aside before he swallowed so she wouldn't hear the gulping sound. Then he was clearing his throat of any shake-sound. He didn't know why it was this particular woman who could make him feel like a lad without wits. He didn't like it, either.

"You'll na' fight me?" he asked, finally.

She shook her head. It was such a surprise, he pulled his head back slightly.

"Truly?"

"You have shelter planned. At some point? True?"

"Aye," he replied.

"And food?"

He chuckled, sending a huff of air about her covered head that he could have sworn ruffled the wisps of hair at her forehead. He felt the pressure about his heart again. He worried again. Fought it. And then he feared it. There was just no reason it was this woman to do this thing to him. None.

"Well?" she asked.

"Aye," he replied finally, and felt a bigger fool.

"Then, I'll na' fight you. Just get us there."

"You hungered?" he asked, swiveling them in tandem and going into a bend in order to fish about in the pack at Orion's rump.

Her immediate response was a gasp, followed by a total cling with her arms about his neck and one leg hooked about his waist as if he was in danger of dropping her, and not just getting her a biscuit. Payton hovered in midtwist, one arm still holding her to his chest, his other arm getting the bag, while his mind was filling over and over with more silent curses on everything.

He didn't need a reminder of what ecstasy he'd found with her! He didn't want any ideas to tempt him, and he sure as hell didn't desire anything more than his distance from her. Then he spent time ordering his body to listen.

"We're going to fall!"

She wasn't screaming it, but she might as well be, since the night was projecting sound. Payton could hear the reaction from about them with snorts of amusement from his men.

"We . . . are . . . *na'*!"

He gave the last word more inflection than he meant to. That's what came of tempering everything, especially his reaction. But he had the biscuits and had pulled back into place, and then he was doing his best to ignore how she'd wrapped about him, shoving her breasts into his belly while her woman-place pressed into his upper thigh. He spent the next moments trying not to show that it had been as difficult a maneuver as it had, as well. He still had one arm wrapped about her and was knocking her head about with his chest muscles until he slapped the bread sack onto where her groin was astride him.

"Here," he announced. "And doona' do something so dense again."

"Put me with a better horseman, then."

He breathed in deeply, lifting her with it. Then he exhaled. Words came out with it. "The lone one in danger of falling is you. Now, sit nicely like a good lass. Jesu', Mary, and Joseph."

She giggled, and Payton's chest went thick with how that felt. He couldn't determine if it was an angered reaction at her amusement or more of the same curse of emotion she was giving him. He decided it was anger.

"I was just . . . remembering," she told him, as if he'd asked.

And then he remembered when he'd used that phrasing before, as well. When they'd created the babe. Payton grit his teeth on the new spate of cursing that his mind filled in for him. It had to be the exertion. That's what was making him weak and turning his chest and now his belly into a mass of heat. He must not be healed enough . . . which was odd. He'd been working with the stone weights, eating fully, and wrestling his men and any other clansman that wanted to take a challenge from him, preparing for whatever battling he might encounter. He should have spent some time working through the other things, such as the reaction to this one particular woman.

"Can you just eat?" he replied with a gruff tone.

She was shifting, removing the arms locked about his neck and sliding her buttocks back into place between his legs and turning his night into hell. That's what she was doing before she got back sideways to him again, settled herself with more movement than seemed necessary into the space he'd created for her, and worked the ties of his bag loose. And then everything got worse.

"You have bread?"

She clasped the bag to her bosom and raised her gaze to him; her eyes wide, as was her mouth. Or the light was lying. Payton surprised himself by keeping the groan from sounding as he lifted his eyes from hers, and looked over her head at where all of them were waiting. They were riding double, and it looked like Redmond had the old woman. And they all looked to have the same grins on their faces.

"Why . . . are you sitting about?" Payton asked them, but he had to lower his voice after the first word.

"We're waiting," Redmond replied with more laughter to his tone than was voice.

"Waiting for what?"

"The command."

Payton sighed hugely, pushing the hair off his forehead with the rush of air. "Christ! I am na' the lone one here. Get to riding."

"We are your Honor Guard, Payton. We follow you. Always."

Sometimes, he truly hated Redmond MacCloud and his way of speaking. This could easily be one of them.

Chapter 10

Dallis tried to sleep, yet the more she tried the more it eluded her. She knew the reason. Her mind wouldn't cease thinking long enough for sleep to take over. She didn't dare let it. That was the lone thing keeping the sensation of being held by Payton Dunn-Fadden in abeyance. So, she suffered through each step of the horse, rocking her slightly backward and forward with a pace set for endurance, and tried to keep everything where it was supposed to be.

Especially her thoughts.

It shouldn't be difficult. She should be exhausted.

First there had been the general slow starvation she'd suffered for weeks now, accompanied by the lack of sufficient movement. Such a thing made listless movements and weak limbs. She knew that, which was why she'd paced her chamber seemingly without end prior to this rescue. And then she took into account the ordeal of Payton's rescue; the boat ride chilled by the bone-shaking elements and hampered by her own stubbornness. And then this forced contact atop a horse.

She knew they had the equivalent of a half day's ride. She'd heard them. That calculated to be perhaps a league and a half in distance. Less, if they'd made allowance for the weather hampering their animals. And if the tales Lady Evelyn told her about Dunn-Fadden skills were true, Payton would have a camp set up with a nice warm fire, shelter, and a warm cot. He might even have it suspended from poles, with furs and satins . . . he might even have pillows.

Dallis shifted slightly, and felt the corresponding movement of the thigh at her backside as he allowed for it and compensated. She wondered if he managed that in his sleep, of if that state was eluding him as well, and then she cursed the perversity that gave her the thought. She didn't want to think of her husband! She didn't want anything to do with any man—especially this one! She wanted her freedom. She always had. And this man was taking her right to freedom.

Dallis had never been to Edinburgh and the castle. Her father had deemed it unnecessary and of little moment until she was wed and off his hands. He'd told her it was due to her winsome face as well as her dowry. She didn't believe the truth of her features, but she well knew the wealth and position that had come with her hand. She wondered if the courtly skills Lady Evelyn had tried to bestow upon her were enough to compensate for arriving in little more than a nightshift and a borrowed length of plaid. She should be adorned as befit the greatest heiress in the Highlands, in velvets and white satin as was her creed, with a jeweled headband to hold her wimple in place, and a heavy golden girdle about her hips. All of which she'd lost years past. She hoped Payton had made allowances for her appearance.

He seemed to think of everything else. The two hard rolls she'd nibbled on had calmed her belly's ills and the little bit of whiskey she'd sipped from the sporran he'd offered up had done even better, warming her clear to her toes. They should have given her time to don boots. And thick socks. That way, she wouldn't be out in the elements with little more than slippers on her feet. Satin slippers weren't known for warmth. Payton must have guessed it, though, for the way he'd wrapped the cloak about her lower legs and brought it back up beneath her had made a warm and secure and comfortable cocoon. It had also put the start to her need for constant thinking, since he'd used the wool about his shoulders to enwrap her to him, effectively sealing her in from the elements, but cursing her with this problem of sensation at the same time.

Dallis shifted again, felt the arm at her back tense slightly as if to keep her from falling, while the thigh she was settled against did the same thing. Again. It happened as many times as she shifted. It was truly amazing how he managed such a thing while sleeping. She knew he was slumbering. He had to be. The deep movement of the chest and belly she was snuggled against sounded too much like sleep-breathing. As did the faint rumble of snoring he made.

Dallis giggled and turned her face to rub her cheek against the fabric-covered hardness that was his chest. And then she wondered where the insanity that made her do such a thing came from.

He wasn't asleep. He was startled, though, if the immediate tautness through all of him was any indication. There was a halt in his breathing and the sound of snoring stopped as well. She felt the cover over her head lifted and looked up to meet snow-flecked lashes around very wide eyes. And if it hadn't been pre-dawn and snowing, reflecting what light there was, she wouldn't have seen that much.

And then he made it so much worse as he pulled in on his cheeks, narrowing his face, while a hint of a smile touched his pursed lips.

"I . . . uh . . ." Dallis's whisper stopped. She didn't know what to say. She supposed it was a full-body blush that rushed through her, heating her even more than contact with his body was. She didn't know enough about it to be certain.

"Aye?" he asked, and then he licked at his lower lip.

Her entire form lurched, all of his limbs seemed to react immediately to seize at her, and then he finished the pulse of motion as if it was supposed to transfer directly from her into him. Dallis's mouth dropped open slightly to gain enough breath.

"'Tis hard enough to keep a seat in the dead of night," he informed her, bending his head slightly to fit it beneath her covering, allowing a soft sift of snowfall to twinkle in the space between and about them.

His movement also put him so close to her, she could feel the breath from his words atop her nose. Worse, she could sense his proximity with some part of her she didn't know enough about to defend.

"With a snowfall. And nae path."

"I . . . uh . . ." Dallis repeated the phrase, in the exact same fashion.

"And with you in my arms."

He just wouldn't cease the slight murmur of his words as they grazed her skin, and then it was his lips doing the touching.

"It is na' what you—"

"Hush."

He said it against the skin of her lips, and that was most brutal of him. And unfair. And enticing. And a thousand other things that marked him a base scoundrel and a cheat.

He wasn't so much kissing her, as he was lapping at her lips with his, lifting her in place with the soft suction against her skin. And then Dallis made it easy for him! One hand looped up and over his shoulder, twined about his neck, and then she could have sworn it was her body lifting slightly, locking her to him, so she could deepen the kiss and blend her moan with his.

He lifted his head away, pulling the skin of her lips awry with the movement, and ended their kiss with a look deep into her eyes. Bottomless deep.

"Easy . . . my love."

She didn't truly hear it, so he must have mouthed it. Either that, or her ears weren't functioning. And he couldn't have called her his love. He just . . . couldn't.

"Nae, I—" Dallis stuttered.

"Lass . . . Lass." He interrupted her, his free arm moving her about, while the hard lump of his sporran seemed to have sprouted bulk, since it was in the way. And then she knew why as he just kept shifting in place and talking. "You're way too gifted. I must have forgotten that, although 'tis beyond me how."

She knew for certain it was a blush now, as he finished arranging himself to his satisfaction and turned his face back to her. Then he lowered his chin to look at her through his lashes. If it was any closer to dawn, he'd have no trouble spotting her flushed skin with a slight skim of moisture.

His face split with a smile. Dallis called him a wretch and then a buffoon, followed by a simpleton, a rake, and then she named him a cheat. Silently. Not one word came out of her mouth, although her lips were parted for them. This is what came of spending a sleepless night atop a horse, she decided. Witlessness.

"Verra gifted. And now you must stop. We both must."

He was clicking his tongue as if to chastise her. Dallis's eyes went wide.

"Wait! Payton, I—!"

"Of course I'll wait," he informed her, shaking at the covering atop them, which made flecks of snow fly about. That added even more sparkle to the pink and yellow tinted air. "Grant me some wits, Wife. We're atop a horse in a blizzom . . . covered in snow. And 'tis cold. I've a meal prepared, a fire burning, and a tent erected and warmed and readied. For my lone use. And I have a pallet. A large one."

And then he winked.

He was right about the fire. And perhaps the meal, since there was a kettle of oats bubbling atop their fire, suspended by a tripod of unevenly chopped and peeled sticks. They'd used wet wood, though, or something of a worse nature, since the smoke cloud was easy to spot. They'd also selected a site open to the elements and any watchers, rather than any of a dozen strands of trees that could have hidden a smaller tent. Worse still, they only had one tent erected and it looked the size to accommodate a horde and not just their leader.

Dallis saw all this a moment after the horse halted and Payton pulled in a lung full of air, dislodging her from a spot against him. Then he was bellowing something, splitting the words into nonsense and making her ears ring with the volume of sound reverberating from his chest. It wasn't until the third time that she realized it was a name.

"Edwin Brennon MacGruder! Edwin MacGruder! Ed! Win!"

Dallis had the coverlet down beneath her nose then to peek out. It wasn't anyone named Edwin that came out of the tent in front of them. It was the servant wench, Bronwyn. The lass hadn't gained much in strength or courage, for she just stood there, wringing her hands as the five horses approached. Dallis watched as Redmond's horse passed by Payton's, Redmond taking the lead and speaking before Payton could.

"Morn, lass. We expected Edwin MacGruder."

Redmond spoke in a calm voice that Payton wouldn't have been able to achieve. Not if the heavy breaths he was taking against Dallis's back were any indicator.

"He—he's . . . hunting," Bronwyn stammered.

"Hunting?"

Redmond was continuing to speak in a moderate, calm tone. He was also dismounting and assisting Lady Evelyn to the ground and holding her shoulders as if waiting for her legs to do it, all of which looked chivalrous and gallant.

"Game . . . is scarce. He told me of it . . . when he left. He had to go! He was under orders to have a deer roasting. Or . . . at the verra least, a hare."

Her voice had gotten stronger, and accusatory. It was easy to see who she was aiming that emotion at, for she slid a

glance to Payton's form before looking back to the ground.
Payton responded with a sigh of disgust and the removal of
his arms from Dallis. It was to lift the cloak from atop him
and bring it down in front of them, leaving his form free to
the elements, and making hers suffer the same. That made her
realize just how cold it was. About the only good thing looked
to be the snowfall had stopped, although the sky was leaden
with a gray color promising more. There was just a slice of
space between the cloud cover and the horizon for the weak
winter sunlight to peek through, granting light but little in
warmth.

"Redmond," Payton spoke with a warning tone, putting his
hands on Dallis's waist with more force than he needed to.
She wasn't going anywhere.

"When did he leave?" Redmond ignored Payton's outburst
and continued the questioning of Bronwyn.

"Last eve. Just after getting the tent set up."

"So . . . he left you all alone. All night?"

The girl nodded.

"And you made gruel for our arrival?"

"A-a-and . . . bread," she stammered.

"You have been verra industrious, lass. Verra."

"Oh, for the love of God!"

Payton launched himself in a twist motion off the side of
his horse, using the handholds on Dallis's waist as his ful-
crum. She barely had time to grasp to the horse's mane in
order to hold her seat and keep the stallion from bolting. It
was a good thing he was well trained and she knew how to
ride a horse, since this was all the regard Payton showed her.
Watching him, she was grateful she didn't have his attention. He was advancing on where Bronwyn had turned back
into a pitiful hand-wringing waif again. From the height of
a seat on his horse, it was easy to spot how he dwarfed even
Redmond.

"I give orders. I give ample time. I expect them followed!

Na' have to deal with a simple-minded lass that I need to placate with soft words!"

"My laird," Redmond replied in the same evenly modulated tone. "There are ladies about."

"What?" Payton stopped midstride and pulled himself back.

"Ladies . . . and they are na' as strong as you are."

Payton shoved out another breath and put both hands out. "What are you talking of now? And why must we mill about bandying senseless words when we have shelter at your back? And it better be warm!"

"Because there are ladies accompanying us, and ladies require more clothing than you have left them with, warm gruel to put before them, and a pallet upon which to rest. Especially after the ordeal we have just put them through."

Redmond gestured to where Dallis probably looked a sight, since she had both fists full of horse mane. That left her unable to hold any of the material that was trailing to the ground, due to Payton's exit from her. She watched as Payton glared over at her like it was her fault all she had on was a plain shift and was outdoors on a winter morn. Then she returned the look.

"We'd best get the ladies into the tent, then," Payton responded finally. "And Davey? See to the horses. Get your brother's assist." He was advancing on her as he said all of it.

"Perhaps I'd best see to the wife," Redmond spoke from behind him, and took one step in that direction.

"I doona' need your assist," Payton replied.

"You certain?"

"I'll see to the wife. You see to getting every other *lady* into the tent."

Payton sounded like he was talking through closed teeth. It wasn't hard to imagine why. Hers were chattering enough she had to clench them to keep the sound at bay. She hoped it was the cold, and yet the closer he got the more she knew that was a lie. And then he stopped, directly at the side of his horse, put his hands on his hips and looked up at her.

Dallis didn't have any way to clasp her hands to wring them and, stupidly, that's exactly what she felt compelled to do. Which would look weak and frail and too much like Bronwyn's reaction to him had been. She was probably in luck that her stance atop his horse gave her no option other than to sit upright in order to keep her seat with both hands full of mane to remain that way.

He probably should wear more than a linen shirt and his *feile-breacan*, since the dawn light was kissing the side of him it touched, while the shadows carved out the rest of him for her to observe.

"You should wear more," he stated, as if he were reading her mind.

Dallis blinked, felt the cold reaction through her eyes at the frost-filled air, and nodded. "As should you," she replied.

He grunted. Then, he put his hands out and up toward her. "Will you come nicely with me?" he asked.

"You're . . . asking me?" She knew the surprise filled her voice. She didn't know how to hide it.

"Aye," he replied.

"Truly?"

He swore, put his hands to his temples to push his hair back, and glared up at her. "I said aye," he finally said.

Dallis's eyes flitted to the purplish scar he'd revealed at the edge of his hairline before she could help it. When she returned to his gaze, something looked to have changed about him. All over him.

He looked stern, disgusted, and angered. All at once.

"I near forgot," he said, as if she'd asked.

"What?"

"My mark. And what it means."

Dallis couldn't prevent the shivers that took over. She'd

never seen such a look, and since it was coming from the icy blue of his eyes, it seemed worse. She told herself it was the reaction to being in winter conditions with one layer of material on and no way to gain more. Then, she worked at believing it.

"Are you going to come into my arms like a good lass? Or am I going to look like a bear again?"

She smiled slightly and then nodded more to herself than him, and went into a slant in order to slide off. The ground was patched with new snow. It looked cold and wet, and ruinous to satin slippers. She stopped and looked over at him again.

"You'll catch me?" She asked.

He looked heavenward for a moment and then back at her. "You're a slip of a thing and I'm the King's Champion. Does it look as if I canna' catch you?"

"You swear?"

He didn't make a reply. He didn't have to. He reached over and plucked her into his arms, gaining himself a squeal from her, and a few strands of hair pulled loose from his stallion.

"Jesu', Mary, and Joseph. Everything has to be a fight with you. Everything. I canna' get you to do the simplest thing. Even when you say you will, 'tis a lie." He was stomping his way toward the tent, putting emphasis to his words, and then he finished his tirade with another bit of swearing as they reached the door flap.

Dallis giggled then, snuggled a bit closer, and when he moved her to one arm in order to fuss with lifting the door flap, she did something so unbelievable and horrid, everything on her went board stiff. His reaction wasn't far behind as he did the same. She'd lifted her chin, put her nose against his throat, and pressed a kiss to the skin there that was throbbing with a pulse.

He pulled his head back, stunned. She probably had the same expression. The door flap landed atop his head, putting them right in the door, blocking the elements somewhat, and yet letting them in at the same time.

There was another fire inside the tent. There had to be, for warmth blessed Dallis's back, while flickers of firelight touched on his face. That was almost too much to handle since the light showed all too clearly the beautiful blue color of his eyes, especially as wide as he had them.

"What did you do that for?" he asked it softly, but with a rumble of sound that went straight through her.

"I dinna' . . . ken," she replied. She didn't know, either. She was as surprised as he was.

"Wife, you need to pick one reaction to me, and stay with it. You're perplexing me, and that in turn, annoys me."

"I . . ." Her voice stopped.

"I'm na' certain I like it, either. In fact, I'm fairly certain I dinna'."

"I—" Dallis tried again. She couldn't think. She couldn't even speak if he didn't move his gaze.

"I already ken you're the bonniest woman I've met. You keep me all twisted inside . . . and now you add to it?"

"But, I—" She didn't have an answer. Again.

"You dinna' have to keep letting me see it. And feel it. Jesu', Woman. Have a bit of sympathy. We doona' even have our own tent."

Dallis gasped. That pushed her bosom fully against him. She watched him glance that way before a tremor ran through him, and then transferred into her. Her increased breasts had been the only change to her body because of his bairn, and her bosom hadn't been a small size to begin with, anyway.

He'd finished off looking at her body's increase and returned to her gaze. Dallis would kick herself later for still having it wide and rapt and ready for him. Everything was going wrong, and she couldn't think if he continued holding her, lifting her with his increased breathing while his arms tightened even further.

"Could you either come in, Payton, or stay out? Either way, allow the door to fall. You're chilling your own tent and making the ladies suffer."

It might have been that Redmond speaking again, but there was enough amusement to the voice, it could be anyone. Aside from which, Dallis couldn't hear much over the hum within her own ears. She knew what caused it, too. Payton's gaze as he looked into hers. Caught. Held. Enthralled. Stricken.

He was moving forward . . . a step, then another. The door flap slid off his head and dropped into place. Dallis didn't move her gaze from his.

"Good. You've made a choice." Someone was still talking. Dallis barely heard it.

"Aye," Payton replied.

"You should unhand the lady," the clansman remarked.

"Aye," Payton said again.

"She probably needs some sustenance," the man continued.

"Do you?" he asked.

Dallis shook her head slightly.

"She has probably tired of your stench by now, as well." The disembodied voice said it from somewhere over his right shoulder.

"Are you?" Payton asked her again.

Dallis shook her head again.

"Payton Alexander Dunn-Fadden."

The name was announced like it was justice being meted out. Dallis watched as Payton shut his eyes tightly, putting little crinkles into existence at the corners, and then he opened them, shook his head as if just awakening, and turned his head toward the voice.

"Unhand the wife. She has a seat set up and a bit of food. All of which she is needful of. And na' more of your attention."

"We *are* wed, Redmond."

"And we are attempting a breakfast. You are rapidly putting me off my appetite."

Dallis giggled again. Payton's arms tightened as if in immediate mindless response to hearing it. And that had her gasping again. All of which got her his glance back to her breasts and then back to her. And then he smiled wryly.

"You make it powerful difficult to remember that I hate you, Wife. Powerful difficult," he whispered it, which made it worse.

"You . . . hate . . . me?" She didn't even give it voice, but he must have known because he replied, with an even larger smile.

"Oh. Absolutely."

Payton moved forward the required space, eased his arms loose and lowered her. Dallis didn't even feel the pile of folded blanket that he set her atop. She wasn't aware of anything sensory beyond the smell, feel, and sight of her husband . . . who hated her.

Chapter 11

Dallis couldn't sleep. Again. She shifted against the body beside her and tried modulating her breathing again. None of the others sleeping in the enclosure seemed to have this problem. Most of the earthen floor was given over to sleeping mats of one kind or another and snoring could be heard from several of the plaid-covered lumps. The men weren't all sleeping. Two men were posted outside as guards, but that had changed twice in the time she'd been lying, snuggled under a fur and trying to stop her thoughts so she could at least rest.

It wasn't entirely her fault. It was too hard, too warm, too bright, too loud, too strange . . . and that was before she added Dunn-Fadden. From across the width of the firepit, she felt the disturbance that came from being in proximity of him . . . and it just wasn't fair!

Her presence obviously wasn't bothering him.

Dallis moved her head slightly to look across at him, the motion rubbing her cheek against the heavy linen weave of the pallet. Payton was on his side facing her, bundled up in his cloak with his head pillowed on a crooked arm. He was sound asleep . . . on a mat made from coarse hemp resembling the sling they'd used. He didn't even have the stuffed pallet he'd described to her.

She and Lady Evelyn did, while Bronwyn rested across the bottom.

That bit of gallantry hadn't needed to be urged. Payton had retrieved the pallet from his horse's back and unfurled it with an emotion bordering on animosity. She suspected the reason, as did everyone else. He'd fully expected to be sleeping on it, and probably with her.

Dallis grimaced a bit with that memory. She'd never been around so many fighting-aged men before, and never in a tent or on a journey, but she would have thought clansmen obeyed their future laird with more alacrity than this group did. They seemed to act more like a quorum all possessing an equal vote. It was difficult to believe these were the same men that had taken the Caruth keep in such a bloody battle three years ago. It was impossible to believe it planned. Not when observing them now. They argued over every little thing, including where they bedded down to sleep.

Of course, everyone wanted to be near the fire. It was warmer. It was most protected. New snowfall the consistency of powder filtered through the opening in the peak but was melted before it reached the floor. Dallis wouldn't want to be at the outer edges of the tent, either. That's where the cold seeped in. So they'd had an argument, a discussion, reached a decision, and it had been Payton's decree that the men coming in from guard duty could have the spot closest to the fire, while those at the edge would be sent out to patrol. Dallis longed to point out that this wouldn't prove restful, since they'd be jostling about when anyone returned, but they didn't ask her opinion, and she wasn't offering it. They also decided that the man who returned had to bring a bit of the sliced peat and lay it to dry at the door prior to adding it to their fire.

That order came after the first returning men used wet peat and turned the enclosure into a smoke-infested, cough-inducing torment. That had been the youngest one's fault . . . the big-eyed one they called Alan.

Dallis blew out the disgust at herself. She really had to get some rest!

Due to their argument, she knew the plan. Edinburgh would take a sennight to reach, if they weren't waylaid by bad direction or another storm. There was also the shelter of Ballilol Castle. It was within four days' travel, and they'd be safe enough there. Except for Payton. Dallis didn't know what the jostling and grinning as they chided Payton meant, but if it was worrisome to Payton, Ballilol Keep couldn't be that much protection.

They were also cursed to travel by night. At least until they reached Ballilol. It was the man, Martin, with that idea. Dallis had a difficult time keeping her tongue during the listen, while she'd pretended to sleep. They weren't risking the main road. They weren't a large enough band to protect her should they come upon brigands, pursuing Kilchurnings, or even Caruth clansmen. And they were riding double. Not only did that slow them, but it also gave the appearance of weakness. It was better to be unseen and avoid trouble. At least until they reached Ballilol Castle or Canongate. That was when her husband spoke up that he courted trouble, and he didn't see the issue, which got him more discussion.

Dallis watched him sleep now. He was getting easier to decipher. That man was primed for battle and seemed to expect one. At any time. As he'd been blessed with a frame guaranteed to bring on a challenge and he'd worked it into strength and brawn and substance that made him nearly omnipotent, it was probably not all his fault that a test of strength always seemed to find him.

She sighed softly and accompanied it with a pursing of her lips as she studied him.

Not only was he the largest male, but he was also gifted with amazing coloring and truly breath-stealing handsomeness. Slumbering as he was, it was even more apparent. Soot-shaded eyelashes grazed his cheeks, and lips that were almost feminine

in shape were parted slightly for breath. He had the slightest
skiff of whisker coating his jaw and should he cease scraping
it off with a skean, his beard would probably come in as dark
as his hair was.

She was glad he slept. That way he wouldn't know how she
roamed her eyes where only her imagination had gone. Back
when she'd been his wife in name only she'd been tormented
with dreams of what might happen when he returned. Now
that she'd lain with him and carried his child, the dreams had
an eroticism to them nobody had prepared her for. Her tower
hadn't contained it. She'd gone to her knees and tried to pray
the images away. She'd bathed in cold water without light to
avoid waking Lady Evelyn. She'd tried changing into a clean,
fresh, cool night dress when hers clung to her body as if mim-
icking where his hands had been.

Nothing had worked. It wasn't working now, either. Dallis
licked her lips and sucked in on the lower one, tried to breathe
shallowly to prevent the pinpricks of her nipples from straining against the fabric like they were, reminding her, plaguing
her . . . tormenting her.

That's when Payton's eyes opened.

He looked across at her without one change in his breathing. Dallis's eyes went wide as they met his. She could only
pray it hadn't been somewhere on her face before she could
halt it . . . and then hope it was true!

He peeled back the sett that had shadowed his head, lifting
it slightly from where he'd rested atop his arm, and then one
eyebrow rose while the smallest smile quirked at his lips.

Dallis gasped and turned her head into the pallet at her
cheek so swiftly, she scratched her nose on the weave.
She stayed that way for long moments, breathing straw-
smell through the material, while ripples ran over her
back and shoulders as she sensed him, felt him coming to
her. The impression that he was moving toward her grew
into certainty. Her breathing quickened, the trembling got

worse, and despite everything, she couldn't get her body to cease reacting.

That was the most mortifying.

She knew he was nearing. There was a whisper of sound so soft, primed ears wouldn't have heard it, and there was a tinkle from metallic objects. Then, another. Again. As if weaponry was swaying with Payton's movement. He wouldn't dare try to gain intimacy with her now! Not when they had so many about them—and not after claiming his hatred.

Besides, she wouldn't let him. Would she?

Dallis hunched her shoulders, drew her knees slightly up, and struggled with the wellspring of want deep in her core that answered. This was horrid. Worrisome. Elicit. Exciting. Enticing. . . .

She held her breath and heard nothing but the steady cadence of deep slumber, accompanied by grunts and snores. Nothing else.

Dallis tipped her head just slightly, moved her eyes to the corners so he wouldn't spot the movement, and then knew it didn't matter. Payton was back atop his arm, heavily asleep if the rise and fall of the sett covering him was any indication, and nothing about him looked primed to see to his wife's discomfort. Except perhaps the small smile that graced his lips.

"'Tis easier for both of us if you'd unbend a bit, Wife."

Dallis kept everything on her body stiff and unyielding, just as she had for what seemed hours now. Despite what discomfort it caused. She wasn't enjoying one moment of being in his forced proximity, atop his horse, and bundled together with his blankets. She hoped her stiffness demonstrated it.

"'Tis easier for both of us . . . *Dallis,*" she replied.

He chuckled. That felt horrid when combined with the way his chest muscles jostled her head. Dallis straightened even more.

"Unbend a mite. I'll na' bite."

"I'm na' afraid even if you do," she replied haughtily.

He grunted, which probably went for a reply and gave her silence again. It was just as well. They'd been traveling since before the sun set. After everyone but her had eaten a filling meal of roast venison since the clansman named Edwin had returned and awakened everyone with his hunting prowess. All of which the men must appreciate since they'd spent a massive amount of time clapping him about the shoulders and praising him. Loudly. That had made it impossible to get further rest, once she'd finally dropped to sleep.

Dallis was exhausted, mentally and physically and emotionally. And she was out-of-sorts. She was also queasy when she first awoke. Lady Evelyn could have told them that. It was his fault, too. She added that to her other ills and found a direct blame: Payton Dunn-Fadden. It was just as well that he hadn't spoken a word to her beyond the order for her to get atop the horse without issue.

Until now.

"Well, I'm na'," she repeated, as if looking for an argument.

"I've na' made the claim of it," he replied. "Here."

He was holding something toward her beneath the blanket, or he was shifting for no reason other than to unseat her.

"What is it?" she asked.

"Hard biscuit. You need something for sustenance."

"I ate fully," she lied, and then her belly rumbled in direct discord.

"I doona' wish to force it, Wife. Take it. 'Twill do the bairn good."

"I am na' hungry."

"Verra well. I'll force it."

He slapped it into her hand, surprising her with how he managed to do that, since it was beneath the blanket and he wasn't looking anywhere near it. He seemed intent on where they were heading and all she got from a swift glance at his face was a view of a set jaw. He had her bundled with a length of plaid, while he was wrapped in his cloak, leaving only their heads and his one arm outside the blanketing. He needed that arm for the reins.

It was easy to see since the moon-imbued mist threading through the trees about them and across the moors wasn't thick enough to swallow a partner atop a horse. It was thick enough to cover over the others, though, making it look and feel like they were alone. Dallis trembled and blamed it on the elements. It was colder than last eve, too, with the absence of snowfall. She set herself to munching on the roll he'd given her.

"You readied now?" he asked when she'd finished.

Dallis's eyes widened. "For what?"

"You need your rest. Unbend. Sleep. I'll hold you."

"I already got my rest," she argued, and then couldn't stop the yawn that gave that lie away.

"I will have to do something about that lying tongue. I truly will. But for now could you please be a good lass, and rest?"

He took away her choice with the hard pressure of his free arm, the one beneath the blanket. She couldn't fight such strength when used without warning and he knew it. That's why he did it. Dallis slumped into the enclosure created against his belly, settled her head into the enclave beneath his throat, and almost kept the sigh of relief from sounding.

"I am . . . na' . . . tired." She murmured the last of it against the center of his chest, right where his heart was thumping with a solid, steady rhythm.

"Fair enough," he replied above her, and the flesh at her ear echoed it.

"I doona' wish anything to do with you . . . Dunn-Fadden." Her whisper was fading toward the end. That's because he was cradling her in place, with his hand holding her head, and his arm against her back.

"Fair enough," he agreed again.

"It's true," Dallis continued. "I'd rather be with any other man than . . . you."

He snorted, ruffling her hair with the force of it. "The next thing you'll be averring is that you doona' lust after me, either," he replied.

The moment he said it, she stiffened. Everywhere. It was in preparation for smacking at something and he must have known it. It was his fault she couldn't move, since the arm at her back hardened to the consistency of iron, making a struggle worthless.

"I don't lust after you," she said through clenched teeth, which was the best she could manage.

"You should save it for when we reach Edinburgh. Or, at the verra least, Ballilol. That would be the fair move."

"I doona' lust after you," she repeated.

He chuckled a sound that echoed through his chest, and the arm at her back loosened slightly.

"You denounce it without reason, Wife. I ken the look you give me. I just canna' act on it. Na' yet."

"I doona' lust after you!" She wasn't clenching her teeth any longer.

His response was full amusement. The belly she leaned against rocked her with it.

"The lasses have been lusting after me since I arrived in Edinburgh and gained myself title of King's Champion. Actually, I mis-speak. They'd been lusting after me a-fore that. Even a-fore our marriage. A-fore I'd even reached my manhood. I ken the look. I just told you. And you have it."

"You are the most self-satisfied, arrogant, conceited, boorish, unchivalrous, maddening . . . !" She ran out of adjectives before she ran out of breath and resorted to finishing it with a scream of sound.

"Payton, we attempt silent progress through here," one of the clansmen about them said.

Dallis's gasp was lost against his chest. She was mortified. Out-of-sorts again. She didn't need him to clamp her to him, either, since she shoved her own head against his chest with the embarrassment and stayed there.

"'Tis only Redmond," he advised her, in a softer tone.

"I know," she replied.

"You ken 'tis Redmond speaking?"

"Your men all have distinctive voices. His is easy."

"He has little regard for the vagaries of the flesh. And a woman's desires."

"I am na' interested," Dallis informed him.

"And he sees a stalker behind every tree, a threat about every boulder, while an ambush awaits at every turn."

"We *are* in Stalker's Wood," Redmond replied from somewhere beside them.

"And he eavesdrops," Payton told her.

Dallis giggled.

"Stalker's Wood." Redmond continued. "'Tis known for hiding reavers and murderers and the like. We've little by way of force and weaponry."

"I thought we were attempting silence," Payton replied to the lesson.

There was a huff for an answer, and then came the heavy thudding sound of a body. Falling from a horse. And then a scream.

It wasn't Dallis making the sound. Her throat wouldn't open enough for it since the dark blobs of tree limbs looming from the fog seemed filled with even blacker blobs, and these turned into silent, claymore-wielding men.

Chaos filled the fog, alive with grunts and anguish. It was peopled with metal against metal, more thumping and the swish of material, including Payton as he tumbled from the back of the horse, leaving her shoulders and back open to the elements since he'd taken his cloak with him.

Dallis grabbed for the reins just as the horse reared, caught sight of Payton's lunge from a crouch to a spinning maneuver that looked to take off an opponent's head, and then the horse reared, nearly unseating her. Dallis split her legs and slid into the saddle, warmed from Payton, just as Orion's hooves reached ground. Then he was racing, dodging trees that advanced without warning, while he appeared to be trying to unseat her from the way he chose the lowest limbs to pass beneath.

She had Orion halted before he could succeed, and made him stand, trembling and heaving for breath beneath her while she did the same. And then she knew her real jeopardy. If Payton and his men perished . . . where did that leave her? She didn't even know where they were, except that it was known as "Stalker's Wood." What good would that do a lone female—without an escort and without a weapon?

Damn that Payton! None even knew she was missing. As far as the Kilchurning or the Dunn-Fadden laird knew, she was still in her tower. None would assist her or come looking for her. No one would even mount a rescue. Blast that man for calling her into an argument tonight—and damn her own tongue for doing this! Heartbeat sounds grew until they flooded everything else, making it impossible to hear what had happened . . . or was still happening.

This reaction wouldn't do. And she'd been trained better. Fright-filled thinking and defeated attitude gained one naught save heartache and waste. What was it she'd been schooled to do? Dallis went over it wordlessly: Stay emotion. Gather knowledge. Assess belongings for use. Act as needed.

Dallis hugged the blanket closer about her and tried to modulate her breathing so she could get past the spooks and banshees that every fog was peopled with. To hear. That seemed the lone sense available for her use.

There was nothing making sound. Nothing to see. Nothing to sense. There wasn't anything in the woods except Orion beneath her, a cold no amount of blanket diminished, and her own heartbeats, although they'd tempered to a hum just shy of a spinning wheel's vibration.

She had no injuries. She had a strong horse, also uninjured. She had a blanket. She had freedom. She had her wits. She was just on the assessing part of her belongings when a shrill whistle split the night, carried easily on the fog. She shifted her head in the same direction Orion did, although it pulled on the reins. Dallis loosened them and let him go.

"God's blood, but you have more sense than to bolt from a fight!"

Payton was angered, but he wasn't speaking to her. He'd yanked the horse's head level to his and was lecturing his steed. He and several others were congregated at a copse, defined by slanted limbs above their heads. They were breathing hard, covered with muck and blood, and they were adding to the opacity, since the heat of their bodies was making more mist.

"How many did we lose, Martin?" Payton lifted his head away to ask it.

"One."

Dallis's back clenched.

"Davey."

She echoed Alan's cry, although his turned to sobs that someone tried to comfort.

"Davey? God *damn* my hide."

Payton carried a great amount of heartbreak in his voice, Dallis decided. It made her own heart twinge. He dropped the reins, although it was more like he flung them, and turned away.

"Injured?"

"Seth took a blow to the head. I doona' ken how bad. He canna' say."

"Bronwyn will see to it. She lives?"

"Aye. And the spinster. Seth was guarding them. 'Twas why he took the head-blow."

Payton grunted. "They paid?" he asked.

"Fully," Redmond replied.

"What clan?" Payton barked it.

"None that can be seen. I counted eleven dead. Differing setts. Misfits. Driven from their own clans. The world is better without."

Dallis decided that was probably Dugan with that information.

"'Twas fourteen." That was Redmond again.

"Fourteen."

Payton's voice sounded disgusted, but to Dallis that couldn't be. His band had just taken on fourteen men intent on murder and robbery and lost but one?

"They carried good weaponry, though."

"Take it," Payton ordered. "And get Davey." He turned toward her. Dallis pulled back and didn't even know why. "Davey Dunn-Fadden was my cousin. He worshipped me. *Me*. And now he's gone. Every time I'm around you, I lose someone close to me. Your presence comes at a high cost, Wife. Still."

"I lost more than thirty," Dallis replied without one inflection.

He shrugged. "I care little what losses to the enemy. I care about *my* losses. Close losses. Come. The journey just got worse. And it dinna' get shorter. Mount up, those that can. And someone stop Alan's wailing."

He plucked the reins from where they dangled, turned away from her, and he started walking.

"You'll na' ride?"

It wasn't Dallis asking it, although it had barely penetrated her mind that he wasn't even willing to sit a horse with her, so it could have been her with the question. It sounded like Dugan again.

Dallis was shivering. The question would have stammered if she'd asked it. It was frigid atop Orion without Payton's bulk. Or, the reaction was settling in, taking her strength in consequence.

"Until I find a burn and cleanse the leavings from myself, I'll na' sully Orion's coat. You ken as much." He was leading the horse, fading as he did so.

"Payton?"

Dallis whispered it and wasn't certain he'd heard. She couldn't tell visually, since the length of the reins took him into the opacity and rendered him a vague upper body shape with no discernible lower legs.

"Aye?" he finally replied in such a soft voice it could have been a goblin as easily.

"I'm sorry about . . . Davey." Her voice broke on the name.

"Save it for your maker." He wasn't whispering. Then he got louder. "And someone see to Alan's wailing!"

Chapter 12

Payton found a burn about midmorn, although it was more like the burn found him. Dallis was slumped forward into her blanket, willing the cold and misery away, when the crust of snow Payton was atop collapsed, sending him into the rushing freeze of an ice-water stream.

She'd never heard some of the words he filled the air with, although Lady Evelyn's gasp from somewhere behind her was easy to hear and decipher about how shocking such language was. It didn't stop Payton. He pulled himself out of the water and onto the snow, cursing all about him, including the daylight that had weakened the ice crust atop the ravine. She gaped as he started stripping, without one care or thought to any ladies present.

Dallis averted her eyes. Not so Lady Evelyn. That woman had a blush about her that was easy to spot in the daylight Payton was still using blasphemy on. Dallis watched her aunt watch Payton, and felt a momentary anger before letting it subside. He'd said he was lusted over. It must be true.

Lady Evelyn didn't turn aside until Payton was covered over in a large hank of plaid that Redmond pulled from a pack and took to him. Dallis knew that from the glance she gave that direction before wishing that move undone.

Payton was swathed in the sett, pulling it close which defined everything, he had it hooded atop his head, and he was directing the ire directly at her.

"Most souls await shelter a-fore bathing in an ice burn, My Laird. And a change of *feile-breacan*. As well as a fire." Redmond said it in his usual unhurried fashion, but there was an urgency to the higher tone he used that had another of the men shouting orders.

"Quick! Get a fire started. We've peat in Davey—I mean Alan's bags. And get the tent up!"

It was Martin directing them this time. Dallis watched as they got a windswept spot selected, since bare ground was better than snow-melt to sleep atop, pulled the tent from a bag, unfurled it, and had it erected before Alan got a firepit marked out and a spark going. Dallis had to help him. There wasn't anyone else, and the lad looked awkward and untrained at it.

Payton wasn't much help since all he did was shiver in place and glare at her. Lady Evelyn remained perched in a ladylike fashion atop Redmond's horse, Bronwyn was supporting the fallen clansman atop another steed, and the other clansmen were needed to hold tent poles, drive spikes, and tie rope fastenings.

That was when Dallis realized something. Payton may allow his group to argue and discuss and take over leadership, and she'd just watched what might be the reason for it as they set up camp without one word of direction from him. She'd suspected it was a Dunn-Fadden weakness. Now, she wasn't so sure.

She tired of watching Alan's attempts at fire. It was a simple matter to slide from the horse's back and approach. It wasn't the lad's fault he looked unsure and ungainly. The cold hampered every move, making anyone look clumsy and ineffective. No wonder Payton had stripped so swiftly, regardless of propriety. A dunking in water was tantamount to a death sentence.

Dallis put her face as close to the spark as she dared and blew, ignoring the proprieties herself with the stance she was in. Someone had to do it and Alan looked more than incapable. He looked like a ghost, his big eyes were moist and red rimmed— although he averted them, and all of him was shaking.

So, Dallis did what he wordlessly was asking. She ignored it.

That woman was going to be the death of him, yet.

Payton hadn't fully regained feeling in his fingers or feet, and there she was, putting her nicely shaped ass into the air toward him, and then swaying it! As if offering him her woman-place when any fool would know a dunking in freeze water wasn't conducive to what she desired. And a greater fool would know to stay away from her in the first place. She was to blame for everything. He nearly groaned.

"You should na' blame the wife."

Payton sighed, slid his glance to Redmond's form beside him, and watched as the black resentment of his expression didn't seem to bother his clansman, either. "And you should na' be my conscience," he said finally. He kept his jaw set as he spoke, not to put emotion to the words, but to keep the chattering of his teeth to a minimum.

"I am attempting to be mine," Redmond replied.

Payton grunted.

"If you blame the woman's lack of silence for Davey's death, then you must blame those that brought on her argument. This would include me."

"She argued when she knew to be silent."

"As did we."

"Are you saying she's blameless now?" Payton asked.

"Those lowlife reavers were in ambush because they had

warning . . . or they were in luck last night. Either way, naught
we did could have affected their attack. Lack of sound or na'."

"It's her fault we're on this accursed trek, then. In death-
defying weather. Without sufficient fare, horses, shelter,
time . . . or men."

"How is the wife to blame that we took her from her tower
without warning?"

"She's to blame that she opened the gates, then. Allowing
Kilchurning into the castle grounds. And nearly getting me
killed!"

Redmond shook his head. "You need to look further."

"And you need to hush."

Redmond answered that with a sigh followed by words.
"How is she to blame for any of it? 'Twas na' your keep in the
first place, but Kilchurning's. Mayhap she was welcoming
her chosen spouse into his intended castle and saving the
inhabitants at the same time. Have you na' thought of that?"

"But it is *my* keep. And *my* castle. And she is *my* wife."

"From a taking."

"So?" Payton responded.

"How is she to blame for that night, Payton? We took her
home, we killed her clansmen, and then you took her. How is
that her fault?"

Payton shifted, worked at his fingers and then his toes.
Nothing felt frozen or numb anymore. The tent was erected,
too. And they'd set the iron rack atop their fire, filled the
kettle with water from the burn, and now his wife was in a
crouch, slicing strips of their cooked venison into the water
as if she was supposed to do such menial chores.

"Where is Alan?" he asked with a frown.

"Mourning his brother. In his fashion. You should na' disturb him. That is why the wife does what she does."

"Preparing soup?"

"Giving Alan time. Away from prying eyes and ears."

Payton pulled back a fraction. Blinked. Looked over at

his man and allowed the surprise to wash all over him as if it was supposed to. "You give her too much credit," he replied finally. "You expect me to believe her blameless? In all things?"

"Well, she is to blame for something. That is certain."

Redmond was on his way to the shelter of their tent. Payton could see by the warm glow of light they had a fire within already, as well.

"What?" he asked, moving after him.

Redmond shrugged as he walked, ignoring Payton. And that was most infuriating.

"We haven't time for this!" Payton said loud enough to stop his wife from her carving. He ignored her.

"We make time."

"We have to get to Edinburgh Castle to prove my claim. Then, we have to get forces enough to rout that imposter from my keep! Dallying about resting is na' going to get us there. It may get more of us killed!" Payton exclaimed.

"We have time," Redmond replied.

Payton didn't answer in words, but if he had, they'd have blistered Redmond's ears, with the sound of his tight-lipped yell.

"Payton Dunn-Fadden. Control. This is the trouble. You lack control."

"Give me a reason. I'll show control," he replied.

"Seth. He has yet to waken from his head injury. That is worrisome. And then there's Davey. We have to get your cousin buried and we have to handle the grief. This takes time. You ken this. We have to make time. Now. And then we move on. Always."

Payton felt the anger dissipate, like blood seeping from a wound. He slumped his shoulders. Redmond was right. Again. He truly hated him.

"Edwin and Dugan are softening ground now. Alan is assisting. On his own. Come. Rest. Prepare yourself."

"I doona' need preparation for grief," Payton replied.

"Agreed. You need it for Ballilol Castle."

Payton groaned the answer, but it wasn't heard over the shouting the servant lass Bronwyn made. Seth-the-Silent had awakened. And was requesting water. That was good.

Payton sighed, and watched his wife move to fetch it.

Ballilol Castle didn't resemble a castle like she was used to. It had no towers, no keep that she could spot, and the battlements were even rounded.

It was also land-locked, with a stream carving through the snow-flecked fields in front of it. It was built atop a knoll, which would grant it greater defense than the wall height would indicate. Dallis sneered as she viewed it. Where her own square tower was five stories in height, nothing about Ballilol looked to be above three. She narrowed her eyes to see better. If the window slits letting out light were any indicator, it looked to be two stories.

It looked stout, though. In the light from an afternoon winter sun, it looked thickly built of a rock that matched the knoll it sat atop.

There were two enormous round gatehouses fronting it, with a wooden portal splitting them. That was odd. Of what use was a drawbridge for defense when there wasn't much of a moat and only a trickle of water from a burn to fill it? And that, only if the burn ran against nature and went uphill. Not only that, but with such low sides, a grappling hook, siege ladder, or even a siege tower wouldn't be hard to use, and any enemy had four sides to use it on.

Of course, they'd have to get near enough, and with nothing save fields about every side, that could present a problem.

The curtain wall wrapped about the entire hilltop, although that didn't make it a pleasing sight. They looked to have built the wall to a specific height, following the ridges of the hill, which made the crenellation uneven and slanted looking in places. Why . . . a bit of tunneling in the right place, and a curtain wall like that would collapse even easier than one on level ground.

They hadn't much by way of defense in Dallis's opinion. And then they ruined even that. The moment Payton's party was spotted, any defense the drawbridge and gatehouses would have afforded was rendered useless as the walkway along the top grew bright with torches, the drawbridge was lowered, and a massive amount of humanity came spilling out, making a swell of sound from many throats as they yelled and ran. As far as she could tell, they didn't even possess weapons.

It wasn't until they neared, crossing the field rapidly like ants emptying from an anthill, that she heard what they were yelling.

"Payton Dunn-Fadden!"

"Payton! Dunn-Fadden!"

"The champion! Payton Dunn-Fadden is here!"

Payton Dunn-Fadden?

She watched the horde surround him, the many arms reaching for him like tentacles from a brine-creature, and then they milled about him as a unit to start an escort to the castle. It was still easy to pick him out since he was atop Orion, with Alan. Dallis had been relegated to riding alone, while Redmond rode pillion with Lady Evelyn. The general melee of crowd enveloped them as well, before moving toward the castle. Dallis looked about her and knew the confusion was easily read on her face. She'd never seen such a mob of people. She'd never been over-run and beset by a horde. And it appeared some of the people in the crowd were crying, and wailing, and some were screaming . . . and cheering.

For Payton?

"Have you nae grasp of your husband's fame?" Redmond was shouting it, but only so he'd be heard.

"Payton's fame?" Dallis replied and then added a laugh.

"Do you na' ken that from what you see?"

"For what?"

"He's the Stewart King's Champion!"

"He's won a few battles. This creates fame?"

"A few?"

He shook his head before reaching across for her pommel and pulling his horse close, although it displaced the men who were walking between them. Redmond didn't even glance down as one stumbled before giving over the space.

"He has won more than a few, My Lady. He has never lost. The king has gained small fortunes from your husband. And he is most grateful."

"I . . . see."

She did see, too, and gnashed her teeth at the vagaries of fate and its implications. Lady Evelyn met her glance. She must be fey. That lady had told Dallis she'd regret what she did. If Payton had the king's gratitude, he owed it to his wife. She was the one who'd sought out and financed his opponents. Actually, she amended it to herself; she was just the financier. It was her cousin, Giles Carmour, who'd sought them out. Giles was the cousin living as a courtier to the king's court . . . and who was always short on funds. The man she'd probably meet up with at Edinburgh.

There was a sinking feeling in the pit of her belly and Dallis forced it aside. She didn't have time for worries of blackmail. She had worse things to face. Things such as being a famous man's wife.

"Doona' fash yourself, My Lady. It will be well. We've attended fests at Ballilol Castle a-fore, when we could find no ready excuse. Payton will be assigned massive, luxurious chambers reserved for royalty, as is his due. He commands it."

"I care not what happens to him," Dallis replied and tipped her nose into the air as if it were true.

"You'll be settled into the same wing. Close to him. Then your troubles will truly commence. I doona' envy you."

If Redmond laughed, he was laughing. Dallis turned from watching her husband's foray across the drawbridge which looked near collapse with that amount of humanity atop it, to sharpen her gaze at Redmond MacCloud.

"The man's name should be trouble. He's brought that since we met. What of it?"

"Ballilol Castle belongs to the Widow Meryck. Of Clan MacKettryck. She has no less than four marriageable daughters to her credit. No sons."

Dallis shrugged.

"She has turned a fair eye on your husband. Verra fair."

"He's wed."

"Aye. That he is." He was laughing again.

"I doona' see the issue."

"You will."

"Why?"

"You have your part to play now, My Lady. And I have mine."

Dallis straightened. "A . . . part?" she asked.

"Aye. And you need do it well."

"A . . . part?" she said it again.

"Aye. Whilst I attend to my laird . . . and do my utmost to keep the widow and her daughters from the indignity that arises from . . . refusal of favors, you need to look and behave the woman the King's Champion has wed. And is well satisfied with. This portends to be vastly entertaining. Vastly."

"I doona' have to do any such thing. And . . . what do you mean refusal of favors?"

He didn't answer. But he was chuckling again as he moved away from her, while the ground between them filled with humanity.

He hated this castle. He hated the stifling air it seemed permeated with. He hated the over-plush bed that felt near collapse with his weight. He hated the amount of attention that got worse each succeeding visit. He hated being on guard every moment with his tongue and his whereabouts, for any slight corner could mean trouble. For that he hated his hostess. And her miserable daughters. Well . . . except for the third youngest, Annalise. That one . . . he tolerated.

He hated the fact the blame emotion was missing. The one that made it possible to look upon his wife without feeling the unsure, shaky unease deep within him. He hated the way his heart pained with each pulse when he'd witnessed Alan's silent tears, and been unable to do anything about it.

He hated his wife, too.

Payton glared across at the door that led to her solar, where she prepared herself, bathing in the warmed scented tub he'd ordered for her. And then she'd dry off, and dress in the outfit Redmond procured. If Redmond managed to gain such a thing.

He hated having to ask it! Asking anything from this family was tantamount to agreeing to the favor of attending one or more of them when everyone else in the castle slept.

He'd refused in the past and made Redmond deal with it. He refused to now, as well. Especially now. His mind filled it in for him. He didn't want any other woman but Dallis. He no longer bothered with the why. He wanted her, and only her. His wife. Naked . . . and wet with her bath. Mayhap reclining on the bedding where she'd sleep, poised . . . for him.

"Bloody, rotten hell."

Payton said it aloud, slapping the towel from his waist against the enclosed bed he'd be using, and enjoying the snap sound it made. That woman truly was going to be the death of him.

"This is the lauding I get?"

Redmond entered the chamber, opening the door without warning. Payton swiveled, reclasping the towel about himself while the five lasses in accompaniment grinned and bobbed their heads and put hands to their cheeks.

"For what?" Payton asked it sourly, with argumentative intent. Redmond answered in kind, which made his eyes widen.

"Negotiating . . . what I have."

"If you think I'll welcome—"

"You? She is na' interested only in you," MacCloud replied. And then he flushed redder than the crimson velvet he carried. "Here. See this to Lady Dunn-Fadden. In her chamber." He pointed and three of the servants left with the garments trailing from their arms. They went right to the door that Payton had been fixated upon, knocked, and then went through it.

That left two wenches Payton had to contend with. Both girls moved their hands from their cheeks to their mouths to hide the giggles. They sounded like twittering birds. Payton flung his hands in the air in disgust before turning to glare at the enormous fire they'd built in the chamber.

He truly hated this castle.

"And that was that," Redmond continued. "Aye. I believe we've settled? Good. Now, see to it Dugan Marsh returns to attend the champion, rather than you lasses. You can leave now. And await Dunn-Fadden's appearance later. When he's full dressed and readied."

Payton waited for the door to shut before turning back. It was true. Both lasses were gone. He raised his brows, planted his feet, and put both hands on his waist. Since he was covered only in a smallish towel, it didn't seem to have much effect on Redmond, but it felt right.

"What was that about? You ken that nae man prepares for a feast with women to assist him," he announced.

"I already told you I had to negotiate. And make promises. That was but a portion. And I thank you for making it a simple matter a-forehand with your attire—or rather . . . your lack of attire."

"What?"

"She wanted a glimpse of the champion. Without clothing. That was one thing the eldest lass Marian required."

"Marian was na'—"

"You dinna' pay much attention or you would have noted the smaller one. In the cap."

Payton groaned.

"If you think that shabby, wait until you hear what I have agreed to in order to get what Dugan is bringing."

"Doona' tell me." Payton raised a hand. "'Twill be easier to disavow."

"Do you ken the widow has one of your *feile-breacans* on display? In her weapon room? In its own case? 'Tis perfectly laid out, creased, and graced on both sides with the matching silver brooch and wrist bands. Exactly as we presented it to her. With your regards."

Payton stared. "Nae," he replied.

"Aye. 'Tis what we gifted her last Middlemass in order to get out of here with our virtues intact. One of the setts The Stewart had crafted special, with the silvered threads woven into it. The only one fitting for an appearance at sup."

"An appearance!"

"You ken the woman. She shows you off. To all. I convinced her to have a subdued affair. From our loss of Davey. 'Tis the best I could manage. She's had the fest planned since we were spotted this morn. 'Tis for all of us, actually. You . . . and your young men. For returning. To her side."

"Tell them I'm ill," Payton replied. "It came on sudden-like."

"If you are unwell, My Laird, that woman will be at your side. In your chamber. Or she might have you moved closer to hers which would be worse."

Payton groaned.

"'Tis na' as bad as before. We have the wife with us. She

carries your bairn. I told them of it. 'Twas verra entertaining to watch faces. 'Twill be even more so at the sup. When they meet her."

"But . . . she hates me," he replied.

"Your treatment these last two days would warrant that. Go change it. Nae, wait! Don your champion attire first. Then, go see to her."

"What makes everyone think I'll just dress and appear for them . . . like a puppet?"

"'Tis the price for these rooms, and this welcome, and our safe escort to Edinburgh. And 'tis the price of your fame. That's why."

Payton looked across at his man with exactly the same blank look he was getting. It didn't change it. Nothing did. He decided he hated being the champion, as well.

"Bring me the sett. I'll wear it."

Redmond nodded. "Dugan is bringing it. If he manages to make it here without one or more of your followers attached to him with force akin to a leech. You think it an easy task to be near you?"

"'Tis worse being me. By far."

"Fair enough. Which is why you'd best make a bargain with the wife. A-fore they summon us to the fest. Long a-fore."

"I would rather bargain with the devil than my wife," Payton replied.

"Then take this." Redmond held out a large brass key with a shiny silver ribbon tied through the handle.

"Where does that go? And nae. Dinna' tell me. I doona' wish to hear!" Payton put his hands over his ears for dramatic effect, but still heard it.

"The widow Meryck's chambers. When the watcher calls midnight. Doona' be late."

"Damn your bloody hide, MacCloud!"

"Cease cursing me, and approach your wife. I'd wait until

you're dressed, though. And a bit less angered. She'll be more apt to listen to entreaties."

Payton sat onto the edge of his mattress, felt the give in the feathers as it absorbed and settled under his weight, making it hard and lumpy, and then dropped his head into his hands.

"What if she will na' assist me?" he asked the floor.

"Convince her."

"What if I fail?" he asked.

"I would most appreciate it if you do," Redmond replied.

"What?" Payton raised his head.

"The bargain was na' just for you, Payton Dunn-Fadden. If you doona' arrive at that chamber at midnight, someone will have to."

Redmond flushed again.

"Jesu', Mary, and Joseph, but I hate this castle," Payton said.

Chapter 13

Lady Evelyn slept deeply and peacefully in the chamber she'd been given on the other side of Dallis's own. She had Bronwyn's message to thank for that, and then she dismissed the servant back to Lady Evelyn's side. Her aunt deserved her sleep. She wasn't young, and although she'd undergone this journey without complaint and without slowing anyone, her years were telling on her. She'd said she felt weak. She needed the rest.

Or so, Bronwyn repeated.

Dallis suspected Lady Evelyn just wanted her niece to be alone with her thoughts. Because she deserved them.

She didn't have to be alone. She'd had a trio of servant girls chattering and working and hovering and making the space alive with chaos until Dallis's head ached worse than the pain their administrations had created.

That was the reason she'd dismissed the trio of servant girls, and not just the damage they'd done to her appearance. After assisting her with the drying of her hair with a fluffing of rough towels guaranteed to make each strand crackle and fly about, they'd started teasing and twisting and looping great ropes of hair about her head, as if that sort of style was appealing. Dallis watched them at it in the chamber mirror and ignored them. And then one of them pulled a vial of something from her pocket and poured some on her hand as if Dallis Caruth allowed a concoction mixed without her knowledge smeared about her.

That was when she'd dismissed them, without argument and with the stern voice she reserved for lecturing her own servants. Their crest-fallen faces and looks of malice showed how right that had been! She even noted how red the girl's hands were from just rubbing that unguent on before Dallis slammed the door behind them.

Stupid women! As if Dallis Caruth Dunn-Fadden couldn't see through a ploy of that nature!

She'd turned then to the crimson bliant they'd brought and hung from a rafter by the neckline as if that would take the creasing from such a material. They'd included a high, pointed headdress with charcoal-colored veil, black slippers, and a flaxen sleeveless underdress in an indeterminate shade of gray. Her lips twisted as she unfurled the wad of materials and checked it for prickly pine, vermin, or other substance. It smelled of storage and was musty, but all of it looked clean. The underdress even appeared to be woven of soft threads and draped like liquid from her hands. It might be safe against her skin.

She smiled to herself after she'd checked everything, and then sprinkled her new clothing with water to spread it out in front of the hearth. A bit of steaming would take the worst of the wrinkling from it. And they'd over-done their plotting. They should have sent her usual white. The gray shades should bring out the fairness of her skin. They hadn't counted on that.

With the inclusion of the crimson velvet, and the charcoal tone of her wimple veil, though, it was going to be muted and dull and uninspiring. Aside from which, such a color scheme was guaranteed to jar with the orange streaks in her hair. She sighed.

She'd been warned. Not sufficiently, but Redmond had warned her.

She bent to the task of untwisting and pulling out every loop they'd made in her hair, before using the tub of luke-warm and used water to smooth her fingertips through each strand. And then she'd plaited it into one long braid that ended at her hip, perfect for tucking beneath the veil.

Hours seemed to have passed before she'd finished, and was mostly satisfied with the results. They'd been thorough, but they must think Payton wed to a lass with little in wits and nothing in skill. She'd had to pick apart the Dunn-Fadden sett of black, white, and green plaid he'd given her, and then braid the wool strands into long colorful strips, but her attire was effective. It was modest. Eye-catching. And it was unique.

She'd used plaid strips to bind the veiling about her braid, enclosing it in shadow, until the bottom peeked out well below her waist, showing the length and thickness. That should bother more than a few of these women! She'd used more of the wool braid to affix the gown to her body, show-ing a womanly shape none could dispute. And then she used more of the strips to accent the vast gap in the skirt of her gown, allowing the gray underdress to show as it filmed and highlighted every bit of her lower leg, as if she'd designed it for that purpose. She didn't have a choice on that portion of her attire, unless she wanted to wear the bliant backwards, and that had been worse! Used like that, too much of her bosom was exposed. No man wished his wife to appear a harlot!

So, she'd tied a batch of strands together into a knot at the back of her waist as if it belonged there, and brought each one succeeding lower on the gapped portion of her skirt, cutting little slits in the velvet to make it work. And then she did the same with smaller strands of his wool at her shoulders, loop-ing each one a little longer than the previous one to give the illusion of sleeves that reached just past her elbow.

When she'd finished her ministrations, sipped a bit at the wine one of his men had passed through from Payton's rooms, and couldn't think of one more enhancement to her appearance, she settled down on a padded stool in front of her hearth to wait. And when that started boring her, she paced a bit. Sat again. Chewed on a fingernail while she waited, listened at Lady Evelyn's door for her deep breathing. Paced again.

Payton Dunn-Fadden was taking forever to ready himself! How difficult could it be for a man to groom himself, don a *feile-breacan,* and then put on his boots? She hadn't any comparison, but this time span seemed ridiculous. And wasteful. And she was getting hungry.

Dallis sat again, faced the fire and tried to stop her legs from dancing up and down and her feet from tapping in the too-large slippers they'd given her. And then the larger door behind her opened.

It was Payton's man, Redmond. He had torch bowl of coals held high and he was gesturing behind him. And into the light stepped Payton. Dallis watched his eyes widen and then his jaw dropped. Her expression was probably the match.

She'd never seen him in full chieftain attire. He had on his family colors, the match to her own, but there was a sparkle to his every move that she lacked. The pure white of his shirt contrasted against the tan color of his skin and black of his hair, although he had that pulled back into a queue, defining the shaven jaw and perfect features. His shirt had a slit opening at the throat, and it was sleeveless, probably to allow every female to sigh over a hardness and strength that the two silver armbands about his lower arms delineated even more. Dallis only wished she were the exception, as the sigh escaped lips she hadn't managed to close.

He had a black velvet weskit that looked bound about his torso, since there wasn't much space between it and the man it covered. His sporran was of silver, the tassels on his socks

were the same, and the hilt and sheath for his sword were
smelted from the same metal.

Dallis was stunned. Impressed. Awed. She knew exactly
what the emotions felt like now. Everything on her body felt
awash with a sensation akin to being dunked in iced water.
There wasn't any way to hide it other than rub at her arms,
and that would disturb the artistry of her sleeves, so she settled with clasping her hands.

He cleared his throat. Or it was a gulp. Either way, it didn't
make much sound. Redmond appeared to be beaming.

"My . . . Lady? I beg a—a word with you." Payton stammered through the request.

"A . . . word?" She gave the same stumbling sound as she
repeated it.

"Aye. A word. Or two. With you."

He wanted a word with her. *Now?*

"Aye. Now," he replied, as if she'd said it aloud.

"Here?" She whispered it past lips that were actually trembling. She felt giddy. Dizzy. Filled with bubbles. Stewed. It
was horrid. Then he smiled and made it so much worse!

"Aye. Here. In this chamber. With you."

Oh, dear God! Her legs were going to drop her at the instant flash of sensation he created, heated, and then shoved at
her. Without effort. He seemed to know it, too, for he didn't
look hesitant as he approached, losing the torchlight illumi-
nation, but gaining the flickers of her fire in its place. And
then he was in front of her, looming large and heated and
solid. And beautiful.

Stunned wasn't even appropriate, Dallis decided, watching
his chest rise and fall with the strength of his breathing, and
then watching it increase in volume and cadence.

She had her hands plunged against her breast, to hold in
any further reaction, and gripped the fingers together. She
had to. Payton was roaming his gaze all over her from a hand-
span away, and making everything more liquid feeling than

her underdress. She watched as he looked there, tightened something in his jaw, if the bulge out one side was any indication, and then he moved that blue gaze back to hers.

Dallis nearly swooned and actually knew what it was. Her heart pulsed in an almost painful beat before starting a ragged rhythm, and she was in luck she had her mouth open again, for she needed open lips to gasp through.

"What . . . has been done to your dress?" he asked.

"This . . . family does na' keep their storage free of . . . moth damage," she replied, adding a hint of sound to the whisper. "'Twas torn. In . . . obvious spots."

His lips twisted and her heart followed the movement with another jerk from within her breast. Dallis tightened her hands there even more and tried to stop it. Or at least contain it.

"What?" he asked.

She wasn't ever telling him! She was terrified to even admit it. What she felt wasn't love. Never. Ever. It wasn't possible that she loved him. She shook her head and then stopped as he moved a step closer, making her totally aware of the clean man-scent of him. It wasn't fair! She had to look away, and chose the flooring beside his boots.

"You are wondrous fair . . . Wife," he said, in a breath of words that reached the veil atop her head, and then penetrated it.

"You're na' . . . disappointed?" she asked.

"With what?" he asked.

"Me."

His amusement feathered the veil, and then he was bending at the knees to look up at her from the lower level.

"I am overcome. Totally. Words fail me. I am na' disappointed."

Dallis smiled slightly, shifted her glance back to him before shying away, and blushed. Severely. Strong enough that it brought heated droplets to her hairline. She licked at her lip, felt the ground roil beneath her feet, and looked back at him. Nothing had moved about him, and yet everything had shifted, and changed, and solidified, and gone crystal clear. Dallis had to admit it, too. She did love him. Tremendously. To the depth of her being and then further, still. It was worse than horrid. And it was better than joy. She only hoped she had the fortitude to hide it.

Then he answered her smile and when it reached his eyes, her heart stumbled. And that just transferred to her knees. Dallis reached out for him before she fell, and gathered every bit of the embarrassment that swooning in front of him was gaining her. Only she didn't swoon. And she didn't fall. Payton's hand was as strong and stout as the rest of him since that's where she latched on.

"The . . . bairn?" he asked.

She shook her head. That was more stupidity, since she could have claimed the child made her weak. It also proved to make the floor swell about them. She moved closer in order to hold on to more of him, with both hands held by both of his. That had him standing tall again and looking over her head, while his chest moved in and out with a voracious need for air.

"Payton?" She whispered the name, and tipped her head slightly to look at him. That just gained her a view of his chin, and then he shifted and brought his gaze back to her.

"Aye?"

His lips moved, so he must have said it, but Dallis didn't truly hear it. She couldn't hear much over the sound of heartbeats in her ears. And if he didn't move his gaze away, she was afraid she wasn't going to be able to make intelligible words at all. That reminded her.

"You . . . wished words . . . with me?"

The fingers holding to hers tightened slightly, and he sucked in a large breath.

"'Tis . . . more of an entreaty," he replied.

He wanted to beg her for something? When it felt like he

had her heart-strings in their conjoined hands and was massaging them with the pressure of his fingers?

"What?" she asked, narrowing her eyes slightly to diffuse some of his nearness. It didn't work, but not much did.

He licked his lips. Her frame rocked with a response, and then the movement transferred to him, making his eyes widen and that was too much impact to her newly discovered feelings for him. Dallis had to look aside again, or she was going to be lost. In a moment, she'd be confessing it to him!

"This banquet. Uh . . . this presentation. 'Twould go over well—"

He was interrupted by the sound of the torch dropping over by the door. Payton swiveled the moment he heard it, taking her with him. They stood side by side, hands entwined and watched Redmond dance about as he extinguished the coals.

"Blast! Damn! Whoreson! Damn, again!"

Dallis stared at the normally reticent Redmond as he went about cursing and stamping out the fires he'd spilt across the floor. A swift glance at Payton showed he had the same expression. When the last of the coals twinkled and died, Redmond huffed with relief and looked at them.

"Forgive me. That was . . . clumsy."

"I was just about to—" Payton started.

"We'll be late at the fest. Nae time." Redmond interrupted his laird.

"But—"

"Nae need for argue. You're readied. She appears readied. The Honor Guard is readied. We go."

"But I have na' asked—"

"Nae time!"

Redmond's urgency transferred to Payton then, for he looked down at Dallis. She felt the movement from their still-clasped hands.

"You ready then, sweet?" he asked.

If he used endearments with her, she wasn't going to be

able to walk! But, how was she to mention that? She settled with nodding and opened her hands, preparatory to moving away from him.

Payton didn't seem to want that, for he held to her fingers for a moment longer before moving her left hand to the crook of his left arm, while still holding the fingers of her right hand within his own. That put her against his swordless side. It felt and probably looked loving and gracious, especially as he worked at keeping his stride slow to accommodate her smaller steps.

They preceded Redmond into the hall, where there were eight of his clansmen, all dressed in clan colors, and all looking very elegant and official, with Alan standing at the fore.

"You are a grand squire, Alan Dunn-Fadden," Payton told him.

Dallis watched as the lad ducked his head.

"You must take your brother's place now. In my Honor Guard. You ken?"

Alan nodded his head. Gulped. And then stood straighter. Dallis felt tears brimming again and forced them away. Payton was endearing himself to her even more! There was no way to face him. So, she didn't try.

They started walking again, boots hitting stone and weaponry jostling the only sounds. And then Payton spoke, lowering his head to reach her ear.

"I should probably warn you," he said.

The sensation of his breath against her throat made her wish she'd kept some of the veiling free so it would cover skin. That way she wouldn't be trembling with the sensations of want and need and passion. She recognized them and knew if he glanced at her bosom, he'd probably recognize them, as well.

"Nae time!" Redmond hissed at his side.

"She needs to ken the widow's leanings." Payton lifted his head away to argue with his man.

Dallis used the time to concentrate on breathing steadily and sliding one foot after the other down the hall to a corner, in order to keep the slippers on her feet. Beside her Payton adjusted without conscious thought, making it one step to three of hers. She missed the first part of their discourse and what it meant.

"You are a loss at subtlely and a failure at acting, My Laird. And I just dropped a torch to try and force it," Redmond replied.

"What?" Payton replied.

"He is saying that I already ken the widow's leanings. It was apparent with the clothing they sent and the assist I got."

Dallis answered him with a bit of amusement and was ready when Payton looked down at her. Or thought she was. That was until the breathless, dizzy sensation came again. She tightened her fingers on his arm, which just made him harden the muscles in it. She was very afraid she'd be launching herself into his arms and embarrassing herself if he didn't move his gaze.

Redmond cleared his throat. Both of them looked toward him. And then he winked. At Dallis.

"The wife . . . definitely possesses Caruth wits." He said.

Dallis responded with a blush and a nod. And felt the arm beneath her hand flex again. Her fingers tingled oddly, or his skin was supposed to create that sort of vibration. But that was just fanciful thinking and getting her nothing of value.

She was out-of-sorts because she was hungry, and she was overcome by the importance and presence of her husband. That was all.

And she loved him.

"This castle is na' enemy territory. But for those Payton treasures, it might as well be," Redmond informed her.

Treasures.

The word sent an all-over heated feeling through her, and then a stab of tears again. She blinked those away, as well.

"I hate it," Payton added.

"'Tis partially my fault this time," Redmond continued.

"It is?" Dallis queried.

"I taunted her with his marriage. And the bairn."

Dallis's eyebrows rose.

"I dinna' need to, but it felt good. You ken?"

She was smiling now. So was Payton.

"You must eat nothing unless it is given to Payton. Drink nothing unless it comes from his goblet. If you share his trencher, 'twill na' be an issue."

She nodded again.

"You must make her sit you at his side. But if we are na' successful, doona' eat anything unless it is given from one of us. We will be your tasters. We will do our part to keep you and bairn safe."

Her heart was swelling. That had to be what was making it hard to breathe, and harder to see through the film across her eyes. Again.

"Come. They'll send for us, and then we lose the vantage."

"Vantage?" Dallis asked.

"Aye. We doona' use the grand entry. We use the minstrel entrance. 'Tis always this way when the widow entertains. We canna' get Payton to the dais without incident otherwise."

"Incident?" Dallis repeated.

"You doona' wish to know. The lasses . . ." He trailed off.

Martin finished it for him. "They will do anything for Payton's attention. Anything!"

"The last one near started a riot! In the Great Room!"

"Nae. That was the time a-fore. The last one flung portions of her clothing at him! I still have it."

"Edwin." Redmond said the name and the man who'd spoken flushed and stepped back.

"Oh, my," Dallis said.

Chapter 14

The great hall at Castle Ballilol was easily the largest room Dallis had ever seen or imagined, and they'd opened both of the great entrance doors to make it even larger. With squinting, she could just see across to where there was a fireplace exactly like the one they appeared beside, near the dais. Both fireplaces looked large enough to fit whole trees, and the one closest to the grand entrance appeared to have just that burning in it. The room was the height of the walls, making it three stories at best. There were huge posts spaced about to hold up a roof of that size, tables along every wall, and some in the middle of the floor. Large chandeliers of lit oil hung high up in the rafters and so many torches spaced a man's arm-span apart along every wall, that they were countless. It was warm, bright, smelled of fresh rushes, roasting meat, perfumes of every type, and every available bit of it looked filled with something to watch. There was an acrobatic demonstration happening in one corner if the trio of bodies stacked atop each other was an indicator. There was a juggler, and she could see a minstrel and his lute, although he had a sour expression on his face at the moment.

If Payton hadn't put her in a position where she was already clinging to him, she'd have gotten that way the moment they appeared and got treated to a din that rose and contained screams as he was spotted. Dallis shrank against his side as the Honor Guard moved from behind them to surround and shoulder a way through to the long table on a raised platform where their hostess and her family were awaiting them. Along the way, someone started pounding at drums, adding to the melee, and reverberating through the floor and up her back.

They'd reached the steps leading to the partition set above the floor and resting along one stone wall, covered over with a huge shield that had three large drapes of separate colors— gold, red, and black—which she took to be the MacKettryck clan colors. Dallis only had time to glance at the magnificence of such a display before Payton was moving, shifting his hands to her waist so he could lift her up the three steps in front of him.

She knew the reason the moment she arrived. The woman responsible for her discomfort rose from a thronelike chair and from a great height glared down at Dallis, marring the perfection of her face with the expression. And if Payton was worried over her attention, he was the oddest male birthed. The Widow Meryck was a fantastic creature. She had the whitest skin Dallis had ever seen, the reddest lips, the deepest burgundy-shaded hair, and a figure that hadn't been altered from birthing four daughters, unless the emerald-green velvet of her bliant was lying.

She was fair dripping with jewels, too, from the pearl strands wrapped throughout the shiny tresses of her hair that she'd left uncovered, to the goose-egg-sized, blue-cast stone falling into the cleavage just hinted at by the square neckline of her dress. She was a jaw-dropping sight. Dallis embarrassed herself by having that reaction, too. Again.

Then Payton got up on the dais behind her, shoving her forward with the twin humps of his chest against the back of her head. Dallis dropped a small curtsey, before resuming her place in front of her husband. She watched the widow's eyes flick over her before seemingly dismissing her. It wasn't hard to reason why. Dallis felt small, insignificant, and dowdy. And raunchily exposed.

The room was quieting about them and the drums fell silent, until there wasn't more than the sound of whispers and shuffling all through the room.

"My Lord Dunn-Fadden," the widow announced in a hard, loud tone that was easily heard. "I was na' aware I'd proffered an invite to this . . . this . . ."

Her voice trailed off, which was just as well. Dallis could feel the heat of a flush happening, and was powerless to prevent it.

"'Tis the Lady Dunn-Fadden, the heiress of Clan Caruth. Daughter of the Earl of Glen-Caruth . . . and Laird Dunn-Fadden's wife."

Redmond's voice was loud as well, and totally without emotion. Dallis was so grateful, she could have kissed him. Her chin rose, as well as her eyebrows and she smiled slightly.

"I have heard of you."

The widow barely tipped her head in acknowledgment before moving her gaze back over Dallis's head to her husband. Or so, she suspected. Dallis didn't move her head to check. She didn't move her eyes from the woman in front of her. She didn't dare. It felt akin to being in the presence of a snake, a very venomous one.

"I failed to make arrangements at my table."

The woman turned slightly, and gestured toward her ecru-shaded linen-covered table, where an array of jewel-encrusted goblets and two-tined forks showed where each person was to sit. Everything was polished and twinkling in the glow from a massive candelabra in the center. It was more riches than Dallis had seen displayed in one sitting, and she was used to banquets set out at Castle Caruth . . . or what had been Castle Caruth. She was going to rename it Castle Dunn-Fadden when she returned to it.

Payton shrugged, or it felt that way from the movement of his chest at her back. "Then I sit below. With the common folk and my wife. Men?"

He was turning, the people in the room seemed to know what he was about for the cries started up again, and Dallis could sense the worry in his Honor Guard. Payton was mad to go to the main floor! They couldn't keep him safe there.

"My Laird. Please." The widow had a hand toward him. "I beg you to reconsider. We always share a trencher, you and I. And you ken how much I value taking you among my people once the feasting is over and the fires banked. You know this. And you would take that from me? After all my hospitality?"

Dallis heard the threat, even if Payton didn't. She understood fully why he hated this castle. And its beauteous owner.

"My wife?" Payton replied.

The woman moved back and gestured. "A spot will be found for her. At the end. You there!"

And with that order, a seat was located and brought, although it resembled a footstool. Dallis sat, as graciously as possible, although until one of Payton's men brought a heavily padded pillow for her to add to it, she looked more to be crouched at knee level. She smiled at the girl she was to share a trencher with, after Redmond introduced her as Annalise. Dallis noted that she didn't much favor her mother as she smiled shyly. It could be worse. She might have been perched at Payton's knee, fending off the widow's barbed words. Or trying to keep from slapping at her as she trailed a finger once too often along Payton's arm while he speared his portion of meat, or fluttered her hands about his chest. Or leaned close to an ear to whisper.

The only thing that kept Dallis from any reaction to the widow's possessive movements was Payton. His steady regard wasn't on his hostess. It was on his wife. Dallis caught him often, locking eyes with him and feeling the same dizzy-ing sensation. Heart-stopping. Breath-stealing. Overwhelm-ing. And each time the widow would interrupt, speaking more hushed words into his ear, or putting another hand on him, to pull his face back to her.

Through the sup, Redmond hovered at Dallis's other side, seeing her goblet refilled from the one he held, looking about constantly, and probably trying to keep her from tumbling off the dais and hurting herself.

She giggled, and then the girl beside her spoke up.

"I think you are verra brave," she whispered.

"Oh, nae. Just unlucky," Dallis replied.

"With him?"

"And her," she replied.

"'Tis worse being kin to her. Much."

Dallis stared.

"You think me disloyal?"

She shook her head. "Nae. I think you honest."

The girl smiled. "She was na' always like this. Only when *he* first came. On her invite."

"Who?" Dallis asked, although she already knew.

"Your husband," the girl hissed.

Dallis smiled. "Forgive me. I tease. I already ken who you mean. I just doona' know why."

"Why . . . what?"

"All . . . this," Dallis waved her fork to encompass the entire room.

The girl shot a glance toward where her mother sat. Dallis moved her eyes there, too. And was caught. Held. Entrapped. By Payton. He'd given off eating, and just sent invisible ten-tacles toward her, pulling at her. . . .

The widow responded with a pull of his chin, releasing Dallis from the power of his gaze. She ducked her head and grinned. Payton was lucky he didn't get stabbed by that woman's fork.

"My mother was known throughout the Highlands as a court beauty."

"Was?" Dallis whispered.

The girl frowned. "Aye. All feted and adored her. Even the king. 'Twas why she wed as highly as she did. Before she got auld. And strange."

Auld? Dallis wondered it with one part of her, while the other focused on ignoring Payton. She didn't even bother glancing that way. She knew he'd be looking at her. The knowledge sent shivers over her that ended with a tremor. And that had Redmond stepping close from the level of the hall floor to ask solicitously if she needed a wrap.

Dallis nearly giggled. A wrap wasn't going to stanch the growing desire and passion and sensual anticipation Payton was making her suffer!

"Mayhap she is na' auld to you, but you were wed late. Verra late."

Dallis straightened automatically.

"'Twas said your intended left you on the shelf because of your lack of beauty. That was what made it easy for Payton Dunn-Fadden to gain your hand. And your lands. And your fortune."

"Truly?" Dallis replied, for lack of another word.

"All can see the untruth of that now. Tonight. 'Tis what angers her so."

"She does na' act angry."

"My mother is verra angered. She just keeps it hidden. And uses it later." The girl's voice dropped to a whisper.

"Will she use it on you?" Dallis asked.

"Na' if she thinks me rude to you. Could you act a bit displeased? She's looking again. So is the champion."

Dallis pulled back, did her best to glare at the girl, and then turned away toward where Redmond stood, hands behind his back and rocking slightly as if to keep awake.

"Redmond?" she called to him.

"My Lady?" He stepped closer and leaned toward her.

"I am attempting to mistreat this Annalise."

"I heard," he replied.

"I doona' understand the vagaries of this house."

"Not many do."

"They say one thing and do another."

"'Tis court intrigue, My Lady. Unless one is raised and taught such, 'tis difficult to understand. And explain."

"Try."

"Tonight is a good lesson in the methods of the king's house, My Lady. You will need such when we arrive there. In two days. From when we manage to put this household behind us."

"She'll way-lay us?"

"As I said a-fore. Such intrigue is a way of life at court. We will attempt a leaving. She will attempt to keep us here. Until she has what she wants, 'tis always the same."

"What . . . does she want?" And why did she have to ask? She already knew!

"Payton. Always."

"Why did you bring me here, then?"

"None has been ambushed and killed here at Castle Ballilol, My Lady. 'Tis safe . . . in that regard. We weighed the options. For you and the bairn."

"Oh."

"You can turn back to the lass now. Annalise is the only trustworthy one. You're safe. She is waiting."

He turned back to looking at the crowd before him. Dallis tried to put a look of disdain on her face toward Annalise, but probably failed. It didn't matter. The moment she turned, she locked gazes with Payton again. A severe buzzing started in her ears, the pound of her heart joined in, and the thickly padded pillow beneath her had the consistency of clouds.

The widow had her hand on him again and was whispering,

and that contrasted with the sound of Redmond's chuckling, and then Annalise's gasp was added in.

"You are truly brave!" she whispered.

"Why?"

"'Tis clear you have a love match. And then you flaunt it. At her."

"It *is?*" Dallis's voice faltered. Oh, dear God! She'd failed. Already. She could only hope Payton was more obtuse than this slip of a girl, if Dallis's feelings were this easy to spot.

"The champion canna' keep his eyes from you. She will tear yours out!"

Redmond was definitely chuckling, but covered it over in a cough. Dallis slanted a glance at him before looking back at Annalise. She pointedly ignored where Payton was sitting. And then noted he was standing, arranging his sporran, and resettling his sword. With the widow at his side.

She had to admit they made a perfect pair. The woman didn't appear overly tall when standing beside Payton. In fact, she appeared womanly and gracious, and beautiful. Dallis caught her breath as Payton turned sideways and walked to the steps, the widow at his heels, followed by her other daughters. He was leaving her? She felt, rather than saw, Redmond moving toward that end of the raised platform as well. They were all leaving her?

"This is the part I truly detest," Annalise said beside her.

"What?" Dallis didn't take her eyes off where Payton was as she asked it.

"My mother is verra proud to have the champion as her guest. Verra. She treats him like her personal property when she shows him off. It disgusts me."

"She does . . . what?"

"She enjoys the attention. She enjoys cleaving herself to his side and basking in the accolade that is his. My sisters, also."

"You doona' go?"

Annalise shook her head. "Nae. This is when I take my leave. To the nursery and my littlest sister, Mary. I usually have the minstrel serenade us. I feel sorry for him when his talent is overshadowed at times such as this. You can come with me, if you wish." The girl held out her hand.

She had the choice of watching Payton traverse the room, being fawned on by every female there . . . or go with this intriguing girl? Dallis sent one more glance after his retreating head, easy to spot due to his height even surrounded as he was by humanity, and then held hands with Annalise. It was a simple move to get from the room, or it would have been if Redmond MacCloud hadn't stepped in front of her at the bottom of the steps.

Dallis and Annalise dropped the hand-hold at the same instant.

"Mistress Annalise? Your troubadour awaits." He moved sideways, allowing the girl off the dais, and then went back to blocking Dallis.

"Why . . . can't I go?" she asked.

He gestured with his head to the crowd beyond them. "He needs you. Which means I need you."

"He does na'," Dallis replied, but there was a doubtful note in the words he couldn't miss.

"Now, more than a-fore."

"Why?"

He held out his hand to her and assisted her back up to the stool, but he didn't reseat her. He untied the pillow-form they'd given her, and set it behind the stool, showing the hard surface.

"Well?" Dallis prompted, when he just stood there, looking at her.

"Look about. What do you see?"

"I doona' wish to play this game with you. Just tell me why and have done."

He sighed. "'Tis better if you see it, than if I tell it."

Dallis lifted her chin to peer up at him. "You speak with riddles. I doona' appreciate it."

"I know. Neither does he," he replied, with a grin. "So tell me. Look about. What do you see?"

"Richness. Wealth. On display for all to note. Serfs, freemen and freewomen, and housecarls. And women. All kinds of women. All in one place. All waiting about patiently for the man that *woman* is clinging to."

He grunted. "Stand," he told her.

"There?" She motioned to the stool.

"Aye. There."

He held out his hand and kept holding to her after she stepped up onto the stool.

"Now. Look out again. Describe what you see again."

Dallis sighed heavily. Looked heavenward for a moment and then brought her head back down. "Why?" she asked.

"You are verra stubborn," he said.

"And you are verra dense."

"Humor a poor dense man, then. One who will be needing such bits of charity in the future . . . the verra near future."

"I thought you left me," she replied.

"For a moment. I returned."

"You left me alone."

"I was protecting Payton."

"By assisting that woman down the steps and kissing her hand?"

He flushed. "You saw that?" he asked.

"As did everyone."

He nodded. "Good. 'Twas na' in vain, then."

"It . . . wasn't?"

"The woman needed a reminder. I gave her one."

"A reminder of what?"

"That there are other men—I doona' wish to continue these words."

"What do you wish to continue, then?" she asked.

"I need you to tell me what you see."

Dallis scanned the room. From the additional height she could see Payton. Easily. He was surrounded. She could pick out the heads of some of his Honor Guard about him. She could see the widow from the pearls reflecting from her head, and her proximity to Payton.

And then he turned toward the dais as if searching, locked eyes with her from far enough away she knew she was imagining it, and smiled before turning away. Dallis gasped, her knees trembled atop the stool, and if Redmond hadn't tightened his hand, she might have fallen.

"What is it?" he asked.

"Payton."

He nodded.

"Go on."

"With what?"

"Describe what you see. As if I were blind and unable to view it myself."

"This is foolish."

"Trust me. All will be clear. Just tell me what you see."

Dallis pulled in a breath. "The great hall at this castle is large. Huge. Probably has a lonesome echo when empty."

He smirked.

"They have two fireplaces, one at each end. They can burn whole trees in those fireplaces. They have windows . . . high on the walls, but they're small. And slitted, although it appears there are leaded panes in them."

He nodded.

"The entire room is built of stone. From the archway width, it looks thicker than Payton is tall. They have little in decoration, though, and the walls could benefit from tapestries or other covering. 'Tis unfriendly having to look at all this stone."

"They have nae decor on the walls?"

"I dinna' say that," Dallis replied. "They have a great big, hammered silver shield, too large to be wielded except by a giant of legend. 'Tis mounted on the wall behind the dais. They have streamers of cloth attached to this shield, and this cloth unfurls, making a draping of sorts, until it is attached against the wall. I see it attaches where they need to lower and raise their chandeliers. What an intriguing design. That must save on dusting and such."

He smiled again.

"What about the floor?" he asked.

"A floor is a floor. Like any other. This one is so packed with boots and such, that 'tis difficult to tell. . . ." Her voice trailed off as Payton swiveled his head again, searching for her, finding her, locking gazes with her again, and then he smiled. Again.

Dallis gasped, felt the stool tremble beneath her and had to consciously lock her knees to keep standing.

"What is it?" Redmond asked from a position at her shoulder. He was still sideways to the room in front of them.

"'Tis Payton," she whispered. "Again."

"What does he do?"

"I swear he looks for me. Sees me. And returns to those about him."

Redmond nodded.

"What else do you see?"

"Payton," she replied, and didn't even care that her voice got dreamy and soft on the name.

"What is . . . Payton doing?" Redmond said it with his usual nonemotional voice, but there was the slightest waver of amusement in the midst of it.

"I doona' ken. Greeting those in the crowd. I canna' tell from here. Why?"

"Another reminder," he replied.

"Of what?" Dallis asked, and this time it was in a sour tone.

"What truly matters in this world." Now his voice had gotten lower, and carried such emotion it trembled.

Dallis turned from looking at the room and stared at him. Redmond cleared his throat. "Forgive me," he said.

"I doona' understand," Dallis said.

"Look about you," he commanded. "Look about and tell me how much of this is real and has value."

"'Tis all real. And verra valuable," she replied. Now, she was getting cross. It sounded in her voice.

"Look out into the room and tell me what's real enough to touch."

"Nae," she answered.

"Why not?" He was getting just as cross. That was amusing.

There was a murmur of sound growing in the room about them, and Dallis turned her head to see why. It was Payton. He was carving a path through the humanity about him, directly to her, putting him close enough she could see him easily. It wasn't a popular move if the crowd noise was any indicator. When she looked at him he stopped, lifted his eyebrows and waited.

Dallis smiled, blushed severely as everyone had to note what he'd done, and then Payton nodded and turned back. She watched him shake hands, nod constantly, draw his sword and pose with it before sheathing it again, and bend down to whisper something to a shrouded woman, heavy with child.

"What did you want to know?" she asked Redmond.

"'Tis na' important now," he replied.

Dallis wrinkled her forehead and turned to him again. "Why na'?"

"Because you already have the answer. So does he. I only hope you both realize it."

"What does that mean?"

"It will come to you. Trust me. Now, look. He'll be searching for you again. Trust me on that, as well."

"'Tis odd that he does that."

Redmond was grinning now. And then he nodded. "He lacks control. I told him of it. This is more proof."

"He looks for me because he lacks control?"

"With that woman attached to him, you need ask?"

Dallis considered that, with her head tipped to one side. And then Payton turned his head again. She nearly waved and felt a flush of pleasure clear through her before he turned away.

"Is it this way every time?" she asked.

Redmond didn't answer, so she turned her head to him. "Well?"

"There are too many answers to that. What way?"

"The crowd. This movement among them. The adulation they seem to smother him with."

"The crowd is a spawn of nature. 'Tis there sometimes, and sometimes na'. The way he moves among such a crowd is Payton. He has ever been so. He kens they waited for him, so he gives them his time in repayment. The adulation? Well . . . 'tis na' so much at Edinburgh. The king holds court there. He would frown on such idolatry and probably seek retribution. Unless 'tis directed to himself. Payton knows this. As do we."

"We?"

"We're his Honor Guard. We deflect attention toward the king. 'Tis nae easy task, I assure you."

"Mayhap we should na' journey there, then. Dunn-Fadden may have gained control of Payton's castle, making it moot for us to go to the king."

"We have na' enough men to reach the keep safely. We have nae choice now. We go to Edinburgh. And then we return to his castle. With masons to rebuild what needs rebuilding. Unlike a-fore."

Dallis colored. "I had my reasons," she informed him.

He nodded. "Dinna' we all," he replied.

Payton was turning toward her again, swiveling at the waist to look over his shoulder, and Dallis connected with him and nodded. He returned to his followers, and she returned to waiting.

"How long must we await him?" she asked.

"Hours," came the reply.

"Hours? I canna' stand for hours," Dallis informed him.

"'Twill na' go to midnight," Redmond advised her. "She'll end it."

"How do you ken?"

"Trust me," he said again.

The oddest, faintest tingle of sensation spawned from her womb and she placed her free hand on it in wonder and shock.

"It moved! Sweet heaven . . . the bairn *moved!*"

She lifted her head toward Payton and met his gaze over the top of the crowd. As if she'd called to him and he'd heard. And that's when he tilted his head back, brushing the small of his back with his queue, and bellowed out the most joy-filled sound.

Dallis had been right, too. The great hall echoed.

Chapter 15

"Edwin? See to the chamber."

Dallis stirred from the comfortable spot in Payton's arms at the sound of his voice through his throat. It had to be close to midnight now. Payton seemed to wait for that event before coming back to the table where Dallis sat. She'd long since given up standing on the stool, and had moved to the comfortable chair he'd gotten to use. That's where he'd lifted her from, and she hadn't demurred one bit.

"Seth-the-Silent. Alone. Awake," Edwin came into the hall to report, shutting the door behind him. "He was only disturbed twice. By the daughters. Marion and Elyse. Or so, he says. Here. You ask him." The last came as Seth left the chamber behind him, shutting the door as he did so.

"Jesu', Mary, and Joseph. 'Tis worse than a-fore!" Payton swore.

"Why . . . was Seth in Payton's bedchamber?" Dallis lifted her head to ask it. None of them met her eye, Payton included. And she looked to each one.

Edwin cleared his throat. "The Widow Meryck serves mead that is too strong. Her daughters need a father's hand with directions. That's what 'tis."

"You should na' try to be Redmond. You lack his way of speaking." That was Martin. He chuckled when he finished.

"Well, mayhap MacCloud should be here to assist with this. Then, I would na' have to take his lead." That was Edwin again.

"Well, doona' look to me. I dinna' see him leave."

"He has pressing business, lads. Pressing." Payton informed them.

"What could be so pressing at this hour—?" Edwin stopped his words and his eyes opened wider.

"We have our own pressing matters, lads. We've sleep to gain. And escape to plan. Early. First light."

Dallis snuggled back against Payton's throat. "Escape? Again?"

Payton nodded, rubbing skin against her nose with the motion. "We dare na' give the widow another day. Or, her daughters. Why, if it weren't vastly cold outside and the dead of the night, and if I'd na' already lost a man this eve, I'd be for marching right to the stables and taking my leave now, Lady Dallis Dunn-Fadden. To do so would create more incident than MacCloud could contain, but that would be his problem, na' mine."

"That is na' verra generous of you," she told him. "Considering."

"Considering . . . what?"

"Dismiss your men, and I'll tell you," she answered.

"One stays. As guard. Martin? Two hours on. Then relief." He nodded.

"You need a guard? Still?" she asked.

"The women doona' sleep in this household, My Lady. That means we canna', either."

Martin answered her and then nodded at the look she couldn't prevent. Dallis let the shock and disgust seep into her, and that's what he saw.

"Have I told you yet that I hate this castle?" Payton asked, to no one in particular.

"Ceaselessly, My Laird," came the reply. "Go. Rest. Both of you. We'll na' let anyone disturb you."

Rest was not on Payton's mind when he entered the chamber, setting her on her feet before he turned and dropped the bolt down. And then he moved to the adjoining door to her assigned bedchamber and slammed a bolt down on it as well. She giggled when he went to the slit of a window, before shaking his head. He'd obviously decided it wasn't wide enough to allow entry.

"What?" he asked, when he heard her.

"You. And this . . . this." She couldn't define or describe it, so she let her voice trail off.

"Safety measures?" he asked.

She giggled again.

"What is so blasted amusing?"

"You. And this. . . . You ken. This."

"This . . . what?"

"This lust that the lasses have for you. That."

"Well, you saw it! You heard."

Dallis put a hand over her mouth to stifle the amusement that time. "You fostered it, though. Worked at it. Created it. And now you seek to deny it?"

"I dinna' make one of those lasses lust for me. Na' one!"

Dallis replied with a huff through her open lips, making it a low sound. It was doubt and disavowal, and she hoped he recognized it as such.

"You saying that I *want* lasses lusting for me?"

"I've na' said a word," Dallis replied.

"You're saying more than a word. You're arguing with me."

"Give me your wrist band." She commanded him.

He pulled back slightly and stared at her.

"Why?"

"Because these lasses are lusting for a reason, withal this argument. I've a desire to ken why. Now, hand over the band."

He made a move as if to pull one of his silver bands off. Then stopped. "What will I get if I do?" he asked.

Dallis pursed her lips, rocked slightly as if considering, and then tilted her head. "What do you want?"

"Your headdress."

"For one band? I think you overestimate your charm."

He grinned at that, and toyed with the band, rotating it so the firelight could flicker all about it. "How about both of them?" he asked.

"And the sporran."

"For a headdress? This is too much. Add more."

"The headdress has a veiling. That is included."

"Will you also unbind your hair?"

"Why?'

"Because I love the color . . . and I want it caressing me . . . swirling about me. Like a cloud."

His voice lowered nearly a full octave and her heart made the same move.

"Who said anything about caresses?" she asked in an argumentative tone.

"You wish to see what they lust after . . . or na'?" he asked.

Dallis considered that for a moment, and then lifted her hands to the strap at the back of her scalp that secured the headdress. It wasn't an easy matter to remove it, because of the wool strips she'd fastened it with. That kept her occupied, and away from any view of what he was doing.

Or not doing.

One of the silver bands rolled across the floor near her feet and Dallis squealed before looking over at where he'd crouched in order to launch it.

"You take too long," he informed her. And then pitched the other band.

Her fingers fumbled more than they worked as she

watched him stand, pulling at the back fastening of his sporran belt, before lowering it to his knee level with a sinuous movement, and then dropping it with a thud on the floor. By then she had her veiling unlatched, slid it from her braid with as sensuous a motion as she knew how, and stood across from him, wrapping it about her hand.

"The braid?" he reminded her, and put his hand up as if to emphasize his point.

Dallis pulled it over her shoulder and started working at it, pulling each lock as straight as she could before she had it completed. She hadn't been successful at keeping the waving from it, for ripples of orange-brown mist looked like it enwrapped her.

Payton responded with a guttural noise and then he was leaning a bit onto a table for support, and looking to bend the structure if the way his arms flexed was any indication.

"What . . . is it?"

"Fortification," he replied.

"You need fortification against one wench? When thousands lust for you? You are a weak man, Payton Dunn-Fadden. Weak."

That straightened him. And angered him. And made everything on him look tense and male. Totally male. Dallis had to part her lips to let the sigh out.

"I doona' have to take such abuse, you ken," he warned.

"Oh, aye," she replied, twirling a bit to let her hair swirl about her. "You do."

"Damn it, Dallis!"

She put her hand up, when it looked like he was poised for an approach. "Show me more."

"More?" he replied.

"Aye. I have a full hankering to see this champion that the lasses so lust over. Or so he says. I need to see more. To evaluate. Fully." And then she licked her lips.

The response was immediate as his frame wavered and

then firmed again, looking almost like she'd weakened him at the knees, just as he did her. Which was only fair.

"Not unless you give me something in exchange," he replied.

She pushed her lower lip out as if his request warranted consideration.

"What do you want?" she finally asked, lifting her brow. And then, she ran her hands down both sides of her frame, emphasizing the way her waist tucked in, and her hips did the opposite.

She didn't dare look in his direction. The growling noise he made was too illicit, tantalizing, and sexual. He almost frightened her.

"The slippers, and any socks they gave you."

"They dinna' give me any."

"Then add . . . any underthings."

"You wish me to take . . . from beneath?"

"'Twill save time later," he replied.

"You seem to believe I want this champion that is you. Hmm. . . ."

"You do want me. And it is a vicious want. Consuming. Heating. Overwhelming."

He was naming the emotions he was causing, exactly as he was causing them, and that just wasn't fair! He had too great a grasp of this lust thing. She was a novice. Dallis looked away for a moment. Swallowed. And then, turned back.

She shrugged. "Mayhap," she replied.

His reply was narrowed eyes, a slitted mouth, and a hugely indrawn breath, if what she was observing was any indication.

"All of your underthings. All of them. Now."

"What will I get?" she asked.

He started pulling at the lacing of his weskit, and when he got it loosened, he was pulling it apart with a vicious movement that had nothing graceful about it. The leather they'd laced it with wasn't giving, and he had to settle for yanking it over his head, and then he was throwing it to the floor beside him with an emotion that looked like one he needed for his fights. The firelight was doing the caressing she longed to as it flickered about the shine of his arms and what chest she could see through the opening in his shirt.

"Satisfied?" he asked.

Dallis's hands were shaking as she lifted her skirts fractionally, and then kicked first one slipper, and then the other in his direction. Then she smoothed the skirts back down.

"Where is your shift? Your chemise?"

"I'm na' wearing any," she replied.

That appeared to anger him more. Dallis watched as he straightened to his full height, put his hands on his hips and glared across at her. It didn't gain him much, except hardened nipples and rivers of shivers, but she wasn't telling him of them.

"Cheat." He launched the word at her.

"Liar," she replied.

"I have na' lied," he argued.

"You claim to be the King's Champion. The man all women lust over. Well! I've yet to see why. And that makes you a liar." She stuck her chin out at the same time, and ignored the trembling that overtook her, all of her.

"The bliant." He pointed to it as if she didn't know what he referred to.

"Too much," she replied.

"Too much?"

"What . . . do you claim that has as much value?"

He lowered his chin and glared at her. From the width of the chamber she could see how his nostrils flared and his eyes narrowed. Everything on her responded as it pulsed toward what he was revealing. Promising. Threatening. Tormenting her with.

"My belt. All my weaponry. My *feile-breacan*."

"Is that all?" she asked, putting a sweet tone on the words

that had him yelling something at her, but through his closed teeth, so she couldn't make it out.

"What more do you want?" he asked, finally, when he seemed to have his breathing back under control.

"What more do I want? Oh, please. You're the champion. The great warrior. Surely you ken what a woman wants."

"Dallis, I swear to you that I'll—"

"Agreed."

She interrupted his threat and started working at the fastening of her strips of plaid. The one that was knotted at the back of her waist.

"To . . . what?" he asked, and he actually sounded confused.

"I accept your sett, your belt and your weapons. For this dress. And I'd na' appreciate the wait."

The belt fell, making a thud on the floor.

She had to ignore it in order to work at the bow-tie of strings she'd made earlier. When the knot gave, so did the tension on her skirt as it fell forward, pulling from her with the weight of the strips she'd used. Dallis didn't dare to look anywhere near him as thud after thud peppered the floor at his feet. Then there was the sound of metal striking against metal, as if the floor didn't have enough room to hold all the dirks and skeans he carried.

She pulled the lacing apart on her upper body, yanking the strands of wool when they wouldn't give quickly enough, and then she had the bliant open and wide, and was lifting it over her head. And that's when she looked again at him.

Payton was standing clothed only in the long shirt that grazed his upper thigh. It did nothing to hide him, since his manhood was stretching the broadcloth in a distorted angle, and making the material hold him in. He was also filmed with moisture, making every muscle gleam in highlight or shadow, as it was graced with the firelight.

Dallis could very easily see what the lasses lusted over. She had her lips open to make certain of breath over the seeing.

"Your underdress?" he asked, in a raw, low tone.

"Come and get it," she replied, and tossed her head.

She shouldn't have called him on. She realized it as he launched across the space as if it wasn't at least two body lengths and had her pulled against him, and lifted up and onto him, and placed so he could shove the male part of himself onto her linen covered loins. That just added to the moisture-imbued sensation of him to her own liquids.

"Dallis. Dallis. Love."

He was murmuring the words against her chin, and then he was sliding his tongue along her jaw, against her neck, and then onto her shoulder, where the underdress straps stopped him.

"I . . . doona' see . . . what all the . . . fuss is about."

She panted the words into the cavern of space above her, since that was all he gave her. And then he was lifting her farther, his hands gripping almost painfully into her buttocks in order to bring her breast within reach of his mouth. Then he was ignoring the linen covering her in order to suckle at her. And Dallis was screaming.

The linen got wet, and then it got clingy, and then he was moving to her other breast tip, shoving his face between her breasts to do so, and making her scream again once he got there.

"You doona' see?" he asked her, when he'd finished turning her into a wavering liquid ephemeral being, and just stood there, looking up at her as if she could find her tongue, let alone make it say words.

Dallis looked down at him, watched how the blue of his eyes looked dark and deep, and endless, and then she smiled. And shook her head.

"Jesu'! Mary! And Joseph!"

He cursed it while opening his arms slightly, turning her

existence into a slide of motion as she lowered farther, arching herself into and against him when her groin reached his. And then he just stood there, holding her in place, and twinging against her, and making the strangest grunting noises each time.

"I'm a-feared . . . you'll have . . . to show me," Dallis whispered, blowing slightly at the end of her words onto his lips, and totally enjoying the lurch of his frame as he felt it.

"You are a stubborn woman, My Lady," he finally replied.

"I know."

"I doona' ken what it will take to make you—"

"The shirt," she interrupted him, and felt the same tremor score through her that started with him.

"The . . . shirt?" he repeated, cocking one eyebrow as he assimilated it.

"Aye," she replied. "The shirt. Now."

Now?" He was trembling worse, if the shake of him was true. And he was going to drop her, if it worsened.

"Aye. . . . now."

Her command had a gap in the center because he'd set her down roughly, onto feet that weren't ready to feel anything like the stability or inflexibility of a chilled wooden floor. He backed from her. Two full steps, then three. And then he pulled the shirt over his head, heaving when it seemed stuck to the moisture on his skin, and then it was done. He tossed it to one side, put his hands into fists at his waist, and shoved the full engorged man-part of him toward her with his stance.

Dallis's entire being answered, as it pulsed toward him, reaching without conscious thought to what he possessed, offered, and expected to be received.

"There!"

He growled it, but she didn't hear. She was too busy, caught up with an approach, silently skimming the wood floor while the linen of her underdress did the same to her limbs, and reaching toward the jagged, purple scar in his abdomen that nearly halved him, and stopped before she got there, as he grabbed both of her upper arms in his hands and lifted her well above him.

"Oh, nae. Na' yet."

He bared his teeth at her as he said it, making a wellspring erupt within her at the sight. Dallis reached for his hairline with hands that trembled, and then she pulled some of the black tresses free of the band, to end with both palms caressing his face. She smiled. Slowly. And watched his eyes narrow.

"I still do na' see what all these lasses lust over," she whispered.

"Well, by God you will!"

He was walking with her, making the linen clinging and hot and sweaty where it was melded between them, and then he was at the enclosure that was his bed. There was nothing gentle about the look he gave her, or the motion he made that set her down onto the mattress, either.

Dallis squealed her surprise at him, but that didn't seem to affect him. Nor did her frightened breathing dent much as he started pulling her shift over her curves, rolling it as he went, yanking it when it clung to her thighs, and shoving when it reached her hips, and then he was putting his mouth to the exposed skin the moment it was revealed and licking everywhere.

Dallis went wild with it. She couldn't contain the ecstasy when he reached her nipples, plying each with a motion that had her crying and shaking and sobbing, and then grabbing his head and screaming at him.

Then he was alongside her, before putting his entire body atop hers, lifting himself with his arms, and hissing commands in her ear as if she could comprehend and obey them. He fitted himself into the space she created when she split her legs for him, and she lifted herself to him and tensed for the pain she knew would come.

But it wasn't pain. Payton slid himself into place, filling her so completely that Dallis slammed her eyes shut, grabbed at the sensation he was giving her, and then was grasping for it back when he moved away. Before returning. Again. Filling her, making her lust for it, and then making her beg.

"Oh, please. Payton. Please. Payton? Please?"

She crooned it to him when his mouth wasn't attempting to suck hers dry with the strength of his kisses. And that was adding to the power of his movements, and the force of each driving thrust into her body, that just made it impossible for anything to make sense other than her cries for more.

"Oh, Dallis. Oh, Jesus. Dallis. Love. Oh, Jesu'. Oh, Dallis."

The cadence of his words deepened, hoarsened, got broader, thicker, harder, stronger, gaining in volume and intensity and strength, until the bed was groaning in time with his words. Through it Dallis clung to him, pushing herself into him again and again, creating and existing and striving and fulfilling, and then spinning into a spiral of pure bliss that had no boundaries she could sense.

And then he was doing it again.

It was as if he was existing in a realm of his own making and taking her with him. Her eyes opened so she could watch him, feast her vision on the shine of skin, rippling with his movements and rosy with his flush. It was then he moved, bending forward to angle his head into the mattress beside her head, while his hands grabbed her hips, moving her, and holding her, and lifting her, and then making certain she couldn't move more than a hairsbreadth as all of him went taut, stiff and unbending, while the longest groan came from his mouth. It was only halted and interrupted by small gasps that matched the pulsing his loins were making against hers.

And then he collapsed, fully, shoving all the available air from her body before he rolled toward the enclosed side. He took her with him, by the pressure of both hands still exactly where he'd left them. He was still shuddering, too, in smaller motions that matched the vibrations that were existing and tempering all along her. Dallis watched him, adoring every bit of watching him, and didn't even care that he caught her at it, when his eyes slit open finally, and he ran his tongue over his lower lip.

"Jesu', Mary, and Joseph," he said.

"I know," she answered. "Where did I learn to tupp like that?"

He grinned, but it was a shaky-looking affair. Then, he raised his brows twice in rapid succession.

"Do you have an answer yet?" he asked.

"To what?"

"What the lasses lust over?"

Dallis reached the slight span they were separated and traced one of the large humps of muscle in his chest. Then, she moved her eyes directly back to his.

"I may need more testing a-fore I'm certain," she replied and then blew a kiss at him.

Chapter 16

"I've changed my mind."

"Hmm?"

Dallis shifted her head sleepily on what she was using for a pillow. She hadn't really heard him, since she'd been close enough to slumber to claim it. The rumble of his words came again, echoing through the chest at her ear.

"I have. Changed my mind, I mean."

"About . . . what?"

"Well . . . na' about this bed."

She lifted her head, put a hand atop his chest to support her chin and peered up at him from that position.

"'Tis too soft," he continued.

As he was starting a movement with one hand along the back of her thigh and onto her buttocks, Dallis wasn't thinking clearly. Or doing much of anything save arching slightly.

"You doona' like . . . soft?" she asked.

"Na' in my mattress," he returned.

Dallis stretched. "Nae," she dissented. "'Tis wondrous hard. And warm."

He growled slightly. "That is me. You have the advantage in an over-soft bed such as this one. I sink. You doona'."

Dallis giggled. "Is that what you call it . . . sinking?"

"'Tis too late for that. I'm a-feared I'm already sunk. Full ended."

Dallis lifted her head, narrowed her eyes, and felt the familiar push-beat to her heart as it stumbled before recovering. "What are we speaking of?" she whispered.

"Well . . . I am referring to this mattress. I doona' ken what you are speaking on."

"Oh." She kept the disappointment from her voice with an act of will, and was very proud that it worked.

"That woman seems to think a man wishes a bed that swallows him. All I can say is she hasn't a real grasp of men."

"You . . . would na' know?" She asked it and held her breath.

Payton lifted his head from where he had it atop his other arm, crooked at the elbow to make it comfortable. "Do I look that dense?" he asked.

He had lifted one eyebrow with the question to make it more difficult to answer him. She had to settle with smiling and tilting her head.

"That looks like an answer I doona' wish to hear," he replied.

"Uh . . ." Dallis's voice trailed off as his fingers started a roving caress all about her lower extremities, defining and trailing, and starting shivers.

"Are you saying I look dense enough to have graced that woman's bed? Or . . . I look dense enough to admit such with my wife?"

"I dinna' say anything," Dallis replied.

"Well, the answer is neither. And this is worse than an inquisition. I swear, you best my sire at it."

"That poor woman," Dallis answered and smiled slightly.

"Are you admitting the lasses have a reason to lust for me? Finally?" He was lifting more than his head with those words, and the muscles at her side pulled and tightened as he made the half-sit and stayed in that raised position.

"I've said naught. Of any kind. You fill in blanks. This is what happens."

"So . . . they doona' have a reason?"

Dallis was trilling along the bumps and knots in his belly that he'd put into play, as if for her fingertips to follow. That was causing tingles to move clear to her elbows. It was a nice sensation, and she was highly attuned to it, even as he moved to suck air in and out.

"Well . . . I admit that the Widow Meryck definitely lusts for you."

She answered him finally, after pulling her lower lip into her mouth and chewing on it. And then releasing it to gain gasps of air as she moved her eyes to his. The muscles beneath her fingers bunched tighter still as he lifted up, taking her with him to a full sit, before settling her into a well of space between his crossed legs. The underdress slid down, partially covering but mainly defining. She watched him look at it, although he didn't change it.

The mattress was definitely too soft for a man of his weight. She knew that as her flesh met the unforgiving surface of wood through the mattress. That position put her far enough below him, she could press her cheek against the hard mounds of his chest, and still meander about his belly with her fingers.

"The widow does na' lust for me," he told her.

Everything stilled, and Dallis slid her cheek along his flesh to look up at him.

"She does."

He shook his head. "Nae," he replied.

"She does. I saw her."

"What you saw was na' real, Dallis."

"I saw that woman. She could na' take her eyes . . . or her hands from you!"

"You believed that?"

He hooted a bit with amusement, and that displaced her

face from his chest and her fingers from his belly. She didn't mourn the loss. She was ready to slap at him.

"Of course I believe it. I have eyes."

"Oh, Dallis. Such a treasure you are. Truly."

The expression when he looked down at her was so tender, she caught her breath, the fist she'd made with her hand relaxed, and her eyes widened.

"I'd forgotten such naiveté exists."

Her face fell. She felt it. That's when she pinched her lips together and narrowed her eyes, and glared at him.

"What?" he asked.

"That woman lusts for you." She said it with a tone that usually brooked no argument. She should have known it wouldn't work on him.

"That woman lusts for power."

"Exactly as I said."

He grinned, showing very white teeth, and then he sobered. "That's a compliment. I think," he said finally, and then flexed everything on his naked frame that she was supported by. Everything.

"Payton," she said in a warning fashion. "You get off subject too often, and too easily. You are to cease it. I tire of it."

"Best go tell the lads I've changed my mind, then. Although you should do it."

"Why me?" she asked.

"You're dressed."

"They're your men," she shot back.

"You're their lady. Sworn to protect and cherish."

"Do you always argue?"

Both eyebrows raised. "Do *I* always argue?"

"'Twas what I asked."

"Never mind. I've changed my mind again."

"On what?"

"First light. I'd decided to miss it. 'Twas a grand idea a-fore."

"A-fore what?" she asked.

"Your arguments. Ceaselessly."

"Payton."

Every other man had stopped everything and kept a respectful look about him when she'd used that tone. Not Payton. He responded with a bigger grin.

"Verra well . . . Dallis. We'll both miss it. And I'll go speak of it with them, saving you the issue. In a bit."

"Why?"

"Why?"

"Why canna' you keep on task? We are na' leaving at first light, and I wish to ken why."

He sighed heavily. "My wife is na' letting me sleep. I'll be stuped and blunt if I try and leave. I may even fall off my horse."

That time she did slap at him, but he must have known, for she'd never seen such fast movement as he made to block her hand with his. And then he kept it, brought it to his lips, turning it over as he did so, in order to place a kiss on the vulnerable underside of her wrist. Then her palm. Dallis couldn't prevent each lurch of her frame as he tongued flesh that had never felt the like. He knew it, too, for he was chuckling when he'd finished, and put her hand back into place atop his chest.

"You wish me on task?" he asked.

She didn't even nod. Her entire body felt too tensed and readied, and irritated.

"Well?"

He repeated it, but he was trailing a finger up her arm, and watching it until he reached her shoulder. He moved the gaze to hers, and completely stole her wits with the roar that seemed to crest through her, to end as a wave sound in both ears.

"Aye." The word was croaked.

"Then, give me a task I want."

Dallis leaned back, using the back of his thigh as her bulwark to give herself space and breathing room, and stop the vexation that seemed to be emanating from the naked frame she perched atop. She put her hands to his shoulders to make certain of it, and straightened her arms.

"The widow lusts after you," she said finally.

His reply was a hooted sound, but since he'd flung his head back to make it at the canopy above them, she couldn't get what it was. Or what it was supposed to be. He was still grinning and rolling his eyes when he looked back down at her. Dallis didn't change expression.

"You are devilishly stubborn, Wife."

"So I have been told," she returned. "The widow?"

"She can have any man she fancies . . . and probably has. Why would she want me?"

"You're the King's Champion."

"Na' any more. I retired. 'Tis why I journeyed to my castle . . . and my wife."

"The greatest warrior in Scotland? Retired?"

"I fulfilled the king's requirements of me. He had nae other choice."

"His . . . requirements?" Her voice shook.

"Are you starting to see yet?"

He was entirely sober as he said it, and that just sent a ripple of shiver through her. It wasn't pleasant.

"Our sovereign is a wealthy man . . . when his mistresses are na' taking it from him. He required funds, and I was a means to getting them. That is all I was. Ever. Nae doubt he has another champion battling for him already."

"But—this eve. This presentation. Those . . . followers . . . I doona' understand."

It sounded it too. Her arms were relaxing and she was settling back to the enclosure he'd made for her between his legs, welcoming the hard surface beneath her for its tangibility.

"I have a certain drawing value, Dallis. 'Tis what the

widow wants. And what I am required to give." His voice spat the last of it.

"Then why do you visit here? You hate it. You said so. Yet . . . here we are."

"To ignore Widow Meryck's invitation is a grave insult. One does na' insult a woman with this much power, Dallis."

"But if she already has power . . . why does she want you?"

"I turned my back on The Stewart. That has value to her. Revenge value."

"Why would the king care?"

"Who do you think sired her youngest daughter, the infant Mary?"

She was reeling in place, and nothing on her showed it other than the way she inhaled air and held it for long moments before letting it out. "She's the king's mistress?" she asked.

"Former. She was replaced . . . discarded. Ignored . . . and then rejected. So now she is bitter. And vengeful."

"Then, what good will it do for Redmond to go to her this eve?"

His eyes went wide and he stared at her. "He told you that?"

She shook her head. "I'm na' as naive as you believe. I pieced it together myself. So, why is he?"

He shrugged. "Women must lust more for him, than they do me."

Dallis lowered her chin and glared up at him through her eyelashes in a pose reminiscent of his. He responded with more amusement. She had to resort to looking away from him and pretending an aloofness her body wasn't assisting with.

"Ah . . . Dallis. Doona' act like this to me. Na' now. Please?"

She smiled at the carved wood of the enclosed bed. All it took was a bit of play-acting like she didn't care? He was too easy. He sighed heavily, brushing the side of her shoulder with air.

"All right. I forfeit. MacCloud seeks his own legacy in a different manner from how I got mine."

"You got yours through killing and taking."

"I prefer conquest and victory," he replied easily.

"He . . . told me it was charity."

Payton chuckled. "Fancy bit of charity that is. He tries to get the widow with child. A male child. 'Twould be the best way to force her to the aisle."

"He wants to wed with her?"

"Only with the king's blessing. And the king would bless him fair should he remove this thorn from his majesty's side. With titles and property and more funds that the king does na' have."

"So . . . Redmond planned this?"

"Let's agree . . . that MacCloud does na' fight against it."

"What does the widow hope to gain?"

Payton put both hands on her shoulders and pulled her back into his embrace, twisting her torso so she'd be shoved against his chest and unable to move from it.

"You need ask?" he asked. "I must be a verra poor teacher." And then his lips came down on hers.

They didn't wait for sunrise, making it a moot point that neither he nor the woman slumbering atop him went to tell the guarding clansman of the changed plans. He hadn't wanted to move her from where she snuggled, warming his side, and brushing a bit of breath across his chest, and making the entire area warm and tight and odd-feeling.

He couldn't sleep, and that was completely off-kilter. Payton never had trouble sleeping. Especially after feeling as drained as this vixen of a wife managed to make him feel. He still couldn't place it. He felt all torn up over her, and knew it wasn't love emotion he was suffering. It couldn't be. He didn't trust her. He had a scar on his temple to prove that much. And without trust, how could there be anything as perfect as love?

But he did feel something. Something more vast than he'd felt before, and something so consuming, he was willing to stay in one spot while she used him for her mattress and pillow, even though it numbed his legs not to shift. That's how much he cared. And that was just wrong.

The tapping on the door was barely noticeable, but Payton turned his head toward it. They had but one high slit for a window in this chamber room, and there was nothing resembling light coming from between the shutters.

It couldn't be daylight yet. Not only were the nights longer, but he'd noted the log in their fireplace sometime after she fell asleep, and there'd been enough deep-burning wood to keep them into the morn, and partly into day as well.

"My Laird? Payton!"

Now they were calling for him, and in this castle with a volume loud enough to pierce wooden doors, that was unsafe. And unwise. Payton maneuvered from beneath Dallis with difficulty, disentangling her arm from about his neck, and her hair from every part of his torso it clung to.

"Payton!"

"Aye?"

He had to speak it before he was loose of Dallis, because they were starting to pound at the wood, and that would just rouse the entire household, making any kind of an escape impossible.

He was almost to the door before they started hitting at it again.

"Cease!" He had the bolt drawn and the door cracked, and then he was looking at several of his men. Dressed. Cloaked. And glaring at him.

"'Tis na' dawn," he mentioned.

"You've moments. Dinna' waste them." Redmond shoved past him and walked through the door, before averting his eyes from the goddess stretching in place on the bed.

"Already?" she asked.

"Here." Redmond flung his cloak at her. "And Payton. Dress. Quickly."

"What did you do?"

"'Tis na' what I've done, or dinna' do," he hissed. "'Tis fate. And cunning."

"Cunning?"

"I eavesdropped. I overheard her messenger. And her orders."

"What message?"

"The Stewart is journeying here. Due tonight! She was told to make ready!"

Payton put both hands into the air. "Fair enough. I'll dine with My Liege on the morrow. After he visits her. You should have stayed. It would have been amusing."

"She does na' wish to be caught with me in her bed."

"And so you are na'. What of it? She's getting what she wants."

"Nae! She wants revenge! And she has the means for it right here. Right now! Dress faster!"

Payton had donned his shirt and socks. He looked over while unfurling the length of plaid that was supposed to wrap about his frame as a kilt and chest band and held it to his waist for the start.

"I doona' see the issue, Redmond. Unless you left her unable to desire him. And if so, I'm verra proud of you."

"Can you na' think quicker than this! She dismissed me! With one word. And it was nae lover word. And then she sent for her personal guards. I stayed in the doorway long enough to hear. I'm telling you, we've nae time. Move!"

"Go through to the wife's chamber. Awaken the Lady Evelyn."

"Already done. With luck, she's already in the stables, awaiting you. Everyone awaits you!"

"Why?"

"Because she wants to be caught with *you* in her bed! What better vengeance could there be? And she does na' wish you aware at the time."

Payton felt his eyes widen, and his hands tremble. He tossed the sett over his shoulders for donning later, fastened his belt, shoved the sword into its sheath and slid into his boots. He looked across the chamber at his wife. Locked eyes. All his wife had for clothing was a cloak. And the very wrinkled underdress she'd pulled back into place the moment Redmond had entered. She was still the most tempting vision imaginable.

He smiled.

"We doona' have time for this! Any of this! If we take the unused wing, beyond your wife's chamber, we may get to the stables without getting spotted."

"Then what are you waiting for?" Payton held out his hand for Dallis and they were at the other door as he said it.

Their progress was silent and steady, with three men in front of him, while the others trailed behind, constantly checking. Constantly moving. Making sure of the path before allowing Payton and Dallis to use it. And then using the first available door to access the walkway along their wall. That way, they only had two worries: cold, and being spotted. Payton crept along the battlements behind his men, going to a crouch-walk between merlons, and Dallis kept pace the entire time. She was even giggling at one point, and that sound made his heart stumble, like always.

Then, they were at a series of guard steps, carved without much skill, and difficult to see through the fog of each breath. Payton skimmed his back along the rock wall for stability, and silently cursed the entire miserable plot. It was blister-raising cold and sinister dark, and only a king's fury over wounded pride could get man or beast out on a night like this one.

They spotted the stables easily, as the lone brightly lit building, and the one generating the most steam into the air. The volume of horseflesh inside it guaranteed it.

"How will we get through the gate? And over the draw-bridge?"

Someone asked it as they readied mounts for riding double again. He'd been promised an escort of fifty men. Mounted. That's why he'd postured and posed and played at being a fa-vorite. It had been for naught. And it wasn't real. But he'd always known that.

Payton didn't even ask Dallis if she wanted a berth atop Orion and in her husband's arms. He didn't want to hear if the answer was nay. He lifted her into position in front of his saddle, and arranged the cloak over her legs.

"We doona' use the gate."

Redmond answered him, as he pulled another hank of plaid from his bag to replace the one covering Dallis. Then he lifted Lady Evelyn into the saddle and started walking toward the back of the stable.

"We don't?"

"Nae need. They built this castle with a tunnel. Come lads!"

Payton looked at his man in surprise. He didn't even know Castle Ballilol possessed a tunnel. He decided the man was better than cunning.

"Slowly now. And watch your step. I dare na' use the path. We'll have to wait by the crypt wall. In shadow."

"But, if there's a tunnel, and we're na' near the gate—"

"The tunnel will be in use, lad," Redmond answered.

"It will?"

"Aye. We need await the party using it to enter. In silence. And then we use it to leave. None will even look twice."

"What party?" Alan was hushed the moment he asked it.

"The king's. I hope," Redmond finished.

"Damn, but I hate this castle," Payton whispered.

Chapter 17

Dallis shivered in the pre-dawn light and that got her Payton's arms as he pulled her even closer to his belly, and wrapped more of his covering about her. She hated to think of how exposed he might be, but the warmth was too intoxicating and addicting to think of refusing. Aside from which, she wanted to be right against him, listening to his heartbeat, and waiting for the occasional grunting moan sound he gave that transferred weirdly into her ear.

She nestled her chin into the depression below his throat, breathed deeply of the man-scent of him, and gave her own moan. And got tighter arms about her.

The horse's movement was gentle and hypnotic, with generous steps across a beaten path, and it was so close to perfect contentment, she was at a loss on how to tell Payton.

"Dunn-Fadden?" She whispered the name.

He lowered his head, running a breath all about her features. "Aye?" he replied, with the same whispered tone she was using.

"That widow definitely lusts for you. Admit it."

"Jesu'."

The word was accompanied by a general shake of his entire

torso that was probably laughter, although he withheld the sound of it. His features were in an open grin, though.

"Well, she does. There is nae more dispute."

"Wife, you feel verra fine in my arms, and even better in my bed. If you say she lusts for me, then I'll na' argue more."

"Well, she does."

"I know," he said. "Every lass lusts for me."

"As long as you admit it." She turned back to contemplation of the throb of motion in his throat that matched his heartbeat.

"Is there another . . . widow . . . at this new castle? This . . . Canongate?"

"There is a lady of the keep. But she's wed. To the laird."

"I will na' be forced from my bed and sent fleeing into the night due to her lusts, will I?"

He chuckled. Moved something on him enough that it lifted her to his chin level, and then he turned and placed a kiss there.

"If it gets you in my arms again atop my horse, then I am na' adverse to such a thing," he replied finally, teasing her skin with more of his breath, hued with the frosted air.

"I find it uncomfortable and difficult to sleep," she informed him, using a haughty tone to the words.

"And the next you'll be averring is you've a fancy for mattresses that are too soft and lack proper support."

"I had nae issue with support. Perhaps you should eat less."

"You are wicked amusing, Wife," he informed her, after his chuckling was finished. "I rather believe Laird Kilchurning was na' aware of such."

"Why would you mention that man?" she asked.

"He dinna' ken the prize he had."

"He dinna'?"

"He'd never have left you on the shelf. Ripe and ready to be plucked by a man with the fortitude to do so."

"You were lucky with your ramming of the gate," she told him.

"Aye. That I am. Entirely too lucky. By far."

"By farther than that. You have the luck of—"

Her gasp was followed by wide eyes. Dallis fumbled beneath the blanketing to put both hands to her belly as the tingle deep in her womb came again. And then she moved her gaze to his, and lost all thought.

The sun had decided to peek onto the snow-flecked landscape, shedding a gold and pink glow that spread out, carrying little in warmth, but a mass of use in light. It lit upon the vivid blue of his eyes, making them look unworldly and vivid as he gazed into hers. Deep. Probingly deep.

"The . . . bairn," she stammered. "It . . . moved. *Again*."

If she had thought him handsome before, it was based on ignorance. He pursed his lips into a kissable shape, color rose to temper his cheeks, and his eyelashes swooped down rapidly to cover over and eliminate a shine atop the blue of his eyes that had made them luminous.

"The . . . bairn?" he queried, with a voice that shook.

Dallis nodded, the motion moving her cheek against the skin of his upper chest where she'd been lowered to.

"Aye. Our son," she told him.

She had to move her eyes from his or she was going to lose the ability to think, breathe, or speak. Or all three. She settled with moving it to the vista in front of Orion, where the dawn was picking shapes of crofts and fencing and swollen humps of snow delineating fallow fields, and everything else that meant humanity and civilization.

The tingle came again, stirring within her, and making a whoosh of emotion so vast it threatened to overtake and consume her. Dallis held her hands to her belly, cupping the slight swell there, and waited for the movement to happen again.

Above her head, Payton cleared his throat. "'Tis terrible

small. He does na' take up much room. You doona' even look to be breeding."

"He may be small yet," she replied, "but I am na' a large size."

"Well, I am. And I sired him." His voice actually warbled slightly on the words. Dallis had to blink rapidly to keep the emotion to a manageable level.

"Aye . . . that you did." Her voice went dreamy, and soft, and nearly inaudible, and then she was turning back into the chest behind her in order to gain more warmth.

Canongate Castle was a fortified structure that was using the word castle falsely. There wasn't one crenellation on the wall, showing the royal house hadn't granted permission for such yet, and there wasn't a high enough curtain wall encircling the whole. For defense it was vastly incompetent.

For luxury and comfort, it was unsurpassed, according to Payton.

Dallis had to take Payton's words about the amenities, since her first exclamation of disgust remained unaltered by their approach to the structure. Why, if she wasn't mistaken, they had few, if any defense mechanisms designed into the structure. Such a design was faulty, weak, and useless for anything other than entertaining.

That's exactly what Payton told her the castle was for.

Canongate Castle sat on the road to Holyrood, which started the Royal Mile, covered in shops and dwellings, until it reached the mountain where Edinburgh Castle perched. That meant it was in the shadow of the seat of Scot power, and hadn't much need for defense.

All of that explanation was a poor reason for calling this structure a castle.

She was still denigrating it as the wooden drawbridge dropped, showing they'd been spotted, and then the horses all came to a stop as humanity started spilling out onto the ground in front of them. It was exactly what had happened at Ballilol. There was the same swell of noise, as well.

"Your followers," Redmond said from beside them.

"Aye," Payton replied.

"This is full great, Payton . . . I mean, My Laird!" Alan's squeaked voice was full of excitement and vigor. Neither of which was an easy thing to find after such a sleepless night.

Payton and Redmond swiveled back to look at the lad. Dallis had the same motion. It looked like the entire grouping of them were looking at the lad. He did look excited, then crestfallen as he interpreted their looks.

"What?" he asked.

"Ah . . . the young."

Redmond had turned back forward first. The others followed. Payton looked over at him from atop her head.

"Were we ever that excited?" It was Martin asking it, and Dallis cocked her head for the reply.

"Aye. Perhaps in those first few months. A-fore we knew the falsehood of such adulation. And the aftermath." Redmond was doing the answering.

"Running in the middle of the night?" someone offered.

"Nae. The other aftermath. The depth of the landing."

"Look! They approach! Running! And listen. They scream even louder than those at Ballilol! Especially the lasses. Look!"

Alan was still excited, if the tone of his voice were true. He was right, though. The cries of Payton's name were louder. More distinct. Dallis pushed against Payton's chest as the onslaught reached a fence-line and then toppled it.

"'Tis true fantasy! Jesu'. You are so lucky." It was Alan again.

"Lucky?" Payton asked, and surprise stained the word.

"If I had this amount of wenches waiting for just a glance at my face or touch of my hand, well! I'd be for jumping into the midst of them, I would."

"Men?"

Redmond moved his horse forward and into a position in

front of Payton. Four others followed, making a half-circle about Orion, with each double set of riders facing what appeared to be hundreds. Alan followed.

"Does this happen every time?" Alan asked.

"More times than na'." It was Martin answering now, and he'd lost all patience. It was in his voice.

The men drew swords then, although the sound of metal sliding from scabbards couldn't be heard. And all of them set the blades across their laps. She watched as even Alan followed suit. Dallis was frightened. It was showing in the quick, short breaths she was taking. She knew Payton would sense it. Then they lifted their swords and started glinting what sun there was off the blades, speckling the crowd with bright flashes of light. The effect stopped the front of the horde, then those behind it slowed and by the time they'd reached where Payton's party was standing, they were at milling speed, with bursts of applause and sounds of awe coming from them.

If she hadn't seen it, she wouldn't have believed it.

"Have you come to escort The Champion?" The clansman called Edwin stood high in his stirrups and bellowed it, with a volume and power of voice he'd been hiding.

There was a general chorus that sounded positive, and he yelled again.

"Then turn about and escort him!"

They were surrounded by humanity that no longer felt threatening, and instead sounded cheerful and delighted and thrilled. As a unit they moved, crossing over the fallen fence and then to the drawbridge, where two of the larger freemen put themselves to either side and began directing the crowd, maintaining a mass that wouldn't collapse the bridge.

"Where did they learn to do that?" Dallis asked Payton when they awaited a turn to cross the bridge and go beneath the portcullis.

"Do what?"

"Use the sun that way. 'Twas brilliant!"

"We were lucky." He was frowning slightly.

"You've done it a-fore. That was na' luck. That was timing and practice and forethought."

"And we were lucky. Some winter morns do na' have much sunlight. It does na' work as well with torchlight, either. Unless you have more men and more swords. A lot more men."

"How many more?"

"The fifty mounted men I was promised at Ballilol. That many. I assure you, Dallis. We were lucky today. And I tire of luck."

He did look tired. And something else. Disillusioned. It hadn't changed when it was their turn to move across the bridge, with Dunn-Fadden clansmen in front and behind, and no gap between. As they rode beneath the portcullis and entered the courtyard, she could see the wisdom of that. The folk who had already passed through were waiting, and lifting grasping hands, and tugging, and jostling . . . pulling, and then a horn blared out so loudly, it startled everything, including the horses. Payton had Orion's rearing halted the moment the stallion attempted it, with legs hardened to the consistency of wood. Since Dallis was perched atop them, she felt it. Alan and Seth-the-Silent weren't as prepared, as their horses reared. Dallis watched as Bronwyn fell off the back of one. The horn came again. Longer and louder this time.

"What are you doing lazing about? Back to work! All of you!"

There was a burly, bearded fellow standing at the top of a span of steps that brought him above a horse rider's level. The man carried in girth what weight Payton probably did, but it didn't seem to hamper him as he moved a step down, and started directing his guards with an arm.

"And Payton Alexander Dunn-Fadden! King's Champion! How dare you ride into my castle, unannounced?"

"Greetings, Dunrobin!" Payton answered, using the same volume of speech and making Dallis's ears ring.

"And without warning! I should challenge you myself!"

That started a wave of laughter through the crowds. With the assistance of guards, they were dispersing, and changing back into the serfs, freemen and women, and housecarls that a household this size needed in order to be maintained. Dallis watched as it happened. She wondered briefly at her ability to fear such pleasant-faced and industrious people, but knew she hadn't imagined it. None of them had.

"When you said you hadn't enough men for safety, you dinna' mean mine, did you?" Dallis asked it as he moved Orion forward to meet the man who was descending the steps.

"Dallis," he replied.

"Well?" She was still encapsulated in his arms, making it impossible for him to avoid answering her.

"There is naught more precious to me than you and the bairn," he replied, without moving his eyes to her.

"That is nae answer."

One side of his lip lifted. "True," he replied.

"I doona' believe I care for this fame of yours, Payton Dunn-Fadden," she informed him.

His smile took up both sides of his mouth this time, and he was nodding, but not to her. The horse had stopped and that meant they'd probably arrived, and that meant he wasn't going to answer.

"Laird Dunrobin!" Payton swung from the saddle, holding to her waist for a base. And then he clasped the man in greeting by a hand to his upper arm.

"Come in. Come in. And bring your lady with you."

"You ken she is my lady?" Payton asked.

"You would na' bring a woman other than your wife to my home. And into the company of my lady wife. Tell me this is na' true. Welcome, My Lady Dunn-Fadden. Welcome!"

The man was beaming and nodding and gesturing for them to follow. He didn't look at all like that man who'd sternly reprimanded Payton. Dallis would have asked why, but Payton was bringing her down and into a berth in his arms, making her a bit dizzy and not at all certain of which direction he was heading as he mounted the steps and entered the hall.

She heard some wording about the lady's solar, felt Payton climbing again, while more than one set of boots accompanied him through cavernous halls. And then he entered such a light-filled room, that it hurt her eyes. Which made it harder to see the balding woman that was peering at them through a glass held to her eye that made it look four times the correct size.

"Laird . . . Dunn-Fadden?" She gasped during the query, and then dropped the glass. She disappeared for a bit and Dallis looked down to watch her slapping at the floor as she looked. Alan was the one who assisted with retrieving it. They all watched as she stuck it against her eye and peered again, with an even larger eye.

"In my solar? Men are na' allowed in a lady's solar."

"I bring my Lady Dallis Dunn-Fadden. To beg your assist." He bent his head toward Dallis. The woman pushed her face forward and blinked with a huge set of eyelashes behind the glass.

"But—we are na' prepared. You're na' due until tomorrow. This eve at the earliest. And this woman canna' possibly be your wife."

Payton straightened at the insult, and Dallis did the same move, putting her firmly against his chest as she looked across at the woman.

"This woman most definitely is my lady wife. And you could na' have prepared for my arrival. I sent nae word," Payton replied.

The woman's snorts of amusement were apparent as the glass trembled in her hand.

"Laird Kilchurning has already given word to the entire court about your wife. I'm told she is a great heiress." The huge eye inspected Dallis again, moving up and down about her. "They expect her at the castle any day. And that is why we knew you'd arrive here." She tilted her head to look up at Payton again. "Why did you allow your wife to wear such garments? You have too much renown to allow your wife to be seen . . . thusly." She put out a hand and flipped a loose fold of Dallis's cloak with disdain.

"I already begged for the assist, My Lady. I would na' trust Dallis to any other. Doona' tell me you dinna' hear it?"

The woman looked back up at him. "Na' a moment too soon, then. Set her down. And you!" She motioned toward a spot where no one was standing. "See to getting some porridge sent up. And send for my seamstresses! And all my fabrics and gewgaws! And then you men get out of my solar!"

Payton stepped around her, revealing such extravagance and opulence amid immense clutter that Dallis's eyes widened again. She was forced to narrow them and rub at them, with the fingertips of both hands as he walked.

The room this lady claimed as her own was speared by morning sun, coming through a leaded glass wall of windows that stained the flooring and furnishings with colored hues of light. They appeared to be in a tower, but it was a large one, looking to be twenty paces across. There was another, smaller door on the left wall, a rock-framed fireplace on the right, sending out more glow and warmth, and the remaining space was lined with every conceivable form of stitched tapestry, hanging from the ceiling to the floors. Lady Evelyn was even impressed. Dallis could hear her exclamation at seeing such consummate artistry.

Where she could see floor, it appeared highly polished, reflecting the colored light coming through the windows. There were armed chairs, backless benches, and tables covered with items in various stages of progress, and along every wall was another stack or pile of fabric.

Payton was used to such a sight, or ignored it, since his pace didn't slow, and he was at a long bench and placing her upon it before she had time to assimilate and evaluate her surroundings further. The sofa he set her on was filmed with satin, stuffed to a thickness that didn't seem possible to dent, and pure heaven to slide down on and rest her head. She was asleep the moment it touched.

"With this one, I used real horse hair."

"Wasn't that . . . slow? And tedious?"

"Oh." There was a laugh. "Verra. The strands are na' much longer than my hand. I had to rethread my needle over and over."

Dallis listened to the sound of two ladies moving, a rustle of fabric, and more low-voiced talking.

"What did you use on this one? I've na' seen such fine stitches. They're near impossible to spot."

"You're so gracious. I'm trying out a new method with these tones. What do you think?"

"What is it?"

"These are bits of silk, special purchased for me in London." There was a cooing sound coming from two throats. "And then I dipped some of them in the vat of vinegar and set them in the sun to dry. See how white they are? It does na' work well with fabric, though. The strands gather and knot easily. I had to be verra careful, and extra cautious."

"But how do you get such coverage? I canna' even see . . ."

"Crosses. You need to peer verra close. Here. Little crosses throughout my work. Much better than long-stitching."

Dallis opened an eye and looked over at the ladies who were analyzing what looked to be an altar cloth.

"That's . . . beauteous." Lady Evelyn put a hand to her bosom and sighed.

"My passion," Lady Dunrobin replied.

"Mine, too. I just dinna' think of what you have. And I haven't access to such materials. Nor such thread . . ." Lady Evelyn's voice got wistful. "I was working on a piece when we left. I only hope 'tis still there when we return."

"You dinna' bring another with you?"

"I only work one at a time."

The Lady Dunrobin giggled again. "One? Why, if all I did was one, I'd be bored within moments. My lord husband kens this. He keeps me in projects. I am so far behind! This altar cloth was supposed to be ready by Middlemass. You note I already missed that. I shall just try for next year's sessions instead."

"Your husband . . . wants you to sew?"

"Oh my, yes. He is such a love. He keeps me in materials and thread, and what-all I need. He goes out of his way to please me with it, although he always gets the wrong thing if I am na' most specific. Sometimes he is so maddening!"

They both tittered with giggles, and Dallis stretched, alerting them.

"Thank heaven! She's awake. And probably hungered beyond all reason. Call the kitchens! Get some more porridge sent up! And some freshly baked bread! I do so love my bread when it's just pulled from the ovens. And crusty. 'Tis rather like touching a man's thick belly. You ken?"

Lady Evelyn giggled behind her hand, acting like a lass in the first flush of youth, rather than a spinster of sixty. Dallis was hard put not to laugh herself at her aunt's expression.

"I'm unwed, My Lady," Lady Evelyn told her.

"Fair sorrowed I am to hear that. Every woman needs a man. And every man is lost without a woman. So the Bible says. Or, so my husband tells me it says."

"You love your husband verra much," Lady Evelyn replied.

"Oh. Aye. He is a bear of a man, but the lone one I'll ever lust for. Aside from the champion, of course."

Dallis blinked rapidly, lowered her chin, and glared across at the women. Then she realized the futility. That woman couldn't see a finger-length in front of her face. And she was suffering a severe misunderstanding. Payton would never be interested.

"You . . . lust for my husband, Payton Dunn-Fadden?" Dallis asked.

Lady Evelyn knew what the look on Dallis's face portended. She was looking uneasy, with frown lines all about her features.

"Of course! Does na' every woman?"

"I knew it! The wretched bastard! He lied!" Dallis was on her feet and approaching where the older women looked defensive. Especially with the altar cloth held in front of them.

"The champion does na' lie. He's forthright, and honorable. Aside from being large and muscled and brawny . . . verra, verra brawny. And handsome. Overly so, but I am na' complaining. Bonny lads are for looking over and lusting for. He is also the best warrior on the land. How can any of that be a lie?"

"You want him?" Dallis asked, in a harsh voice.

"She's a mite jealous," Lady Dunrobin apprised Lady Evelyn in a loud whisper. "You should have warned me."

"Nonsense," the lady replied. "She does na' even care for him."

Lady Dunrobin's eyes went wide, making one four times the size of the other. They were a very watered-down shade of blue, Dallis noted.

"She does na'?" She gasped after the words.

"I more than care for him! I love him!" Dallis shouted it at them, as if the woman had trouble hearing, rather than seeing. And then she went beet red with the blush.

"You . . . do?" Lady Evelyn asked.

Dallis felt all the emotion, trauma, and passion welling up inside, from her failure to control her own destiny, this journey, finding out about the babe, and admitting the love for him she'd just shouted out. She couldn't prevent the tears that overwhelmed her and started spilling.

"Please doona' cry, My Lady. I would na' say a word to hurt you."

"But you did!" Dallis wailed. "You lust after my husband."

"Na' in the way you believe."

"What other way is there?"

"I would na' ken what to do with a man like that if I had him. Good heavens! One look at my frame, and he'd be running for the nearest door. I'd die of embarrassment a-fore it got that far. I only meant that . . . well . . ." Her voice lowered and she looked to the right and left of them as if it helped with her vision. And then she whispered the rest. "Doona' tell my husband, but sometimes Dunn-Fadden's image comes in right handy when my husband gets randy. Right handy. If you ken my meaning."

Dallis couldn't hold the sad feeling. Not when all of her felt like laughing. She had to give it up and wiped at her face before the mirth overtook her. Lady Evelyn wasn't as demure and poised. She roared with it.

Chapter 18

"You should cease moving, Dunn-Fadden, and partake of this feast."

Payton looked across at his host and the others, all shoving food into their mouths and drinks into their bellies like that was what mattered.

"I ate," he replied, and resumed his constant circuit of Castle Canongate's great hall.

"That's true enough, isn't it, lads?" Laird Dunrobin's announcement was loud and raucous sounding, which was a condition brought about by drinking too much of the spirits provided. "And we should drink to that!"

"Aye!"

The answer was chorused as they lifted their tankards toward Payton and then their host, before drinking them empty and calling for more.

"You truly should sit, Champion. You are dizzy-fying my view."

That comment got the laird more laughter.

"I canna' sit down," Payton informed him. "And I canna' decide the why."

"He worries," somebody said. Payton thought it was

Martin, but he couldn't be sure since he hadn't been looking and they all sounded stewed.

"Over what?" The Earl of Dunrobin asked. "He slept a bit, ate my buttery and pantry empty, drank a bit, and then annihilated everyone foolish enough to accept his challenge. I vow Dunn-Fadden, I've na' been that entertained in months! And all a-fore sup! Drink again, men! Drink to the champion!"

There were more shouts of agreement, sounds of liquid sloshing and being drunk, poured, or spilled. Payton resumed his walk. He should be exhausted. But he wasn't. He was alive, and tense, and Martin was probably right. He was worried.

"Why . . . I avowed my guardsmen to be strong men. But look here. One bit of scuffling with you on the list, and they're reduced to wretches that have to soak away their pains in the loch!"

There was more laughter at that. Payton smirked. He'd joined them in the pool of water that wasn't large enough to have the name loch attached to it, but it was cold enough. That was after he'd worked with four of his men, and then eight of the Dunrobin men, until they had to be removed. A brisk dunk was a good way to chill heated bodies and hotter tempers once a man was pronounced beaten and removed from the list.

Strange, how a bit of practice with his clansmen had turned into a contest once the earl came out of the keep. And then it had turned into challenge, with angered words and excitement staining the air. It was a good thing Payton hadn't allowed killing weapons when he'd started, only clubs and shields. That was a better way to work the knots from a man's limbs, and put a fresh wind in his head. Exactly how Payton liked it.

Several of those on the benches and filling their mouths looked askant at him. Most looked untouched, for Payton

worked at body blows, not head ones, and knocking a man
from his feet was a sure way to manage it. There were a few
blackened eyes, and one swollen nose, however. That hadn't
been Payton's fault. The man moved too quickly. Payton had
a heavy bruise along his upper arm as proof of it. That man
had deserved it.

Dunrobin had a large great hall. It was a full three stories
in height, with arched cathedral ceilings that made it possible
to have such a space without poles intersecting the floor
below. The family table was on a raised dais at the far end,
overseeing whatever might take place. They weren't seated at
that table. They were at one of the long, common ones,
stretched along the walls, leaving the center open for the
dancing the earl had assured him would come. Once the
ladies showed. If the minstrel who was at the end of the table
near Alan stayed sober enough to play his lyre, anyway.

The reason they'd chosen this particular table to await that
event was its proximity to the fireplace, the kitchen entrance,
and the kegs. All of which were getting full use during the
wait. The walls were stone, cut in large blocks. There were
elaborate stitched tapestries gracing nearly every speck on it,
showing battles, murals of heaven, and on one wall, was a
span of tapestries that inter-related. They showed the story of
a dragon-threatened maiden, and the knight that eventually
was depicted atop it with a lance through the throat. There
was even a maiden resembling Dallis tied to a tree while she
awaited her rescue. The kiss that would be rewarded after
the rescue must not be finished yet. That spot was taken up
by a scene of roses, thistles, and sky. Payton knew the lady
Dunrobin was the skill behind the needle, and she was immensely talented, even if it appeared to have ruined her sight.
He moved on after studying the dragon's death scene.

"Payton, I beg you. Sit. Eat. My head is reeling from
watching."

Payton waved away the complaint with his hand and moved on to the next tapestry they'd mounted on their wall.

"Well, someone satisfy my curiosity, then. One of you tell me . . . what is it that worries the champion to the point he canna' sit down?"

"The wife."

"She's in good hands, lad. My wife will see nae harm comes to her."

"That is na' what worries him."

Alan Dunn-Fadden had a developing young man voice that moved octaves every time he spoke. Since he'd been imbibing with the others, the squeak when the low tones took over was apparent and made everyone laugh.

"What?" he asked when several pointed and laughed harder.

"You seem to know much, lad. Tell me. What does worry him, then."

"She carries a bairn."

Alan announced it like he was the proud father, turning the Dunn-Fadden clansmen into statuelike stillness while they looked at Payton for guidance. He regarded them for a bit and then turned back to the tapestries when Dunrobin spoke again. He was just starting to evaluate a religious one when the earl spoke.

"I already ken that. As does the king. 'Tis Kilchurning's word that the bairn is his. And that means the keep and castle are his. 'Tis what he sent a messenger to Edinburgh with. A sennight past."

Payton swung about rapidly enough it swirled his kilt about his knees. "What?"

The word was thundered. Payton didn't realize the extent of anger he'd flavored it with until the entire table of revelers swayed back from him toward the wall at the other side.

"The bairn . . . is na' his?"

The earl was the only man brave enough to say anything.

The high tone of his voice acted like a needle put to a bladder puffed with air, as the tension rapidly deflated into chortling men and more calls for ale.

"She carries *my* son," Payton announced.

"On whose word?" the earl asked, lifting a joint of meat and starting to pick away at it. "The Kilchurning had possession of her at the time of conception."

"Mine," Payton replied. He was starting to finger the sword at his right hip, massaging the design with the pressure of his fingers.

"And hers," Redmond inserted. Payton flashed him a glance.

"Is she the trustworthy sort? Or would she say what the man holding her longs to hear?"

Payton moved his left hand to the scar on his forehead subconsciously, rubbing at the spot until it started to heat up.

"You ken . . . when you rosy up that way, the Dunn-Fadden crest at your brow is even more purplish. Look."

It was Alan again. Standing and swaying and pointing, and making everyone else look.

"You have a Dunn-Fadden crest in your temple? What a peculiar idea. And unique. Did it hurt?" the earl asked.

Every beat of his heart was making it hurt. Payton cursed the moistness in his eyes, making the tapestry-covered walls a blur of color, even as he blinked rapidly to change it back. Each inhalation felt like it burned, and then when he let the air out, it burned more. Kilchurning was not getting the castle. Payton would handle the issue of the bairn in good time, but Kilchurning was not getting Payton's castle.

The lie he'd harbored for two years and thought forgotten, shifted in the pit of his belly, reminding him of its presence . . . and its power. Payton locked his jaw and glared at all of them.

"The wife is verra trustworthy." Redmond spoke up from his end of the table, rising to his feet as he did so, and keeping his eyes directly on Payton. "I would stake my life on it. And do so. Now. Right now."

The earl slapped his hands together and rubbed them with vicious-looking glee. "This is working toward a verra entertaining season. I will tell the wife as soon as she arrives to make arrangements to move to Edinburgh Castle."

"You're within sight of the castle. Why move there?" someone asked.

"I canna' keep abreast of all the workings of The Stewart from here. 'Tis why he placed me here in the first place. He dinna' wish one of his father's by-blows any closer to the throne."

"You're a Stewart bastard, too?"

Alan really needed someone to put a hand on him. Redmond must have decided it at the same moment Payton thought it, as his hand came down on the lad's shoulder, and forced him back onto the bench with an ungentle move.

"Of course I am, lad. We're scattered all through the Highlands. Hard to keep track of each other, but it does give me rights to visit the castle, force the hospitality, and await this new event."

"What . . . event?"

"The birth of this bairn! 'Twill be the deciding factor . . . nae?"

Payton swallowed around a knot in his throat so large and tight that he had to rub at his throat to make it work.

"Well? Dunn-Fadden clan is well known as siring black-haired infants with blue-cast eyes. Kilchurning is pale. His bairn will be the same. True?"

There was a general chorus of agreement, followed with more tipping of tankards. Payton turned back to the viewing of the tapestries, although he wasn't truly looking. He was absorbing the newest curve to his life, reliving the moment this same morn when she'd told him of the bairn's movement, and cursing the agony that seemed to emanate from his chest to spear through every limb he had.

He was blinking rapidly again, and focused on controlling any shudder of his frame, in the event anyone noticed. And then Redmond joined him, looking at him with his normal emotionless stance, and that made it harder to control.

"Come. Walk with me," he said.

He didn't wait for an answer, and Payton shuffled out after him, holding a thumb and forefinger to his eyes once they'd reached a hall, and pulling in shuddering breath after shuddering breath.

"Payton," the man began.

Payton put his free hand out. He couldn't speak. Not until he had this accursed weakness handled.

"Payton," Redmond spoke again, stepping a bit closer and lowering his voice. "Dinna' let the workings of an auld fool do this. 'Tis your bairn."

"How do you ken?"

Payton was failing. The shudders were happening, and he couldn't prevent the wavering of his knees, and then his thighs, and he was in luck there wasn't anything between him and a wall as he sagged against it.

"She told me so."

Payton huffed a disgusted amusement sound. It disguised the sob.

"All about you is jealousy and greed, and avarice, and hate, and falsehood. You knew nothing of real . . . until that lass."

"But . . . it is na' . . . real!"

Payton had totally failed then, as the last word showed the depth of his grief and he had no choice but to stand there and shake with the sobs. Redmond shoved a heavily embroidered napkin at him then, pilfered from the table. That showed not only his instinct, but his sure knowledge that Payton would need it. Payton felt even more disgust at himself over it.

"Payton." Redmond tried again, using the same unaffected tone. "I swear to you the lass carries your heir. I swear it."

Payton pulled in a breath that trembled and wiped at his eyes with a vicious gesture.

"You dinna' ken anything."

Redmond sighed. "I've watched the two of you. You may have noted it, you may na'. That lass could na' act as she does, nor have the look she does when she looks at you, if she was living a lie and carrying another man's child. I swear it to you!"

"What . . . look?" Payton asked.

"Have you ever known me to go to the widow's bed willingly?" Redmond asked.

Payton pulled himself from the wall and gave Redmond a level look. "You canna' be serious," he asked.

"Do I na' look serious?"

"Can you na' just tell me what I asked? Must you turn it into a lesson?"

Redmond's lips lifted slightly. "A lesson," he repeated. "I fancy that. And agree. I must."

"I hate it when you do this."

"I know. So does she."

"So does she . . . what?" Payton asked.

"Hate it when I do this. So answer. Have you ever known me to visit the widow's bed willingly? As I did last eve?"

Payton thought for a moment, and then shook his head.

"And you dinna' question it?"

Payton smiled fractionally before shaking his head. "My mind . . . was on other things," he answered.

Redmond's smile got a little larger, and lifted both sides of his mouth. Then he sobered. "I went because it felt right. And just. I still feel it is so."

"You pleasured the widow, who has a reputation for taking a man and leaving a mouse . . . and now you call it right and just? I dinna' see where this is heading, Redmond. I truly don't."

"Humor me," Redmond replied.

"Verra well. Why did you go to the widow's chamber last night . . . without hesitation?"

"Because when I see you and the wife together . . . it moved everything in my thinking. I swear it to you. That little lass has pulled at my heart and opened my eyes. That lass of yours has a heart as large as heaven and a soul as pure as snow. And she *is* real, Payton. All of her. I went so your wife would be protected from all that is cheap and tawdry and evil. And that is why I stake my life on the bairn being yours now. Nae woman that pure in spirit could harbor such a lie as Kilchurning's seed within her. It would show. When she's with you . . . *it would show*. Do you understand what I speak of?"

Payton had fresh tears in his eyes and had to blink them away. Then he was sniffing away more evidence of his lack of control. And that made him sheepish, and shy-feeling. Even around the man he most trusted. Then, he nodded.

"Then, doona' let the intrigues of some auld fools and a jealous, vindictive monarch change anything!"

"I will na'," Payton answered as solemnly as Redmond was speaking.

"You vow it?"

Payton nodded. "Aye."

"Good. You may na' understand the true value of what you and that lass have. The only ones who do . . . are those who have missed out on it."

"What?"

"She loves you. Vastly. As much as you love her."

Payton straightened, stuck his chest out and curled his hands into fists. "I doona' love her," he said.

Redmond hooted, which was so rare that Payton stared.

"Lie to the others. But na' to yourself. I already told you.

'Tis apparent to all those who go about this loveless existence, thinking they ken what is real and what is na'. Trust me. You love her. And it is as vast as her love for you. You doona' have to admit it, but that does na' make it change. That is why I stake my life on it, and still do. The lass is yours. The bairn is, also. And you are the most lucky man alive, I think."

Payton blew his nose into the napkin. And then looked back at his man.

"I should find the laver and wash my face in it," he said, finally. "I saw one in the upper hall. I'll return. A-fore the ladies join us."

"That would be a fair assumption," Redmond replied. "And, My Laird? I would na' wish this time mentioned."

Payton looked at him with horror. "You think I would?" he replied.

"Good. We are agreed."

The man nodded, turned on his heel and went back to the great hall. Payton turned toward a staircase and was running them, strength and vigor pounding through his veins with every step.

Chapter 19

Dallis followed the music strummed with an unsteady hand and accompanied by a voice that clearly had musical talent, if there weren't so many hiccups taking place throughout the words. Lady Dunrobin had gone down earlier, claiming an ache in her head wrought from trying to see detail for as long as she had. Lady Evelyn had accompanied her. Dallis had no need of sustenance after the enormous feast they'd brought to the solar, not once but twice more, as four ladies clever with their needles had worked and trimmed and altered a gown to not only fit her, but to present her.

Present her, it did. Dallis had never worn anything as becoming. It made last eve's effort at Ballilol Castle look crude, lewd, and poor. The ladies had spared no words on how disgusting they found her gray underdress. Lady Dunrobin had gone on at length how she'd seen better clothing worn by the poverty-stricken beggars at her back gate, waiting for the old trenchers to be distributed as their lone meal.

Dallis had blushed uneasily at that, and silently thanked the fates that they wouldn't ever see the overdress, with the indecent opening. Her attire now was nothing less than ladylike. Elegant. Demure. Graceful. Refined. All of which made her feel that way.

The rustle of satin accompanied every step, reminding her of the underdress's material, although that wasn't the first layer she'd donned. The chemise they'd given her was of the finest lawn imaginable, sheer to the point of transparency, yet still able to hold minuscule stitches adorning it with thistles, and puckering the bodice for support. Her underdress of white had the same pattern of stitches, made in the same shade of white, only seen when they caught the light from the sleeves that had been tied on.

And her bliant was another work of art. Embroidered throughout the bodice and trailing to the hem in several winding places with more stems of thistles, sewn with silver thread, on a background so blue it was akin to gazing into a loch on a clear sunny day. Lady Dunrobin had told them all it was silk from the Orient, and added that her husband traded for all her fabrics and threads and notions, just to assure his wife's happiness.

And everyone had smiled, and sighed.

Dallis's hair was left loose tonight, but the scented oils they'd rinsed through it during her bath had guaranteed a shine and texture to it that beckoned a touch. Lady Dunrobin had brought out ropes of little tiny colored stones, that twinkled when they caught the light, and someone had the idea of lacing them throughout Dallis's tresses. And so they were. Catching the light whenever the sheer white of her headdress veil allowed it.

She had a silver girdle at her hips, fastened low and left that way, since she had such a small waist it would have necessitated removing links to fit it properly, aside from which no one wanted to harm the bairn. She'd declined wearing any further jewels that belonged to her hostess. It hadn't stopped the woman. She'd given orders for more gowns and underthings created, adorned throughout with stones and gilded threads. Then she'd dispatched the seamstresses to work on their assignments. Throughout the night, if need be.

There was a clansman standing at the entrance to the great hall. Dallis smiled shyly up at him. It appeared to be Seth-the-Silent. He lifted a hand to show his mission in escorting her. Dallis ducked her head and accepted it, lying her hand atop his outstretched one.

Then they entered the great hall.

There was dining happening still, as the tables clearly showed, and drinking. More than one man appeared to be without ability to stand, and so was reclining on benches or the floor. The minstrel was still singing and playing, and keeping a good enough melody that there was dancing about him. Then she saw Payton, rising from behind the table, and Dallis didn't see anything beyond that.

He didn't bother with stairs. He turned and disappeared from view as he must have jumped down to the common floor and she lost sight of him before he reappeared on the right end, moving through people, some of whom reached out toward him, intent on waylaying him. He didn't even break stride. Everyone else might as well be invisible. All his followers. Everyone.

When he was within a body-length in front of her, he stopped, pulling in great breaths that expanded his chest and made the doublet he wore strain at the fastening before he exhaled it.

"Dallis . . . I. . . ." He licked at his lips, and his eyes actually looked away from her, before returning.

"My Laird Dunn-Fadden." She curtsied, watching the gown billow beside her as the material shuffled through the dried rushes on their floor, before lifting her eyes again to him.

"I . . ." His voice stopped again, and he cleared his throat. Then, he looked away from her again.

Dallis moved the four steps to him, pulling Seth with her.

"Payton?" she whispered.

His eyes met hers for a moment, moved away as if burnt, and returned to lock glances with her for long, heart-pounding moments, and then he moved his gaze over her head. Pulled in some more large breaths. And if Redmond hadn't come from around him, Dallis didn't know what else she was supposed to do.

"Allow me to see the both of you back to the dais. Seth, bring the wife. Payton. Follow me. We'll be trampled if you stay here longer."

It looked to be true, since the crowd about them had increased tenfold in the moments of their greeting, but Redmond and Seth had them to the dais without incident. And then, a page was sent to find the chair since Payton had toppled his from the dais when he'd stood, and someone had actually stolen it for a keepsake. All the time, Redmond was shaking his head and smiling.

"Nae. Na' that one. A short bench. For two. The champion canna' sit in such a flimsy affair. And the wife refuses to sit elsewhere . . . doona' you?" he asked her, and then winked.

She nodded with a questioning look.

"Exactly. Now, go," Redmond waved at the page. "Fetch the bench. And Seth . . . as the lone Honor Guardsman that abstained from My Laird Dunrobin's fine ale this eve, could you fetch a trencher? For two. Sweetmeats only. And grapes. And perhaps those little cakes. Go now!"

A smaller bench was brought, possessing a short railing along the back that was useless for leaning, and placed behind the table. Dallis was seated with the assist of Redmond, and spent a moment arranging her skirts. Payton was still acting odd. He hadn't moved or said anything.

"Payton?" She asked him, looking up at him as she did so.

He dropped, shaking the wooden support with the move, and making Dallis gasp.

"Payton . . . ? What is it?"

He turned his head toward her, caught her glance for a moment before moving it away, and then he reached for her hand and took it to his lips.

"I've na' seen you in correct dress a-fore," he told her fingers.

"You . . . approve?" She couldn't keep the uncertainty from her voice.

He moved his gaze from her fingers to her eyes, and the moment he did so, everything about her silenced. Or perhaps it was the complete stoppage of her heart making it so, before it decided to keep beating. Or maybe it was the way his eyes intensified, until they lumined the glow of candles back at her.

"There are nae words for how beauteous you are, Wife. None that my tongue can find without stumble. I will have to settle for 'aye'. I approve." And then he moved a kiss to the tops of her fingers, and made everything in the room start up again.

"I doona' recollect why, but Seth is here, annoying me. With a trencher for you. My Laird? Lady?"

Redmond placed a hard bread plate onto the table before them, and then he retreated again. Beyond a quick glance Dallis didn't even look at it before returning her attention to the man at her side. Payton didn't even glance at it.

"I have something for you," he told her.

"You do?"

"Aye. But I should have given it earlier." He looked up and out at the swell of humanity all about them, and grimaced. "'Tis too crowded here. I'll wait."

"Payton!" She said the name with an exclamation of frustration.

He responded with a smile, and a movement of his fingers across her knuckles on the hand he still hadn't relinquished.

"Aye?"

Dallis couldn't hold his gaze! It was sending trills throughout her upper body to center at her breast tips, making the chemise seem bulky and heavy against her skin. It was also sending shooting darts through her spine and into her scalp, and making everything an itch of irritation, a prick of sensation behind her eyelids, and an urge to burst into song. She moved away before something on her reacted, and caught Redmond's eye again.

His eyebrows lifted.

"Seth? Perhaps the wife would find wine a bit more pleasing to her palate. Laird Dunrobin does have a fine winter garden, and grapes. Everywhere on one wall are vines. And the wines he has created?" He kissed his fingers. "Truly magnificent."

Dallis didn't look to see if Seth had gone on the errand or not. Her thoughts weren't focusing, and her entire being seemed to be pulled by the man sitting right beside her. He shifted, moved a kilt-wrapped thigh closer to her, making the bench sway slightly, and sending heat from where he touched. Dallis dropped her eyes, lit on his lap where the kilt should have been draping between his legs, but instead it looked uncomfortable enough he had to shove his sporran to the side with his free hand. And that just gave her a reminder of how virile and masculine he was.

Everything rocked inside her, and yet nothing moved.

"Wine? Of course, they'd appreciate two goblets of it. Honestly, Seth. One would think you'd never served the laird and his wife a-fore."

There was a hissing noise to the other side of Redmond when he'd finished, and then two goblets of the proffered liquid were set in front of them, just past the ignored trencher.

Dallis shifted to look at the liquid, darkening the sparkled facets of the drinking vessel whenever the candlelight flickers caught it, and then moved her gaze back to Payton. It wasn't by choice. But she felt the pull of it, and could no longer resist.

"You hunger?" he asked, in such a soft tone, she had to tip toward him to hear it.

She shook her head.

"Thirst?" he asked.

She shook her head again.

"Well, I do. And 'tis na' for food and wine." And then before her eyes, he blushed.

Dallis didn't dare blink for fear anything changed, as two spots of color touched the tops of his cheeks and then faded. He'd turned his head aside, as if to hide it, but wasn't successful. She couldn't prevent the swell of joy within her anymore than she could prevent the smile that broached the tip of the emotion. He was acting like a man in love! And the moment she thought it, she couldn't contain it. It was her turn to blush and turn aside.

"Well . . . what can I tempt them with next? We can try a bit of the blood pudding. Go, Seth. Fetch a bowl, and mind it's the right temperature." Redmond's voice came as a disembodied sound, buzzing over the top of the other noises: the minstrel's drunken singing and playing, the laughter and talk of a large swell of people in a warm enclosed space, the sound of snoring, and dogs whining and barking as they waited the bones and hand-outs from the tables above.

And over all that she could swear she could hear every single one of Payton Dunn-Fadden's breaths from beside her. Dallis tipped her head toward him again, and wasn't surprised to see the steady regard he'd decided to bestow upon her, although her entire form lurched with the reaction of getting it.

He smiled slightly, putting a crease to one side of his mouth, and then he nodded.

"Blood pudding? Finally? I truly doubt they'll find that tempting, Seth. Especially now."

Dallis glanced at the table in front of them, where a large bowl of black-looking jellied confection was just getting set, and wobbling slightly with the motion of it. Then, she returned to Payton.

"Would you be caring to dance?" he asked, cocking a head slightly toward the floor.

"I—"

"Dance? Nae. I canna' allow it." It was Redmond replying.

Dallis watched the confusion take over Payton's features, and then he turned to where Redmond was standing, adjusting the grapes and other items on the trencher platter as if to make them more appetizing.

"Redmond?" Payton asked.

The man stopped and lifted both hands. "And Seth. Who do you think is orchestrating this courtship of yours?"

"Court . . . ship?" Payton stumbled over the word and Dallis ducked her head.

"Just because you pass over something, does na' mean it has no worth. I said courtship and I meant courtship. And while dancing would be a perfect accompaniment to your endeavor, I really must balk at this point."

"I dinna' ask it of you."

Payton grumbled it, Dallis giggled, and there was more hissing sound as Seth appeared to also have something to say.

Redmond's face went even more expressionless. "Have pity, My Laird. Your men have mostly over-imbibed and are useless. Save for Seth and me, you have none to guard you. And your lady. Should you take the dance floor, we'll have a riot, and nae way to stop it."

"Oh." Payton said it, but it could have been Dallis as easily. "But what if I long to dance?"

"I can attempt a serenade in your chamber. I've na' much talent but I can strum a decent enough tune for you."

Payton wasn't amused. It sounded in his reply. "What if I want to dance here? I long to be seen with my wife, na' constantly hide her away!"

"You're victim to your fame, Payton. As are we. Most of the time."

"Well, what do you suggest then, Redmond?"

"You have done remarkably well for yourself. I will send Seth for a bit of mulled, spiced jellies. I haven't decided how, but they have used honey to glaze bits of tallow, and then rolled them in spices. Verra tasty."

"I'm na' interested," Payton replied.

"Then what are you interested in?" Redmond put his hands on his hips, and she could see Seth had the exact same pose behind him.

"I just want to be alone."

"Payton Dunn-Fadden!" Redmond exclaimed, and behind him Seth was making grunting, chirping sounds.

"*With* the wife! Jesu, Mary, and Joseph! You think me dense?"

Payton announced it and stood at the same time. Since he'd never relinquished her hand, Dallis either had to let it rise with him, or stand at his side. She stood, and got clasped to him with an arm that trembled slightly.

"Well. There are moments—"

"Move."

Payton interrupted him. He didn't turn fully. He'd have to release his hold on her to do so. He chose instead to step sideways, meeting Redmond the moment he shifted.

"'Twas na' a question? Well, you need cast your words better if you wish them answered correctly. You wish a serenade, then?"

"Can you na' move? I wish to be in my chamber . . . with my wife. And I doona' wish anyone else there! No one." His head had lowered, as had his voice. It looked like a challenge. Those watching them must have had the same thought, for they were starting to get noticed. The floor in front of the dais thickened with Payton's followers.

Redmond backed. Seth didn't at first. He was gesturing at all the items he'd procured for them that were still on the table.

"Well, of course they're leaving. They are na' hungered. What fool would think that? Hmm? Perhaps you should think a-fore doing my bidding. You ever consider that?

Doona' raise your hands. We need see our laird and his lady to their chamber. Assist me with it. And cease that. I canna' believe I am having an argument with a silent man!"

"I can," Payton replied.

The chambers assigned to Payton were dark with the volume of rock, while only his banked fire lit the interior. It didn't stay that way long, as another clansman she ignored rose from a chair and started poking at the fire.

"Visitors?" Redmond asked.

"A few," the man replied. It sounded like Dugan.

"There are three of us tonight. Three hour shifts. Outside."

"Forgive me," Payton said. "I never considered what this fame of mine costs the rest of you."

"Why should you? As your Honor Guard, we serve. Loss of sleep is nae great issue."

"I still—"

"Payton," Redmond interrupted.

"What?"

"There are large bonuses attached to being your Honor Guard. Trust me. The lasses doona' all crave you. Seth? Get us from this chamber a-fore I say anything more. And you have first watch. What? Doona' argue with me again! Of course I'll get you the foodstuffs. Why dinna' you think of that when we were leaving. That would have been . . ."

Redmond was still remonstrating the silent clansman as he pulled the door shut behind them. Dallis only knew that from the loss of his voice and the light from the torch-lit hall. And then there was just her and Payton, and the strength of her heartbeat against his.

From a berth in his arms, she heard it easily, and snuggled even farther into the space below his chin.

"Dallis?" he asked. The name rumbled through her nose at his throat.

"Hmm?" She moved slightly, willing to look at him while he spoke, but deciding it was too heavenly to stay where she was, encapsulated within his arms, where it was safe, warm, and vastly blissful.

"This fame . . . of mine. 'Twill na' always be so."

"I ken as much."

She hadn't asked to be in his arms. He hadn't given her time. The moment they reached the lower hall just outside the great room, leaving through the minstrel gallery as was their usual, he'd swooped her up. She didn't bother questioning it. She knew. He wasn't willing to alter the pace to her smaller steps. Redmond had approved the move, too, and received Payton's curse for his effort.

"You do?" Payton asked.

Dallis wasn't given the choice of staying against his neck, since he pulled back, and lowered his head in order to see her.

"Nae man can grasp such fame forever. There will come a champion to best you. One with more brawn, and more skill . . . or more youth. And after that, there will be another. And after that, another."

"More brawn?" he asked, lifting one eyebrow.

"Did I say that?" Dallis teased, lifting her hand to brush a stray black lock of hair from blocking her view of him. "I must be crazed."

"And was there a claim of more skill, as well?"

"Falsehoods. All of them," she replied.

"Falsehoods?"

"I find all manner of weakness takes my tongue . . . and makes me say . . . words I dinna' think through first. 'Tis na' my fault, though."

She was lifting toward him, using the arm she had looped about his neck to bring his head down, as well as her legs against his forearms to shift up, and then she put her tongue out, touched a scratchy bit of chin, and licked her way to his lower lip, stopping there as the man holding her trembled in place.

"Nae?" he asked, punishing her with the breath of air from his lips to hers.

"I canna' think when I'm with you, Dunn-Fadden. I nae longer have a will or wits."

"Truly?"

"Truly . . . I—"

She almost slipped and said it. *I love you.* Dallis stopped, finding her wits somewhere in her body to keep from damning herself with her own tongue. Then she was shuddering with the ice-cold feeling that seemed to invade everywhere.

"I . . . ?" he prompted.

"I . . . recollect that you said . . . you had something for me." The words limped out, sounding trite and stupid, and awkward.

Payton didn't seem to note any of that, as he failed to move his mouth the entire time she'd been speaking, and instead, started plying her lips apart with his own.

"Aye, love. I do have something . . . for you."

It was said between kisses that drained her will further and scattered more of her wits. Dallis let them go easily, blending her moan of hunger with what had to be his. She was startled to be set on the floor, attempting to find stability with legs that felt as strong as the blood pudding had looked to be, and finding it truly chilled in the chamber when she wasn't locked in his arms.

She crossed her arms about herself, and rocked in place, and fought the tingle of tears that stung at her eyes.

"Ah . . . Dallis, love. Doona' look to me that way. I will na' be able to find it."

He was fishing about in his sporran with a hand, without looking. He hadn't relinquished her gaze, and didn't appear to want to, until he was forced to peer down at what he was doing.

"There!"

He stepped closer, sending waves of warmth radiating from the nearness, and he was holding something out to her. Something small. Sparkly. Round.

She moved her eyes back to his.

"'Tis the smallest one I own. A ruby. I had it made smaller. For you."

Dallis was shaking, and the hand she held out to him showed every bit of it. Payton suffered the same, as the way he fumbled with her new ring indicated.

"Doona' take this one off."

"I will na'," she said.

"Na' even to wash."

She nodded.

"I want the world to ken that you belong to me. Only me. Ever-more."

She nodded again. And lost out to the tears that had hovered at her lower lids before tipping out without her blink to assist them. The ring fit snugly and perfectly, and had a dark red stone in the center of it that reflected back at her.

"You vow it?" he asked, stepping close enough he blocked the light.

"Aye," she whispered.

"Then . . . say it," he commanded.

Dallis looked up at him, caught the wonder before she burst with it, and blinked more tears into existence.

"I . . . love you, Payton Dunn-Fadden," she replied.

His yell was heard clear out into the hall. Then they had to deal with Seth, carrying a trencher of food, and behind him Redmond, as the door shoved open so hard, it rebounded from the wall. Dallis hadn't had time to gasp. She was hugged against Payton with one arm, getting shoved toward the back of him, while his other had already unsheathed his sword.

"You might consider bolting your door," Redmond informed them. And then he sighed hugely, turned, and pulled Seth back out into the hall with him.

Chapter 20

They entered the Royal Mile two days later. Dallis nodded and waved from a seat atop a white horse, the shade replicating the white cloak she was wearing, covering over the green and black bliant that showed her clan allegiance. Payton was right in front of her, mounted on Orion, who'd been brushed and plucked and groomed with braids in his mane and tail, and seemed to know that it was all for this show, because he walked with a head held high and large head nods to the crowd as well.

And there was Payton.

As the heir to the Dunn-Fadden clan, he was dressed in full Dunn-Fadden chieftain attire in a *feile-breacan* of green, black, and white plaid, which were awe inspiring by themselves. But, as King's Champion, he also wore the solid silver champion belt, and silver or gold adorned everything else they could put metal to. Payton sparkled and shone every time he waved, or stood in the stirrups or turned about to check her. And the crowd lining the streets, tossing ribbons, and leaning from balconies or rooftops appreciated every bit of it.

Dallis wasn't worried. Canongate Castle had been filling with Dunn-Fadden clan over the two days, and the Dunrobin earl had seen to it that they were mounted and rode with more than a fifty of his own clan, all mounted and accompanying them, riding four abreast on either side of Payton and his Honor Guard, while a vast retinue of them led the way, parting the throngs with their horses, if the bagpipes, drums, and warnings weren't sufficient.

It was stunning and meant to be so. It was also time consuming. Walking a horse a distance one sixth of a league should have been done without any forethought and no need to sustenance. This trek, with Payton stopping often to speak with a grouping at the side, or slowing to wave at the lasses who were pouring from balconies, and from their blouses, which she still wasn't used to, took more than three hours to accomplish. Dallis was beginning to think she should have brought one of the breakfast breads from Dunrobin's table with her. Or she could always ask one of the men beside her to pass in one of the muffins, rolls, or hard biscuits that were being held out to them as they passed the bake shops.

Through it all, the shape of Edinburgh Castle, looming high atop the mountain overshadowed and clouded, and darkened. Always muted. Always there. As if overseeing and controlling everything beneath it.

The ground changed, beginning the ascent. The massive, black shadow quality of the castle started such a deep unease within her, that it chilled her. Dallis gathered her fur-lined cloak closer, and frowned a bit at the pieces of misted freeze hanging about in the air as if opaque fingers had to be pushed aside to get through.

She knew it was fanciful, shook herself mentally, lowered her chin and focused on Payton's back while they climbed. The tree cover thinned, and they went beneath a gate. A higher climb, and then another gate. And then a third. Each with a portcullis lifted, bagpipers playing, and men-at-arms standing at attention. They still fit, nine across, although there was no need. Payton's followers had dropped away. They either couldn't take time from their chores, or weren't allowed inside the castle itself. Dallis didn't know which and had no one to ask. So she surmised.

They were halted somewhere in the front of them, in the shadow of walls so high, they blocked what morning light was available. Dallis looked up, gazing with awe at the might and strength, and impregnability of Scotland's majesty, and shivered worse.

"Payton Alexander Dunn-Fadden! Heir to Clan Dunn-Fadden and current champion of the list. Granted such title through valiant service to the crown! Dismount and show yourself! At the king's command!"

The entire greeting was repeated all along the walkway above them, interlacing and overriding the telling as it went. And coming from throats that must have been chosen for their projecting ability.

Payton was dismounting, making a clank from all the metallic objects in his accouterment, and he walked the short distance over to her to assist her to the ground. His smile was secure and comforting. As was the kiss he pressed to her forehead, when she was on the ground and pulled into him with a hand behind her head.

"Doona' fear, Dallis, love," he whispered.

"I canna' help it."

"'Tis our destiny we go to meet. I'll na' let some wizened, stunted, cock-nibbed, son-of-a-banshee steal it from us. You ken?"

"You canna' say such things of the king!" She was horrified. It sounded in her voice.

Payton stood straight, and let her free. She watched as he adjusted the diamond-bedecked brooch holding his kilt band, his heavy championship belt, rearranged the dirks inserted throughout it, and ended with settling his sporran in front of his groin. Then he looked over at her and grinned.

"I refer to Kilchurning. Jesu'." He held out his hand. "Come. You worry for nae reason. The king is a fair man. Usually."

She followed him as he joined a mass of clansmen and king's men, their boots echoing from long halls of floors and lofty ceilings in the halls, until she lost all sense of direction. And distance. And then they were stopped again.

"The king commands the champion attend to him! In private. He may bring four clansmen with him. And his wife!"

The men outside shouting orders and edicts must have earned that duty because they lacked the acoustic quality of the man blocking their further movement. As she got close, Dallis saw he was standing on a three-step block, giving him room to better project his voice above any crowd. He must have massive respect for Payton, she decided, since he backed to the edge of his block as Dunn-Fadden walked through the opening the others about them had made, and nearly tumbled off the back of it.

"Redmond. Seth. Martin. Dugan."

He listed the clansmen when he got there, but it looked unnecessary. Those were the exact men and in the exact placement that were at his heels.

The man on the block must have thought that Payton's words insufficient, since he lifted his chin and repeated them. Standing directly in front of him, she could tell that while he did have a massive voice, his shouting upward reached the echoing capacity in the room, as well. Dallis smirked slightly. It looked an excellent way to keep one's livelihood.

"What mood, MacIlroy?" Payton leaned a bit toward their announcer to whisper it.

The man gulped. "Nae good," he answered.

"Current mistress?" Payton continued.

"Nae. Bad spirits last night."

"Hung-over, is he?"

The announcer looked uncomfortable and then tipped his chin again. Dallis saw the reason as a thud sounded and then two men-at-arms pushed the doors outward, sending light from the old throne room into the antechamber. Then MacIlroy was announcing Payton, Dallis as a Caruth Dunn-Fadden, and then the accompanying clansmen.

Then there was a yell coming from Payton, followed by everyone pulling swords and claymores and skeans, and Dallis felt the pressure as Payton shoved a dirk into her hand.

"Kilchurning!"

The quintet of men facing them, from an area to the left of the king, were also drawing swords and claymores, making such a sound of grunting and metal, nobody heard her gasp.

They were halted by a shrill bagpipe blast, and then yet another fellow with a great set of lungs was shouting.

"Cease! You are in the presence of His Majesty, King James! You are to cease this or face imprisonment!"

"Only if he's na' dead!" Payton replied.

"Silence!"

"My Laird . . . Dunn-Fadden. Here. Finally. My . . . champion."

The voice was coming from the throne, but it wasn't possible to see him through the bodies that had stepped in front of her and blocked her.

"He holds my castle. I want his blood," Payton replied.

"Not true. According to Laird Kilchurning here, your sire Alexander Dunn-Fadden holds the castle. At the moment. Now, sheath your blades. All of you. And act like the civilized men we are."

The shuffle of boots and clang of weapons showed that his command was being followed.

"Now. Show me the wife."

"Why?" Payton asked.

"Because I say so," the voice from the throne said.

Payton sighed, lifting his back in front of her. Then, he was turning sideways and giving her his hand for an escort.

"Without you, Dunn-Fadden."

Payton's jaw looked locked. He had his lids lowered and

his chin as well. Dallis was grateful she wasn't getting the look he was sending toward the throne.

"Now." The monarch repeated.

Her husband moved back, to allow her to step through the opening. Dallis listened to the satin as it slid along her legs, and forced the chill feeling of the slick material from her. When she was within a circle shape, splied with carved wood into the floor beneath her, she curtsied, going nearly to the ground in deference. Then she rose and lifted her head.

"My Lady."

The man stepping down from the throne was wearing more jewels than necessary, including a huge cross about his neck and massive crown atop his head. He wasn't exactly handsome, although he was definitely a presence, as the shivers careening over her shoulders warned her. His beard was red-tipped, he had a purplish red birthmark scoring one side of his face, a narrow nose, and very high pointed heels on his shoes. Even with that, he was her exact height.

Dallis caught the giggle before she made it, and immediately forced her back to bend, slouching to lose height. Then she added a bend in her knees, that he wouldn't spot through the skirts and cloaking. She knew it was the correct move when he reached her, lifted her hand, and then stepped back slightly, looking her up and down, evaluating the exquisite attire she wore and probably the cost, as well as the fact she was shorter than he by a hand-span in height.

"Charming. She's truly . . . charming."

"She's wed," Payton replied from his side of the room. King James looked over at him, releasing her from his scrutiny.

"Please, my Laird Dunn-Fadden. Grant me a moment. I ken very well that she's wed. To you. And I already have a favorite." He turned back to Dallis. "Come, Lady Dunn-Fadden. Sit with me. We need to be apart from men and their lusts for power. 'Tis too taxing so early in the day. You agree?"

She was fortunate he led the way, because she lost her knee scrunch and back slouch. If he'd turned he would have seen it. Dallis didn't know what he'd do then.

She hurriedly slid into a seat at his right side, lower than his, and not as elaborate as the one on the other side of him. She closed her eyes in silent thanksgiving that he hadn't put her in the queen's throne. Her heart wasn't ready for that test of how rapidly it could beat.

"Now. We can discuss at length why I have brought you here."

"Me?" Dallis asked.

He lifted her hand to his lips. She kept it loose and flexible by a sheer act of will. It didn't sound like Payton was having the same reaction, if the sounds coming from that side of the room were accurate.

The king waved with his other hand, and metal sounds grew. Dallis forced herself to concentrate on the man beside her and nothing else, but it started sweat beads all along her hairline.

"I could have had you brought before me in chains, Laird Dunn-Fadden." King James's threat was worse since there wasn't any sound of a warning to the words. Dallis gulped away the moisture in her mouth and smiled shakily. He released her hand and swiveled back to look over the two clans assembled before them.

Payton had two men on either side of him, each with a lance spearing the space in front of him, the blades facing each other and crossed for more effect.

"Now . . . we can talk," the Stewart announced.

Nobody answered. He flipped at the lace on one sleeve and looked out at the men again.

"My Laird Kilchurning sent a messenger to me a sennight past. With an odd tale. Of battle and siege, and murder. You all know I frown on that."

He encompassed the room with his look. Dallis relaxed slightly as he didn't direct all of that warning toward Payton.

"It was a surprise. I had already decreed that the Caruth Castle and the heiress and all the holdings were yours, Laird Dunn-Fadden. It makes me very angered to find that in dispute."

Dallis watched as the Kilchurning clan appeared to be frowning as they shifted about, fidgeting with their weaponry.

"I gave the holdings to the man who'd earned them, and then demonstrated to me and everyone in the land why. They belong to my champion. Payton Dunn-Fadden."

The lances in front of Payton tipped slightly at the approval in the king's voice. Kilchurning looked very uncomfortable, as his face went red.

"But the news Kilchurning brought me . . . I can't overlook. You do understand? Or have you not heard?"

Dallis watched the men below them, and all had the same expression: stern. She must be the lone one questioning it, but bit her tongue to hold back any such words.

"You know the law. And my edict was law. The keep, the lands, and all the holdings go with the heiress. And I cannot change it at this juncture."

"Fair enough," Payton replied.

"Well, how can I give over the keep, lands, and holdings to you, if she is carrying Kilchurning's bastard?"

"He told you . . . *what?*" Dallis couldn't help it. She blurted it out, her mouth went open with shock, and the last word was almost a scream.

"Now, my dear. Calm yourself."

"Calm—! But . . . he lies! It's a lie. I swear to you—" she began.

"He says the same of you."

"What? He says I lie? How would he ken? He's na' met me but twice!"

The king chuckled. "Well, he must have been very intimate on short acquaintance then."

"He's never touched me!" Dallis's voice shook. She was so angry, nothing else mattered. "Never. I swear it!"

"And he swears the same. Don't you, My Laird Kilchurning?"

Dallis turned with the monarch and watched him nod. Her mouth went into a snarl and she turned back to the king.

"But I can prove it. My aunt was with me. Every moment in my tower. She would ken his lie!"

"He has already told me of Lady Evelyn Caruth. And her leanings. I'm afraid, my dear, that she is also branded a liar in this mess."

"But . . . it's na' true."

She was close to sobbing now. And she could hear the reaction on the floor as the lances slapped against each other in warning. Dallis clenched her hands together and sucked for breath. She had to calm! She had to find the state she'd been taught of, the one that makes it possible to absorb tremendous suffering and shock without complaint. She had to! She didn't know what Payton might do, otherwise, she didn't know what the diminutive king was capable of, and she was afraid to see it.

"What . . . are you going to do?" she asked finally, in a voice that was steady-sounding and sharp.

The king pulled back into his chair and regarded her. "Well, her antecedents are not in question here. She is definitely a Caruth. No other clan has their stoicism."

"Well?" she asked again.

His eyes narrowed at her. "Firstly, I'm going to fine My Laird Kilchurning for disobeying my edict in the first place. He will find this fine onerous. Especially when I add it to the bill he will incur by my hospitality."

"I'm na' staying here!"

The king looked over at Kilchurning. "I have a dungeon

for those that displease me. And if they displease me enough, I have them executed," he said.

Dallis's heart beat a staccato rhythm in her breast, and she concentrated on modulating it . . . calming it. Just then the babe moved, sending the tingle through her womb and making everything crystal clear and focused.

"I was telling the Lady Dunn-Fadden my plans. I am also going to have to fine my champion. For the same transgress. I will also be adding in the cost to house that bastard, Dunrobin. And his household."

"For how long?" Payton asked.

The king sighed heavily, and turned from her to the floor again.

"I am trying to discourse with the lady here. If I have much more interference, I'll be issuing other orders. Is this understood? Both of you?"

Payton nodded. After a moment, Kilchurning did also.

The king turned back to her, put a hand to his forehead and squeezed it with ungentle fingers.

"I was just preparing to inform her ladyship that my hospitality will match hers. As long as she carries this child. That is the length of her stay."

"Over four . . . months?" Dallis whispered.

"I need to see if you birth a Dunn-Fadden or Kilchurning. The bairn's heritage, my dear, cannot lie. So, it is decreed."

"What will happen then?" Dallis asked.

"If it is Dunn-Fadden's bairn, he goes about his way, with his wife and child and his legacy. As I already decreed once a-fore."

"And . . . Kilchurning?" Dallis asked.

"If the child is his, then I'll have to make the castle, and lands, and all holdings over to the child. Not to the sire . . . although he will have control of it, as is usual."

"I meant, what will you do to Kilchurning when his lie is discovered?" Dallis asked, turning a narrow glance over at the man she almost wed.

"My head hurts too much for this."

"Then, allow me to devise the punishment," Dallis replied. "Decree that."

King James removed his hand and looked at her. Then he smiled. He looked genuinely amused. "Agreed," he finally said.

Dallis put all the hatred and malice she felt into the look toward Kilchurning. She had to be satisfied with his lack of color because otherwise he didn't move.

The king stood. There wasn't a breath of anything happening on the floor. He was almost to another door before he turned and then returned to her. "It must be the ache throughout my head. I forgot. One more thing I must make clear. And I need a hold put to my champion, first."

Dallis looked at Payton as men-at-arms seemed to come from everywhere to surround him and his clansmen.

"The lady will be kept in solitude. With my guards about her."

"Nay!" Dallis's throat hurt to scream it, and it actually hurt worse that it was in unison with Payton's cry.

"I canna' guarantee her safety otherwise. And the safety of the bairn. Come with me, Lady Dunn-Fadden. Quickly. A-fore I have to make good on my threats."

Dallis could see the wisdom of that as steel was getting pulled in the area about Clan Dunn-Fadden. She ran to the door, and then stopped.

She called out to him. Waited. Called again. She couldn't see through the tears streaking her face and had to shove an arm across her eyes to blot them away.

Payton had all four of his clansmen holding to him, and several more arms putting up a wall against his progress toward her when he heard her. He ceased struggling, looked across the chamber at her over everyone, and locked eyes.

I love you.

She mouthed it and disappeared through the door.

Chapter 21

"How long has it been? Why are there only six marks? Well? What does the six mean? 'Tis been only six? Why does na' somebody answer me?"

"Because you already ken the answer, Payton. Sit down. You're driving us mad with your pacing about."

"You saying the six is true? That's it, is na' it? Six? We've been here six days . . . and I have na' seen her? Na' once!"

"See? You already knew the answer."

"Curse you, Redmond!" Payton let fly one of his skeans, hitting the shield target they'd set up in their chambers with a thunk of sound.

"And that's what I feel for you, Kilchurning. And that!"

Payton had his skeans depleted, all ten of them, and was grabbing his hand-ax when Redmond stood.

"Now, cease that, Dunn-Fadden. You'll be putting a hole through another tapestry, and we already have to pay a fine for the last one."

"Fines! Fines! I pay a fine for breathing in this accursed rock! Tell me something I doona' ken!"

"Dunrobin is useless as a spy. Thus far."

Payton stopped the cocked motion of the hand-ax and looked across at Redmond. "Spy?" he asked.

"Aye. He tells me he can get word. He's been trying to find her whereabouts. Without success. Thus far."

"Thus far? All have failed at finding her whereabouts, thus far! I am nearly desperate enough to beg."

Redmond sobered. "You want to see her?"

"Aye."

"Maybe . . . speak with her?"

Payton lowered the hand-ax onto his shoulder and welcomed the weight as something tangible . . . not like the dreams he'd been cursed with, and the worries he'd been suffering, and the ache in his heart that nothing cured.

"Aye."

"Then, do as the Stewart requires. Give him battles."

"Nay!" Payton retaliated with a fling of the hand-ax, slamming into the shield they'd set up that was already thick with knife hilts. They all watched as the wood slowly cracked, and then split, sending the unattached half to the floor.

"Why not?"

"I will na' fight for him. I vowed it when he last forced me. And I am keeping it. There is nae glory in it anymore. He can find another champion."

"What . . . if I can get him to have a different kind of battle?"

Payton stopped, with his bow pulled and an arrow set, ready to split the twine holding the upper shield half to the wall. He let the bow string slacken and turned back.

"What . . . other kind is there?"

"First blow, perhaps. Nae pain."

Payton shook his head, and pulled on the bowstring again. "Nae good. I am too quick. You ken it. I'd have a challenger to the ground within moments, and then it would be over. First blow from the sod!" He let the arrow fly, it glanced off the rock after splitting the twine, and everyone dove for the floor until they heard it crash into a corner. Then, the sound of the target falling added in. Payton was on his feet again, dusting at his knees, and looking sheepish.

"Show them, then."

"What?" He looked across at Redmond, who was coming up from beneath a table.

"Give instruction. Show them how you manage to get a man onto the ground and in the defensive stance so quickly and easily."

"You truly take me for the thickest-headed lout, Redmond MacCloud. Why would I show a man I may have to battle against—and who might be Kilchurning clan—how I do that move? Would he na' use it on me?"

He walked over to the ruined target and started pulling his skeans out, with a jerking motion on each one.

"The Stewart will let you see her. One hour a day. At a place of his choosing."

Payton stopped all movement, felt his heart twinge along with it, and then he restarted yanking at knives. "Alone?" he asked.

"I can get him to agree to a companion . . . Lady Evelyn. What say you?"

Payton considered it, waiting until the last skean was removed from the wood, and then pitched it toward the fireplace. "Find us another target, Alan," he ordered his cousin. Alan went sprinting toward the door. Payton looked back at Redmond. "What would I have to do?"

"An exhibition."

"Exhibition?"

"Show of your skills. But not against an opponent."

"Those are my skills," Payton replied. He was shoving skeans into his belt along his waist as he said it.

"We're na' in agreement. Are we, lads?" There were some grunts of agreement. "Look about you. We have nothing left you can attack. We are now sending Alan about to pillage items for you to work your skill against. For six days now.

And you have four months of days still to go. Why na' show this skill to the court . . . and gain rights of visit with them?"

Payton waited four heartbeats to answer. They were speeding up, too, at the same rate his hands were starting to tremble. "Go. Arrange it," he said.

"I canna' get the stitches straight! And I canna' see well enough to try!"

Dallis pulled her hands away from the needlework she was attempting, put her face in her hands, and barely held back the sobs as wave after wave of them rushed through her breast, filling her throat, then her nose, and finally her eyes, making a welling of tears inevitable.

Lady Evelyn handed her another heavily embroidered handkerchief, sighed heavily, and went back to work. Beside her, Lady Dunrobin didn't do more than shuffle to another spot on their joint project.

Dallis was embarrassed by her loss of control from the moment it happened, and that helped dry the tears, while she mopped at her face.

"Forgive me, Aunt Evelyn. Lady Dunrobin. I . . . doona' ken what has come over me."

"'Tis the bairn," Lady Dunrobin said sagely, while she put another stitch in what she was studying from a distance of an inch.

"Nae," Dallis's voice shook but she couldn't help it. "The bairn was why I was sick. This . . . this is different."

"The same thing happened to me when I carried our eldest, Harold. I'd be happily stitching and having a spot of tea, and the next I'd be sobbing. For nae reason."

"I have a reason," Dallis complained.

"Aye. We ken. Your husband."

Both old ladies said it, although one was behind the other,

and then they giggled. Dallis had to smile. And then they were all looking toward the door as someone knocked.

They'd given her two servants for her use. Mary and Bess. Both were rose-cheeked lasses from a goodly family in town. They were also quiet, efficient, and fairly dense. Dallis watched as the door to what felt like a prison cell was reached. And then opened.

"'Tis a message," Mary said, coming into the sun-filled antechamber where the ladies were stitching.

"From the king," Bess added.

"Here." Dallis put out her hand. Both girls looked uncomfortable and unsure.

"Beg pardon, but the message is addressed to Lady Evelyn Caruth."

They were handing it to her on the silver salver it must have been delivered on. As if it were a supreme delicacy. And she supposed it was.

Dallis tried to ignore what was happening. She didn't care if he wrote to every other lady in his castle. If it didn't concern Payton, she didn't want to know.

She rose, walked over to the long window that had real glazed panes in it. The view from her room was uninspiring, but everything was. She was above the curtain wall level, so that put her too high to reach by grappling hook. She appeared to be near the castle herb garden, from the snow-locked stubs of plants in rows that were one wall over. She couldn't see straight down, or how high she was. The walls were too thick, and they were too high.

She could see the sun in the distance, however, trying to peek through the cloud cover. She knew it wouldn't succeed. It hadn't for a full sennight, so far. Scotland's weather was always harsh and unpredictable and wet. This week had proved it.

"His Majesty appears to be relenting a bit, Dallis."

She tilted her head toward her aunt. "How so?"

"He's granting us an audience. At dusk. We are to follow the guardsman that comes for us. Oh, my. Whatever shall I wear?"

Dallis turned back to trying to pick out the horizon from the slivers of sunlight. It didn't matter what she wore. He'd already adjudged her a woman capable of adultery. What did it matter what more he thought of her?

"But . . . if he wants to see you . . . why did he send a message to me?" Aunt Evelyn asked.

"I'm in disgrace, Aunt Evelyn. I should think it obvious."

"As am I. He thinks me just as much a liar as you. I still doona' ken why he'd write—"

"I have the added disgrace of possibly being an adulteress, Aunt Evelyn."

"Possibly. Hmm . . . but is na' that a bit like back-wash? You know . . . he fornicates with adulteresses daily. I still doona' understand why . . ."

Lady Dunrobin looked up from the tapestry with her watery-blue gaze fixed on the wall to Dallis's left. "He considered his options, ladies. Mary, Bess, and I canna' read. Simple. Now, you really should get back to this rose right here, Evelyn. You've left a hanging thread."

The other ladies returned to sewing, and Dallis went back to looking out the window.

Dusk had shaded the clouds a darker gray when the summons came. Dallis had changed from her daygown. She'd brushed her hair and changed her wimple, and added a drop of Lady Dunrobin's perfume to the area between her breasts. Then, the guardsmen came. There were four of them. They blindfolded her, the same as they'd done when she'd first been brought there. She knew they did the same to Lady Evelyn by her aunt's protests. It wouldn't do any good, and she longed to hush her, but didn't. She had enough with trying to keep her courage, and her mind on what she'd say. And how fast she'd have to say it.

The child within her moved more than usual, and that altered her steps occasionally. The man holding to her elbow either didn't note it, or didn't care. They'd left one arm free, and she used it in front of her, spanning the space as she'd seen Lady Dunrobin do.

She heard sounds with ears high-tuned for them. The scrape of their feet on the flooring. Doors opening. The swish of clothing. Another door. The boom of something falling.

"God's blood! None said anything about a blindfold!"

"Payton?"

"Get it off of her! Now!"

"Payton?"

Dallis was pulling the blindfold down and managed it a split moment before he reached her, coming from across a far span of room at a near run.

"Payton!"

She was lifted from the floor and into his arms. And then she burst into tears.

"Oh, dearest heart . . . doona' cry. My heart canna' contain it." He crooned it to her.

"Payton. Payton. My love. Payton."

She couldn't stop weeping, even as she had her hands all about his face and then to his shoulders, and then she was putting kisses in their place.

"Darling heart. We have an hour. A short, short hour. Doona' waste another moment of it crying. Dallis? Do you hear me?"

He was walking with her, and crooning to her, and so solidly real that fresh tears started up.

"An . . . hour?" She managed to get it through the teardrops, that filled and overflowed, without any blinking on her part.

"Aye. An hour. 'Tis all the king will part with."

"Nae. Payton . . . nae."

"Please, my sweet?" He sat, cuddling her on his lap, and whispered it in her ear as he did so, lifting her hair out of his way. "This hour will be all I have."

"How can he . . . be so mean?" she cried.

"He is na' one of the lucky ones, love. He does na' ken how it is between us. Redmond did his best orating for us, but he failed. In a fashion."

Dallis shoved the heels of her hands to her eyes, shuddered through three breaths, then four. She held the fifth one. Held it to the point of pain before letting it ease out. Payton continued the strokes of her hair and back.

She moved her hands away, opened her eyes to his, and was lost. Eyes that blue and that soul-filled couldn't exist. Yet, they did. For her.

"You're treated fair?" he asked.

She nodded. "You?"

He replied in the same. "The bairn?" he asked.

She moved a hand to cup the swelling that hadn't seemed to change. "He moves much more oft. 'Tis impossible to count the times." She tried to laugh, but her voice croaked and she quieted.

"I ken I should be grateful for this time. But I am na'. I am even more angered." He'd lowered his chin and gave the watchers his challenger look.

"Nae, Payton, nae." Dallis touched his chin and brought his gaze back to her. "If I have the same hour, I doona' wish it spent on anger. Please?"

"I should be grateful he does na' allow Kilchurning the same hour." He ground it through clenched teeth, and Dallis cried out.

"Nae! And if he does, give me a skean. I'll carve his heart. Gladly." Her voice hardened and that seemed to release him from the angered look on his.

"Dallis? You must na' have thoughts like these. And you truly must na' act on them."

"Why na'?" she asked bitterly.

"Because it may harm the bairn. And after you, my son is what matters most to me. Ever."

"Payton? I swear this bairn is yours," Dallis said solemnly.

He grinned. "You think I doona' already ken that? Right here?"

He put his fingers around one of her hands and placed it on his chest, right above his heart. Dallis's eyes filled with tears again, and she blinked rapidly to dissolve them away. It was a vicious effort to do it, especially as he moved his gaze from her and blinked in the same rapid fashion.

"This is na' what I wished to say. And I have rehearsed all morn."

"At least you knew. I wasn't even informed!"

"I knew . . . because I earned this. And I'll earn it again on the morrow."

"The . . . morrow?"

"Aye. Redmond has made my bargain. I get one hour. Every day. At dusk."

"Oh, thank him! Thank him, Payton. For me."

She was peppering his face with kisses again, and stopped only when he put his hands about her waist and put her back on his lap.

"You . . . doona' fight again. Do you?" She whispered it.

"Nae."

"Truly?"

"I would na' wish to come to you with a face battered and bruised and a body marred with more scars. Not when all I get is an hour."

"Redmond is a wizard to work such a bargain!"

He nodded.

"You have one quarter hour remaining."

Both of them turned to the gathering at the door. It was impossible to note who'd spoken. Lady Evelyn was standing with her back to them, looking small and frail amid them.

"It canna' be!" Payton said.

One of them nodded. Dallis turned back first.

"Check your timepiece. It's wrong, I tell you!"

Dallis moved his face back to hers with her hands. Gazed lovingly and for long moments into eyes that had spellbound her from the moment she'd met him, and then tilted her head.

"Time is short. I must spend it na' in angered words, but with my hands, and my eyes and my ears. To memorize and hold dear to my heart. You ken?"

"Dallis?" He whispered.

"Aye?"

"I love you. Only you. Ever."

She caught a breath, and then couldn't stop the smile that was so wide, she knew it split the sides of her mouth. Then she was pressing kisses against the perfection of his lips again. "And I love you. I love you, Payton. I love you."

Something broke within him, and she was hugged to his chest, while his mouth devoured hers, and his heart thudded to a race of sound, with hers right behind it.

"Five minutes."

The announcement broke them apart. Dallis sat atop him, watching him inhale and exhale in great motions as she did the same.

"Time is short, my love," she whispered, when she had her heart and breathing back under control.

He nodded.

"I'll write you, Payton. I'll bring you letters. Each night. I swear it."

"I would return it, but I have never been friendly with a quill and ink," he replied, with a self-conscious smile.

"I will treasure anything you give to me, Payton. Anything."

The babe moved then, startling her, and making her gasp.

Dallis watched as he seemed to note exactly what had happened and nodded.

"My bairn is strong."

"Of course," she agreed.

He huffed a huge sigh. "This span of time we are apart . . . it will be as nothing when compared with the life I will give you once we are free of here. You ken?"

"I ken," she whispered back. "'Tis all I think on."

"One minute."

They both jumped and watched as their eyes both widened.

"So little time."

"I love you," Dallis told him. "I will dream of you. Of this time. Of the time we can be together, and when nae king can keep us apart."

"As will I."

He lifted her hand to his lips and kissed her fingers reverently, and then stood, with her still in his arms.

"'Tis too soon," Dallis told him.

He nodded.

"They have na' called the time, yet."

"Parting will na' get better with the fight of it, Dallis, love. I know verra few things, but that I ken well."

She nodded, but didn't dare blink in case the moisture in her eyes obliterated him for her.

"Time!"

Payton placed her on her feet at the door.

"Must you blindfold her?" he asked, using his angered voice.

Dallis put her hand on his arm. "If it gets me my time with you, they can blind me and tie me. You ken?"

He looked at her for long moments, spellbinding her as always.

"You must leave now, Laird Dunn-Fadden."

Payton bowed to them and swiveled, placing his back to her as he walked to an opposite door and went through it. And then slammed it so hard the door jamb rattled and the torch in the closest sconce blew out.

Dallis put her hands out for her blindfold, and that's when she saw that Lady Evelyn was sobbing silently with the tears Dallis was forcing back. She went to the old woman and held her. The guards didn't stop them. Holding her aunt's hand tightly, with a guard on either side of them was how they were sent back.

Chapter 22

"Oh . . . please, Payton?"

He shook his head.

"But . . . nae one will see. Aunt Evelyn assures me."

Payton looked over at where the spinster aunt was studiously ignoring the couple, her eye on a delicately wrought treasure box.

"The spinster does na' control the king's guards," he replied. "Now, cease that!"

He had a hand caught to where she'd moved hers, stopping her exploration of his thigh right above the knee where the kilt barely covered. Dallis looked up at him through her eyelashes, and moved sinuously and amorously against him. He made it easy, since he'd put her into a slant on the bench seat, after kissing her into a state of desire and frustration that made everything on her body tremble and shake and lurch. And crave.

"We've na' had guards watching over us for over a month. Longer. They trust us. Or they tire of us."

"Your aunt will see."

Dallis giggled. "Aunt Evelyn will na' say a word."

"She'll still see," he hissed.

"This room has angles, Payton. Closets. Shadowed . . .

recesses." Dallis lowered her voice, and wriggled again where he still had her buttocks on his lap. Then she smiled slyly as she felt the stirring exactly where she wanted it. He must have known what the look meant because he immediately pushed back into the bench, and away from her.

She responded with a fingertip, moved from his knee to his arm, bare, warm, and powerful. She trailed her nail along sinew and skin, feeling the bumps of his shivers before she reached his shoulder. She got more firm substance against her buttocks, as well.

"Dallis." He had a pleading expression in his voice that was replicated in his eyes. "I'm a man. Verra desirous of you. And your . . . body. You canna' call on my response this way, and leave me wanting."

"We have time," she replied, licking her lips.

"We've used half our time. I ken. I'm watching the clock."

Dallis put her finger to her mouth and licked it. Then she put it back on his arm. He wasn't just shivering. That was a tremor scoring his frame, making the wood support of their bench respond to it, as well as making his groin stiffer, and larger, and stronger, and hotter.

"You doona' ken what you do!"

He was snarling now, making absolute thrills course her body, centering to where the darts of her nipples were barely contained in the dress's bodice as it was. She watched him glance there, scrunch his eyes shut, and shake some more.

"Payton. . . ." She drew his name out like a caress, moved both hands to the neckline of her dress and slid it even lower, until the dark shade of her breast tips were near to popping out. Then she licked her fingertip again and touched it to his lower lip.

His eyes flew open, moved instantly to where she was displayed for him, groaned, and then he moved his gaze to hers. There wasn't much blue color showing through the black of them. Dallis studied them, and couldn't see any blue color at all in the shadows thrown by the torches far enough away as to be useless for close scrutiny of any kind.

"Vixen." He said it between his teeth, but he was on his feet, holding her tightly against him and moving to the darkest reach of the room, far from prying eyes and listening souls.

"'Tis your son . . . making me so," Dallis whispered, urgency staining her voice as she pulled at his head, lowering him to grasping lips, and taking everything he was trying to keep from her.

"That's right. The bairn. What will he think of this?"

He was swiveling her, facing her away from him, lowering her to her knees onto a settee, and Dallis near cried out at the loss, until she felt the lift of her skirts, the touch of skin, and then she was filled. Completed, totally, and with such relief, she gushed her pleasure with more than mewing sounds.

"I have . . . some time . . . a-fore I worry over our son's opinion. Or lack of one." Dallis replied, ending the whisper with a moan of sound.

Payton rocked back, before shoving forward again. Filling her. Moving away. Filling. Dallis bit on her tongue to keep the cries of pleasure from sounding, while the slight grunt noises Payton was making filled her ears.

"I mean . . . what of him . . . now. Jesu'!"

He was moving, leaning forward in a curve, pressing warmth and weight all along her back, and making the back of the settee she leaned on creak with the motion. Then, she knew why, as both hands shoved her bodice down, filling his palms with her, and making it even harder for her to contain any noise from the sparks of ecstasy flowing through her.

"Ah . . . Dallis. Love . . ."

The whisper was hoarse and rough, and filled with a low tone that sent Dallis into more raptures, and more release, and more bliss. She held it to her, keeping the breath as long as possible, before going back to panting small gasps that matched his increasing tempo.

He moved a hand, gripping it to the sofa back at her nose. She knew it was for stability, as the strength of his thrusts got harder, stronger, swifter, alternately filling and then emptying from her. Again. Over and over and over until Dallis had to lower her head, and hold her breath through another burst of pure bliss. Payton moved the other arm then, looping it around the space between her growing belly and her breasts, to hold on to her.

"Dallis. Ah . . . Dallis . . . Love. You're a temptress. An enchantress. A siren." He moved a knee onto the bench beside hers, making the structure groan worse. "Brought to life . . . just for me. To torment me. Torture! Ah . . . Dallis! Doona' move. Na' now! Na'—!"

His whisper had intensified throughout the words, as well as his strokes, pushing her with dominating effect at the settee, making it rock backward with them. Filling her, lifting her, and shoving at her until the back of the bench stopped him. Dallis arched her back, grabbed at his head and twisted enough to join lips with him. That's how she contained the full breath of groan he gave, filling the cavern of her mouth as he stiffened completely, and held her in place for what seemed an eternity of pleasure. Then he was shuddering with discordant tremors while the arm tightened even further about her.

"Oh, my God. Dallis. We should na' have done that."

Payton was pulling from her, dropping her skirts into place as he did so. Dallis turned around to sit, pressing her thighs, knees, and ankles tightly together to hang on to the heavenly feeling for just a bit longer, while she rearranged her bodice back into place with hands that trembled.

She looked up at the shadow outline of him, since any torchlight was at his back, and smiled. "Perhaps, na'," she replied finally, "but I thank you. And my attendants will thank you even more this eve."

"What? And you're to cease that!"

He had his hands on his hips now, and nothing about his stance displayed a man who'd trembled in place sheer moments earlier. He looked massive, virile, and fit. Dallis licked her lips. She knew he could see her face, since the light was full on her.

"What?" She was all innocence and lack of guile, but ran her tongue all about the bottom of her upper lip anyway. And settled for the swift, strong outlay of breath he made, since that was all he gave her.

"That! You are to stop that! You doona' understand how it is with a man! I live in torment! I sleep with torture. I think of nothing but the sweet pleasure I receive from tupping you . . . and I canna' think! I work at the list in a rough attempt to escape it. Take dunks in the cistern at the top walls of this castle and beg the fates that 'tis cold enough to assist me. And then it starts up again! Jesu'!, Dallis! Assist me with a bit of this!"

She giggled.

"You laugh? I bare my soul . . . and you laugh?" His voice caught.

"Payton . . . I must confess."

That stopped him. "To what?" he asked in the stillness that came from holding his breath.

"I have been a termagant. A shrew."

"Nae." He answered. "You?"

"Aye. And I think all knew why, although I dinna' tell them."

"Why?"

"You."

He straightened. She had to imagine the perplexed look that would be on his face, since she couldn't see it in the shadowed alcove he'd put her in.

"Me?"

Dallis nodded. "Aye. You. There is an issue with my frame now, Payton. I canna' rest, either. I canna' sit and sew as they require. I canna' sit still long enough! I am restless. My every thought is beset with . . . images. Sensual images. And if I seek sleep . . . 'tis worse! My nights last forever, and I daren't nap!"

He'd tilted his head. "Women . . . suffer this, too?"

Dallis looked down. "I doona' ken if all women suffer it. I only ken that I do. And it is a massive need, Payton. Near consuming."

He moved to sit on the bench beside her, making the wood give slightly with his weight.

"You doona' think less of me?" Dallis whispered.

He pulled her into his embrace, holding her against the scratchy wool of his kilt band.

"I think I love you more, if 'tis possible."

"Five minutes!"

The door opening somewhere around the side of the wall portended the entry of a guard. Dallis heard her aunt answering.

"Thank you, Reginald. We will be ready."

Dallis giggled. "You see? We had time."

Payton was smiling, too. She had the torchlight to thank for showing it.

"You are verra gracious to me, dearest husband. I am now replete and famished. And your son needs feeding."

She stood, put her hands to the mound that had rapidly outpaced her bosom in the six weeks she'd been in captivity, and put a hand toward him.

"Well, then. Go. Eat. Feed the lad."

He stood with her, looking down at her, and the babe responded with a roll move as if readjusting. Dallis gasped.

"What is it?" he asked, instantly solicitous.

"Your son," she replied, and watched the look of total satisfaction cross his face.

"I thank you, Wife. For this visit."

"One minute!"

Both of them looked in the direction the words came from, turned back, and yawned. In tandem.

"I just may be able to sleep. Deeply."

He lifted her into his arms and carried her from the alcove, and into the brightness of torchlight over by the door they used. Then, he set her on her feet next to Lady Evelyn.

After a nod to both ladies, he turned, leaving without a farewell or another look at her. They'd decided it from the first week. She knew it was best, but still she watched him until he went through the other door. But this time, he didn't slam it.

"I've brought something to show you."

"Beyond what you've already shown me? You've a wicked streak, Wife."

He was teasing. It sounded it. He couldn't be angered. Not after the romp she'd put him through the moment the guards had left and Lady Evelyn had gotten engrossed in her needle-work. His wife had the most luscious body. She had a haven made for a man's loving. He hadn't been mistaken the first time, and he wasn't now. She was the best at tupping. Ever. He was too content to argue, almost too drowsy to pay attention.

He shifted on the sofa they were using, grimaced at the heavy bruising his left side had taken, and hid it. That was odd. He hadn't felt it at all when she'd been having her way with him. Making him sit on the settee over in the hidden alcove that she'd taken to calling theirs, while she did all the movement and possessed all the power. Or so, she'd claimed. All he'd had to do was guide.

He let her. It was exciting and enticing and satisfying to watch. And receive. He shifted slightly at the remembered passion, and then sucked in a breath as his left side connected with Dallis's shoulder. She didn't appear to notice, and he relaxed again.

Slowly.

"I've finished it! And 'tis more beautiful than I'd hoped!"

She was gesturing to her aunt. That lady brought over a wrapping of some kind and handed it over. Payton watched without comment. His expression must have said something, for after a quick glance to him, the aunt curtsied and returned to the door.

Payton turned his attention back to where his wife was busy, unfurling a long, small gown with lace all about the edges.

"See here? Lady Dunrobin has taught me her method of stitching."

He nodded. And then yawned.

"Payton!" She lowered the item onto her lap. "'Tis a christening gown for our son! I made it. And you yawn?" Her eyes were tearing up, and he hated that.

Payton leaned forward quickly, pulled in the ragged gap in his breathing as she connected with his side again and had her in his arms before she turned the emotion into full-out tears.

"Dallis, pray doona' take on so. 'Tis verra fine. I swear."

"You doona' even care!" She was whispering it, but she might as well be wailing it for the way his heart pained him.

"Doona' allow the workings of a man's mind to harm you. I would na'—" His voice caught as she touched his left side. He'd gone stiff with remembered pain, and held it as she blinked the tears away and stared.

"What is it?" she asked.

"Naught."

He tried to reply quickly, since that was the best way to

ease her mind. It didn't work. He didn't need the calculating look that came over her features to prove it.

"What has been done to you, Payton?" she asked.

"Little."

"Let me see."

She was lowering her chin and giving him the look he used with enmity on any challenger. On her, it was just adorable, and whimsical. He grinned and bent to kiss her nose. That went awry as a sore rib jarred against flesh, and he sucked for breath again.

"Damn . . . !" His curse whooshed out with the released breath. He was forced to sit back again. And take as shallow breaths as possible.

"Payton?"

He'd hidden it to keep the concern from her face. And then he'd stupidly betrayed it. He groaned. She took it as pain.

"If you doona' let me see . . ."

She didn't finish her threat. Silence grew for a bit, and then he looked toward her.

"'Tis little, Dallis. I promise. And means naught."

"You lie."

"Doona' let it spoil our time. I beg of you."

She tipped her head and studied him.

"You are fighting again," she accused.

"Na' . . . true."

"Then, let me see."

Payton turned his head and met her gaze. "There is nae fight, Dallis. I swear it. But His Majesty claims he canna' get any bets unless there is a challenge. And if he canna' get any takers to his bets, then I canna' see you."

Her eyes filled with tears, and Payton swore again.

"Then . . . how can you say . . . 'tis nae fight?"

"I will na' fight for him. I made him that vow, and I'll keep it. The little runt knows this. So, he sends challengers into the list that I have to . . . fend off. Without injury. Nae weapons."

"How do you fend them off?"

"I am verra good, wife. Verra."

"Then why are you hurt now?"

He blew the sigh hard enough to dry his eyes. "I was na' quick enough, and the Frankish knight he found was stout. You ken? Short."

"So?"

"I took a head-butt when I thought him cowed and beaten. I was na' looking. Why would I? They'd played the pipes and called the match. And then he cheated."

"A head-butt?" Dallis asked.

He nodded. "Aye. With a helm. He had a lot of spines on that helm, too, the rotten Frank."

"Dear . . . God," she whispered.

"Dallis." He moved sideways, rather than twist, to face her, since it might prove painful, and he didn't want any further pain reflected in her eyes. "I would take ten times more if I could see you. You ken that."

"But—he makes you fight."

"What makes you say that? I dinna' give a blow to any man."

"Then how did the Frankish knight lose?"

Payton lifted an eyebrow and smiled. "I told you he was short."

"So?"

"Short men, who find their heads held in place, canna' reach another man with their arms. Nae matter how much they flail about."

"You held him in place?" She giggled. Payton's smile broadened at being the one to bring her to such a heart-warming sound. He loved the sound of her laughter. Much more than her tears.

"Aye. Until the guards got there and took him away, dragging his sorry carcass from the list. With the title of cheat added to the loss. I doona' think he will appreciate the king's hospitality, henceforth. I hope his family has a large purse.

To pay his fine. Now, show me this christening gown that you have created."

Payton concentrated on giving correct responses of appreciation for the tiny slashes of thread she'd worked in vinelike patterns across a bit of material. And he enjoyed every coo of pleasure she gave as she showed them to him.

Chapter 23

Payton slammed the scrawny bit of a man to the ground again, and jumped back as more foam-flecked blood was spat at him. The man wouldn't stay down. It was as if demons controlled his frame, and Satan his will. Payton went back to blocking fists that flew nearly too quick to see, and a mouth that continually bit at him.

He barely moved his hand away again, as teeth slammed shut, without Payton's skin between them, and then he was flinging the slim body through the air and watching him thud into the mud quagmire the list was turning into. That's what happened when a battle took place that wouldn't end. And that's what happened when they tossed buckets of water at the participants when the late spring sunshine turned them into opponents who didn't look active enough to keep the crowd entertained.

That wasn't the case with this duel, but since it was the third Payton had been in already, the mud was getting slippery, and the holds harder. And then they'd sent this scrawny ghoulish fellow into the fray.

The lad was up again. Yelling and spraying more foam about, and then coming at a dead run for Payton. The fellow slipped, almost going down, and Payton put a boot out to make it a certainty. Then, he had to leap backward as the lad bit at his calf.

"This one . . . appears rabid!" Payton called it out from a side railing, as he watched the lad get up again.

"He is," Redmond replied. "We were just told!"

Payton turned his head in shock.

"What?" he asked.

"My Laird!"

Redmond's warning came with enough time for Payton to twirl about the lad's attack, giving him nothing but air to the launching of his frame.

"Rabid?"

Fury was starting to pump through him, warming blood he'd tried to keep cold and calculating, and aloof. Payton speared a glance up at the king's balcony before going back to the battle, with an opponent who was on his feet again and lowering his head. And foaming from the mouth even more.

"Give me the hand wrap."

Payton went to a crouch stance, willing his heart to accept what he was about to do, and waited for the lad's next move. And then he was catching the body in midair before using the movement to slam it face-first into the turf. He ignored the huge roar of crowd approval. He ignored everything, save the lad who was starting to stir again. Payton was at the railing by then, grabbing the loop of steel from Redmond and sliding it over his right hand, to settle it atop his knuckles. It was a mark of extreme cowardice, and he'd never used it, but this bit of steel that a knight could wear beneath his gauntlets, would change the course of any battle if used correctly.

The lad was up, shaking his head and looking even more maddened with blood trailing from his chin this time, mixed with the foam. Then he fixed his eyes on Payton, lowered his head and came again. Payton didn't move. The lad slipped, recovered, came again. Just before he reached him, Payton stepped to one side, bent at the knees, and launched an arm across the lad's throat, sending him onto his back with a thud the mud absorbed. Payton was astride him instantly, his left hand holding the lad's throat, although the lad struggled and twisted and snarled and bit at him. Payton squeezed, watched the fluids coating the skin come oozing from between his fingers. Payton arched up, and slammed his right fist into the boy's chest, directly at the heart.

He was off the lad the next moment, looking down at him without expression as the lad grabbed at ground and struggled for air that his stopped heart no longer craved.

Payton stepped away and moved his gaze up to where the king sat, perched at the front of his chair as he watched. They all watched. And waited. The entire crowd was hushed as it listened for the lad's death rattle, holding a collective breath as it came before the body went still. That's when the entire crowd came alive again, roaring wildly with approval. Payton ignored it and took the steps over to his men with legs that trembled, while he pulled at the steel ring.

"Quick. Redmond. Get me to the cistern. The one atop the latrine. Just you. None other."

Redmond nodded once.

"Why canna' we all go?" Alan asked.

Payton turned to the lad, and he must have read the panic, because Alan's eyes went wide. "I need water to wash. I need to strip. I need Redmond to look me over. 'Twill be most . . . uncomfortable."

"Look . . . you over?" the lad asked.

"For tears in the skin. Any. You heard them. He was *rabid!* If I have any scratches . . ."

"Oh, God. I'm going to be ill." The lad turned away before he made it true.

Payton didn't bother with anything else. He was already running, with Redmond on his heels.

* * *

"My Lady Evelyn Caruth? The king sends a missive."

Dallis looked up from composing the letter she was writing to Payton. She'd given off needlework for the day, although it never seemed to bore her companions. A letter might be just the thing to take her mind off the discomfort that came from carrying a barrel-sized belly around, adjusting from every time the babe kicked or punched, or made sitting difficult. And all that did nothing to mute the wait for the moment when her hour with Payton arrived.

She stood, using the table for balance, since Payton's bairn stretched far enough out she was off balance and couldn't see her feet. She wobbled toward the door, but Lady Evelyn got there first. It was an unfair contest, even if Dallis had made the challenge. Her aunt might be past sixty, but she was spry, and slim, and light on her feet in comparison.

It didn't truly matter who got the message, or who read it. The missive may be addressed otherwise, but they all knew it was for Dallis.

"It say . . . it says . . ."

"Aye?" Both Dallis and Lady Dunrobin answered.

"He's granting you an additional hour. In the same chamber. Earlier."

"With Payton?" Dallis couldn't contain the joy. It was in her voice, covering her skin with shivers, and in her eyes as they misted over.

"He does na' say that. But there is nae other reason. Is there?"

"Well, assist me with my bath, then! I must wear the new dress. The one that does na' make me look like a pig! And my hair. We must do my hair, in the loose fashion he likes so much."

"Dallis," Lady Evelyn stopped her before she could put any of her plans to action. "I doona' believe the man notes what you wear. Or how your hair is arranged. Or anything other than that it is you."

"Truly?"

"Well . . . I doona' note much, as you ken . . ."

Both Evelyn and Lady Dunrobin snickered.

"But I am na' lying when I tell you the man is smitten. Totally. He thinks you the most beauteous woman birthed. And he thinks the sight of you carrying his son is the most heavenly sight on the earth. Aside from which, I doona' believe he cares much for any of your clothing, unless it is in his way."

Dallis gasped. And then she was giggling, too.

"Oh, please, Aunt Evelyn. You ken we have na' done anything like that in some time. At least a month."

"A sennight. Mayhap. And that only because the bairn has made it too difficult. 'Tis what I suspicion, anyway."

"The king is granting us another hour. A whole hour!"

Dallis tried to twirl but only managed a half turn before having to grasp at a table for balance. And then she sobered. "Oh, I do hope he has na' done something horrid to earn it," she whispered.

The same guards came to escort her. They didn't use blindfolds any longer. They weren't needed. The lesson was learned. There was no escape from a Stewart King's hospitality, and no reason to try.

Dallis longed to run, once they'd opened the door and let her and Lady Evelyn through, but her weight and condition forbade it. So she settled with leaning backward and waddling. As was normal anymore.

The room was deserted.

Dallis looked about in the waning sunlight. The torches were lit already, but they weren't needed. Sunlight was still lighting the area, especially the alcove she considered theirs, coming through glazed, thick green glass. Dallis walked a circuit of the room, at a slow pace that necessitated stopping and waiting for the bairn to subside movement, or to make breathing easier, before continuing.

The room felt oddly empty and lonely without Payton there.

She sat on the padded settee they always used, heard the door he used opening, and tried with every bit of control at her command not to yield to the instant stab of fear she felt at who walked in.

"Cousin Dallis! I vow it's been months! Years! An eternity! So pleasant to see you. And you look so . . . so . . . large."

Dallis didn't bother moving from her seat as her cousin, Giles Carmour, walked toward her. Her mind was racing through so many avenues, she almost didn't hear the slur he cast on her form. And then she sneered slightly.

"May I say the same to you, Giles," she answered sweetly. He stopped and his face fell. That was gratifying. Giles hadn't improved since she'd seen him more than a year ago. He was a flirt, and she'd always thought his orange-streaked brown hair attractive. As was the hazel color of his eyes, and the fancy dress he wore, that she now knew matched the king's penchant for European fashion, and not Highland wear.

Now, she decided he was wearing so much frippery, he looked ridiculous. And effeminate. And weak. She hadn't missed in the accuracy of her greeting, either, for the large volume of flesh about his middle almost prevented the buttons fastening on his doublet. He wasn't even wearing a kilt, but strange tight-wrapped pants, with a heavily embroidered tunic atop it. He was carrying a sword that looked incongruous with such tawdry finery, as well.

"What do you want, Giles?" she asked.

"What? The pleasantness of our greeting is over? So soon?"

He moved to sit on the settee beside her, where Payton always did. Dallis knew she paled as she considered it.

"What do you want? I've nothing for you."

"I'm beset by duns," he replied.

"Nonsense. Your attire is new. In fashion. It reeks of wealth. And you've na' missed many sups, if the girth about your belly is any show."

"May I say the same of you? As well as the richness of your own dress."

Dallis tipped her head. "I carry the champion's bairn. Why would I be small?" she replied.

"I'm na' fashing you, Dallis. The money-lenders truly are after me. I am destitute."

"So?"

"I need funds."

"I doona' possess any," she replied.

His eyes narrowed. "And here we just went over how expensive your attire is, how fashionable . . . considering. And how many sups you appear to have consumed."

Dallis glared over at him. "I used to find you charming. I doona' ken how."

He grimaced. "You have a sharp tongue. Too bad. I was trying to work with you, here."

"On what?"

"Is na' your husband due . . . soon?"

"Long after you have vacated. That's when he'll be here."

"Oh. I doona' think so," he replied, and turned a look to her that started her heart into such a speeded thumping the bairn complained.

"Payton is na' to see you," Dallis replied.

"I beg to differ, My Lady Dunn-Fadden. But I am here for that verra reason. And he is going to see me."

"I'll have the guards remove you. Aunt Evelyn!"

"You'd allow me to find him in a quiet corner and tell him what I have to tell him? When you have the means to stop me?"

"Wait, Aunt Evelyn! I spoke . . . too soon."

The spinster aunt wasn't listening. She kept coming and

stopped when she was at Dallis's other side. Giles looked up
at her and then back to Dallis.

"She can hear this, too. She already kens most of what you
did, anyway. I fear the champion and his Honor Guard are the
lone ones in the dark. I wonder how he'll take word of how
his wife betrayed him, paying for his death, over and over, and
over again. Why, she even sent her wedding ring for me to
sell . . . in order to see him perish."

"You always were a snake, Giles," Aunt Evelyn said. "'Tis
why the clan sent you out. Away."

He nodded and then shrugged. "Clan Caruth is too small
for my talents, Aunt. You ken that."

"Please, Giles?"

Dallis looked toward the clock on one of the tables. The
one Payton must have positioned while he'd been waiting
for her. So he'd have advance warning of how much time
they'd have.

"Nae need to plead, dearest cousin. I've come to make certain your disloyalty stays hidden. You have my word."

"Of what use is the word of a scoundrel and a cheat?" Aunt
Evelyn hissed the words.

"You really need to ask our aunt to keep a civil tongue, if
you wish me to keep mine, Dallis. You truly do."

"Aunt Evelyn?" Dallis moved her eyes to her aunt, and
silently pleaded.

"Doona' listen to him, Dallis. Tell Payton yourself. He is a
fair man. He might even find the humor in it."

"Nae," Dallis replied and put her hands up to hold to her
aunt's. "I canna' take that chance."

"He'll be angered. Enraged. But it will pass. Trust me on
this, lass."

"Please, Aunt Evelyn?"

"Doona' let this—this—"

"Careful, Aunt Evelyn," Giles warned.

"Doona' do something more you'll regret, Dallis lass. I'll hold my tongue."

"Then, mayhap you'll also hold it verra far from me," Giles requested.

Dallis squeezed at her aunt's hands and beseeched her silently with her eyes. Lady Evelyn finally smiled, but the gesture was as sad as her eyes.

"Verra well. I will be at the door. In my usual place. I will try na' to interfere."

Dallis watched her walk away before lowering her empty hands to place them atop the enormity of her belly. Then she turned back to Giles.

"What do you want?" she asked.

"I need funds."

"I truly have none, Giles. I swear."

"He's been earning pay. With his exhibitions. I want some of that."

"The king keeps me prisoner! I canna' get to his funds!"

"You expect me to believe that?" he asked.

"'Tis true." Dallis looked down at the white satin of her overdress, pleated and draped for fullness, and watched it waver before going solid again.

"Then, give me that ring."

Her eyes went wide. "I canna!"

Even if he wasn't looking at her, he had to sense the panic in her voice.

"Of course, you can."

"Nae, Giles. He made me vow to keep it on!"

"So?"

"I doona' vow lightly. I canna' take it off. You'll have to wait. I can get funds."

"I would wait, but time is short; I've been promised a hand-chopping if I doona' come up with funds! I'm desperate. Or . . . perhaps you dinna' note that in my tone when I said I'd await the champion."

"He will na' give you funds," Dallis told him.

"If he wants my information, he will. Or wait. I've been short-sighted." His tone changed, and he stood, starting to pace in front of her. One step past the length of the settee. Back the other way. Return.

"This knowledge I have. 'Twould be worth more to someone else, I think. Someone like . . . the king."

"Nae!" Dallis stood with the cry, and then had to put a hand to her side as the child kicked mightily. She had to sit back down before she fell there.

"Or perhaps . . . better still . . . I could offer it to Laird Kilchurning. Now, there's an avenue I'd na' considered. Imagine how much he'd pay to know the wife paid to have her husband killed. Imagine how he'd use it."

"Nae, Giles, nae. I beg of you." She no longer cared if he saw her tears.

"I hold all the options, Dallis. You ken that now?"

"Please . . . Giles?"

Her nose was running, and she was going to be red-eyed and emotional, and a glance at the clock showed that Payton would be arriving momentarily.

"The ring, Dallis?"

"All right! All right!" She twisted and turned it, and worked at it. Then, licked at her finger to twist some more. It tore the skin of her knuckle, but it came off.

"You must promise me na' to sell it here."

"I doona' have to promise you anything."

"I'll get you more, Giles. Please, Giles! I'll find a way to pay you all you need! For as long as you need, but you have to promise me na' to sell it to anyone outside of Inverness, or . . . or Glasgow. Or perhaps Aberdeen! You have to promise!"

He took the ring and lifted it, frowning as he did so.

"The champion gave you this . . . trifle? 'Tis na' worth the time it took to gain it from you. I only hope I get enough funds for it that I will na' bother you again a-fore your bairn is whelped. You'll have more funds for me?"

She nodded.

"You vow it?"

She nodded again, looked at the clock, and couldn't prevent the widening of her eyes.

"I vow it! I do. Now go! Go!"

He turned.

"And doona' use the door he uses! Go through the one Aunt Evelyn is standing beside. Now, Giles, now!"

Her urgency must have translated to him. Or the promise of more funds if he did as she wanted worked the same, because Giles was at a jog before he reached the correct door.

Dallis watched it shut before pressing her fingertips to her eyes to wipe every hint of tears away, and then she gasped. There was a blood streak on the white satin from her finger. She licked at it, creasing her dress with the other hand into a fold that should hide the spot, and put the barren-looking hand beneath the curve of the bairn. Then, she moved along the bench to the left, making certain he'd sit on her right.

And then she prayed with all her being for the ability to deceive the man she loved. That's when his door opened.

Chapter 24

Payton had an unsure, uncertain, and odd look about him. And that's when he finally got close enough to tell. The one quick glance Dallis had of his approach showed her. She looked quickly back to the lump of belly, sniffed, and forced what she hoped was a welcome expression to her face.

"Dallis?"

His voice sounded different as well. He sat beside her, making the wood bow slightly with his weight, proving not only that Giles was the smaller man in that category as well, but that Payton wasn't sitting with his usual forthright, self-confident, and assured manner. All of which was odd-strange. Dallis cast another glance at where he sat, cradling one of his hands within the other one. That made her grip to her skirt on the left side with the injured one.

"Aye?" she answered.

He didn't answer at first. He just sat there, rolling his left hand over the inner one. And then he slid a glance to hers and shied away.

"I have something that needs saying," he said.

"I have something to tell you." She blurted it out almost as a harmony to him. Then they both laughed, but it was an insincere, uncomfortable sound. Dallis frowned at the white satin.

"You do?" he asked.

She nodded.

"You must hear me out first."

Dallis swallowed, stilled where the left hand was clutching to material, and waited.

"The bairn . . . he's well?"

"Oh, aye." Dallis brought her right hand up to cradle the mound that was their child. It responded with a kick into her palm. "Payton! Quickly!" She turned to him and reached for his hand.

"What is it?" His whisper was light and caught up with the indrawn breath.

"He moves. Right here! Put your hand . . . right here." She maneuvered his hand over the spot and held it in place. Waited. Looked up into perfectly lashed blue eyes and felt her heart skip. And then the babe responded, kicking rapidly three times. Right where she held him.

Payton's eyes widened, went moist with an instant sheen, and then he was pulling his hand from beneath hers and looking at the far wall.

"Did you feel it?" she asked.

"Aye," he replied.

"Is it na' . . . wondrous?"

"Aye," he repeated.

"He is such a strong bairn. The image of his sire. I just know it."

He nodded.

"Then . . . why did you move away? You dinna' want to feel it? You find it . . . offensive?"

"Nae, Dallis. Never that. 'Tis . . . me . . . who is offensive."

Payton rose and walked over to one of the plastered walls, keeping his back to her. She would have gone to him, but something about him stopped her. She was forced to look at the back of his kilt, the wedged shape of his upper body, his bent head. Then, he straightened his shoulders and turned to her.

"You've made vows. Have na' you, Dallis?"

"Aye," she replied.

"And have you kept them?"

She lost her color. She almost lost her senses. She had to grip the seat bottom with both hands to stay in place until the floor ceased roiling beneath her and went back to being polished slats of wood.

"I . . . tried." Her voice warbled. Now was the time to tell him. She opened her mouth but he filled the space with words.

"What if trying is na' enough?"

"Some . . . vows are na' possible to keep, Payton. The things against them are too . . . large. Too strong. Too . . . evil." Her voice dropped.

"Then you will understand?" he asked.

She nodded.

He took another huge sigh. She could see the size of it from where she sat as it expanded his chest.

"What vow have you broken, Payton?"

"I have just come from seeing the king, Dallis."

"He has na' made things worse for us, has he?"

"He wants me to fight. A great battle. Against a champion of his choosing."

"What will you get?"

"Your freedom."

The babe lurched to one side, and she moved her hand as if to balance it, before hiding it again.

"And . . . yours?" she asked.

He nodded.

"And you dinna' agree?" She was shocked. Angered. Dismayed.

"'Twill be to the death, Dallis."

"You must na' do it then. Nae, Payton. What if you lose?"

"I doona' lose, Dallis. And I will be able to get you to our home. Our bairn will be born in our home. If I do this for him."

"What of Kilchurning's claim?"

"He nae longer believes Kilchurning."

"What?" She was on her feet now, even if the bairn didn't like it and made her arch backward to balance the weight.

"He says Kilchurning told him of the lie already."

"When?" she asked.

"A month past. Does it matter?"

"Does it matter?" Her voice was rising. He'd never heard her at screech level. It wasn't going to be pleasant.

"He's na' going to let me go. Kilchurning must have guessed that. And used it. To save his head."

"When do I get my revenge on the little bastard, then?" Dallis said between clenched teeth.

"Nae one gets such on a Stewart," Payton replied.

"I mean Kilchurning! The king promised me Kilchurning when his lie was discovered!"

"Our king . . . is a verra sharp man, Dallis. Verra. His cunning and skills are difficult to grasp if one has na' been about them for long."

"He's na' going to give me Kilchurning?"

Payton shook his head.

"Why not? He decreed it!"

"You should sit down, love."

"I'll sit down when I'm damned good and ready to sit down. How dare that man cheat me?"

"He is na calling it a cheat."

"Of course not. He's a man. And a king, above that. They never call themselves cheats and frauds, and scoundrels!"

"Dallis—"

"That man has made this entire time horrid for me! For you. For us! What excuse could he possibly use to prevent me from having Kilchurning's head in justice?"

"His decree was that you could devise the punishment when the lie was discovered."

"And?" Dallis waited.

"The lie was na' discovered. Kilchurning gave it up."

"Nae. I refuse to accept such! You march right back in there and tell that man—"

"Dallis. You're upsetting yourself, and the bairn. I canna' tell a king anything. He's a king! Aside of which, I'm a-feared to be back in his presence."

"You? A-feared?" She spat the words with her disgust.

"Aye. Of what I might do to him. And what that will cost. Now, please. Sit. Calm yourself. I told you our sovereign is a verra sharp man. Verra. 'Twill take more in smarts to escape this trap he has set for me."

Dallis closed her mouth. Sat. And folded her arms across her belly.

"Are you going to fight for him?" she asked.

"I doona' think so."

"Good. He should na' win everything."

Payton smirked. "He always wins, Dallas. One way or the other. Look at us. 'Tis a perfect example."

"Why?"

"He has me where he wants . . . because he uses you as bait."

Dallis's eyes went wide enough, the babe kicked his displeasure.

"And Kilchurning used it to get his pardon."

"He *pardoned* him?" She lost her voice on the word. It was the shock.

"Fifteen minutes!"

The door opened with the information. Dallis cursed at the man. His brows rose, and then he shook his head and shut the door.

"Laird Kilchurning gave the king the power he needed to

use against me. He wanted me back on his list, making him money. Kilchurning gave it to him."

"Then, cease fighting."

He shook his head.

"The bairn will be birthed any day now, Payton. You ken it. I do, as well. We can last that long. We can."

"His vengeance is far worse than you can imagine, Dallis. Far worse. If I wait for my son's birth . . . I give him another target."

"Jesu'!" Dallis cried out.

He was coming toward the settee now, and Dallis barely had time to hide her hand beneath her skirt before he arrived and sat beside her and picked up the other one.

"Aside from which . . . the king said something to me. Something . . . that I had to admit the truth of. And I have to live with now."

"What?"

"He said I may claim na' to fight anymore, and I may vow otherwise, but the moment I agreed to enter a list in order to see you . . . I made it false. All he has to do is set terms and negotiate the sum. I am the one who disavowed my own words. Me."

"You doona' believe such swine-sop . . . do you?"

"Here." He held out his right hand, bruised black across the top knuckles. "Do you see that?"

She nodded.

"That is a man's life. Taken this day. On the list."

Dallis moved her hand to his, lifted it, and then kissed the bruise mark. "He deserved it," she told him. "You had nae other choice."

He smiled. "I do love you, Dallis Dunn-Fadden. I may na' deserve you, but I do love you."

"You do deserve me, Payton. And I understand. Every-thing. Some vows are difficult to keep. Things conspire against one. Sometimes—"

"One minute!"

"God damn you, Randall!" Dallis was on her feet and hollering the curse at the guardsman. Payton was the one hauling her back into his lap and laughing when she got there.

"Jesu', Mary, and Joseph. You've gained four stones in weight, Wife. I can barely heft you, anymore."

"You just wait, Payton Dunn-Fadden. I'll show you heft."

Dallis lifted her right hand to his cheek to cup it and hold him, while arching up for a kiss. It only worked because he helped, lifting her to assist with the embrace. They'd just connected when the guard opened the door with the expiration of time.

"There's someone here to see you, My Laird."

Payton looked up from the writing desk, amazed that he'd made sensible sentences in the love sonnet he was attempting, and not just dribbled massive quantities of ink. He was rather proud of the execution of her name, as well, with high swirls and calligraphic style.

"What does he want?" he asked, and redipped his quill tip . . . just barely, and then he patted it with a gentle motion, to keep the ink where it belonged.

There was some verbal murmuring happening in the antechamber and then Martin came back to the archway. "He says it's something of immense value. To you. And only you."

"Everyone has something of immense value for me," Payton replied with a smirk, and started on the next line of his poem. "Find out what it is."

He heard more voices, louder this time, and then Martin was back.

"He will na' say. He will na' release it, and he will na' leave."

"Then shut the door." Payton lifted a bit of sand from the tray and sprinkled it across his latest word, and then bent sideways to blow it gently away. He probably looked and acted contrary to everything his followers believed of a king's champion. He didn't care.

"He says if you doona' want it, he'll take it to Kilchurning, then. The offer there is for forty-two gold crowns."

Payton finished blowing, put the quill atop his letter, and pushed the stool back. It was just as well. He'd over-filled the last loop of the word love. It had filled in with ink and no longer resembled a letter, let alone the one it was supposed to be.

"Forty-two gold crowns is a lot of gold. Verra few men can even heft it. Let me see what he has."

Payton was sandwiched between two of his Honor Guard as he went through to the antechamber. He didn't need them, but their curiosity was aroused. As was his.

The man at the door looked vaguely familiar. Payton couldn't quite decide why. His hair was reminiscent of Dallis's, but there the resemblance ended. He was a courtier. That was obvious. No Highland wear corrupted the frills and beribboned attire he wore.

"What clan is he from?" he asked Martin. Martin turned from him to ask it.

"You dinna' even ask that. Jesu', Martin. You are a poor agent. Give the item here. I'll decide if 'tis worth forty-two gold crowns, or forty-two blows from my fist."

The man backed three steps into the hall, almost reaching the opposite wall as if Payton would really act on such a threat. He turned to his men and grinned.

"Na' much for bravery, is he?" he asked.

"Do you want the trinket, or not?" the man asked.

Payton's eyebrow rose. He stepped out into the hall, as well. "Trinket?" he asked.

"Of a sort."

"Show me."

The man put both hands out with nothing in them. "Do I look fain stupid enough to bring it with me?" he asked.

Payton pulled himself up straighter, folded his arms across his chest, and lowered his chin. Most challengers knew the look. This man was right. He wasn't stupid. He immediately seemed to fold and looked like he was near tears.

"I only thought your lordship would want it because it belongs to the wife. Well . . . it used to belong to your wife, but I have it now. That's all."

Payton rubbed at the scar on his temple, and wondered if he was lucky enough to have his first ring sold back to him. He smiled.

"Give the man forty-two crowns," he told Martin.

"The price is now forty-three."

The man was standing tall again, which was Payton's shoulder height. For some reason, he was reminded of an eel, a slippery slimy eel. His eyes narrowed. "Verra well. Give him forty-three."

"But, how will we get the trinket?"

"Follow him. He fails to produce it, he dies. You want the chore, Seth?"

Seth-the-Silent played his part perfectly, going so far as to pull a skean from his belt and lick it across his tongue.

"Jesu'! All right. I have it. I do. Give me the crowns, and I'll pitch it to you from the end of the hall. Right there. Should you not think it worth that sum, send someone after me. I'll probably die of fright a-fore they reach me."

Payton chuckled. The men about him did the same. "Done. Martin? Give him the gold."

The bag they handed him was so heavy, the man's arm dipped when he took it and he had to use both. He was grinning widely, before turning.

"Are na' you going to count it?" Martin asked.

"No reason, is there?"

"What's your name, gent?" Payton asked.

"Giles. And tell her I'm sorry. Truly . . . but I am desperate!"

Payton was frowning when Giles stopped exactly where he

said. He bent down to put his sack of gold on the floor. Then he was fishing about in his waistcoat, for what looked to be a small trinket box. He pitched it at Payton.

Payton didn't even have it in his hand before the man was picking the sack back up and running. Payton jerked his head in that direction and Seth took off.

Then he opened the box. And slammed it back shut. A horrible ache started then, stirring with each beat of his heart and getting more and more painful as it grew in volume and cadence and strength.

She is buying my death? Again? Even . . . the rabid challenger?

His heart couldn't handle her betrayal. He couldn't handle it. The beats got harder, thumping with painful precision within his chest, and then down both arms. Consuming him. Until it consumed his hearing.

"Nae!" The cry came from the depths of him then, erupting through the fire of red that filled his vision, making the hall dim and warp until it was her face . . . so beloved, beautiful . . . so eloquent as she spoke on her love again and again.

Pretending all the time. Which meant none of it . . . was real.

Payton didn't realize he was crying until the moisture blurred the red into a haze. That was worse odd. The champion didn't cry . . . and if he did, it should at least quench the burn erupting with each heartbeat, and getting thicker, denser, louder. More painful. More agonizing. That's when he moved.

Voices bothered him. Yelling at him. Angrily hollering. He ignored them, and shoved anyone aside that tried to stop him. Every weapon he could carry, he loaded onto his frame. Skeans, three hand-axes, two claymores—one on either side of his belt. His sword. More skeans. The arrows . . . bow. If anyone tried to stop him, Payton slammed them to the ground. It was easy. Slam a foot to the instep of a challenger at the exact moment of impact. A man without a foot to move went down.

The Honor Guard went down. One after another. Again and again. Martin went down. Redmond. Alan was flung aside and glanced off a wall. Dugan went down. Four more clansmen went down.

Redmond again.

The red filling his vision changed to the blood-red ruby of her ring. Twinkling up at him from the box, instead of from her finger. The ring she'd vowed to keep on her finger for all time. She'd *vowed* it!

Payton gave a huge yell as he slammed through his chamber door and entered the hall. He didn't know where they kept her. But he knew where she'd be . . . at the appointed hour.

The door to their special room crashed open, and this time the hinges didn't just protest but fell, especially since Payton took a claymore to the wood until the door sagged in defeat. Then he moved on to the clock, making it a jumble of garbage metal. The settee. He took particular joy in smashing the padded settee into as many small pieces as possible, with an ax in each hand. And then he flung one of them at the other door. The one she'd come through.

His men caught up to him when he was sending arrows through the chamber, after dipping them in the lit oil in the sconces, until every tapestry in the room was alive with fire.

"Fire!"

He didn't hear the cry, as a boom resounded behind him. He didn't care either.

Redmond was in front of him again. And Redmond went down. Again. Payton held his man by the throat with his left hand, took a long-bladed dirk in the other, and affixed Redmond's shoulder fabric to the perfection of the wood floor. Then it was Martin going down, again.

He saw a body running, silhouetted in the flames, and pulling a tapestry down to slap it against the floor over and over, killing the fire. Payton nearly sent an arrow through him, and sent it, instead, right through the center of a chair.

Someone threw water at him. Payton side-stepped it easily, and watched as it slid across the floor and leaked around the wall corner. Into the alcove. Their special alcove.

He threw his head back and yelled the pain at the ceiling, sucking in cough-inducing smoke from the fires his men were still putting out behind him. Then he had to wipe at the tears his body was still cursing him with, regardless of the fact they weren't doing anything other than pouring acid through his soul.

He advanced around the alcove, with his sword in one hand and a hand-ax in the other, and then he was chopping at the bench where he'd found so much pleasure and so much bliss. Nothing changed. The anguish increased until he was bleeding it, and nothing changed.

Payton had the little wooden settee obliterated to little more than kindling, and he was still sobbing and hammering at each little piece, willing the solid ache of his heart into the same oblivion.

And nothing changed.

"Payton."

It was Redmond. Payton pivoted on his knee and sent the hand-ax whirling across the floor, until it slapped against an opposing wall.

"Payton," Redmond said his name again, using the modulated, calm, precise way of his.

Payton hardened everything. He started it with the area around his heart, since he couldn't get that part of him to cease spurting pain with every beat, but the rest of his body he controlled. The sobs wouldn't die, but he stood anyway, yanking a forearm across his eyes when he did, and faced the smoke-blackened faces of eight of his men. And more than a dozen Stewart guardsmen.

He lowered his chin, narrowed his eyes, and glared at all

of them, heedless of the fresh tears that slid from his eyes and just kept coming. More than one of them backed a step. Then, another one.

"Take me to the king," he told them.

"Now?" Martin asked.

Payton lifted the remaining hand-ax.

"There is no reason to take him anywhere."

"All bow! 'Tis King James Stewart!" The king's announcer yelled it.

"Oh, cease that."

The king was picking his way through debris with pointed-toed shoes and making clicking noises with his tongue as he did so. Then, he was at the front of the group facing Payton, although it looked to have swelled in number.

"What have you to say for yourself, Payton Dunn-Fadden?" he asked.

"You want a battle to the death?" Payton asked, with a growl throughout the words he didn't need to force.

The king put his little finger against the side of his mouth. "What have you to offer?" he asked.

Payton lifted the hair from the left of his scalp and shoved his head forward. "Find the man that wears this ring . . . bearing the Dunn-Fadden clan crest. He's in Kilchurning's camp. Find him. And then match him with another man. I'll take on two. Two to my one. To the death. That's my offer."

"Payton, nae." It was Redmond, and now he sounded close to tears.

The king had lifted both eyebrows and he was genuinely smiling.

"Agreed," he announced.

Payton snarled. "And what do you offer?" he asked, just as the king was turning around.

"You mean, aside from freedom from my tower over this . . . this . . . shall I say? Bit of destruction?"

Payton nodded.

"What do you want?"

"My *wife*." Payton put all the hatred and anger and agony in the word. Everyone gasped. "Released to me."

"Will she . . . be safe?" the king asked.

Payton narrowed his eyes even further. "The wife. Released to me," he repeated. "Those are my terms."

The king looked him over for long moments, while smoke-choked lungs led to coughing and sputtering about them, and then he nodded.

"Agreed," he said.

Chapter 25

Dallis entered the room, with a bit of embroidered handkerchief in her left hand. It was better for concealment. And her latest letter to Payton in her right. Lady Evelyn was right with her as they beheld the complete destruction of what had been a rich and elegant room.

Dallis put both hands to her mouth as her eyes watered up, with the smoke-filled air and the emotion. And she knew exactly what had happened.

"Sweet Jesus. What's happened?" Lady Evelyn was in shock.

"Payton," Dallis replied, picking her way into the center of the room, and standing forlornly in the center as absolutely nothing looked the same. It didn't seem possible to completely destroy a room, but it appeared Payton had managed it. There wasn't even anything left to sit on. And no tapestries, other than the fire-ravaged bits of material littering the floor.

"Oh . . . dear God . . . why? Why would he do such a thing?"

Lady Evelyn just kept asking it. She must not be able to hear Dallis's silent cries responding.

"I was hopeful you could tell me."

Redmond MacCloud came from the alcove area, where

he'd been sitting on the floor. He looked beaten. His face was smoke-blackened, which appeared to be covering over a blackened eye, that was near closed with the puff of it. His clothing was ripped, bloodied in places, and there was a large hole rent in the shoulder of his shirt that looked like it had been hacked away with a blade.

"Well?"

He was almost to her. Dallis was standing, her mouth open with the silent cries, and the bairn was kicking and pummeling her with his distress, as well.

"What could bring on such rage?" Lady Evelyn asked.

"Giles," Dallis whispered.

"Aye. It was a fellow named Giles. Said to ask your forgiveness when he sold My Laird a nice trinket for forty-three gold crowns."

"The little bastard!" It was Lady Evelyn. Going against all her teachings with the curse. There was complete silence for a span. "Well, he is," she added.

"What did he sell Payton?"

Dallis still had her mouth open. She forced words. Nothing came. Lady Evelyn said it for her.

"The ruby wedding ring."

Redmond's face reflected nothing. No shock, surprise, or consternation. He nodded. "I guessed as much. Why would you give him Payton's ring? I saw you with it. I've watched you twirl it. I doona' understand."

Dallis still had her lips open, and that gave her silent tears an avenue to run. She couldn't answer anything. She was standing in place, and feeling a great numbness happening . . . coming from her ankles and moving up her legs, and she started shaking her head back and forth while her hands moved to clutch at the baby before the numbness reached there.

"Because the bloody bastard was black-mailing her." Lady

Evelyn spat after she'd finished. "Rotten, filthy, scum . . . ! Slimy, black-hearted . . . bastard!"

"That pip? On what grounds."

"I . . . have to see him," Dallis mouthed the words, but they weren't watching, and nobody seemed to care.

"That pip? Black-mailing a Dunn-Fadden? On what grounds?"

"Dinna' you ever wonder why the Kilchurning laird never came to claim his bride?" Lady Evelyn asked.

Dallis watched them standing and conversing amid the destruction and it felt like they wavered getting closer, then farther. Closer.

Redmond smiled curtly. "Just tell me. I doona' have time for games."

He was closer with that answer, and Dallis moved her eyes to him, before shying away. *Payton!* Her heart was crying it, and nobody heard.

"'Twas due to my ladyship's tongue. Her wit. Her habit of ordering others about. She was nearly shrewish at times. She dinna' want Kilchurning."

Dallis's mouth closed, and she licked at the saltiness trailing from her eyes. The numbness faded slightly . . . hovering. At midthigh.

"He turned her belly the one time they'd met."

"So?" Redmond replied.

"And she dinna' want Dunn-Fadden, either. What respectable Caruth would?"

"Where is the black-mail in this?"

"The lone way to stay in charge of her estate is . . . widowhood. So, Lady Dallis starts sending every bit of funds that Payton sent her to Giles, that bastard, who's been outcast from Caruth Clan. He purchased challengers that would take on Dunn-Fadden in the list. The plan was to get Dunn-Fadden killed so Dallis would be a widow. That way she'd keep her castle and her lands, and Kilchurning would be left out in the cold, with nae claim, whatsoever."

"Payton . . . was paying for his own . . . fights?" Redmond's voice was showing the surprise. Then he started snorting. "'Tis priceless!"

"Exactly. His gold was just circling about him, with him none the wiser."

"The first ring? The one with the crest?"

"She sent it to Giles, as well."

"So . . . to keep him silent now, she gave him the little ruby ring."

"Near tore her skin off getting it to him, too. The craven little bastard."

"Well. This is a puzzle now."

"How so?" Dallis had her voice back. It croaked, but it was back.

"Payton has agreed to fight a battle. To the death. On terms."

"What . . . are they?" she whispered.

"He wants the man who knocked the Dunn-Fadden crest into his head with a blow from his own ring."

"That's a crest . . . from the ring?" Dallis queried. "Dear God. All this time, and he . . . he thought—"

"He thought you traded it to Kilchurning. For the same result. His death. He may suspect the rest. He may believe you'd do it again. And that would make everything about you . . . false. Everything."

Dallis had both hands to her mouth. She was shaking her head.

Redmond continued. "'Tis worse, My Lady. He requires the king to find the man with the ring. And another. Payton will only take on this challenge if the king puts forth two men at the same time."

"Nae," Dallis moaned it. "Please nae. You have to stop it."

"I have nae power to stop it."

"But he'll be killed!"

"You should worry more over when he wins, My Lady."

Her eyes went huge, and she watched as both Redmond and Lady Evelyn warped to farther away again, looking very tiny in comparison.

Why? Her mouth made the motion, but no sound came out.

"Because the king has agreed to Payton's terms. You're to be delivered to him. At the fight's end."

"'Twill give me time then! He'll listen. I know he'll listen."

"Look about. We all tried to stop him. And a good force of king's men. Does this appear a man who listens . . . a-fore acting?"

Dallis welcomed the numbness to her then, hugging it close to use against what had to be horror and fear. The room was swelling to a huge size, too, just before it started rotating, circling about her until it went dim. Then dark. It was still rotating when she crumpled onto the floor.

Demons had her body and were attacking from all sides, the blood they were spilling flying about to fleck the rooms she'd lived in for months now, with anguish and sobbed cries and hushed whispers.

"'Tis too early!"

"That bairn would na' wait another moment. And you ken it!"

"Too soon . . ."

Then the room warped before her eyes, turning into the same one where she and Payton had met. For their hour of time. And then it warped again, the beauty ravaged and ripped to oblivion, and then sent even further than that.

Through it all banshees and gobbshites and creatures of the night continued their hammering at her body. Twisting her into contortions while they worked their evil on her. Dallis screamed long and hard and with a wailing sound that should

have carried for leagues on the winds of a summer night . . .
but nobody heard them.

Because nobody cared.

Rotate. Again. Dive. Belly-roll, to his knees. Leap back to
feet. Knees. Feet. Launch to flat back landing, losing air and
precious time. Twist to front. Push up with arms. Leap to feet.
Sword at ready. Again.

Kill the agony of the heart.

Payton stood panting, letting the ground mists stirred by
the rain-filled day caress him, cool him, and revive him. The
moon had decided to come out, and had finally reached a
high enough apex that light managed to filter through the
walls of the enclosed barren garden the king had given him
to use.

The sound of a banshee wail, carried on the night caught at
his ear, made him lift his head and move it about on his
shoulders, releasing any cramps. Payton smirked to himself,
and picked up a hand-ax, hefting it for a time atop his shoulder while he waited for the cry of pain to come again. It had
sounded a bit like her. And that was good.

The twinge deep in his chest came again, and he hunched
his shoulders forward while he fought it. He already knew he
couldn't kill it. He'd tried. For two days now. Ceaselessly.
He'd tried. And failed.

But that was his secret.

The lie that he'd always harbored deep in his innards came
alive then, keeping him focused and taking his senses from
the pain, for sharp, intensely centered periods of time, but it
still worked. Payton pulled in a breath, and started swinging
again.

The wail came again, lifting the hairs along the back of his
neck, and adding a ghoulish accompaniment to his movements. Twirl. Thrust. Dive. Roll. Leap. Staying on the ground

after being knocked to it was a sure way to get killed. And on that leap back up, he used a slashing motion of the ax that could cleave an opponent's manhood clean off.

And would.

Payton grabbed up another ax. Put them under his armpits, handles backward. He was spinning when he opened his arms, crooked both arms behind him and caught both axes, making deadly slashes at the air at the end of one full rotation.

Again. And again. Doing the same maneuver until it was natural and perfect and instinctive. The banshee cried out again, filling the night air with pain and suffering. Payton's heart reacted, sending heat and pain shooting down both arms, through his belly and then into both legs. He hunched forward again, hugging himself as he waited for it to recede.

It would. He knew it would. And it got a little easier each time. Not much, but a little. And that was better than never.

He picked up his sword, moved the blade about in front of his face, within a hairsbreadth of space. His eyes constantly moving, checking for the glint that betrayed the blade's path. Closer. . . .

Payton shaved a stray eyebrow hair or two while he practiced with the blade, using it as an opponent might, making certain that no matter what the cost, he'd know where the blade was at all times, and wouldn't even blink.

The woman-cry came again. Stronger. With more agony involved, and it sounded so much like her, that his knees wavered and then dropped him. Payton hunched forward . . . struggled, and nearly had the weep emotion killed before it reached his eyes.

This time.

Payton blinked rapidly at the moonlit span of turf before him, where shadows showed where he'd been shoving weapons for balance, or using clods of earth as a weapon. He focused. Turning all his attention to every minute bit of darkness before moving on to the next one. His reward was a domination over the weakness that made a man cry. Tears were for the weak and for the faint-hearted to spill.

And her to spill.

He conquered the emotion again. Straightened. Flexed. And rotated.

Dallis awoke to a rain-filled day smelling of freshness and renewal and bringing heart-pain with every moment she had to look at it. She shut her eyes again, and that allowed the tear to ooze from beneath her lid.

"My Lady?"

Dallis trembled and hunched a shoulder, hoping the speaker would get the unspoken message. She should have known Lady Evelyn wasn't that easily put-off.

"You canna' ignore him all day."

Dallis shuddered through a breath. Then, another. Nothing muted it, nothing tempered it, and nothing changed it. If she opened her eyes she had to face the vast vista of nothingness that it was.

I . . . ken as much." She whispered.

"And you truly should give the lad a name. He's keeping the wet nurses up all night, sleeping all day, and na' one soul kens what to call him. Going on six days, and nae name. The devil will snatch him up if you doona' give that lad a name!"

"His father . . . can christen him," Dallis replied.

"Dallis."

Oh, God! It was Redmond MacCloud. In her bedchamber and speaking just as he used to with Payton. Dallis's heart twinged so swiftly and painfully, that she very nearly cried aloud with the pain of it.

"Aye?" she whispered to the wall.

"The challengers have been located. Yester-eve."

She nodded, the motion allowing more tears to slide through her closed lids and down her cheeks.

"They are both hardy looking. Tough. Large. They appear to be able to give . . . him trouble."

"They may . . . kill him?"

The possibility was making everything that she couldn't consciously numb spurt with agony.

"Aye," he replied.

"Oh, God," she whispered.

"'Twas already a given, lass. The king could na' get any takers to this bet of his without challengers that would make a fair fight."

"And . . . Payton?"

"I've na' located him, yet. None of the Guard has. The king has him locked away so tightly, it's worse than looking for gray hairs in the king's beard."

His attempt at humor fell flat. Dallis licked at the dry feeling in her mouth. Everything felt flat, anymore.

"You sent word?"

"Through the king. Daily. He claims Dunn-Fadden was informed of his son's birth. There is nae other answer. Yet."

Dallis sighed. "Then . . . the bairn has nae name. Still."

"You are so stubborn!" Lady Evelyn told her. "You already ken that the longer he goes un-christened, the greater the risk."

"May I suggest a name?"

Dallis struggled to open her eyes again. The room was dreary with rain-leaden skies outside, and the candles sputtering along the wall. She had too many pillows, too. She knew better than to complain. Nobody was listening.

"David. 'Twill do until Laird Dunn-Fadden adds to it. We shall call him Davey."

Dallis struggled with the fresh tears, and then lost out. She watched as Redmond's eyes looked moist, too. She nodded.

"I'll go and tell young Alan."

"Redmond?" she asked.

"Aye?"

"You are too good to me."

He looked at her for a bit. And then winked. "I know," he replied before sauntering out.

Chapter 26

The drums had been going for hours, legions of drummers making a beat of sound that infiltrated the walls, searched down all the corridors, and even into the dungeon, to the slab of stone that Payton Dunn-Fadden was lying atop. He'd been awake the entire time, looking inward, rather than feeling the damp, decay, and fear that the entire space seemed filled with.

"My Laird Dunn-Fadden?"

It was MacIlroy. As Payton had requested. He watched the king's announcer grimace at the choice of hospitality, looking incongruous in his tunic of a satin so fine it shone, even down here, with only an ancient torch for light.

"In the end room, MacIlroy!" Payton called out, and smirked again. "'Tis the only one with the door open."

"I have never seen the likes of—"

The man stopped at the door to Payton's chosen room and his mouth dropped open. Payton guessed he was looking at the moss-draped walls, which was all some had for water. Payton pulled himself up, feeling every muscle in his abdomen making the move, and then he was on his feet and stretching.

"You bring my attire?" he asked.

"You could have anyone assist you. Anyone. Your entire

Honor Guard has been bothering the king daily with messages about it. And you choose me. Me. Why?"

"'Tis the sound of your voice. It echoes. Even down here, with none to hear."

"Have you lost your wits? There are rooms all about this castle for your use. Rooms! With fine lighting, and warm fireplaces, and—and—and padding on the chairs, and blankets. Look there! You doona' even have a blanket!"

"I have my plaid." Payton started unwinding it from about him. "'Tis all I need."

"But . . . it's blasted chill down here! And you had a choice of any of them! Or all of them. The king would probably have moved his wife if you wanted her rooms!"

"I dinna' want any of them, MacIlroy. Too soft. Now. Move from the way. They're bringing my bucket."

"A bucket? For what?"

"Washing. What else?"

Payton moved around the older fellow and took the bucket from the turnkey. The man returned his nod. Then Payton placed the bucket on the floor, went into a full hand stand, and ducked his head fully into it before lifting back out. MacIlroy had a look of awe on his face when Payton finished, was back on his feet, and spitting wet strands of hair from his mouth. Then he was dipping one end of his kilt into the water and splashing himself, unmindful of what the announcer might be calling chilled conditions.

"My *feile-breacan?*" he asked when he'd finished and the man just stood at the door to the cell, staring.

"But—but—"

Payton sighed heavily and went to pluck it out of the man's hands. "I chose you because you're used to royalty, MacIlroy. You'll na' be easily turned by false things. Evil things."

"What things?"

"Fame. Appearances. Wealth."

Payton was unfurling one of his plainest kilts. One he

hadn't worn in over a year. There was no shirt. No loin wrap. No brooch. No shine. Anywhere.

"And look. You have attire that is jaw-dropping. Suitable attire. And you make me bring you what? That?"

"I'm killing two men tonight, MacIlroy. And then I will see to the killing of a heart. Mine. There is nae suitable attire for that. You ken?"

The man gulped. Nodded.

"Good. Now, hand over the belt. Boots. You did well, MacIlroy. Verra well. Your service is to be commended."

"But—"

"Now, go. Lead the way. You're the chosen escort to the champion! On the eve of his great battle! You need to start acting it!"

"Well, I've a message a-fore we go."

"What?"

"They called him Davey. I doona' ken what it means, but there you go. Your message."

The solid spurt of his heart sent such weakening emotion through all his limbs, that Payton swayed against the door. The slam of it hitting the wall was loud and abrasive in this otherwise silent place. He willed the sensation dead, and within two more heartbeats he'd succeeded, gained the focus back. And the intent. Payton straightened, looked forward again and followed MacIlroy.

The drums were still thumping out a steady rhythm, making certain all in the complex knew of the challenge, or had no excuse for not knowing it. Payton followed the announcer, who was starting to get ribbons and kisses flung at him, and women leaning forward for glimpses of full bosoms. He watched as the announcer straightened and started waving back.

It brought the shadow of a smile to his mouth before he let it drop.

He'd been spotted. The drums ceased then, and bagpipes

started up instead, filling the grounds at Edinburgh Castle with swells of sound. And over that was the enormous crowd sound, drowning out the king's hand-picked bagpipers, as cheers and shouts rang out.

Payton ignored it, turning a deaf ear to all but the inner workings of his mind. The spins. The twists. The gyrations that would see him through this.

Although it was late afternoon, they had tents set up all along the list, their roofs keeping the light mist of rain off all the torches they'd lit, and putting the light back onto the field better.

Payton watched his challengers. They were both large men, packed with muscle. They were proud of themselves and strutting about the edges of the wide swath of field that was marked with poles. Greeting the crowd. Puffing out their chests and posing. Hollering for the effect.

Payton watched them, looking silently at how their muscles moved beneath the skin. Evaluating. Checking. One had a slight limp, left side. The other had a large scar along his back . . . also left side. The limping one looked all shiny with sweat. Already. But he might have used oil on his skin. That would make him slick to hang on to.

Payton stepped into the list, standing for long moments as the din grew to encompass the sky. He was watching as it interfered with the challengers. He waited for them to turn and eye him. Payton lowered his chin and observed. He didn't glare. He didn't threaten. He didn't move.

The scarred one shifted first, breaking eye contact as he jostled the other.

He was going to go down first.

"Ladies! Clansmen! All rise for King James!"

Payton turned toward the raised platform that the king would sit on. He had his current mistress at his side. And courtiers surrounding everywhere else. Everyone waited until the monarch was seated and then the announcements came again.

"The challengers! Derrick Kilchurning of Clan Kilchurning, and Edward the Lion from Clan MacKettryk."

Derrick was the scarred one. He'd had the ring. The widow must have put in the other challenger. That was interesting. Payton's lip lifted as he wondered what reward the widow had promised the man.

"And the King's Champion, Payton Dunn-Fadden of Clan Dunn-Fadden."

His applause was deafening. And Payton lifted both arms toward them and turned in a slow circle, waiting as they all evaluated, noted, and exclaimed. He'd lost a bit in weight, but gained sinew, strength, and endurance. And it was obvious.

He put his arms back to his sides and approached the center. There was another announcer fellow standing there. And beside him were three other men, all holding weapons.

"You get one weapon each. Dunn-Fadden can have two."

"Nae," Payton replied. "I take one."

The man nodded and turned to his opponents. He watched as they talked amongst themselves. From the way they were talking, it appeared they were speaking of strategy. And timing. They were far too late for that. And they hadn't practiced together much. All of that was apparent.

He watched as they went forward. The limping one chose a hand-ax. The scarred one a sword. They stepped back, one of them circling to the left. The other to the right. Just out of arm range.

Payton stepped forward and took another broadsword. He checked for balance and dexterity by swinging it in elegant swift slashes through the air. He nodded his approval and moved back, also, keeping in mind where the opponents were with a constant scan.

Circling. Scanning. Payton bided his time, swiveling with the sword held out in his right hand, and his left with nothing.

Spinning on the ball of one foot to scan from a different direction. Limp lunged slightly, waving the hand-ax with small, jabbing motions. A solitary drummer started thumping the large drum, sending throbs of sound through him. The crowd was chanting, too.

The scarred one moved slightly inward, with a swift quick motion, his sword slashing the air in front of him. Payton was already turned for the other's charge, and at the moment of impact, one foot went down on the opponent's foot, with punishing force since it was his limping side, and then Payton slammed his shoulder into the man, knocking him to the ground.

A moment later, Payton was up, swiveling to face the other's sword, catching the blade with his own and sending it uselessly to the ground. And going in close to land a powerful blow to the man's scarred side. The man's release of air told Payton what he needed. Then, he was on his hands and knees and whirling with one leg to take the legs out from under the limping one again.

Up. Spinning toward the scarred one. Parrying the sword thrust once, twice. The third time, he turned the hilt around, and used it on the man's sword hand, hearing the crunch of bone.

Scar cried out and dropped the blade, only to pick it up with his left hand.

Limp was back on his feet, and charging. Payton spun, planted his sword point in the ground and launched himself straight up atop it, doing the same hand-stand as before, only in midair, for the one moment of time it took for the limping one to stumble past, his ax swinging at air.

Payton fell, pulling his sword the moment he was on the ground and staying on his knees to swing at that level. He got Scar across the lower legs, the blade slicing nearly bone deep, and the man went down. Useless. Payton grabbed up the discarded sword, ignoring the blood spurting from his opponent's legs, to spin with both blades out, in the event he'd miscalculated Limp's mobility.

The other challenger was charging, his limp even more noticeable as he moved. His face was a grimace of hatred, and his eyes were ugly with intent.

Payton tossed the unneeded sword, bent his knees, willed the tenseness into his legs, the spring, the readiness, the ability.

Limp was using his hand-ax in a lever motion as he ran, pumping it from side to side. That made it a matter of rhythm to launch at him, grab the ax on one slashing move, and use it as a base to pivot around the man. The rotation made Limp spin too, sending him to his knees because of his injured leg. Payton slashed him deeply, in a horizontal motion, through the muscles at the backs of both legs, sending that opponent to the ground as well. Useless.

It was the champion's signature. Get the opponent to the ground. And keep them there. Battle over.

Payton went over to his second sword. Took it up and walked back over to Scar, working the swords through the air as he went. The man had pain etched all through him, and something else. Fear was huge in his eyes, and he stiffened, preparing himself. Payton locked eyes with him, put one blade against the scarred side, letting it pierce the already ravaged skin, and then he was demanding his ring.

Scar had a sly look to him. Payton had no choice.

"The ring or your hand," he replied, moving his other sword there.

It didn't surprise him that the man moved. Death was one thing, deformity another. He watched without expression as Scar rapidly pulled the Dunn-Fadden ring from his hand. Payton put the sword tip out and Scar slid the ring onto it.

Then Payton was walking, crossing the length of the field toward the king's dais. The crowd roar was blistering to the ears at the intensity of it. For the entire time the walk took.

He hadn't a mark on him.

"Laird Dunn-Fadden."

Payton was stopped short of the dais by more guards than he could count. He was forced to wait for the noise to abate, looking up at where the king reclined the entire time.

"You do seem to have failed, Dunn-Fadden," King James remarked.

The announcement was trumpeted over and over all along the walls.

Payton turned around, held his sword up, and listened as the noise swelled even louder than it had been. He brought the sword back down, and turned back to the king. And waited to be heard.

"Leave them out there long enough. They'll die," he replied.

His words were also trumpeted around the walls, the criers talking over each other as it went. The crowd got a bit unsettled sounding, and disgruntled.

"Or . . . let them live!"

Payton put his sword in the air again as the criers circulated his words. The swell of approval was enormous again. Payton lowered his sword.

"'Twas a battle to the death, Dunn-Fadden," the king replied.

That was met with a gathering hush as the king's remarks went about the field. Payton could tell his sovereign wasn't appreciative. He wasn't as well liked as he wished to admit. No king wearing fancy European court dress would be. Payton watched as the king frowned. Payton raised his sword again.

"'Tis clear I won!"

Once again the crowd noise showed how much they appreciated Payton's remarks. He lowered his sword and the noise seemed to dissipate with his movement.

King James wasn't frowning anymore. His face hadn't one expression on it.

"You dare change the rules?" he asked.

The criers started yelling the words about the walls. There was a strange hush happening as any cheers or approval was withdrawn, and angry calls were heard. The enormous volume of humanity felt like a cloak about the courtyard, stifling the very air.

"Grant them clemency, my king! I beseech you!"

Payton's words were announced, and the crowd approval was so loud after the silence of a moment before that Payton wasn't just imagining the movements of some of the courtiers, to leave the podium, sliding from the back, where King James couldn't see them.

"Verra well, Dunn-Fadden," the king remarked when Payton had lowered his sword and the crowd seemed to be waiting. "You win. They have clemency."

As the king's words were announced, the crowd went absolutely wild, and began spilling from behind the rails onto the field. They were running with abandon at the fallen warriors, and toward the king's podium. King James wasn't waiting. His guards were surrounding him and moving him off the stage. Payton vaulted over it and was moving amidst all the finery and colors and fabrics of the courtiers, without thought to how different he looked.

It wasn't until he was solidly inside the walls of the castle again, that he realized what he'd just done, and what he'd lost. The king wouldn't hold to a bargain when Payton hadn't stayed true to it. He'd failed.

In everything.

The summons came late into the morning. After a night spent sleepless and staring at nothing other than the rock above his head. The cavern he was in was hewn from the rock, with uneven walls and an even more jagged ceiling.

What shadows he could see depending on the vagaries of the torch and its flares.

She'd called him Davey.

The reaction made him tremble atop his stone berth, shivers rippling unpleasantly through him as the fiery lump of heart reminded him with every beat, that the pain was still there. Undead, and waiting.

The turnkey brought the news, moving silently in the same large-framed, hunched fashion Payton was familiar with. The man probably didn't walk straight because he'd been down here too long, absorbing the place, and the sheer defeat it harbored.

"They sent guards for you. As an escort." The man grinned, showing yellow teeth. "Now, that has never happened. An armed escort from my lodgings." He was chortling, but had to end it with a cough.

"To where?"

"Nae telling. A-fore you go, I need to thank you. I do."

"For what? Being a model . . . guest?" Payton's lips twitched.

"Nae. For the silver you brought me. From my bet. From the fight."

"I dinna' win," Payton replied.

"I bet you'd live. And you'd let them both live. Down here, you tell a man's character a bit quicker, if you ken my meaning."

Payton stared.

The man nodded and smiled. And led the way.

It was the four clansmen from his Honor Guard. Redmond, Martin, Seth-the-Silent, and Dugan. Payton nodded to each in turn and waited.

"The king has sent us for you," Redmond informed him.

Payton nodded, ignoring the twist in his lower belly at the same time. For the first time, he'd failed in gaining a win for the king. He didn't know what the consequences were. All he knew was they weren't getting smaller with the wait.

They didn't speak as they marched through lengths of halls and up series of steps that lightened the farther you walked them, whether due to reality or atmosphere. Payton didn't know for sure, and he'd ceased letting it bother him the second day. It seemed to bother more than one of his men. He noted it as the pace quickened without conscious volition.

He was taken to the throne room. King James was already there, surrounded by guards. His men marched with him to the circular area, marked with the placement of the wood on the floor. In front of, and below the raised throne. Payton stiffened everywhere. He bowed his head.

"Payton Dunn-Fadden! King's Champion!" MacIlroy had followed them in, which was odd, and he yelled it from the door.

Payton lifted his head and looked across at the king, noted that the birthmark on his face looked more florid than normal, and waited.

"Payton Dunn-Fadden."

The king was stewed. Payton's eyes narrowed on him as the words slurred, the man warbled, and then he slid down the chair slightly.

"I find myself in an odd position."

There were some smiles all about the king's own guards. Payton kept his face stone still.

"I should be designing your torture and imprisonment. Someone, get me a tankard!"

He turned and spoke to one of his guards. The tension relaxed as a brew was brought. Payton's body started doing the same thing.

"I find myself the receiver of all kinds of good will. Thanks to my magnanimity toward you and your challengers yesterday, I have had nothing but tankards lifted in my name, cheers called to me throughout my castle . . . and my town, and even the French ambassador has been in to see me, about a possible alliance with their royal house and my first-born daughter once I have one."

He stopped, put the tankard to his mouth and drank a long draught while everyone waited. He was smacking his lips when he'd finished.

"And then, there's the matter of the bets."

Payton's shoulders both went taut, his right hand tightened on his sword, while the left felt it was warping the hilt of a skean tucked into his belt. He forced his shoulders to rest, set his mind to relaxing his fists, and his breath to continue in the same modulated, calm motion.

The king slammed the tankard to one arm of his chair, sloshing a bit of ale.

"Do you ken how much gold you have made me? Good God, Payton! I am amazed! And it just keeps adding up!"

The surprise flooded him, overtaking the taut pressure he was exerting on everything to keep the reaction hidden. Payton stood a bit taller, remained silent, but couldn't halt the frown.

"Not that it wouldn't be much, much more, if you were na' so damned famous. And accurate. And deadly. And acrobatic. Did you all see that move into the air? I vow, my court near collapsed with the awe. Oh! And I must not forget, that you are a wonderful warrior, as well. My troubadours are penning songs to you for my fest this eve. The Lord of my Bedchamber tells me 'tis almost readied and quite lovely." He hiccuped. "And melod—melod—mel . . . it has a grand sound to it."

"I doona' understand," Payton said.

The king snorted. And then he was standing. "Well. When the mayor brought me his proclamation this morn, and included taxation monies . . . *advance* taxation monies, well! I was already four sheets to the wind over my great mag—mag—kingly ability. Better make that five sheets. I was drunk. And then the man wanted to drink to my health as well. My health."

He lifted his tankard, took another long drink, and then lowered it before looking back out at Payton.

"I really need to keep on task. This audience is taking bloody ever, and I need my rest. What was next . . . ? Ah yes. The decision. 'Tis my decision, I'm told. It is being yelled out all about that my decision is that anyone betting on the challengers has forfeited their wager. 'Tis most obvious that the challengers dinna' win. 'Twas obvious . . . was na' it?"

He encompassed the room, and the guards about him nodded and chuckled. They looked nothing like men called to lynch a traitor, which is what Payton had been preparing for.

"These funds will all be used toward the common good of Scotland . . . and they will be! But—because I so . . . mag—magnamaneously and graciously, and with great skill and kingly forethought . . . allowed those men to live, then anyone betting on your win forfeits that. Because you obviously dinna' win, either. They'll get their wagers back. Of course. That is good sportsmanship. So, all wages on you are getting returned. I have accountants working through it right now. And 'tis more of my great fortune that you had lousy odds. So, the bets are na' much more than a piddle in the wind."

The king took another swallow of his brew, brought the tankard down, swayed a bit, and then collapsed back into his chair. Payton watched as one of his guardsmen covered his lap with a fur wrap. Then, King James was adjusting the crown back atop his head and looking over at Payton.

"Which does bring me back . . . to the problem . . . of what to do. With you."

Chapter 27

"Quick, My Lady! He's coming!"

Dallis shifted her head on the pillow, looked out as it appeared to be Bess, and lifted her hand. "Assist . . . me," she replied.

She probably shouldn't have asked them to put her in white satin atop the swathing of linens about her to ward off a chill that no summer day should have. But she wanted the pristine white. It had always been her favorite. And it gave her a sense of invulnerability and purity.

She clucked her tongue at the wrinkled appearance, once she was on her feet, waiting for her legs to hold her there, as well as the dancing dots before her eyes to cease being abrasive and annoying, and disappear altogether. There appeared to be a dark tone along one portion of her skirt, and Dallis frowned a bit at it, while she fussed and shuffled it about, hoping the marks of over-heating with an iron weren't noticeable. And then she stopped, smiled at herself and raised her head.

Foolish worry. It probably wouldn't stay white long, anyway.

She had a silver girdle about her hips, made of meshed wire, rather than solid metal. That had been Lady Dunrobin's choice for Dallis's attire today. They all knew she couldn't support the weight of a solid silver or gold girdle. She was feeling shaky and weak just from the work of standing up.

Dallis moved to the chamber mirror, near an armoire, looking to all observers there like she was checking her appearance, frowning a bit at how washed-out and ghostly she looked, bending to tuck a stray hair beneath her pearl-encrusted caplet, adjusting her belt to sit with more security at her hips, fussing at the back of it, where the long drape of her veiled hair hid any movements.

That way no one would see how all of it was put in play for securing the small handled skean she'd had secreted beneath the mattress, into the back of her belt. All of it was orchestrated and accompanied by the greatest whooshing sound in her ear that she pegged as fear, because otherwise she'd have to admit to herself that it was the sound of her heart breaking.

The door opened and Dallis moved to the oriel window of her chambers. Facing outward, she looked over the high wall that had been her view for almost as long as she'd known Payton. There wasn't much to see. There never was.

She turned, composed herself, and watched as Redmond entered the room first, followed by more of the clansmen, and then there was Payton.

She couldn't bear it. Dallis spun, kept herself from falling by gripping the rock opening to her alcove, and cursed the cry that came from her own throat.

"Payton Dunn-Fadden. King's Champion."

It was Redmond stating it, and something in his voice spoke just for her. Dallis waited to hear more, listening for any sound in the room behind her that might penetrate the odd whoosh of thrumming noise through her ears that matched her pulse. Nothing. She heard nothing. She straightened, blinked around the dots that were hampering her vision, and turned.

If she could have died the moment the cold of his blue

eyes touched hers, she would have. Gladly. Instantly. With joy. Because then she wouldn't have to continue holding his gaze, despite every ripple of shiver that coursed over her body unpleasantly, and the tremble of her knees as they knocked together, and the tightening of her hand on the wall to keep from falling.

That's when her Caruth heritage returned, reminding her. Dallis pulled in a large breath, lifted her shoulders and chin, and gave him the exact same look he was giving her, despite how it made the air-sound in her ears even louder. She had to concentrate to hear, and that made it all a bit easier.

"She is well enough to attend me below," Payton said.

"The king granted this. True. But she is na' well enough to be moved. Even in a litter!" It was Redmond answering.

Dallis sneered. "I'm well enough to meet with him . . . anywhere, Redmond MacCloud. As you can . . . plainly see."

She'd chosen well. The rock at her hand didn't give away her weakness as a wood support might have. Dallis pulled from inner strength, locked her knees, and remained standing, through the narrowed eyes, lowered chin, that was his warrior look. None would guess if she was too weak or not.

Exactly as she wanted it.

Payton nodded. "Then, step down from there, and meet with me," he said.

Step away? She'd fall. Dallis shook her head and returned his regard.

"You disobey? Why?"

"I want . . . this . . . day. This sun-filled . . . day. Out there." She gestured to the view behind her. "I want *that* to be . . . the last thing I see," she replied.

Lady Evelyn's cry rent through the chamber, starting a prick of sensation to Dallis's eyes before she stanched it and sent it away. Her aunt had the same blood as her niece, but the backbone was missing. Still. Dallis straightened even farther, feeling the strain along her back at standing so long for the first time since Davey's birth, and locked it away as her secret. That way, she returned the steady regard of her husband, with exactly the same lack of emotion.

"Dunn-Fadden is allowed a word with you, My Lady," Redmond informed her. His lack of words said more, and she knew it.

Dallis endured the swelling of the noise through her ears as it reflected the quick surge of her heartbeat. She didn't have another choice. As usual.

"Allowed?" she asked.

Redmond nodded. Dallis watched the movement coming from Payton's side. Payton didn't move his eyes. Consequently, she didn't move hers. She smirked slightly. He'd let the men live. That had angered the king. And that meant she lived.

"What else is he . . . allowed?" she asked.

She could tell her word choice bothered him, by the way he clenched his jaw, sending a nerve bulging out the side. It showed the control he was exercising, as well as how much that must affect him. If she hadn't had her gaze firmly affixed to his face, she wouldn't have seen it.

"What would you have of him?"

Redmond's word greatly angered Payton despite the rigid control he had on himself. Dallis watched as a red flush stained the exposed flesh of his chest before it flooded his chin and cheeks. She lowered her chin and smiled, showing she understood. The king had granted her the power. That was the punishment Payton had reaped.

How it must bother him!

She watched how much his increased breaths moved his chest. He probably should've changed from the attire it looked like he'd worn to the battle, if Redmond's description had been accurate. Payton should've shaved what looked to be a day's growth of beard, narrowing his cheeks. He should have pulled his hair back. And done a thousand things different than angering his monarch.

"Leave us," Dallis said.

The eruption was immediate and vociferous. And loud. Almost loud enough to over-ride the noise she'd gotten used to listening around. That made it easier to ignore all of them, Redmond, Lady Evelyn, Martin, Dugan, big-eyed Alan, Lady Dunrobin, Bess and Mary. Dallis even had to listen to Seth-the-Silent as he grunted and pounded at his chest, although Redmond was the loudest. And he was last.

Dallis had her hand up for silence, and then had to drop it. She hadn't realized how heavy a hand could be, nor how shaky. It was too easy to spot.

"My Lady! I must protest!"

"Why?" she asked, when they quieted finally.

Payton wasn't reacting at all, although he'd narrowed his eyes even further, and was looking at her with such enmity, she could feel it. Everything on her sensed it, and hammered at her with it, and frightened her with it. Dallis worked at dampening the fear enough it wouldn't interfere, and watched as the knowledge reached him, and brought the shadow of a smile to his lips. She didn't have another choice. She wasn't moving her eyes, and neither was he.

"Payton . . . means you harm."

Dallis tilted her head on one side, lifting her chin at the same time. That had an odd benefit of sending the whoosh noise to the lower side. She hadn't guessed that.

"Then take his weapons," she said.

"Jesu', My Lady! He can kill with his bare fists. I've seen it!" That was Alan. Somebody hushed him, but too late. And foolish. Dallis knew what terms he'd fought for and what he wanted. They all did.

"Take his weapons . . . anyway," she replied.

They didn't have to take them. Payton didn't move his regard as he reached behind him and handed over a battle ax tucked into the back of his belt, then he skimmed along the belt, back to front along both sides, pulling a plethora of knives from it. Then he flipped the fastening clasp of his scabbard to get it released from his belt as well, before handing his sword over. And then he lifted one leg at a time, to pull the *skean dhu* from each sock.

"My Lady, I truly protest. 'Tis foolish in the extreme!"

"You say the champion is allowed words with me. I have words. For his ears only. The rest of you leave. Now."

"I want his word that he will na' harm you."

"Redmond MacCloud."

Dallis said his name in exactly the same non-emotional way he always used. She probably would've appreciated looking at his reaction, but she didn't move her eyes from Payton.

"Aye?" he asked, finally.

"Leave us."

They were still dissenting. They didn't have to put it in words. Not one of them was leaving. Dallis pulled in a huge breath and sighed.

"I doona' need his word. I already ken he will na' harm me."

One of Payton's brows lifted, in that annoying, endearing, heart-skipping way of his. Dallis's heart pulsed in reaction, sending whooshing noise throughout the side she'd tilted down. She had to move her head back upright or go crazed with listening to it.

"How do you ken that?" Martin was the one asking. Redmond appeared to have stepped back, and the others were following.

"He dinna' kill his challengers . . . did he?" she replied.

"The next room. With the door ajar. 'Tis all." Redmond again.

Dallis hadn't moved her gaze from Payton, but she saw the satisfaction overtaking his entire frame. It was in the way he'd straightened, puffing out his chest to an even more impressive size, put his hands on hips and lifted his chin from the challenger look.

"My Laird?" she asked him.

A slow smile split his face, the teeth white against the swarthiness of his skin. And then he nodded.

"Jesu! Mary . . . and Joseph!"

If Dallis wasn't mistaken, that was her prim Aunt Evelyn cursing and muttering and gesturing, but she was leaving. They all were, filing one, sometimes two abreast out into the antechamber the ladies used for their sewing and chatting and dining, and living.

The room went so quiet, it was near deathly in quality. If it wasn't for the continued sound in her ears, she'd have heard nothing. Payton didn't move, either. He just stood there, eyeing her.

"Join . . . me."

Dallis put out a hand toward him, controlled the shaking with an act of will she didn't know she possessed, and watched as he walked toward her. He stopped just shy of the window opening. Within reach of her hand, but not deigning to touch it.

Dallis lowered her eyes for a moment, to hide whatever might be reflecting in them, and then she lowered her hand, too. It was just as well. That digit felt ice cold. He'd know the fear she hid if he'd touched it.

"What . . . do you think of my . . . view, Payton?" she asked, turning sideways to him so he would look.

He grunted.

"Tis na' much. I ken."

Body heat from his nearness radiated toward her, intoxicating her, and Dallis took several breaths of it before she continued. So beloved! She trembled, hoped he wouldn't notice, opened her mouth, and started speaking.

"I . . . always wanted . . . to be a widow," she said. "Until you showed me different, that is."

He'd taken a step closer to her. She heard it with ears primed for such a thing, even over the blasted sound of her own heart breaking. She had to admit what the whooshing noise was then, and then she had to hold the knowledge as close to her as possible, and never let it out.

"I . . . thought that way I'd have power . . . over my life. My . . . keep. My people. It was na' until our stay at Ballilol Castle that I knew the falsehood of that. Being a widow is nothing. Nothing."

Dallis frowned out at the view, as her voice cracked a bit. She bit at her lip, ducked her head and spoke again.

"I . . . I dinna' wish to be wed. To anyone. And so I spent all the funds you sent me. All of it I gave to my cousin, Giles. To buy challengers. To kill you."

There was absolutely no reaction from the body standing right beside her. She couldn't even sense his breathing, and he was right beside her! Within touching distance. Able to reach out and take her neck in his hands, and squeeze the life right out of her.

"I know. 'Twas stupid. I dinna' ken then that there is nae challenger capable of killing the King's Champion, but you'll have to forgive that. I dinna' ken what that meant. From my castle . . . in that section of the Highlands . . . how was I to know what being champion was? And . . . how famous you are?"

Nothing. He probably wasn't even listening. Nobody ever heard her anymore. She should be used to it.

Dallis sucked in another breath.

"But then you came. And gave me . . . Davey. 'Tis only what we call him. I left the christening of him to you. When this . . . is over."

Dallis dared a glance over and up at him. And wished she hadn't. His features looked gray and the hate in his eyes was so visceral, she could reach out and touch it. If she wanted. Her lower limbs wobbled, threatening to drop her. If she hadn't a grip on the stone beside her, she wouldn't have been able to prevent it. As it was, her body swayed toward the wall, connected, and then clung. That put her back to him, and she didn't dare stay in that position.

Then, to her absolute dismay, her legs wobbled worse, betraying her completely. Dallis was forced to a slide, keeping her face turned toward the window opening so she wouldn't see Payton.

The oriel had a ledge at the bottom of the cupola that comprised her window, constructed mostly of glazed glass. Dallis ended on the ledge, using it for a seat. She had one leg bent beneath her, while the other trailed to the floor.

"Stand up," Payton said.

"You'll need to pardon me," Dallis replied. "But I doona' believe I can. Davey's birth . . . was hard. Over two days. I was a banshee, too. I screamed mightily. I—I lost a lot of blood. And damn me for admitting it. To you."

Her voice ended with a whisper, and then she got treated to more silence. She had her hands clasped before her on the white satin of her skirts, looking so pale, her skin was only a shade off-set from the material. Dallis frowned at that. Her hands better not betray her! She was going to need them. She pulled in another extremely shaky breath and started spouting words again.

"When Giles threatened to tell you . . . I could na' think! I should have done the accounting to you months a-fore! I ken that now . . . but I—I—I couldna' let him destroy what we had! So, I broke my vow! It was wrong . . . but you said—you said sometimes a vow couldn't be kept. Sometimes things are too vast. I would have done anything to prevent Giles from killing what you felt for me. So . . . I gave him the ring. And I . . . destroyed it myself."

She'd failed. Dallis realized it as the emotion she'd hidden filled the last of her words, making them almost insensible. There was no place to hide. No place to run. Nothing.

She moved her hands to the back of her waist, fumbling for the knife, her eyes so awash with tears, vision was useless anyway. She watched the teardrops fall, over and over, staining the material with each one.

She sensed him moving, going to a squat beside her, and if he had pity in his eyes, she was going to scream at the vexation of it!

His hand came into her vision, reaching for her chin. Dallis jerked to one side, felt strength flooding her frame as her right hand locked on the handle of the skean, and then she was bringing it forward, slicing the material of her skirt a bit before she had it in her lap. He went ram-rod stiff beside her.

"Oh, Payton, Payton. I love you. Only you. Ever. I dinna' ken the scope of it. Nobody ever told me. But I know it now! I do! And there is nothing worse . . . than living this life without you! Nothing. It is already death."

She shoved the skean into his hand.

"Do it quickly, Payton," she whispered. "Quick and clean. And when 'tis done . . . I beg of you, doona' mount my head on a spike like Kilchurning did with Leroy . . . and the others! I ken . . . a betraying wife has such happen, but please, Payton. Please? Doona' let anyone see me . . . like that. Please?"

She raised her eyes to him then, knowing only then that she didn't want a sunlit day to be her last view on this earth. She wanted it to be him.

"Dallis."

Dallis slammed her hands to her ears and looked away. She was wrong. Looking at him was worse.

"Payton, please! Please! I beg of you! Doona' make me suffer one more moment! Please?" Her whisper was wild with intensity and emotion, and filled with anguish as she failed every single bit of Caruth Clan creed.

She heard a clank sound of metal striking something in the room behind them, and then she was in his arms, he was transferring from a crouch to a seat on the floor, and everything about him was trembling.

"Dallis. Dallis."

He was crooning her name against her throat, stroking her hair with one hand while the other arm was still locked about her, cradling her. As if she was something precious.

Treasured.

The word slid through her head easily and Dallis blinked moisture from her eyes that was just replenished. Over and over and damn! Why did fate have to curse her with so much weepy emotion it disgusted even her?

"Dallis . . . I dinna' ken. Forgive me, love. Forgive me." Payton was murmuring words along her throat and into her ear, speaking love words, and that's when it hit her that the whooshing noise was gone.

Completely.

"Pay . . . ton?" The name was split in two and barely made sound.

He lifted his head and moved his love-filled gaze to hers. Dallis felt everything on her reverberate with the hammering of her heart as it rammed at her throat, making it difficult to swallow.

"I love you, Dallis. Ever."

"Even . . . with my betrayal?" she asked.

"You make a verra good argument, Wife."

His voice was deep, gruff with the tone he was putting on it. And full of feeling. And real. Totally real.

"Aye, love. A grand argument. I only have one answer."

"Oh, Payton. Anything. I swear."

He was splitting his legs, settling her onto the hard surface of the floor. She didn't know it was so he could wrap both legs about her and tighten them, too, until he did it. Then, he leaned backward, holding his back from touching the floor while conjoined with her, confining her and holding her until the tremble of them was moving both of them with it. Such strength was awesome. Jaw-dropping. He was leaner, too. More delineated. Everywhere she was touching had the consistency of iron. Dallis shifted, and fidgeted, and finally got a hand free enough to reach his chin and turn his face downward.

"What?" Payton asked.

"You need to release me. A bit. I canna' move." And she wriggled for effect.

"You think this bad," he replied. "You should wait until you see the ring I next design!"

He put back his head then, and gave his huge battle yell, making Dallis jump, and bringing the door crashing open.

Redmond was at the front, sword drawn. Behind him were other clansmen, all armed and poised. Dallis looked at the shock on their faces, and then the grins as weapons lowered and eyebrows lifted. She ducked her head beneath Payton's chin.

"You continually come to my rescue, MacCloud." Payton stated, moving to a sit with her still locked in his arms. That released the tension from the ropelike texture of his muscles, throbbing everywhere along her side, since she was still pressed to them. "And at the oddest times."

She heard Redmond clear his throat, but he didn't sound like the only one.

"Fair enough," he finally said, and she heard the sound of his sword getting sheathed.

Chapter 28

"'Tis a lovely song. And to think . . . 'twas penned just for you."

Payton slid his gaze to the side to meet his wife's upturned smile, perfectly shaped nose, and mischief-filled eyes. He smiled back.

"Too filled with blood lust, I feel. Na' much for gaining a wench's eye and attention with gore such as he describes."

His remark had her dipping her head. "But you said the last minstrel's song was full of courtly love and foolish banter," she complained.

Payton lifted the hand he held, that he hadn't relinquished throughout the banquet, and placed a kiss atop first the ruby ring that was on her ring-finger, and then the overly large Dunn-Fadden clan crested ring that she had on her middle digit. He took his time, stroking his lips over the hard surfaces of gem and metals before moving on to the delicate skin.

Beside him, he felt Dallis tremble. It would have been impossible not to, since he had his entire right side, from waist to ankle, right against hers. She flit a glance to his, and stayed, and then the rose shade of her lips parted slightly.

He'd finished his caress of her hand and moved it back to his lap, unwilling to let her have it back. It was a good thing she was right-handed, he decided, as she reached for another morsel of lamb from their shared platter. She had an immense sense of grace and direction. He watched as she unerringly picked up the bite-sized portion of meat, without losing one moment away from his enthralled gaze.

And then she brought the lamb to his mouth, waited until he opened, and slid it in. Payton chewed subconsciously, and then stopped as her hand fidgeted within his, before he loosened his fingers. She didn't take it away. Instead, she was sliding it up, brushing the fine wool of his champion kilt, raising the hair on his upper thigh, and then hovering, poised atop where lasses shouldn't be. He had a moment to realize she wasn't finished, before she pressed down, stroking with a gesture that had him choking.

And her giggling.

"I truly . . . adore . . . *kilts,*" she leaned toward him to say, rubbing her hand along flesh that went instantly aware, alert and desirous, and too large for one hand.

Then they banged one of their large drums, King James stood onto a box placed in front of his chair for the move, and started what was probably going to be one of his long-winded, boring speeches. Payton closed his eyes, twitched himself solidly back into her palm, and was watching for the gasp of surprise she gave. And the slanted, upward-cast glance, meeting his again. Payton was caught, held, enchanted. He couldn't move his gaze, even if he'd wanted to.

The king was yelling something, the announcers were sending it out about the room, and then Redmond nudged him.

"What did you do that for?" Payton swiveled to ask, and then turned back the other way as it appeared the king had been addressing him.

"Stand, My Laird Dunn-Fadden! King's Champion! My Champion!"

He went to a full flush, realizing he had to do it. Dallis

wasn't helping at all. She'd moved her hand away, to a ladylike posture in her lap, and was giggling, making everything worse.

Payton groaned, shoved their double-seated bench backward the same time he was pulling his sporran forward, and stood, at a half-bow, somehow making it look deferential to the king, and not what it really was.

Then he sat back down, rocking the seat slightly as his buttocks met the small raised back to the bench, and listening to the swell of approval the courtiers were making.

"'Tis true! We must bid farewell to Laird Dunn-Fadden! He's served me well, and true, but alas! The man canna' stay forever from his lands!"

Payton ceased listening. He'd already heard it anyway. He had much better plans in mind. Real plans, with real emotion. With his wife.

Then Redmond slanted a shoulder against his other side again.

"What?" Payton looked over again at him.

"You need to pay attention to the king's words."

"Why?"

"Both of you."

Redmond was looking down and to the right. Payton flicked a glance down that direction and collided with her glance, looking just a little guilty.

"At least . . . until we can get you to your chamber."

Dallis put a hand to her mouth to hide the giggle, but he loved the sound, and the way it trembled along where he'd plastered himself to her side again. That had him putting an arm about her back and around her waist, lifting her into an embrace against his chest. Where she belonged.

"Payton Dunn-Fadden."

Payton sighed, lowered Dallis back to the bench, and turned again toward his man. "What is it now, Redmond?"

"Behave!"

Payton turned back, sighed again, and reached for her

hand. The one closest to him. The one wearing his rings. And the one that wouldn't behave.

The king was still droning on over at his own table, set farther along the raised dais. There were two long tables on the royal stage, one holding the king and his guests. The other for Payton's retinue. It was the highest honor he could be accorded without being royalty. But it hadn't been the first he'd received from The Stewart.

It had begun directly following a bath, that she'd ordered him to undertake, but stayed to supervise. Payton's eyebrow lifted in reverie, and he caught at her hand as it inched up his knee. From the moment he'd been dressed in this, his newest *feile-breacan,* complete with the championship belt and more silver wrist bands, Payton had been on the move, marching to the king's tune.

They'd been shuffled off to Saint Margaret's Church, the king's own chapel, containing a reverence drawn down through centuries of worship. Payton knew then that Dallis had spoken the truth about her weakness. It wasn't an act put on for his pity. He wasn't allowing a litter for her, either. He was carrying her. Swathed in white satin, and covered over in his clan plaid, and held as close to his heart as possible.

They'd brought in his son then, wearing a familiar-looking gown his wife had lovingly sewn. The woman carrying him walked right over to where Payton was, and placed the babe in Payton's hands.

He was in luck he was sitting. Everyone was. Pride and exhilaration slammed into him so hard, his heart thudded with the reaction, his hands shook and grew wet with the sweat, and his legs had the resilience of bog weed. The lad was barely a week old, but he had very black hair and very blue eyes, and was very curious and alert, and absolutely perfect.

As was the look in Dallis's eyes when he'd handed the lad over to the priest for the blessing and naming and turned back to her. She was weeping joy while he held her and shook with the same emotion. But he kept any tears back behind his lids, where they belonged. That way his voice was steady and strong when he gave them the bairn's name, although he'd had to clear his throat.

"James David Alexander Dunn-Fadden."

There was a sigh of approval throughout the chapel, and such a feeling of peace. It wasn't shaken until King James had requested yet another audience with them.

Her hand was inching again. Payton grabbed at it, and lifted it to his lips, but this time he wasn't kissing her rings. He'd turned her hand over and was tonguing her palm . . . going to her wrist . . . enjoying the goose bumps that were strong enough to tease at his tongue.

"Payton Dunn-Fadden."

It was Redmond's voice again. Payton lifted his head, looked deeply into his wife's eyes, and then turned to his man again.

"What now?"

"The king is still speaking."

Redmond gestured with his fork. It was true. King James was still pontificating and droning, and making more than one courtier yawn from behind a hand, or a fan. Copying proved impossible to resist, and Payton tipped his head backward for his own yawn. That created titters and crowd noise that showed even here, in the king's house, his followers hounded him.

His eyes burned, and then he remembered. He'd been sleepless last night. All night. And most of the prior one. Working his muscles and mind into a sharpness he'd need. It was totally appreciated, however, so it must have been worth it. He knew that from all the caressing and finger-touches, and cooing she'd done when he'd bathed, and she'd supervised. And he'd tried to keep from her, due to her fragile state.

Her hand was back atop his leg. Just above the knee, squeezing on either side of his leg with her thumb on one side and fingers on the other. Payton sucked in on his cheeks, looked directly at the king, and slid just a slight bit lower on their bench.

Beside him he heard her giggle again. God, how he loved that sound! He was just about to tell her of it, when Redmond spoke again.

"We leave at first light."

"I ken as much," Payton replied.

"'Tis best. You dinna' wish to stay about here any longer than needed."

Payton nodded, concentrated on not showing how she'd moved her hand to the inside of his thigh, to wrap about his leg while continuing her lascivious squeezing.

"The king already mentioned how he has tired of paying for our hospitality. And the earl of Dunrobin. We are to leave and na' come back until summoned. And only if summoned."

Payton nodded again, and eased his legs open, making room for slender fingers that were trailing up his leg, well past midthigh.

"He's sending supplies, foodstuffs, mounting all your clansmen, and providing an escort of his own men for protecting the wagon of gold he says you've earned . . . but heaven alone knows how."

"'Tis probably issued under the 'Good of Scotland' portion of his latest decree," Payton replied.

The last word came out squeaked, sounding a bit like Alan when he was excited. Payton couldn't help it. Dallis had reached her objective, and flicked a finger, making him not only jump slightly, but it altered his voice. Payton concentrated on looking at the king, and tilted his head toward Redmond, as if awaiting more grand, wise words.

"With an escort like that, we will na' reach your home for nigh on a fortnight. Perhaps longer."

Payton didn't even nod. He couldn't reply to anything. He was afraid to. He was holding a breath and easing himself farther down on the bench, putting weight and heft and heat where she could access it easier, run her hands along it better, squeezing . . .

"You two may wish to cease that for a bit. I believe you'll be standing again. Soon."

Dallis's hand stopped. Payton turned toward his man. "Cease what?" he asked.

"The king's men are na' for your use."

"What men?" Payton asked.

Dallis was giggling again, and with the addition of where her hand was locked, made it impossible to keep track of Redmond's continual words.

"The escort! They're to turn about the moment we arrive."

"I ken," Payton replied. "The king wants them back. They're to escort his stonemasons."

"Aye. King James got word that the restoration to your entire castle was completed more than a month past. He is na' pleased."

"He sounded pleased."

"With the results . . . aye. According to his messengers, the castle is better than it was a-fore we decided to take a ram to it."

"I doona' ken . . . what you mean, then." Payton said it evenly, looking at Redmond the entire time, but he had no way to stop the sensation she was stirring with the solid stroke she'd just done. And repeated. He was doing his best, but his sporran was lifting, and catching the light from how much silver it contained as it rose.

"The king angers at your sire stealing the stonemason's skill. For his own use. On his keep. Dinna' you hear that?"

"My da would na' do such," Payton replied.

"Alexander Dunn-Fadden would steal the pillow from beneath your head, if he wanted it, and even if you were sleeping atop it. 'Tis what Dunn-Faddens were known for. Reaving. Hiding. Thieving."

"A-fore me," Payton replied.

Redmond nodded solemnly, and then smiled. "Aye. A-fore you. They will na' say the same of Dunn-Fadden clan e'ermore."

"Payton Alexander Dunn-Fadden!"

The king must have announced it, because the criers were shouting his name all along the balcony railings of the room. Payton's eyes went wide.

"You'll need stand now, My Laird . . . and please remember that I did warn you."

Redmond was laughing as he said it. The wretch wasn't just smiling. He was out-right laughing.